Boys Will Be Boys
Their First Time

Boys Will Be Boys
Their First Time

An Erotic Anthology Edited By
Mickey Erlach

STARbooks PRESS

Herndon, VA

Copyright © 2008 by STARbooks Press
ISBN-13: 978-1-934187-32-6

Published in the United States STARbooks Press PO Box 711612 Herndon VA 20171 Printed in the United States

Many thanks to graphic artist Emma Aldous for the cover design. Ms. Aldous may be reached at: emma@starbookspress.com.

Herndon, VA

CONTENTS

Granddad's Woodshed
By Jay Starre

I was chopping firewood out in the back at Granddad's when Bobby rode up.

"Look at those muscles," he laughed brightly as he dismounted and tied his horse to the hitching rail.

"How ya doing, Bobby?" I asked, stopping what I was doing to stare at him.

He'd grown. I hadn't been up to Granddad's ranch in the Colorado Mountains for two years, the last time back when I was eighteen. Bobby's family lived on the ranch down the road. He'd only been sixteen then and quite chubby. I looked him up and down, noting how the chubbiness had been replaced mostly by a fuller chest and broader shoulders. He was sexily plump.

"You sure are looking me over, Brent. Like what you see?"

And then the little fucker clutched his crotch suggestively and leered at me.

He was always a joker, and I'd liked that about him. Although he grinned now, and so did I, a rising boner in my jeans revealed the true story. Bobby clutched what looked like a stiff bulge in his own rough work jeans.

"I saw your Granddad driving to town on the road a while ago. No one's around. Let's go in the woodshed and fool around."

His dark eyes swam with promised lust. He licked bowed, pursed lips. He was a fucking little cock-tease!

I abruptly decided to test his dare.

Dropping the axe in my hands, I reached out and grabbed his arm, almost dragging him toward the shelter of the woodshed. "Let's see what you got, then, Bobby. I'm sure my cock's bigger than your little snake," I smirked, thrusting my hips ahead and unzipping my fly at the same time.

I fished out my hard dick just as we reached the open front of the woodshed. I figured that would scare him off if he was bluffing.

He wasn't bluffing.

"Nice boner! But look at this, Brent," Bobby chortled, his face flushed and his eyes wide.

He unbuckled his belt and undid his fly in a flurry of fingers. Before I knew it, his pants and his underwear were down around his knees! I felt my mouth dropping open. One big, long, stiff boner thrust up in the crisp mountain air in front of him.

His cock was enormous!

"Fuck! That is a respectable rod you got there," I admitted.

We'd moved into the shed, which faced away from the house and into the thick woods. No one could see us, and Granddad was in town for the afternoon anyway. Bobby and I faced each other, our rock-hard cocks rearing up between us.

"Let's jerk off. The cold air always makes me horny," Bobby said, still grinning.

He was already stroking his cock with both hands. It was so fucking big both hands fit on the lengthy shaft. The purple head poked out above his fists all swollen and drooling. I realized I was trembling. The autumn air did seem to have that horny tension to it. I managed a shaky smile as I began to pump my own tool.

"Yeah! It feels good, doesn't it, Brent?" Bobby muttered, really getting into it as he shoved his hips forward and banged his big meat against mine. His hands rubbed up and down, pumping more of the gooey pre-cum from the swollen slit. His cock had a big cap, wide and with a flared crown that shone bright purple by then. I stared greedily at it as I used one hand to rub my own boner.

"Spit on it, Brent. Rub it good," Bobby suggested in a quavering voice.

I glanced up at his face. He was very cute, with soft raven-dark hair cut short above his neat ears. He had a chubby face, but his features were button-cute. His lips were wet with drool, and as I watched, he raised one hand and stuck out his tongue to wipe spit all over the fingers. He dropped that hand back to his cock and began to rub it up and down, with the other gripping the fat base just above his hairless nut sack.

I followed his lead, spitting on my fingers and rubbing the sticky lube up and down my respectable, but smaller-sized boner. Hell, any cock would look small next to Bobby's gigantic meat! I felt chills of desire coursing up and down my spine as I continued to rub spit into my cock and stared at Bobby's giant bone.

But then he abruptly escalated the action. I'd shed my shirt while chopping wood in the autumn sunshine, and now I noticed how

2

he stared hungrily at my bare chest. Without warning, he bent over and clamped his mouth over one of my nipples.

"Goddamn!" I hissed.

The wet warmth suddenly sucking on my sensitive nub was like an electric shockwave blasting through my chest. Even hotter, Bobby's hands moved to my cock as he sucked and licked my nipple. He began to yank and pull on my boner. I groaned and muttered as I returned the favor and took hold of his big cock to start working it. God it was huge! Fat, rubbery and stiff, it was like a baseball bat of torrid, sexy fuck-flesh. I pulled on it with one hand and thrust my chest into Bobby's hot mouth. He gurgled noisily over my nipple while rubbing spit-wet fingers up and down over my dick. It was awesome.

I don't know how it happened. My hands obviously had a will of their own. One of them was suddenly sliding around Bobby's naked waist and roaming over the hot expanse of his bare butt. I gasped with heightened passion as my fingers kneaded and explored hairless butt cheek. Lush and firm, that ass quivered under my touch. Bobby's fingers on my cock increased their already frantic rhythm. When my searching hand dipped into the parted butt crack, Bobby's mouth went wild over my nipple.

I stroked Bobby's monster meat while I poked boldly into his heated ass crack. The crevice was deep and moist. Slick, hairless and smooth as satin, the plump butt cheeks quaked and shivered as I sought and found the small, puckered asshole between them. I toyed with the tight rim and crinkled lips while yanking on Bobby's big shank.

That did it for him. With a loud groan, Bobby's body heaved and a geyser of warm goo splattered out of the head of his giant cock. The stench of the male juice and Bobby's wild hands on my own cock combined in an irresistible pressure. My balls poured out their seed as I blew a load, too.

We writhed and bucked together, jizz coating our crotches and fingers. My hand in Bobby's butt crammed deeper, and I actually poked a finger up an inch between the tight ass lips. He cried out and wiggled his butt as his cock oozed out the last of its copious brew.

We leaned against one another as we attempted to catch our breath and slow our pounding hearts. Bobby's smirk and wink made me laugh as he pulled up his underwear over drying cum.

"I gotta go home and do my chores before dark. See you tomorrow at the same time when your Granddad goes to town."

3

I nodded in a daze of semi-satiated lust. Bobby's chunky, sexy body was suddenly very alluring. I wanted more of him, and he'd just promised to supply me with it. I watched him ride away with a resurrecting cock in my jeans.

That evening I borrowed Granddad's truck and drove into town. I had to get some condoms! A riot of fantasies ran through my head as I tossed and turned in my bed that night. What exciting things would we do in the woodshed tomorrow?

Although Granddad was retired, he owned a small law office in the nearby town and went in every afternoon to grouch at his partners. Sure enough, while I was out chopping and stacking firewood, Bobby rode up again.

"Let's take all our clothes off this time. You got such a hot chest, and I wanna see the rest of you. I wanna see you butt-naked," Bobby blurted out in a rush as he tethered his horse.

His excited grin and sparkling amber orbs got me immediately hot. My cock leapt and dribbled before I even dropped my axe and chased him into the relative privacy of the woodshed. It was a bright October day, and the sun was pleasantly warm. It shone through the open front of the shed directly on us with only the deer in the woods being offered a view of whatever we decided to do.

The smell of wood chips and fir sap hovered in the shed. I'd always liked that smell. I inhaled it deeply, smiling at the warm sun on my face, my senses heightened in expectation of exploring more intimately Bobby's chunky young body.

Bobby, the horny little slut, wasted no time. He tore off his thick wool shirt and undershirt then hopped out of his jeans, leaving his boots on, so he wouldn't have to step on the woodchips and shavings on the shed floor. I watched him greedily, impressed by the changes in his body over the past two years. He still had a tan, although it was fading, and his skin was smooth and appealing. His shoulders were wide, and his hairless chest was well-shaped with small brown nipples already erect and excited. His stomach was flat, although there was a hint of love handles around his waist. His naked thighs were big and strong.

And, his cock was big and hard.

I began stripping as I looked him over while he returned the inspection avidly. His intense amber eyes spotted my stiff rod, and they roamed over my muscular build with appreciative lust. His look sent shivers up and down my spine, the brisk autumn air partially responsible for that, too.

Bobby couldn't have been greedier for it. He grabbed my cock and clamped his mouth over my chest so quickly I almost fell over backwards. He obviously assumed we'd repeat the shenanigans of the day before. I realized his experience in the sexual arena was practically nil.

"We're going to suck cock today. Okay?"

Bobby nodded his head vigorously, his eyes nearly bulging out of his head. He was actually drooling!

"I want you to bend over and suck on my cock while I play with your hot ass. How's that sound?" I suggested. I hoped he agreed. I'd been fantasizing about that plump, warm butt endlessly ever since I'd copped a feel the previous afternoon.

"Sounds hot! I've never sucked a cock before. I can't wait," Bobby muttered under his breath.

His eyes were on the prize as he bent over and shoved his face in my crotch. I still had a hand on his cock and pulled him around by the big handle so that he was sideways in front of me. I let go of his boner and placed both hands on his white ass. Just as I gripped the hot flesh in both palms, I felt a warm mouth surround the head of my cock. I grunted and bit my lip, my legs shaking as Bobby started licking my cock head.

Reveling in that sweet sensation, I took a minute to appreciate the awesome sight of Bobby's sexy, bare butt. The fading tan line accentuated the swell of his big cheeks. Ivory white skin, totally hairless and without blemish, curved in twin sexy mounds bisected by a deep crevice.

My hands moved greedily over the flesh, kneading and stroking as I pulled the cheeks apart and stared down into the exposed crack. I could see Bobby's asshole! Bobby's mouth slurped up half my cock as I stared down at his vulnerable little slot, and I knew I just had to feel it. I held the plump cheeks apart with one hand and crammed my fingers into the valley with the other. Slick, moist skin welcomed my exploration. I found the wrinkled hole and began to tease and stroke it. Bobby lurched, his back arching and his mouth opening wider to take in more of my throbbing cock. As I began to toy with the slippery, flushed opening, Bobby grunted and buried his face in my crotch, suddenly taking all of my boner into his mouth at once.

I shoved my finger between his tight ass lips. The clamping sphincter pulsed and snapped around my digging digit. I wormed it deeper, incensed at the way it looked, my finger sticking out of his hole as I probed and poked his guts. His hot insides quivered nervously, but Bobby apparently loved it. He wiggled his big sexy butt and slurped greedily over my stiff bone. His wet suctioning was driving me nuts while the nasty smacking of his lips also gave me an idea.

I bent over and spit down into his crack, the gob of saliva landing right on target. I worked the spit into his tight young asshole with my finger. He groaned deep in his chest, and his ass shook like big bowls of sexy Jell-O. I grinned and spit again, working the goo in and out and deeper and deeper.

We were both shaking by then. With my finger exploring Bobby's tight little anus and his mouth bobbing up and down over my stiff whanger, I felt orgasm approaching. I was going to blow! But Bobby lost it first. His high-pitched whine thrummed around my cock as he suddenly erupted. He'd been pumping his own cock, and he grunted out his ecstasy. I felt jizz spraying my naked thighs.

That did it for me, plus the fact his snug butthole convulsed wildly around my knuckle-deep finger. I jammed that finger as far up Bobby's quivering hole as possible and thrust my cock up into his slobbering mouth. I shot.

Waves of hot satisfaction rocked through me as my cock unloaded in Bobby's mouth. He kept on sucking until both of us had emptied our young balls. I pulled out and Bobby stood up, my finger still buried up his between his sexy ass cheeks.

"Will you suck me off, too?" Bobby's innocent smile belied his lusty libido.

I didn't even bother to answer. I still had my finger up his ass, and I wiggled it around and grinned, dropping down to kneel on our discarded clothing. His cock drooped slightly, but was still fat and full.

He was hot for more sex already! Kneeling in front of him, I had my arm wrapped around his waist and one finger still digging around in his steamy ass slot. As he squirmed around that probing finger, he hastily worked to wipe the jizz off his cock onto his undershirt. His cock reared out in front of him, half-hard, when I opened wide and slurped it up.

I'd sucked cocks before, but never one this big. I thought I'd dislocate my jaw! It was fat as hell and had to be a foot long. He was definitely young and hung. I fed it to myself with one hand around the base while I continued to probe into his tight asshole with a spit-wet finger. Bobby's cock rose up to its former stiffness after a few moments of avid slurping on my part. Then, he obligingly spread his legs wider to open up his crack for my delving finger. That's when I released his cock with my other hand and shoved it up under his crotch. Now I had both hands in his crack.

I got my fingers in there, pulling his hole apart with one hand then placing a second finger beside the first and wiggling it around the swollen ass lips to worm it beyond the defending rim. Bobby groaned, and his butt shook as he bent his knees and dropped down slightly over my fingers. That did the trick. I suddenly had two fingers up his butthole.

I bobbed my head over his fat cock head, managing to open my throat and get half his shaft in my mouth. Bobby groaned louder, his butt shaking like mad and his asshole going crazy around my fingers. I snorted air through my nose and took the plunge, sucking in all of Bobby's big boner to the balls.

Bobby cried out, his asshole suddenly opening up like a budding bloom. The sphincter gaped apart, and both my fingers plunged deep. I wiggled and twisted them, probing Bobby's cherry prostate with insistent jabs. His knees weakened, and he reached out with both hands to lean on me, his asshole totally open for my jabbing fingers.

I knew right then that I had to fuck him. Immediately.

I spit out his cock in a daze of lust and turned him with my hands on his ass. He moaned and shook all over, while his asshole remained sloppy and welcoming, as if he knew what was coming and was already giving in to it. Bobby bent over, placing his hands on his knees, and then he looked back at me. Those big brown eyes were soft and dreamy. He wanted to get fucked!

My own cock was hard as rock again. I had to take my fingers out of Bobby's quaking ass-pit long enough to put on a condom I frantically fished out of my discarded jeans, but he remained bent over and waiting without saying a word.

What a sight! The sexy country boy was naked except for his boots, his feet wide apart and his chunky alabaster ass wriggling, bent over, waiting for my cock. Unbelievable!

I stood behind him and shoved my cock between the globes of his plump young ass. The mounds trembled violently as my poker scooted around in search of the hot little butt slot. In a daze of heated desire, I managed to remember about the lube I'd also bought in town the evening before. My pants were at my feet. I hastily bent down and rummaged through the pockets again.

Bobby watched me with his head craned around. When I squirted the clear lube over my cock, he bit his lip and moaned. He closed his eyes and dropped his head. I jammed my cock up into his steamy crack again, so excited I thought I might shoot before I got it inside him. Using my fingers, I found the hole and pulled it open, planting my cockhead at the swollen entrance. I poised for the plunge, staring down at Bobby's sexy, bent-over body. Then I shoved.

Heated, quivering asshole surrounded my cock as I drove it deep. Bobby was wide open for me, but still his cherry butt-hole was deliciously snug. The lips stretched around my shaft, clinging to it as I prodded deeper and deeper.

"FUCK MY ASS!" Bobby howled.

I rammed all the way home. And then I shot my load. Even while I was cuming inside him, I fucked him. Barely able to stand, I held onto his sexy ass cheeks while I drilled him in furious rhythm for a good ten minutes until a second orgasm rose up to erupt once again.

Bobby muttered and moaned the whole time, his body limp and willing beneath my assault. His asshole was accommodating, steamy and slick with lube. But when I cried out with my second orgasm, he rose up, and gobs of cream sprayed the woodpile in front of us as Bobby shot again.

I stayed an extra two weeks at Granddad's that autumn, and Bobby and I rocked that woodshed every afternoon.

I had never chopped so much wood in my life.

Down by the Creek
By Wayne Mansfield

When I was eighteen, the only place I felt truly alive was by the banks of a small stream, which ran through the bushland at the back of our property. I would lie there cushioned by the sweet smelling grass that grew tall by its banks and watch the light dance on the water as it trickled by. Every few meters, the shallow stream would deepen, creating decent-sized paddling pools where tadpoles liked to congregate. Even as a teenager, I would gaze in wonder at them as they wriggled through the water, each at a different stage of metamorphosis.

Toward the far edge of the thicket, there was an old fig tree whose branches, thick with large, dark green leaves, spread out above the grass almost to the bank of the stream. I called it "The Fortress" because it seemed impenetrable, in those days. I loved to climb up onto the smooth, thick branches on a hot summer's afternoon and lie there imagining I was anywhere but in the small town I'd had the misfortune to be living in.

The Fortress was my secret place. It may have been on government land, but in my mind it was an island in a sea of wild bush, hidden from everyone and known only to me. Its bounty, the sweet, succulent crop of figs it produced annually, provided me with sustenance. In fact, I felt I could live here quite happily for the rest of my life, self-sufficient with fresh stream water to drink, figs to eat and no one to bother me.

Summer days could get pretty hot so quite often I would peel off my T-shirt and shorts, leave them hanging safely on a branch in The Fortress and go skinny-dipping. With no one else around, I felt perfectly comfortable walking the dozen or so steps from the base of the fig tree to the nearest paddle pool, slipping into the cool water and pretending that I was the only person in the world.

That eighteenth summer was also the year I underwent a metamorphosis of my own. The smooth, milky-white skin of my boyhood had transformed seemingly overnight into something rougher and hairier. I noticed a shadow of fine hair growing on my top lip, and above my cock, which had also experienced a growth spurt, a forest of black, curly hair had appeared. My voice was deepening, and every morning, without fail, I would wake up with an erection that never wanted to go down and seemed intent on embarrassing me in front of my parents.

One particular morning, I awoke with more than an erection to contend with. There was something else down there, something strange. I put my hand down my pajama pants and encountered a small patch of sticky stuff. It looked like glue and had a kind of starchy smell to it. I immediately panicked. I had no idea what it was. I had never seen anything like it before and wondered if I had contracted some hideous illness during the course of the night. One thing was for sure, I wasn't going to tell Mum or Dad about it. I decided it would be best to leave it a few days to see if it would clear up by itself.

Somehow I managed to get my pajama pants into the bathroom and sponged off before anyone could see what had happened. I hung them over a chair in my room while I had a shower, that way they would be dry enough to fold up and put beneath my pillow before I went to school.

The perfect crime, or at least that's what it felt like. I had no idea why I felt so ashamed, but I did. Had I vomited over my pajamas, I would have gladly given them to Mum to clean up. But this was different. This was something that had happened "down there," and I was feeling fiercely private about the latest developments in that particular area.

It was now mid March, and summer was officially over, although nobody appeared to have told Mother Nature. She always saved the most ferocious heat for March. For the past two days, the temperature had peaked at forty degrees, and the weather forecast wasn't predicting any cooler weather. To make matters worse, it was the beginning of the school year. I was now in my last year of high school, and we had only been back at school for three weeks when the heat wave hit. The only thing that kept me going was the fact that there were only ten months of school left before the end of this year and I graduated. Then I could escape to the city.

I had it all planned. I would go and live with my Aunt Jane, who was divorced and lead a life that evolved around nightclubs and parties and get a job in a record store. Music was my passion and often my only savior. I knew about every band and every singer, thanks to a steady diet of Countdown, Smash Hits, Number One and NME. These were the only qualifications I would need to achieve my dream, and when I had saved enough money I would get my own flat, and I'd have somewhere else to call my own – a place where I could do what I wanted.

But that was in the future. In the present I had to contend with a heat wave, school and a bully nicknamed Bouncer because that's what he used to do to anyone he took a disliking to – bounce them around the playground. He was the bane of my life. He was five-foot-eleven, athletic, had clipped blond hair and a penchant for making my life hell. He liked nothing more than to trip me up, stick chewing gum in the lock of my locker, hide my school bag or anything else he could think of to get a laugh out of the goons that hung around with him. He was so popular that even the older boys, who thought they were the sheriffs of the schoolyard, let him hang out with them and smoke Marlboros up behind the Pre-Voc shed.

However, this year he didn't appear to be interested in bullying me. During the first three weeks of school he'd had numerous opportunities to get a laugh at my expense, but he had passed them all up. I expected things to happen and when they didn't, I was at a loss. It unnerved me not to be picked on by Bouncer.

By Friday of the fourth week back at school, the mercury had climbed to forty-two degrees Celsius. The classrooms weren't equipped with air conditioners, only ceiling fans, which were barely adequate at the best of times, so the teachers let us go home early. We couldn't get out of those classrooms fast enough. Many students headed straight for the local pool or to air conditioned homes, but I headed straight for the stream and my own private sanctuary.

After dropping my bag at home and changing into an old T-shirt and some shorts, I was over the back fence and running through the bush toward the stream. My clothes hadn't even had time to absorb the sweat on my skin before they were off again. I dropped them by the side of the stream and jumped in – the cold water taking my breath away.

The water in this pool was only waist deep, but the hole itself was wide enough to allow me to stretch out and float on my back. I liked nothing better than the feeling of being immersed in the cool water with the hot sun on my face, especially on a day like today. As I lay back on the surface of the water, I dipped my head back and wet my hair. Then I closed my eyes, relaxed and let the sun's rays beat down on me. Behind me, I could hear the water trickling into the pool, creating a peaceful and calming ambience.

As the sun washed over the front of my body I became aware of a familiar sensation in my groin. I felt myself stiffening under the heat of the sun, and my hand, seemingly independent of my mind, gripped my hardening cock and began to stroke it. I had never done this before, a fact I was surprised by since it felt so damned good. The sensation as I began to rub it was incredible, and as this feeling intensified, I wondered if anything else in the world could ever feel this good. My cock got so hard I felt sure the skin surrounding the muscle would split open.

"Well, well," came a deep voice from the side of the pool.

I immediately knelt down so the water, which now came up to my neck, hid my erection. I looked up to see who the intruder was and was shocked to see none other than Bouncer standing there, holding my clothes in his hand.

"Got quite a big cock there, Farmer," he smirked.

I froze.

"Suppose you'd like ya clothes back," he said, the smirk turning into a grin.

"Yes, please," I replied respectfully.

"Well come and get 'em."

I couldn't believe this was happening. If I stayed in the water to hide my hard-on, he might get bored and take off with my clothes. On the other hand, if I got out of the water, not only would he see my erection, but he could still take off with my clothes. In the end, I decided to risk getting out of the water to retrieve my clothes. I figured the humiliation I'd suffer would satisfy him enough to return my belongings.

I stood up and took a couple of steps towards the edge of the pool. My hard cock slapped against my legs as I moved.

"Shit man, you've got a fuckin' hard-on, homo!" he jeered.

I dropped to my knees and tucked my erection between my thighs to hide it. It wasn't possible for me to hate him any more than I did at that moment, not only for humiliating me beyond belief, but for doing it here, in my secret place; for trespassing into the only place that was mine. I felt tears welling up in my eyes, but I was determined not to let him see me cry. I blinked them back and looked him straight in the eyes, although it was difficult not to be distracted by what looked like a large bulge in his shorts. Suddenly I wasn't afraid any more.

"What are ya lookin' at?" he snarled.

"Nothing," I lied, averting my gaze.

"You were lookin' at my cock, weren't ya?" he said accusingly.

Suddenly, a dark look came over his face. He dropped my clothes, tore his shirt off and came storming towards me. I turned to run but he leapt into the pool, landing on my back and pushing me face first into the water. I came up spluttering as he grabbed me around the neck with his arm. He held me in a vice-like grip. My hands went up to try and wrench his arm away from my throat, but of course it was useless.

"Stop it, Bouncer," I managed to say. "I can't breathe."

"You were lookin' at my cock, weren't ya?" he repeated. "Tell me, and I'll let ya go."

His grip tightened, and I could feel my face turning red.

"Bouncer, I ... can't ... breathe," I gasped, starting to panic.

But then I became aware that I could feel Bouncer's cock against my naked buttocks, and it was hard – rock hard – and straining against the fabric of his shorts with all its might. I had an idea.

"If you let me go, I'll do anything," I struggled to say.

Bouncer relaxed his grip a little.

"What?"

"I said if you let me go, I'll do anything you want me to."

Bouncer let me go, pushing me against the far bank of the pool. I got up and turned to face him. I saw for the first time his toned abdominals and pectorals, lightly tanned and covered in a mat of fine, golden hair. Tiny drops of water clung to each hair and glistened in the sunlight. He looked like a Greek god, and in an instant I forgot that I hated him.

"You wanna see my cock, don't ya, faggot?" he asked.

I was not a stupid person. What Bouncer was really saying was that he wanted to show me his cock. So really I had no choice. If I said no, he might lose face and give me a belting, so I said, "Yes."

He looked about to see if anyone else was around, but there wasn't. Our house was the nearest building, and that was quite a long way through the thick bush from where we were. Satisfied we were alone, Bouncer began to lower his shorts, revealing a thick black bush of his own. As his shorts came down his cock slapped up against his hard stomach with a sharp thwak!

"There ya go, faggot. Ya like it?"

"I guess," I replied, not knowing what the etiquette was for talking about your bully's penis. "It's big."

"Yours is bigger."

"No way," I said, feeling more and more comfortable.

"Let's measure them then. Come over here."

I couldn't believe what was happening. As I neared him, he held out his hand, grabbed my cock and pulled me closer to him. He put our cocks together and noted that they were approximately the same size. Then he looked at me in a way that made me want to melt. He closed his eyes and leaned in to me. I had seen this in movies, and without any experience whatsoever, my lips touched his, and we kissed. His hot breath on my mouth made me tingle even though we were standing in icy cold water.

Then I felt his hand come down and grip my hard-on.

"Has anyone ever played with your dick before?" he whispered.

"No."

"How many times have you cum?" he asked, his lips still on mine.

"What?" I asked.

He broke off the kiss.

"You do know what cum is, don't ya?"

"Nup."

Looking back, I can't believe how naive I was, but it was true. I didn't know what cum was. I had few friends and kept to myself at school, all of which meant I had little or no opportunity to find out about these things in the school yard like most other teenagers.

"Come over here," Bouncer said, leading me to the side of the pool by my cock.

He lay back on the grass and pulled me on top of him so that my back was firmly cushioned on his well-developed chest and stomach.

"Now just relax," he told me. "Relax."

I did as he said and let my body go limp. I felt him grip my erection and start pulling it. My breathing became heavier. I couldn't believe how much better it felt when someone else was doing it. I closed my eyes and let my other senses take over. I could feel his hard cock nestled neatly in the crack of my ass. I could hear him breathing and feel his hot breath on my cheek. He began to lick my ear, and I began to make little moaning noises. My body felt electric; so unreal that at any moment I thought I would float off into the sky.

"How does that feel?" he asked, puffing into my ear.

"Mmmmm. Good," I managed to reply, wondering how the hell he came to be so good at this. I didn't have a clue about wanking.

But it was better than good. It was incredibly good. Inexplicably fantastic! I wanted this feeling to last forever and ever. I wanted his hand to keep pumping my cock until the day I died.

"Feel good?" he asked again.

"Oh yeah," I moaned.

And then I could feel an almighty sensation building up from deep inside me.

"I think I'm gonna piss myself," I confessed.

I couldn't believe that at such a critical moment I was going to urinate over us both and spoil the whole thing. However, it didn't seem to bother Bouncer, who instead of stopping, began to pull my cock faster and faster until I reached the point where I thought I was going to explode. And then I did. All over his hand and my stomach.

When he stopped wanking, I looked down and saw the same sticky, white stuff I had discovered on my pajama pants a few days earlier.

"What is that stuff?" I asked.

Bouncer laughed and told me that it was cum. Mystery solved.

He rolled me off him, and I discovered that he, too, had exploded – all over my ass. He put his finger in my crack and ran it along my hole, flicking strings of cum off onto the crushed grass. He did it again, and I felt a little tremor pass through my body.

"If ya tell anyone what we did, I will fuckin' kill ya," he threatened.

"I won't," I promised.

And that was where our passion began and ended. Bouncer stood up, wiped his cock on my T-shirt and disappeared back into the bush. I lay down on the grass where he had lain, completely relaxed and breathed in the smell of crushed grass and sex. I couldn't stop smiling for the rest of the day, and from then on, whenever I saw Bouncer, I couldn't help but wonder if it would ever happen again, if he would ever take my cock in his hand and stroke it until I blew. Unfortunately, it never did, although there was one consolation. Bouncer, the school bully, soon found someone else to pick on which meant he left me alone. I sometimes wondered if he ever did the same thing with his new "victim."

Last Chance
By K. Appleby

Joe hurried down the path passing the music block on his right; the off key notes of some want-to-be musician assaulting his ears. The terrible playing was soon drowned out by the sounds of heavy machinery as he neared the brick tech building to his left. Someone was busily putting the last minute touches on some object, probably a bookend or wooden pencil case.

Joe continued down the footpath between the tech building and the schools boundary fence. The golf course on the other side was pristinely green and isolated. Joe had never actually seen anyone playing golf there, not in all the years at this school.

It had been a long time, from that first apprehensive day he had stumbled in confusion and fear around the huge high school. The school was filled with large sprawling buildings holding many classrooms that seemed to have no order or reason to the numbering system used on their doors. There was added culture shock after being the big kids at primary to being suddenly surrounded by taller, older students. Joe had learned to be tough but fair. He would stick up for the little guy, remembering what it was like being the new kid. Of course, he had grown since then, now it was the last few days of year twelve. Joe was now eighteen, and to his horror, he was still a virgin. Perhaps not a virgin in the traditional sense of the word, he had had girlfriends, but Joe had kept a secret from everyone. He was gay. There were some attractive guys in his year, but none had ever shown any sign of being like him, and besides he always had a huge crush on his former best friend Ash.

Joe and Ash had been best friends since early primary school, but as they grew, Joe came to the realization that he wanted more from Ash than just friendship. When Joe's sexual identity and his secret attraction had started to become a real issue, he had slowly removed himself from Ash and his circle of friends. Joe joined another group of friends, mostly girls, who liked that he never cracked on to them. Joe and Ash were still civil and would occasionally chat and catch up when the situation brought them together. Joe passed the tech building and checked his reflection in the window. He brushed his thick blond hair from his eyes and adjusted his white collared shirt. He noticed the top button of his school shirt was missing, revealing much more of his smooth tanned muscular chest then was appropriate. The shirt was also a little small in the arms. The short almost see through sleeves hardly contained his bicep muscles. Years of working on the farm at home had given him a well-defined muscular build. However, Joe only smiled, with this being his last day of school he gladly wouldn't have to replace the shirt. Joe gave one last smile at his reflection, crossed the footpath and hurried past the bike racks and into the hall.

Upon entering the large, smelly, assembly hall, Joe was glad to see that the exam hadn't started yet. He quickly scanned the room for empty seats and found one just behind and to the left of Ash. Joe hurried over to Ash and gave him a warm smile, which Ash returned with a nod of his head, which sent his long brown hair trailing over his handsome face. Joe took his seat and fiddled with his pen.

Ash said a quiet, "Good luck," as he brushed the hair from his face with his left hand.

Joe sat waiting for the exam to be handed back to him and couldn't prevent his gaze from resting on Ash. As Joe stared at Ash, Ash's long brown hair and broad shoulders fascinated him and stirred his cock into a half mongrel. Joe almost jumped out of his seat when Ash turned to pass the exams to the guy behind him. Ash noticed Joe's stare and gave an odd smile raising his right eyebrow slightly. Joe flushed with embarrassment, realizing that he, too, now had a pile of exams sitting on his desk. Joe quickly took the top exam and handed the rest back to a rather impatient looking guy that Joe didn't really know.

The exam was scheduled to last for two hours, and Joe had no idea how to answer most of the questions on the test paper. It had been almost thirty minutes when Joe had completed all the questions he could answer and had guessed the rest. Joe only had to wait a few minutes more before the teacher finally told those who had finished that they could quietly leave.

Joe watched Ash rise and walk down the isle of tables right past his seat, lightly brushing against Joe's shoulder as he walked alongside, which aroused the shaft contained within Joe's pants. Joe couldn't be sure if it had been deliberate or not, but even if it had been intentional on Ash's part, it would have only been intended as a friendly gesture. Joe waited just long enough for his cock to soften before he got up and followed the small crowd of students out of the hall.

Joe left the hall and saw Ash standing under the shade of a nearby tree waiting for him. Joe headed for Ash while the other students formed small groups and wandered off in all directions.

Joe looked over Ash as he approached. Ash was about the same height as Joe but thinner. He had an athletic build, but without bulging muscles like Joe's. Ash's long brown hair hung gently over his shoulders and wisps of it blew in the summer breeze. A large mound filled the crotch of his gray shorts, and muscular, scarcely hairy legs protruded from beneath. Joe's mind filled with thoughts of what made up the proportions of that mound in those gray shorts.

Joe recalled how one day last year he and Ash had been sitting on the sports oval at the back of school chatting while the rest of their history class did the same. At one point while they sat in conversation, Joe's attention was drawn to a flash of pale movement at Ash's right leg, and Joe had gasped as he spotted only for a second that Ash's cock had flopped from his pants and rested along his inner thigh. Ash had quickly tucked it back into hiding, but Joe had caught a glimpse of the thick smooth cock, and ever since then he had trouble keeping his own cock flaccid whenever Ash was around.

That was one of the reasons Joe had put so much distance between him and Ash. Joe did miss Ash's friendship. However, Joe had felt that he had no choice but to separate himself from the object of his affection. If Joe wished to keep his secret in the small country town where he went to school, he couldn't risk any obvious signs of attraction.

Joe quickly averted his gaze from the shorts and looked up at Ash's face. Ash was watching Joe approach, with a wide grin on his face. Ash's face was long and thin, his features almost angelic but for the few tuffs of facial hair. Not enough that he looked bearded, but just enough to give Ash an almost feral look.

"How'd you go?" Ash asked cocking his head to the side slightly.

"Not too good, I think I failed, how about you?" Joe replied, shrugging his shoulders and rolling his eyes.

"That sucks. I think I did ok though. What you up to now?" Ash asked as he reached out and rubbed Joe's upper back with exaggerated sympathy.

Joe fought against his blooming erection until Ash's hand had stopped caressing his back.

19

Joe thought for a minute. That was thankfully the last one of his exams, and the bus wouldn't be coming to take him on the forty-minute journey back to his home on the farm until 3.00 pm. Checking his watch, he now saw it was only 10.30 am.

Joe shrugged, "Nothing, going to wait for the bus. I suppose."

Ash nodded, "I'm heading home, if you want to come? Beats hanging around school all day"

Joe was hesitating when Ash slapped him on the back and almost pushed him forward.

"Come on, it'll be fun," Ash promised.

Joe nodded, and they started walking out of school, in all the years he had known Ash, Joe had never actually been to his house, living out of town made such things almost impossible.

After a short nervous silence, they started to talk of school, of the teachers both the horrible and the good ones. They remembered all the fun they had had together. Ash remarked of the two Year Seven kids that were too scared to enter the boys' toilets after all the horror stories they had heard. It wasn't until the second term of Year Seven that they were brave enough to enter the boys' toilets. They revealed how they were both rather disappointed by the anti-climax, when nothing untoward had happened.

Ash mock punched Joe's shoulder, sending his cock into heat again.

"We were such dorks," Ash said, and they both laughed.

"What about the time we stole that hose from the agriculture shed, and we set it up on the demountable roof," Joe replied.

It had been a hot summer that year, and there was a rumor around school all summer that if the temperature ever reached 40°C the students would all be sent home. The temperature was 40°C, and everyone was milling about, not going to their classes. An impromptu assembly had then been called over the loud speaker. All the students gathered standing in the hot sun on the asphalt quadrangle, waiting to hear that they could leave school. Instead the deputy announced that it was just a rumor and school would go ahead as normal. He added that anyone not attending classes would be in serious trouble for truanting. Needless to say, none of the pupils were very impressed, and once dismissed moved with lethargic reluctance to there respective classrooms.

20

Joe and Ash's next class was in the demountable, a portable tin roofed classroom that they knew would be hotter than outside, perhaps even hotter than hell itself.

"Yep and when our teacher saw, she just laughed and prided us on our ingenuity," Ash laughed again. "It sure did cool down the classroom, I think she appreciated that." Joe added with a smile.

Joe looked over at Ash; Joe stopped laughing as he saw that Ash had unbuttoned his shirt to catch the light breeze. Ash's smooth well defined chest was gorgeous, his small dark nipples contrasting beautifully with his smooth pale skin. Smooth that is except for a light trail of hair that went from his flat stomach down to whatever delights were hidden within the substantial bulge in his gray shorts.

Joe realized again that Ash was observing his stare. Joe only hoped that Ash hadn't noticed the bulge in his pants sticking out at an obvious angle.

Ash laughed again, "I'm hot what can I do?" he shrugged, causing Joe to laugh, too.

They continued to reminisce, and as they neared Ash's house, they were sore from laughing and had grins fixed to there faces.

Ash unlocked the door and entered first.

"No one's home, come on in," Ash offered motioning for Joe to follow before closing the door once he had entered. Ash moved into the kitchen and offered Joe a drink of water, which Joe eagerly accepted, the cool refrigerated water was a relief from the warm day. Joe tried not to be too obvious as he watched Ash slide the cool glass over his chest, stomach and nipples sighing deeply. Joe let out an involuntary sigh at the sight, himself, his cock again becoming rigid.

Ash just smiled and led Joe into his room. Ash's bedroom was full of paint tubes, brushes and half finished paintings. As Joe looked around at the paintings, Ash sat on the bed, removed his shirt and then picked up his guitar, and started playing something that Joe didn't really recognize. Ash finished his impromptu performance and placed his guitar aside, grinning as he offered Joe a seat beside him in the bed.

They sat in silence for a few minutes before Ash cleared his throat.

"You know we probably won't see each other again," he said sadly breaking the silence.

"Yes, I know," Joe replied leaning his head back against the wall and sighing deeply.

Ash grunted then asked, "Can you take the glasses back into the kitchen for me?"

Ash was obviously frustrated about something. Joe worried that Ash had realized that he was gay or had noticed Joe's affections toward him.

"Yes sure," Joe said as he stood and grabbed the empty glasses and left the room.

Joe so wanted to tell Ash how he felt about him. Joe wanted to explain why he had removed himself as Ash's closest friend, but he didn't want to ruin their last day together. Joe quickly washed the glasses and left them on the sink. He returned to Ash's room to find the door closed. Joe hesitated then knocked gently.

"Come in and close the door," called Ash's voice from within his bedroom.

Joe did just that. He opened the door and entered turning to close the door behind him.

Joe turned again to see Ash lying naked on the bed, his pale fit body almost glowing in the dim lighting. Joe looked him up and down in astonishment. It was all there in full view. Ash's lightly tanned flesh showed off those small dark nipples. The light covering of hair on Ash's arms and legs gave his boyish body a manly touch. That small thin trail of hair did go all the way down to Ash's small patch of light brown pubes.

That trail of hair kept drawing all of Joe's attention to Ash's cock. Ash's manhood was as glorious as Joe had envisioned, and it was lying fat and thick on Ash's tight stomach, and Joe was sure that it must have already been at least half erect.

"What you standing there for?" Ash asked, "You want this don't you?" He proposed.

"Ummm," was all that could pass his lips as Joe stood staring in shock as the blood rushed from his body into his virgin cock, swelling it to proportions he had never before felt. Joe had secretly dreamed of this moment with Ash for many years, but now it was real. Ash was lying naked just a few feet in front of him. It was almost too good to be true. Joe was too scared to move, as if any action on Joe's part would dispel the magic of this dream made reality.

"Joe … last chance?" Ash warned reaching beside the bed for his clothes.

Joe needed no more warnings. He ripped off his shirt, the remaining buttons flying around the room, revealing his broad shoulders, muscled chest and flat stomach. Joe then kicked off his shoes and tore off his socks. He removed his gray shorts with a little less haste and a little more self consciousness, until he stood in only his underwear.

"And the rest," Ash said pointing at the jocks, which could barely contain Joe's throbbing erect cock.

Joe removed his underwear freeing his massively erect shaft, which stood pointing straight up at the ceiling. Feeling self-conscious, Joe practically ran and jumped onto the bed beside Ash.

They lay there for what seemed like an eternity, neither confident enough to make the first move. Joe's cock pulsed with every breath. He watched Ash's cock as it started to grow longer and thicker. Joe couldn't believe that Ash's large manhood was only just becoming erect now.

"Man, you must have a big one," Joe blurted out without thinking.

"Why don't you suck it?" Ash suggested as he reached down to hold his thick cock so it was pointing up into the air.

Joe had never sucked a dick before, but the one on offer looked delicious. Joe gently climbed over Ash positioning his head above the thick shaft that just seemed to be getting bigger and bigger.

Joe hesitated not really knowing how to start or what to do.

"Suck it," Ash urged as he placed a hand gently on Joe's head and ran his fingers through the silky blond hair, tenderly directing Joe's head down toward his waiting cock.

Joe slowly lowered his moist mouth onto the smooth cock, his whole body trembling. As he felt the warm smooth cock in his mouth, instinct must have taken over; he moved his head up and down licking the throbbing shaft of flesh with his tongue. Ash moaned occasionally, and the first few times Joe worried that he had hurt Ash's cock, but Joe soon came to realize they were moans of enjoyment and not pain as he had at first feared. Ash's cock had swelled to almost double its original size. Its length dug deep into Joe's throat, and his lips were starting to get sore from stretching to accommodate its expanding width. Joe could feel every throb of Ash's cock deep inside his mouth, and then it swelled even larger making it difficult for Joe to breathe when he took its full length within him.

As Joe worked the thick shaft, he realized finally, how right it felt, how good it made him feel to have another man's pride in his mouth, giving it pleasure. In time, he noticed Ash's soft hairy balls tighten, and Joe tasted something odd and arousing in his mouth.

"Stop, stop, I don't want to cum like this," Ash said as he pulled Joe's head off his cock with both hands.

Joe looked at Ash's beautiful cock. It was fleshy and thick and a full inch or two longer than his own. Ash was reaching under his bed for something, allowing Joe to see his lightly sculpted back and pale butt cheeks with their sprinkling of soft fluff. Meanwhile, Joe sat and played with Ash's cock rubbing it between his fingers. He was completely fascinated by the differences and similarities to his own aching prick.

Ash pulled out a tube of something called KY. Ash dribbled a little oozing liquid onto his hand and then smothered it all over his cock.

"Lie down, I want to fuck you," Ash said as he stroked his own cock.

Joe lay face down on the bed, his hard cock digging a groove into the mattress, and his smooth pale bubble butt lying naked and vulnerable in the air. Joe was equally excited and scared. He had loved sucking his first cock but was unsure if he could handle having Ash's cock penetrating his virgin ass.

"No, lie face up," Ash demanded stifling a laugh.

Joe did as instructed, and as soon as he had rolled over, Ash moved in close behind him and raised Joe's legs up with his feet on Ash's shoulders, positioning them either side of Ash's head.

Ash maneuvered his engorged cock against Joe's virgin hole, and Joe let out a whimper of trepidation. Ash leaned forward and felt up Joe's heavily defined chest, and in doing so, Ash's roaming hand brushed against Joe's left nipple, which sent Joe's body quivering with delight. Ash smiled and moved both hands to caress Joe's chest and sensitive nipples. Joe's own swollen cock rubbed between their tight young bodies as the pressure on his anal entrance grew and grew. Ash then pulled in closer to Joe's chest and licked his receptive nipples one at a time. Joe writhed in rapture then suddenly the tip of Ash's drooling knob pushed its way into Joe's tight unexplored crevasse. Joe flinched with pain, as the massive dick slowly edged further and ever deeper into his tiny virgin hole.

As the long cock was almost half way in, Joe felt the pleasure overriding the pain and finally started to relax. Joe looked deeply into Ash's brown eyes, reassured that he wasn't in fact being split in two by the massive shaft that was filling his hole. As Ash and Joe's eyes locked in stare, Joe could see the expression of bliss on Ash's handsome face and the look of absolute ecstasy in his eyes.

Joe relaxed and allowed himself to be lost in the moment. It was finally happening. Joe was losing his virginity, becoming one body and soul with another guy.

"This feels great," Joe whispered.

Ash stopped the assault on Joe's nipples with his lips and tongue. Instead, Ash returned to gently tweaking them with his fingers as he begun to really pound Joe's firm butt. With each powerful thrust, Ash's manhood delved further within Joe, and with each deepening plunge, Joe found himself wanting more and more. He knew with no uncertainty that this is what he wanted. Joe was gay, and if this was what being gay felt like, he was glad to be gay.

"Fuck me Ash, fuck me," Joe whispered through labored breaths.

Ash heard and obeyed, fucking his friend with new determination.

"You're so fucking tight," Ash gasped mid stroke.

Ash suddenly slowed and leaned into Joe's face, their lips meeting first only briefly, but then Ash came back in closer. And, they kissed frantically and deeply like lovers, tongues and lips finding each other's mouths, all the while Ash kept gently caressing the insides of Joe's ass with his smooth, thick cock.

Joe was in heaven. He could do this all day, but at the same time, he desperately wanted to cum, and he wanted to make Ash cum as well. Ash pulled himself up and grabbed Joe's rock hard erection in his hand. Ash started to pound Joe's stuffed hole with even more power then before. Pulling his thick dick out almost all the way and thrusting into Joe's tight ass deep and fast, repeatedly.

"I'm going to blow," Ash gasped as he pulled on Joe's oozing cock with fervor and fucked his hairless smooth ass like an animal. Both Joe and Ash simultaneously exploded, releasing the biggest loads either had ever blown before.

Ash collapsed on top of Joe, and they lay there for a time, moist and sticky catching there breaths.

"Thanks Joe, that was awesome," Ash said as he removed his softening cock from Joe's worn ass and got off the bed. Joe just lay there smiling while watching Ash clean the lube and cum from his body before getting dressed.

"Shit! Joe you got to go, its 2.30!" Ash exclaimed noticing the time on the clock.

Joe climbed out of bed exhausted but exhilarated. He wiped himself dry and glanced at the clock. He would have to hurry back to school in order to catch the bus on time. Joe hastily got dressed as Ash disappeared into another room. By the time Ash returned, Joe was fully dressed and heading for the door.

"Does that mean I owe you a shirt?" Ash asked jokingly, looking at the now button-less one that Joe wore.

Joe laughed back abashed and just he shook his head.

"No, its on the house," he replied, closing the shirt to hide his manly chest momentarily in mock modesty, before letting it rest open with a shrug of his shoulders.

"I'll find the buttons and give them to you next time I see you," Ash said through laughter.

Joe looked at his watch. "It's ok; you don't have to come back to school with me." Joe insisted.

"Thanks," Ash replied, "I'm exhausted."

"I'm feeling pretty fucked myself," Joe replied, and they both broke into laughter again at Joe's unintentional joke. Joe chuckled as he headed down the hall to the front door.

As Joe was about to leave the house, Ash stopped him, giving him a kiss on the cheek and a huge hug before he placed a piece of paper in Joe's hand.

"This is my number and address Joe. I hope now we can be friends like before?"

Joe smiled, nodded and pocketed the note.

"I'll have to see you to get my buttons back anyway," Joe called as he dashed out the door and hurried toward the school.

Joe knew that Ash wasn't going to be his boyfriend and that they would probably never have sex again. Joe truly was thankful to Ash for being such a good friend, for taking his virginity and making him a man. As Joe approached the waiting bus for the last time, he realized that he would contact Ash again soon and that their friendship would be stronger than ever now that Joe could truly be himself in Ash's company.

Joe smiled to himself as he climbed aboard the bus. His last day of school had been his best day of school and his first day as a proud gay man.

Six One Thousand
By R.A. Padgett

"... six one thousand, seven one thousand, eight one thousand, nine one thousand – -come on, you pussy! One more – give it to me! Give me that last one – yeah boy, come on, fuck yeah!"

The fucker wasn't going to let me off easy, was he? Sometimes I hated him – when he would push me into hating him. This whole love-hate cycle was driving me up a wall. I wanted what he had to give. I wanted my flabby, out of shape body to look like his. I knew I was stuck with certain traits, my short, stocky body would never conform to, say, the Amazonian body I idealized that I lusted after. But this man, my coach had that sort of body; tall, built like a brick shithouse, amber eyes that could bore right through you and the smoothest, chocolate satin skin stretched taut over his perfectly proportioned frame. Not muscle-bound at all but a body that was well trained and beautifully toned. But right now I hated him. Right now he could go straight to hell, and I wouldn't bat an eyelash. Right now, he could go fuck himself!

"One more set on the bars. I know you want to give it to me. Let's go, Buddy." I always just melted when he called me Buddy – he must have known this as he always ended our sessions by calling me this, and I always forgave him for his tirades. On the last set, I was sweatin' like a pig, and I looked up at him spotting me and got an eyeful of his crotch, which only made me want to push myself further. I lusted after this man in the worst way, and damn if he didn't know it and use it against me – "You did real good, buddy – I'm proud of you and all your work is starting to show ... time to shower up now ... hop to it!"

It was difficult to look him in the eye, but inside I felt proud of myself and warm all over. As I trudged to the locker room, my legs all rubbery and lightheaded, I opened the door and smelled that moist testosterone as I walked in. I turned the corner to my locker just in time to glance at Coach as he bent over to remove his shorts leaving a sparkling white jockstrap framing his beautiful ass. Bent over, I got a great view of his nuts partially escaping the same pouch I salivated over just moments ago. Standing up, he turned to see me staring at him before I could avert my eyes – gave me a little smile and continued with the unintentional striptease, my heart racing. I'm sure my face was beet red. I stood there slack-jawed as he stripped off his jock, freeing a beautiful piece of man meat overhanging two incredible, pendulous balls – over ripe and ready for the picking. As he turned to go to the showers, I couldn't take my eyes off him until he was out of sight.

I looked down at my own crotch that was obviously tented and then to the floor where he had left his jock curled up among his other clothes – beckoning me, inviting me to come take a whiff. I couldn't help myself – I had to get at it. I carefully made my way to this treasure. As I brought it up to my nose, I inhaled deeply almost as I would a drug.

Fuckin' A! This rank, sweaty aroma was everything I expected and more. Intoxicated I fell backwards against the bench, grabbing on my way down a locker door that banged loudly. I heard the shower shut down and coach yelled out, "Are you okay?"

Gathering myself together I replied that "yeah I was fine!" Panicked, I threw down the still warm jock, and it landed, sitting there so obvious on top of his other clothes. But it was too late.

Coach rounded the corner with a towel wrapped around his waist asking, "What's up? Are you sure you're okay?"

"Yeah – I mean yes, I'm fine, sir," I replied. Thank God the panic actually helped me and my boy dick calm down, but not without leaving a noticeable wet spot on the front of my briefs. My face bright red; I looked down at my feet as I continued to pull my sweats up around my thighs. "Aren't you gonna shower, kid??" he asked.

"No sir, I have to get home fast … uh, I mean soon."

His eyes boring right through to my soul, he said, "Well I'll tell you what, kid, obviously you are in need of some more intense training, so what do you say we crank it up a notch? You may not like what I have to say at first, but you will thank me in the long run. We are going to be doing something a little different from now on. We will begin and end our workouts in the pool. You will lap swim for forty-five minutes both before and after our sessions, as a warm-up and cool-down. This next thing, and I need you to trust me on this one, I want you to shave tonight when you shower. I want all the hair off your chest, crotch and legs – not a single hair left on your body! Do you hear?"

This last thing was said with more authority then I was used to from this man.

"You can use a little talc tonight after your shower – this will help with the itch. Get a good night's sleep because you are gonna need to be rested for tomorrow. Meet me at one-thirty instead of three. We are gonna get that shag of yours cut off. You are to have your hair cropped at half inch on the sides and one inch on the top. You will keep it this way from now on."

He was testing me. I knew it. I was powerless.

What was I willing to give up for this man and for the body I wanted, I craved? I had been working for a couple of years on getting rid of my flabby physique and turning it into a classical marble sculpture before I noticed his ad as a personal trainer, which was just what I needed to go on to the next level. That was months ago, and the dedication and discipline he had instilled in me was indeed showing. I was getting a lot of notice by both women and men at work as well as on the street. My shoulders straightened up, and I started walking with not quite a strut but more or less a confident stride. This made all the difference in the world. I felt better then I ever had about myself, and I wanted this to continue. Besides, what would it hurt to follow his directions for a time, just to see what happened?

"And as for these," he grabbed the waist band of my briefs, his fingers creeping inside, grazing my piss slit, "You will lose these panties and start wearing boxers like a man. You will enjoy the feeling of your equipment swaying back and forth as you walk." He quickly let go and the waistband of my jockeys snapped back and slapped the head of my erect dick, causing a small moan; more like a whimper to escape my throat. He brought his fingers up and licked the precum that had gathered on them. "Now be a good boy and clean up this mess!" With that he put on his socks, slacks, and shirt – no underwear – and stormed out into the evening.

I was shocked and stunned. I couldn't believe what had just happened. It was if he had reached into the dark recesses of my mind, grasped my hidden fantasies and wrung them dry for his pleasure. My mind was reeling. A moment later someone entered the locker room and yanked me back to reality. I finished dressing and tucked my things into my backpack and stuffed his stuff into his gym bag.

Turning in my key, the receptionist quipped, "Looks like your friend left you a little present," and winked knowingly. I guess he noticed I came in with just my backpack but left with much more. I blushed red hot, and I was sure this wouldn't be the last time.

That night, noticeably shaken, I succeeded in making myself a brief meal. Just a power shake and tuna on rye. Then sat down to watch some tube. Increasingly distracted by my thoughts, after about an hour,

I decided to turn the damn thing off. Actually I couldn't remember anything at all of what I had just watched. I sat for a while in the silence. Just a few years ago, I was doughy, plump, depressed and lacked any real energy at all. Today, I had energy plus and thrived on life – actually thrived! In the last year, I had decided I needed a little sumpin' extra from having a trainer and went through a couple before I stumbled on Sam – he wanted to be called Coach – in the want ads. There was something more to him than what showed on the outside. He seemed genuine and well rounded. He believed in integrating all aspects of your life including exercise, mental focus, diet and spirituality. He had a certain sadness that made me want to explore his depths. He certainly turned my world around.

Today, I feel alive and rejuvenated. I feel more comfortable in my own skin and more attuned to my emotions, creativity and fantasies. At least that was what I had thought! As I was thinking, my mind kept going back to that vision of that beautiful dark ass. I wanted to see it, taste it, feel it. I wanted to dive neck deep into it! My dick sure needed some attention.

I wondered whether I could do what he had asked of me. I guess more demanded from me. Coach really liked to test my limits and make me reach beyond my grasp. "The only way to grow," he would say. This though was something new, kind of humbling, humiliating, yet exciting. I wasn't sure if I could do this.

Turning down the living room lights, almost in a trance, I went into the bathroom, stripping off my street clothes and throwing them into the hamper. Coach's bag fell down from where I had put it when I came in the door. A rush went through me like a warm chill as I stared at the bag. When I unzipped it, the contents fell out onto the tiled floor. I brought his shirt up and sniffed at where his pits had been, the aroma nearly knocking me over from my squatting stance. It was wonderfully heady, unmistakably a man's odor. I couldn't keep from frantically grabbing his jock and binging that to my nose, too. I loved the smell of this man. I touched it to my lips, my tongue darting out to taste that sweet tang. My mouth by now seriously salivating, it didn't take much to shove the whole pouch into my mouth. My dick was rock hard and starting to drip again. I brought a finger full of my precum to my lips, the same scum he had tasted just hours before. I licked it slowly bridging it from my tongue to my fingertips. I needed this! I needed him … in the worst way!

Gaining some control, I began putting his stuff back in his bag, but there on the bottom of the bag was an small manila envelope with my name, Chris, unassumingly taped to the black bottom, it stood out like a gold ticket in a candy bar, beckoning me. Without too much thought, I grabbed it and ripped it open at the seam. What fell out was a link, just a single platinum link of a chain and note that read, "IN THE BEGINNING …"

That fucker! He had to have known, the son of a bitch planted this before we even got to the gym today. So fuckin' full of himself! Who does he think he is? A wave of fear swept over me, no not fear – more like trepidation for what I thought, (and apparently) he knew what lie ahead. I'll show that two can play at this game. I started my bath water getting it a little hotter than would be comfortable and brought out my clippers. I started trimming away. I'll show that son of a bitch. I used the number-one guard on the clippers and trimmed off all the hair on my chest, pits and pubes. I gathered my tools and stepped into the bath with a three-pack of disposable razors, a can of shaving cream and a couple of washcloths. Slowly lowering myself into the hot water I soaked for a couple of minutes before beginning what turned out to be an hour and a half procedure. I had done this before for swim team in high school as had a majority of my teammates, so it didn't bother me as much as he probably thought it would. After nicking myself a couple of times, I decided to slow down and enjoy the process. I started with my legs and went on to my chest, armpits and butt. I started to shave my pubes and stopped short of it. I ended up shaving around my balls and up the shaft of my dick. I left a patch of hair above my dick, kind of a fuck you statement and let the water out of the tub, which only ended up leaving a mass of stray hairs all over. Steeping back in, I got the handheld and sprayed down my body and the tub surround. Using the shower, I squatted down and paid particular attention to my ass and balls. The water strumming against them felt incredible.

I got out and dried off thoroughly, opening the bathroom door to let some of the steam out. Wiping down the mirror, I was surprised to see how my body looked after denuding all that hair. My muscles that I had worked so hard at looked more defined. I could see the beginning of a six-pack, (a four-pack really) starting to show up. The cleft in my butt cheeks and the shadow of my overhanging chest showed proud and proper. I ran around the apartment buck ass naked for a while to try and cool off. The air against my body felt so fucking good! I wished I had done this earlier. After having a snack, I returned to the bathroom and liberally dusted myself with talcum. My skin turned satiny soft and smooth as – you'll forgive the analogy – a baby's bottom. I shook off the excess powder and trotted off to bed.

I was excruciatingly tired, probably from the workout along with the mental, emotional strain. After setting my alarm. It didn't take long for me to drift off to sleep.

Sometime in the middle of the night, I awoke with a fierce hard on, humping the crisp, cool sheets, fucking the air with an animal lust. The sheets behind me creeping into the crack of my ass, the ones before me encapsulating my dick like a French whore. My moaning and groaning interrupted only by one word – a mantra of sorts. "Coach" "Please, Coach," "Ugh, coach!"

I went over the edge bucking the sheets and biting, crying into my pillow. I came with a vengeance, crying out loudly, the white-hot slag pulsing out of my dick, into the bed sheets and soaking my belly. "Fuck yeah! Take that you fuckin' dickhead," "Jesus H Christ! I yes, I cum fuck! Fuck yeah, please I need it!" "I need you!"

My heart was racing, trying to keep up with me, and I'm sure that if someone was around to take my blood pressure, I would have blown the circuits in the machine. Holy shit! That felt good! I got up and blindly sopped up the majority of my splooge with a towel and trudged to the living room with a blanket and my alarm clock in tow. I slept soundly for the rest of the night.

I woke up refreshed and revitalized, drank me a quick cup of brew and tore the sheets off my bed, starchy pile that they were, stacking them in my hamper along with assorted underwear, socks and shirts. I took a fresh set of sheets out and proceeded to make my bed. Damn, I was in a good mood. I couldn't just waste away such a beautiful day. I called my friend, Ken, and set up at time to meet with him for lunch. After dropping my laundry off at my favorite cleaners and doing some shopping, I made my way to Barney's, our local eatery.

Ken knew me like the back of his hand, and it didn't take him long to figure out that something was up. After grilling me for about a half hour, I finally relented and told him my story.

"I don't know what kinda spell this guy has over me, but my dick gets half-hard just having him around me." Ken didn't offer any suggestions. He wasn't big on offering suggestions, but he was a great sounding board, letting me go on until I was empty. Afterward, I felt ashamed and excused myself curtly. After all, I had an appointment to keep.

After picking up the two loads of laundry, I arrived early. As I was pulling into the parking lot, I found him there, eyeing his pocket watch. I jumped out of the car, grabbing the laundry and shuffled toward him, shyly watching the sidewalk as I came up to him. With a grunt, he directed me to get into his car saying we had somewhere to go and didn't have much time. I don't think I looked at him at all until we came to a stop in front of a barbershop that looked out of place in the middle of this stretch of high-rises. The sign outside read "Buzz cuts $15.00." I looked over at him, and he pointed his eyes at the sign then back to my eyes again. Once more, a small whimper escaped my throat.

As we entered the shop, the barber knowingly acknowledged Coach and finished with his client. After the last customer left, he stepped behind him to lock the door and turn the open sign to close. The barber and Coach both led me to a chair without saying a word. Coach told the barber to crop the sides as usual but leave a little length on top. He added, "Not so much that I can't see him sweat."

Little did he know that I was sweating like a pig under the rubberized cape that thankfully hid my full-blown boner. Coach told me, "You are to look into my eyes the entire time, boy."

I did as he said, his eyes burning into my soul. My dick twitching and leaking under the cape as the barber shaved my head. The clippers found every erotic nerve on my head. Coach grabbed a handful of my crotch through the material as he looked at me, and I him. He started massaging roughly and continued staring right through me.

He said, "I know what you did last night, I'll always know." His gripped tightened catching my entire kit as he continued, "I'm gonna let it go this time, but from now on you are not to cum. Unless and until I say you can! You can beat off and milk that pretty boy dick of yours all you want, but you are not to cum, do you understand?"

"Yes," was all the breath I could spare with the clippers buzzing my neck, his grip on my wet equipment and those eyes, those damn eyes looking into mine, piercing mine. I was starting to shake from the need, my hips bucking back and forth as much as I dared with the crop job going on my topside. Trying to get that gripping, fuck yeah, fist, oh my God! "Fuck yeah! Please, Daddy! Please let me!" I groaned out load and tears started involuntarily leaking from my eyes. "Fuck Sir Please!"

This went on only a few minutes before he said, "Okay boy, you can cum now."

33

Just then he wrenched my dick hard, and the barber dug his hands into my freshly cropped hair. Coach reached up to squelch my moans, covering my mouth and forcing the seed right out of my dick like a fire hose. I came violently and as noisily as I could with his hands covering my mouth. "Fuck yeah! I need it, Sir! Please I ... need to fuck your fist ... Yeah holy fucking Christ!"

He never took his eyes off me, letting go of my mouth, I gasped for air. He let go of my kit, and I felt a tremendous release and relief. He stood back and gave me one of those half-smiles of his. The barber finished up in a few strokes and ripped the apron right off me. I was horrified to find in the crumpled folds of my jeans, a huge wet spot that would be impossible to hide. Nodding his head to follow him, he led me through the door. Outside on the way to the car, we passed a couple, and as they looked down at my crotch I was surprised that along with my shame and humiliation, there was a sense of pride in my stain.

As we drove back in silence, I kept wanting to say something, starting out, "Coach, I ... oh never mind," trying to get words out but failing at every attempt. Finally as we pulled into the parking lot, I blurted out, "Coach. I just wanted to say how much I appreciate, um, the extra attention."

He stopped me before I could continue, and his voice lowered an octave, and quietly he told me, "Look kid, this isn't about your dick! The sooner you learn the better! I'm gonna let you go this afternoon. You have a lot to think about, but I want you to show up here tomorrow at one and bring your suit – we'll warm up in the pool."

As I grabbed my bag from the backseat, he said, "Leave those there with my stuff. Now get along and get yourself some rest – you'll need it."

He got out of the car, and I felt privileged that he would do such a thing. Walking toward my car, my sanctuary, he called out, "Stop!" I turned to look at him palming and playing with some shiny object, making it dance along his fingers like a poker chip. He winked at me as he flipped it through the air. Instinctively, I reached up and caught it midair. Looking at this prize, I realized it wasn't a coin at all but another silver chain link, a perfect partner to the one I found last night. Looking back up, he was already in his car and had started his engine. He didn't even look at me as he drove away. I took my former treasure out of my pocket where it had been stashed and linked the two prizes together. I knew in my heart what they symbolized. I was bewitched, bothered and bewildered. This was how it was that I entered his world.

Hot Shot
By Sedonia Guillone

"Hey, Paul, will you photograph me?"

Paul froze. He clutched his towel and stopped in mid-rub of his wet hair. The room filled with silence, the only sound, the evening spring rain that pelted the living room window. Slowly, he lowered the towel, turned, and looked at Carlo.

Large brown eyes watched him from under a thick fringe of ebony lashes. Carlo had already toweled the rain off his own thick glossy hair and the raven-colored locks tumbled around his face, set off his high cheekbones. His smooth black goatee and mustache emphasized his full lips. Paul had spent countless moments fantasizing about kissing those lips.

Paul's heart thumped. Carlo's beauty always struck him, and in the whole three years of their friendship, he'd ached to capture that beauty on film. "Are you serious?"

What appeared fleeting shyness passed across Carlo's face, quickly replaced by his usual coolness. "Yeah, man. I'm serious."

Paul nodded. His heart pumped in rapid beats now, and his cock stirred and jumped to attention in his jeans. He set the towel aside and cleared his throat. "Okay, then. If you want me to." He forced himself to act casual, far from the emotional chaos that churned his blood. In three years as housemates, Carlo had never expressed interest in getting photographed, not even in his soccer uniform or at his garage where he designed and built the hottest choppers in their part of California. "May I ... uh ... I mean, I'm just curious ..."

Carlo's soft laughter interrupted him. "I know. You can't believe it." He shrugged and looked down. "I don't know, man. Just like this."

Paul stared at him another moment. Carlo was holding something back. But hey, he wasn't going to push. Carlo's asking to be photographed was a fantasy come true, as rare as Halley's comet.

"Well..." he gestured in the direction of his studio, really, a spare bedroom in the back of his house he'd converted into a studio. "This way." He led Carlo there.

"Should I change or something?"

Paul turned around and looked at him. The rain had soaked Carlo's white T-shirt and plastered it to his lean torso. Carlo's skin, the color of light caramel, showed through the wet cotton as did the tiny peaks of his dark nipples, hardened, apparently, from the coolness of rain. Below that, he wore a baggy pair of jeans.

He cleared his throat again. Aside from nudity, Carlo couldn't have looked sexier for the kind of photographs Paul envisioned. "No. You're ... perfect."

A shudder of electricity seemed to pass between them. Carlo blinked. "Okay. Just tell me what to do."

Take your clothes off and let me suck your cock. Paul didn't say the words out loud. He wouldn't dare. Carlo had never given him any indication that Paul's wild attraction to him was mutual. If Carlo had wanted him, he would have included him in the string of lovers that had passed through their apartment over the last three years.

Paul swallowed hard. "Um, just ... I don't know. I guess ..." His hands shook as he adjusted his camera, already set up on its tripod from a job the day before. "Start with something natural." He indicated the sofa draped with sheets he'd set up for yesterday's photo shoot for *Gay Life Magazine*. That had been a joy to shoot. Three gorgeous guys in underwear draped all over each other.

But today? Was better.

Carlo sat down on the sofa and leaned against the cushions, one muscled arm along the back of the sofa. He looked up from under his heavy lashes, lips pouting. "How's this?"

Paul's heart jumped. Electric heat zinged up his arms and down into his groin. Carlo looked incredible. In that pose, he was sexy, alluring and innocent all at once. "Perfect," he said softly. He adjusted his camera, set the lighting in the room and shot the picture.

"Should I do another pose?" Carlo sat up and raked a hand through his thick ebony hair. Inadvertently, he looked off to one side. Perfect. That pose, too, brought out Carlo's irresistible combination of dark sensuality and innocence.

"Stay like that," he ordered. Carlo obeyed, and he shot the picture.

Carlo turned and smiled. "This is kind of fun," he said. He draped his arms over his thighs and leaned forward.

Paul shot another picture. "You seem to be a natural."

"Nah," Carlo lay back, one arm bent behind his head. His T-shirt rode up just enough to expose half of his tight abdomen. "You're a good photographer, man."

A shiver of lust tore through Paul. He forced his attention off the thin trail of ebony hair that ran down the center of Carlo's stomach and onto shooting the picture. "Thanks," he managed to say. Carlo had often praised his work, and he felt ridiculously pleased each time. He'd won several awards for his photos in the past three years and attributed his success to the fact that he worked so hard to please Carlo.

The thought made him ache to confess the raw emotions he felt for his housemate. He remained silent and kept snapping pictures. His tension melted away as he got into the flow of taking pictures. Carlo moved from one pose to the next, as if he'd been a model for years.

Suddenly, Carlo sat up and stripped off his T-shirt. He dropped it onto the floor and looked directly at the camera, his hands on his thighs.

Paul's finger froze on the button. He cleared his throat. His heart took off like a bucking bronc, and his stomach fluttered just as it did when he had his first crush back in high school.

"Is this okay?" Carlo looked worried. "Should I put it back on?"

"No!"

Carlo grinned and chuckled. "Okay." He lay against the cushions, both strong arms along the back of the sofa.

Paul stared through the eyepiece. He pretended to be adjusting the focus when he was really staring at Carlo's rippling chest and abs, at the soft dark hair on his pecs funneling into a trail down his stomach and at the chocolate brown of his small hard nipples. Paul's mouth watered, and now he had a major hard-on in his jeans. Who'd have thought that a pizza out with Carlo and running back home in the rain would end up like this? He shot the picture.

Carlo lifted one arm from the back of the sofa and ran his hand over his chest.

Paul licked his lips. Was the guy making fun of him, teasing him? His eyes widened as he looked through the viewer. He could swear there was a sizeable bulge in Carlo's jeans, just behind the zipper. Was he hard?

Carlo slid his hand down his abdomen. Right down toward that delicious-looking bulge. He stared into the lens. Carlo's dark brown eyes took on a velvety sheen. His lids grew heavy, and his full lips parted, as if he were breathing heavier.

Paul shot the picture. Damn, he couldn't wait to develop that one.

"Hey Paul?"

The husky tone in Carlo's voice made his heart thump. He swallowed hard and looked out from behind the camera. "Yeah?" He forced himself to look and sound calm. No easy task considering the raging boner he had. To him, Carlo was the hottest guy in the universe. Hotter than any movie star.

"How naked do I have to get before you take the bait?"

Paul nearly crumpled to the floor. Because his knees suddenly felt like Jell-O. "Wha … What?"

Carlo chuckled softly. "You heard me."

He let go of the camera and wiped his hands on his jeans, feeling like an idiot. "B … b … bait?"

Carlo raked a hand through his thick, raven hair. That shy look Paul had seen earlier now came over Carlo's face, only now, it didn't flit away so quickly.

Paul's heart thumped again. Was Carlo nervous? He'd always thought Carlo never got nervous.

"Yeah. I didn't know how else to tell you, man. You're so … quiet."

Now Paul's heart was racing almost too fast to breathe. "Tell … me?"

Carlo huffed, but the sound was like mock annoyance. In spite of his seeming shyness, he grinned, that devilish, sexy grin he had. The one that first made Paul go ga ga for him. "Yeah, man. You know, to tell you I … I want you." His hands went to the button of his jeans. He worked it open, slid down the zipper and left them open. He wasn't wearing anything underneath, and his cock, the same caramel hue the rest of him was, Paul noticed, stood straight up from his black pubic hair. The thick veined shaft made Paul itch to touch and taste it.

Paul sucked in a breath. "You … want me?

Carlo pushed his jeans down past his hips and palmed his cock. He rubbed it in slow, light strokes.

Paul stared. He watched Carlo's hand slide up and down the length of his cock. Carlo sagged back into the cushions, and his breath rasped loudly in the room.

"Get over here, man. Please. I mean, if you want to," Carlo sounded insecure.

"I want to." And did he! For three years now.

He came out from behind the camera and crossed over to the sofa. His heart pounded like a jackhammer as he sat gingerly down next to Carlo. Carlo's scent, musk mixed with rain filled his nostrils, made him feel a bit drunk.

Carlo's dark gaze simmered into his. Carlo reached out and cupped the back of Paul's hair. "I love your hair," he said softly. "It's like silky gold." He stroked the back of Paul's short hair and neck with gentle fingertips. A pleasant shiver ran through Paul's body, right into his cock. A brief image of Carlo stroking one of his newly finished bikes this way flitted through his mind, that of an artist appreciating his work. "Th … thanks."

Carlo's lids lowered more. "I like your blue eyes, too." He rubbed the nape of Paul's neck, caressed him with the sweetest touch. "You like that?"

Paul nodded. He glanced down. Carlo's hand still rested on his cock, which he stroked lazily. Wow, he couldn't ever have imagined being here like this with the guy of his dreams. Maybe Carlo was just horny, or lonely. Maybe he wouldn't still want Paul after they came. It didn't matter.

With gentle pressure, Carlo drew Paul's face down to his. "Kiss me," he whispered. He parted his lips and brushed them across Paul's. At the first touch, Paul's eyes fluttered closed. God, so soft, Carlo's lips, just as he'd always imagined them. Carlo's mustache and goatee tickled his clean-shaven chin in the sexiest way.

He sank in closer to Carlo, surrendered fully to the kiss. His nervousness melted away a bit more, and he ventured to slip his tongue between Carlo's heavenly lips. Carlo murmured softly in his throat and opened his lips wider, danced his tongue hungrily against his. Carlo's hands groped at Paul's T-shirt, lifted the damp material up.

"I want to see that bod of yours," Carlo breathed between kisses.

Paul broke their kiss long enough to help Carlo get his T-shirt off. He was glad that he worked hard to keep in shape. He had the same v-shape to his torso and similarly carved abs and slim waist as Carlo. He and Carlo were almost identical in height and physique.

"Mmm." Carlo sat up and leaned into Paul, pressing Paul back against the cushions.

Paul hitched a deep breath. His skin tingled under Carlo's caresses, and through his hazy pleasure, he saw the contrast of his pale skin with Carlo's caramel skin.

Carlo leaned over and kissed him again while he stroked Paul's chest. Carlo's touch was appreciative, soft and reverent. Even the way he pinched and kneaded Paul's nipples only stoked the hard-on raging in his jeans.

Carlo slid his hand down Paul's stomach and worked open his jeans. He pushed his fingertips under the waistband of Paul's boxers and stroked his cock. Carlo gasped softly and lifted from their kiss. "Damn, Paulito," he said, grinning, "I always figured you were hung. Now I know for sure." Before Paul could answer, Carlo kissed him some more, deep and hot.

Paul groaned into Carlo's mouth and arched his hips upward. Carlo fondled the length of his cock and whispered his masterful touch over his balls, which tightened more with each caress. Carlo pulled away again. "I love your skin," he murmured. "So silky over that hard cock." Before Paul could answer, Carlo took his lips again, caressed Paul's tongue with his.

Each passing second, Carlo's kisses grew wilder as he slid down to his knees. He lifted away from his kiss and panted. His hot breath passed over Paul's skin. Paul slipped his fingers into Carlo's hair and sifted the length of it between his fingers. "I love your hair, too," Paul said, chest heaving.

Carlo grinned. Without speaking, he tugged down Paul's jeans and boxers. Paul felt his cheeks heat. Damn, he was blushing! His freed cock stood straight up in a slight curve from his body. Carlo stared. His tongue came out and slid across his full soft lips. "Like I said before, well hung."

Paul laughed. Carlo's praise helped melt away more of his nervousness. "Thanks." He hitched a breath as Carlo wrapped his hand around his cock and stroked it.

"You feel sooo good," Carlo crooned. He leaned forward and took the head of Paul's cock into his mouth.

Paul lifted his head and watched. Sparks of heat danced on his skin every inch that Carlo engulfed in the moist heat of his mouth. Carlo feathered his tongue along Paul's shaft. His dark head bobbed as he took Paul in and then slid back. Paul's fingers remained in Carlo's hair. He couldn't believe this was happening to him; couldn't have ever imagined Carlo on his knees, sucking his cock.

Carlo's hand stole downward, slipped between Paul's butt cheeks. Paul hitched another breath as Carlo caressed his tight hole with that same expert touch. He spread his thighs wider for Carlo, and Carlo pushed a finger inside him. Carlo filled his hole gently, spread him open with soft but insistent tugs. The pleasure was incredible, and Paul moaned. He couldn't think at all. His mind, like his body from Carlo's licks and strokes, was jelly, completely under Carlo's control. Whatever Carlo wanted to do to him, he could.

Carlo sucked Paul's cock for what seemed a long time. Paul made himself hold back, even though Carlo's masterful tongue and lips kept bringing him to the edge. Bit by bit, Paul's shyness completely slipped away. Carlo was coaxing him to a frenzy. He slid his hands from Carlo's hair to his strong shoulders.

Several tugs, and Carlo let Paul's cock slip from his mouth. He looked up, large dark eyes full of lust, lips gleaming. "What is it, Paulito? Am I hurting you?"

Paul shook his head. He'd always been shy about asking for what he wanted. Now, the thing he wanted most was within his grasp and shyness grabbed his words. He pulled again on Carlo's shoulders.

A grin spread across Carlo's sexy lips. He rose up onto his knees. Paul leaned over and pushed Carlo's already loose jeans down his tapered hips and sloping thighs, strong from years of playing soccer.

Carlo's erection sprang free. The thick shaft bobbed close to Paul's mouth, and a drop of pre-cum glistened at the tiny opening. Feeling bolder now, Paul reached out, wrapped his hand lightly around Carlo's delicious, caramel-hued cock and leaned over. He slid the tip of his tongue gingerly across the lobes of the plump head and licked up the tiny salty droplet.

Carlo groaned and pushed his hips forward. One hand slid through Paul's hair, just long enough on top for Carlo to curl his fingers into. "Paulito," he whispered.

Encouraged, Paul took the whole head in. Carlo's answering groan urged him to take the shaft in deeper. As deep as he could. His lips bumped over the small veins, and Carlo's musky flavor filled Paul's senses. Carlo was as delicious as Paul had always imagined he'd be. With his other hand, he palmed the heavy sac of Carlo's balls. Carlo groaned again and tightened his fingers in Paul's hair. Paul tightened his lips and sucked Carlo more. He bobbed his head up and down, faster and faster, and his wildness inside unleashed itself. Every suck on Carlo's cock made his own body tingle. His cock and ass tightened, desperate for release.

Paul pulled back, and Carlo's cock slipped from his mouth. He looked up at Carlo's flushed face. "Carlo … I … want …" Shyness overcame him again, and he lay back, legs spread, hoping that the nonverbal message would work.

It did. Carlo chuckled and collapsed lightly on top of him. The studio lights had warmed their bodies as well as the heat of lust and their bare chests fused together, as if Carlo were making love to him on a sun-warmed beach. Sliding his hands down Carlo's strong back of smooth muscles, down to his perfect ass, he clutched the two hard globes of muscle. Carlo answered him with a hot kiss and the push of two thick fingers inside Paul's tight hole, preparing him.

Carlo pulled out his fingers. "Don't worry, Paulito, I'm safe. I wouldn't hurt you."

Paul nodded, panting. "I know."

Carlo moaned softly, as if Paul's trust in him was a turn-on, and pushed the head of his cock, well lubricated from Paul's mouth, in. Paul groaned and gripped Carlo's ass tighter. He pulled Carlo closer, and Carlo obeyed, pushing his cock in deeper … and deeper, until their bodies met.

"Paulito," Carlo whispered again and plundered his lips and mouth with hot kisses. The passionate way he rode Paul and kissed him made Paul feel as if Carlo had wanted to do this for a long time. Paul tilted his head back and let his whole consciousness shrink to the feel of Carlo's hot body on top of him, his cock inside him, rubbing the soft insides of his ass with perfect strokes, Carlo's male scent and the iron quality of his lithe muscles.

Carlo pushed harder, deeper, moved faster until he groaned. His body stiffened, and Paul could feel Carlo's hot cum spurting inside him, filling him. Paul grasped his own cock and pumped it rapidly, wanting to come at the same time. In moments, he spilled over the edge. His cum made white ribbons of moisture that splashed on his stomach and chest.

He felt the tension run out of Carlo's body just as his own climax ended. Carlo chuckled and kissed Paul's lips. Paul laughed, too. He couldn't stop. The two of them laughed together, and the sound mixed with the patter of rain outside. Paul rested his hands on Carlo's triceps. When their laughter had passed, Carlo kissed him again.

Now that it was over, Paul felt afraid, afraid that this was a one-time thing. At least he'd had that. Too bad he wanted it for always.

"Thank you, Paulito." Carlo kissed Paul's forehead. "I'm sorry it took me so long to tell you how I feel."

Paul looked at him. "How do you feel, exactly?" His voice was timid to his own ears. When it came to Carlo, Paul felt vulnerable. He didn't care, though because he loved Carlo.

Carlo sighed. He remained above Paul, his cock still partly hard, inside him. Paul loved that and wished they could always stay this way. "Well," Carlo said in a soft voice, "I realized I was beginning to love you when I started to compare every guy I was with to you, and he never measured up. I think that's why I've never stayed with anyone. Then … yesterday when you had that photo job with those gorgeous guys, I was madly jealous. I realized I had to do something or I'd lose you. You're hot, even though you don't know it."

Paul stared at him. His heart pounded, and he was overcome with joy and disbelief. "Am I dreaming?"

Carlo returned his gaze. His smile faded. "No, man. I love you."

Paul pulled Carlo down on top of him. "I love you, too," he murmured into Carlo's hair.

Carlo kissed the side of Paul's neck. "I'm sorry it took so long."

Paul squeezed him close and smiled. This was turning out to be the best day of his life. "Don't worry about it. I took a long time, too. At least you came out and did something."

Carlo rose up and looked down at him. He, too, looked really happy. "Finally." He grinned and glanced up. "Thanks to that camera of yours."

Paul chuckled. "Yeah, I guess a picture really is worth a thousand words."

Carlo kissed Paul's lips again and smoothed back his hair. "Not a thousand words, Paulito. Just three."

Noah's Arch
By Ryan Field

One summer a few years ago, there was a young man who discovered he was turning into the wrong person.

He was only twenty-two years old by then, a college graduate with a degree in business but still working as a waiter in a small rural town in eastern Pennsylvania. He was tall and rugged and muscle-toned, with a shock of dark brown hair that fell across his forehead – thick hair that always appeared slightly wind blown. Dark eyelashes framed his deep blues eyes. He had an unadventurous style of dress veering precariously close to Catholic School uniform.

Give him credit. Most guys his age, with his background, would settle for marrying their high school sweethearts and ignoring their innate urges. It's only a phase I'm going through, they would say. Just get married, and it will all go away in time.

It did occur to Noah to say that. But he didn't.

On the night he made his discovery, he was meeting his married lover at the rest stop along the I95 corridor in Chester County, PA. His first and only lover was a man who could curl his toes and make his eyes roll to the back of his head. It was a warm, humid night in late August 1999, and the rest stop was crowded with hungry drivers – men looking for other men on the down-low.

All styles and makes of cars, from mini-vans to BMWs, were parked on an angle in the parking spaces that circled the grey brick public rest rooms. Off to the right, beyond the automobile section, large trucks with motors running endlessly lined a manmade wooded area where truckers could park and sleep in their air-conditioned cabs. Some stood outside, leaning against their rigs puffing one cigarette after the other, while the local tranny would sashay by in red stilettos and a black mini skirt waiting for one of them to say something like, "Hey baby, you got a light."

But it was a safe place, too. For some reason, there were never any cops after ten at night.

For about six months, Noah had been meeting this married guy, Mike, at the rest stop every Saturday night at ten. An ex-Marine-turned-farmer, same age as Noah, who looked really hot in baggy jeans and always wore black steel toe half boots with a crew cut, he was an ex-high-school-jock type of guy. Mike never spoke much, but whatever he said was always a compliment, and he treated Noah like a fragile wine goblet that might crack with the wrong move. He also didn't bother explaining, or hiding, his gold wedding band, and Noah understood there would be no fantasy of having a real relationship. Mike liked fucking good looking young gay guys, and Noah liked getting fucked by straight guys who drank beer and wore baseball caps.

When Noah pulled alongside Mike's beat up Chevy that night, it suddenly occurred to him that he got a sinking feeling in his stomach lately when he saw Mike. But still exciting, too, and Noah needed dick. So he got out of his Honda and slipped into the backseat, where Mike was finishing another bottle of beer. Noah gently placed his palm on Mike's large bicep and leaned forward to kiss the stubble on his cheek.

"Hey, baby," Mike said, as he chugged down what was left in the beer bottle and then belched.

It all went as predicted. No talking while Noah systematically removed all his clothes and Mike watched with a fierce look in his eyes as though he hadn't been fed in months. The exhibitionist in Noah liked this part the most – Mike's glaring, his need to pounce on Noah's smooth body with force. When Noah's clothes (even his socks) were on the front seat, Mike spread his strong legs, and Noah slowly unfastened Mike's jeans and pulled down the zipper. He fumbled for a moment, until he reached through Mike's loose boxer shorts for the thick, hard cock. He leaned over and gently slipped it into his warm mouth while Mike moaned and felt up Noah's bare ass with his coarse hand. It was a good dick to suck – really hard, extra thick and always tasted tangy because Mike hadn't showered since the early morning.

That night, as usual, Noah sucked and slurped the big thing until his jaw hurt, and when it was just about ready to shoot a load Mike pulled out and slipped on a lubricated condom. He stretched his legs and Noah slowly climbed up on his lap. He pressed his hands on Mike's chest for support, straddled the thick, familiar dick and then lowered himself onto it until he could feel the hard denim fabric of Mike's jeans against his smooth ass cheeks. While Mike's hands were firmly positioned on his waist, Noah arched his back, folded his hands at the back of his neck and began to ride. A couple of guys passing by on foot stopped to watch. Though a bit creepy (and never mentioned aloud) both Mike and Noah silently enjoyed putting on a show for the other guys who circled the rest stop on foot; they even slowed down to let the guys watch Mike's cock slowly going in and out of Noah's hole.

Mike enjoyed Noah on his lap, but he preferred to climax on top. So eventually Noah slid off the dick, went flat on his back and put his legs over Mike's shoulders.

Mike, who could fuck like a bull, banged away to the finish while Noah moaned and begged for more, jerking his own cock, so they'd both come at the same time.

When the fucking was over, Mike's eyebrows creased as he tossed the used condom out the back window and shoved his cock back into his jeans. Noah slowly bent over the front seat to gather his clothes, so Mike could gently slap his bare ass. With a turned down mouth Mike said, as he always did, "Thanks, baby, gotta go home now."

But for some strange reason Noah didn't reply, "See you next week," as he usually did. And he didn't bend over to gently kiss Mike's crotch goodbye either. Actually, Noah didn't even bother to get dressed. He just grabbed his shoes and clothes in a heap, pressed them against his stomach and got out of the car totally naked while five guys watched in the shadows.

Mike's eyes popped, and he climbed to the front seat and lowered the window. "What are you doing?"

"I'm changing my life," Noah answered, as he tossed his clothes into the front passenger side of his car and casually walked around to the driver's side, still naked. There were red marks on his smooth ass, revealing paw marks that he'd just been nailed by Mike.

Mike opened the car door and jumped out, ignoring the small audience of voyeurs in the darkness. He reached Noah's car and blocked the driver's door. "What's wrong?"

"Mike, I'm standing here totally naked, at least let me get into the car," said Noah.

"Not until you tell me what's going on," said Mike. He wrapped his strong arms around Noah's body, resting his large hands on Noah's ass.

Noah sighed. In Mike's arms he'd always been safe. He reached up, wrapped his arms around Mike's wide neck and rested his cheek against Mike's chest. He spread his legs and arched his back, hoping Mike would start to squeeze and feel up his ass again.

"Will I see you again next weekend?" Mike asked, as he began to play with Noah's ass cheeks as though he were kneading bread dough. "C'mon baby, talk to me."

49

Noah frowned. "No. You probably won't see me again. I'm moving to New York; been thinking about it for a while. And I don't want this to be dramatic; we both knew it would end sooner or later. You're never going to leave your wife."

"I'm sorry," said Mike, "But you're okay, man?"

Noah smiled. "Yes. I'm fine. And I think you're a great guy, but I need more than this."

"Get in and start your car," Mike said, smacking Noah's ass, "I want to make sure you get out of here okay, and no one rapes that pretty ass of yours ... at least for tonight it only belongs to me."

"Thank you," Noah said. He wanted to say more, but just slipped into his car, started the engine and drove naked onto the dark highway. For a mile or so he felt safe; Mike's headlights were in his mirror. He managed not to look back as he pulled off the highway and headed down a dark country road toward the rural Pennsylvania home where he'd been born and raised.

About two weeks later, after calling his mother and father to let them know he'd arrived in Manhattan safely, Noah was standing beside his black college luggage with brown leather trim and hailing a taxi at the Port Authority. He was headed to his new home; a large, two-bedroom, dream-come-true co-op he'd be sharing with three other gay men. The ad on Craigslist had read, "Three guys, ages 22, 30 and 33, looking to rent a room in Chelsea to a young, nonsmoker, willing to share one quarter of the rent." At first it all sounded too good to be true, but after several e-mails, and a couple of phone calls, Noah decided this ad was the perfect opportunity to leave the rural countryside and begin a new life as a city boy. The situation had been explained faultlessly: three guys were all together – in a permanent three-way relationship. Noah would have his own room and his privacy when he needed it, in one of the gayest urban neighborhoods in the world.

The building, on 18th, just off Tenth Avenue, wasn't awful, and it had a doorman who wore a long burgundy top coat, with epilates trimmed in gold and a matching cap. With a dull golden brick façade, chocolate brown window trim, and a sign over the lobby entrance that read "Penny Lane," the place probably hadn't been remodeled since the early 1970s. It backed up to a restaurant called "The Park" that appeared to go against its name until you figured it out. If you didn't know anything about The Park you would assume a park-like setting, with trees and grass and benches, however, The Park Restaurant was

50

actually a converted parking garage. Until he landed a real job, Noah suspected The Park might be a great place to wait tables.

The doorman announced his name into a metal speaker, and Noah walked through the brown lobby toward the elevator. He pushed a button for the tenth floor and rode up to meet his new room mates.

All three were home. Mike, the thirty-three-year-old, was the one who answered the door. Noah hoped his name wouldn't be a bad omen. "Hey man, did you have any trouble finding the place?"

"No, none at all," said Noah. Mike looked more like twenty-three than thirty-three, with short blond streaks, a painfully thin waist and a chest and arms that seemed to pop from the tight white T-shirt he was wearing. His low-rise jeans with a three-inch zipper were as tight as the skin on his tanned face, and Noah liked that he wasn't effeminate in any way. The small, square entrance hall of the apartment, covered with the most exquisite wallpaper of sage green ferns he'd ever seen, rang with sophistication Noah had read about in magazines. The gray marble floor complimented the sage ferns, and Noah actually touched the walls to see if the ferns had been hand painted.

"I've never seen wallpaper like this," he said to Mike.

"Thank you," Mike replied, "I'm an interior designer, and a collector of vintage Florence Broadhurst wallpaper. She was a lively character from Australia, who didn't begin to design wallpaper until she was in her sixties. She was murdered in her warehouse in the 1970s, and the crime was never solved."

"It's spectacular," Noah said, gazing at the walls, "Where did you find it in such condition."

"I didn't find it," Mike said, "The whole place was already papered; that's the reason I bought it. Originally I'd planned to live in The Village, but when I saw this wallpaper I didn't have a choice."

"Spectacular," Noah said.

"C'mon in and let me introduce you to Randy and Angelo," Mike said, taking Noah's bags and placing them off to the side on the marble floor.

They crossed into a spacious living room with a tall ceiling, also papered with a famous Broadhurst design that included beige, blue and silver foil geometric shapes. Very 1970s and now considered "retro." Two guys stood from the black leather sofa with chrome trim (Noah knew there was a famous designer name attached to it, too, but couldn't recall exactly what it was, and he didn't want to sound stupid) and extended their hands. Randy's hair was black and short with a turned up wave above his forehead. He wore lose fitting kaki shorts that stopped just below his knees, exposing slightly bowed legs covered with more black hair, black sandals on his large feet. His handshake was wilted; a large hand that felt more like a wet sponge than human flesh. Mike mentioned Randy practiced law with a small firm uptown. Then he introduced Angelo, certainly the twenty-two-year-old in the group, a light skinned black man with hazel eyes and a warm, friendly smile who didn't look a day over sixteen. He simply wore a white T-shirt and blue and white stripped boxer shorts; his legs thin and muscular with short ankle socks covering his feet. Mike said Angelo worked in the garment district, but didn't go into detail. Where Noah could have recognized that both Mike and Randy were two trendy gay men living in New York, he would have had to wonder about Angelo, who seemed so straight and un-gay he stood out much too clearly from the other two. When he shook Noah's hand it almost hurt.

After the formalities, Mike walked Noah to his new room; a small antiseptic rectangle with a full-size bed, a beige wood 1930s dresser in remarkably good condition and hardwood floors that clicked when he stepped on them with his new hollow heeled black leather half boots. The bed popped with fitted white sheets, two beige pillows and a white duvet cover. So unlike the rest of the wallpapered apartment; the white walls calmed Noah's senses.

"I like that everything is so neutral," Noah said, "simple, solid shades of beige and white. This is perfect, too."

Mike shrugged his shoulders when he opened the closet. "It's not much, but compared to other NY co-ops, it's not all the bad either."

Noah peered inside. The closet resembled a meager bookcase with a door. No pole that ran from end to end, just a row of four hooks on the back wall where you could hang clothing in short, compact stacks, maybe three or four jackets to a hook, if that.

"You know," said Noah, putting his index finger to his bottom lip, "this is fine, too. I'm not a huge clothes horse, and I can make this work."

"The rest of the apartment is pretty self-explanatory," said Mike, "living room, dining area, kitchen … but there's a really great terrace off the living room. Semi-private, with a great view, where you can sunbathe in the nude if you want."

"Semi-private?"

"There's a teenage boy in the building across the street who likes to watch us and beat off, but he's harmless ... kind of cute in a way," said Mike.

"Oh well," Noah said, but he was already thinking about how to put on a show for the horny little guy.

Mike handed Noah a key to the apartment, and Noah handed him a check for two months rent. And then Mike explained that he and the other guys were meeting some friends in Brooklyn that afternoon to work on some sort of fundraiser, but would be home for dinner. He invited Noah to join them around seven, as sort of a welcome dinner, and Noah gladly accepted.

It only took a half hour or so to unpack, so he decided to take a walk over to The Park to see if he could get a job waiting tables as soon as possible. Taking the elevator down to the lobby, nodding at the doorman as he headed toward the street, Noah couldn't believe that he was actually now living in Manhattan. Tenth avenue streamed with gay men – some walking dogs, some walking hand-in-hand, most stopping to stare at his ass while he passed by. Dick for the taking as far as the eye could see. It wasn't the prettiest section of the city, with trees and cute little shops, but the energy in Chelsea suggested newness and excitement; as though it had all been very carefully planned out ahead of time.

Though the fat, bald manager of The Park told Noah there weren't any openings, he did lead him back to his office, beyond the busy waiters in black and white outfits, for a brief interview just in case one of his staff quit unexpectedly. The dark atmosphere, harsh and sophisticated, portended urban doom. There were more rusted bars and chipped concrete tables than Noah could take in at a glance; filled with a muffled sound of voices mixed with the clinking and clanking of dishes. The hapless lunch crowd appeared gay and straight; some sitting at the bars, others off to the side at small round tables. Waist-high, shelf-like areas lined the walls where people could stand and drink and talk; fast music with a techno beat banged against the concrete so loudly you had to shout to be heard. But this wasn't a cruise bar; just a place to eat and congregate before or after cruising. Next to the manager's office were two outsized glass doors that led to a conservatory type eating area that looked as though it would be awkward at best, and very moist on a rainy day.

After the interview, Noah walked the neighborhood. He came close to getting picked up by a middle-aged guy with short gray hair and tight jeans who'd taken his Boston bull terrier to the little doggie park on Tenth Avenue. When the horny guy noticed Noah, he began to casually wet his lips with his tongue, slowly and cautiously sliding long fingers across his crotch. Though Noah would have enjoyed a quick fuck, he realized it was after six, and he didn't want to be late for his first dinner with his new roommates. Actually, he was tremendously curious about the three guys; clearly they all shared the same bed, but there was something peculiar going on there; they were all too much alike – no sense of balance.

He thought of stopping at a bakery to buy dessert, but then thought twice when he remembered how fit the guys were; men who clearly didn't eat cake. So he opted for a bouquet of white roses at the Korean Grocery instead. He decided to be cautious; watch and learn how urban gay men interacted with each other; and not to make any mistakes that might make him look foolish.

That night, before dinner, the three men toasted their new roommate with martinis.

"Just a small, informal cocktail hour," Mike said, "to show you how glad we are to have you here, Noah."

There was a small rectangle of pate, surrounded by neatly sliced wedges of dark bread, set out on a crystal dish on the glass coffee table. Angelo nibbled, and Noah tasted, but it was a waste of food. Though Noah felt left out, the guys did their best to include him. By eight o'clock, they went to the dining section of the living room and on a two inch thick glass table, with Noah's white roses perfectly arranged in a Waterford crystal vase, Mike served large Caesar salads with grilled chicken and capers on white Wedgwood plates. There were black leather placemats and black linen napkins with thin gold threads running through them. The guys spoke about their day in Brooklyn, and Noah mentioned his interview at The Park. Nothing about this place reminded Noah of his mother's Quaker lace table cloth spread over his grandmother's old mahogany table; the black linen so unlike the paper napkins he was used to placing on his lap. Not to mention the thought of eating dinner at eight. Why his mother wouldn't think of putting the meatloaf on the table later than six.

After dinner (Noah cleaned his plate; the others left half) three went back to the living room for Port; Angelo cleaned the table as it was his turn that night. Now, Noah wasn't exactly off the turnip truck, and he did have a good education with a degree from an outstanding university, but he wasn't quite sure about the Port. So when Mike offered it to him in a small crystal wine glass, he accepted gladly and sat on one of the black lather chairs that faced the sofa.

"God, Dude, port makes me so horny," said Randy, placing the palm of his hand on Mike's ass and giving it a hard squeeze.

"Be a good boy," said Mike, as he sat opposite Noah on the leather sofa, "You don't want to scare Noah away."

"I don't wanna be a good boy," Randy teased, winking at Noah.

Noah sipped his drink, not knowing how to react. The Port tasted slightly sweet, with a rich thickness that reminded him of wine syrup. But he liked it; and Mike was only too willing to pour him a second.

"I'm going into the bedroom to get out of these clothes and get comfortable," said Randy. He had a naughty-boy twinkle in his eye.

Mike smiled at Noah. "I should have warned you about this. We are strictly clothing optional here. On a normal night all three of us would be walking around in our underwear, jock straps, or, most likely completely naked. We're being polite because it's your first night with us."

Noah wondered if he were being tested. "Not a problem. You guys do exactly what you normally do … I want to fit in."

A moment later, Randy returned wearing nothing but a white oversized T-shirt that stopped just at the top of his thighs. No underwear; Noah could tell by the way Randy's dick bounced around beneath the sheer cotton. His legs were strong and solid, like a runner's, covered with coarse black hair that seemed to thin out a bit toward his crotch.

"Can I have a foot massage?" Randy asked Mike. He sat down at the other end of the sofa, spread his long hairy legs out and rested his giant feet on Mikes lap.

"I guess I don't have a choice," Mike said. He leaned over, stuck out his tongue and then ran it all the way up the bottom of Randy's big foot.

"Hey, I'm next," Angelo shouted. Obviously he'd finished clearing the table and stacking the dishwasher, and taken the time to slip into a pair of sheer black boxer briefs. He wore no shirt; just the see-through briefs. Noah tried not to stare but couldn't help it; noticing Angelo had a thick, uncut dick. He wasn't very hairy except for a slight dark fleece on his legs.

"You'll get your turn," Randy said, and then lifted the white T-shirt over his head so that he was totally naked, with a nine inch erection resting on his stomach. A long dick, with a thick vein.

Mike stared at Noah. "Are you okay with this? I mean, we're not getting too informal … don't want you to run out the door screaming or anything."

Noah smiled. "I'm fine, Mike." The Port helped, but his fists were clenched, and he wasn't quite sure what to think. Was it normal for these guys to be walking around naked on his first night, rubbing each other? Licking feet? Cock's bouncing around? After all, he was still a perfect stranger, and they weren't leaving much to the imagination. Needless to say, his cock was now rock hard.

Mike let go of Randy's big feet and stood from the sofa. He stretched his arms in the air and then began to remove all of his clothing, too. His erection was full and thick like Randy's. Angelo, who's dick was also popping from the sheer mesh briefs, walked over to where he was standing and wrapped his hand all the way around it. Mike leaned forward, grabbed Angelo by the back of the head, and stuck his tongue all the way into Angelo's open mouth. By that time Noah's cock pulsed, and he couldn't take his glazed eyes off the men.

Randy stood, pressed his cock against Angelo's ass crack, and said, "Let's go into the bedroom, men."

Mike pulled away from Angelo. "Noah, we don't mind if you follow."

Noah's cock ached from beneath the fabric of his khaki slacks, and when he stood to follow them into the bedroom it stuck straight out as though it had pitched a tent. His knees were shaking; his body on the verge of trembling. It felt as though he were in a dream – three hot guys with big dicks inviting him to join them in what could only be described as a scene from one of his favorite porn flicks. And, so different from the sex he'd always known in the back seat of Mike's Chevy.

The bedroom was dramatic and stark, with more Florence Broadhurst wallpaper that reminded Noah of red Florentine swirls curling and twining into an endless infinity. No art work; just the wallpaper. Gold silk sheets, with matching duvet and pillows, covered the king sized bed. The hardwood floor gleamed in subtle light, shining from two crystal lamps on either side of the bed perched on matching mirrored stands. On the far right wall, a large, uncovered glass door led to the terrace; on the other side of the room a white upholstered antique sofa with a silk throw cover tossed over the back sat on its own. Other than that, the room was bare; the focus of the room centered on the wallpaper, and the men who sucked dick – everything else was insignificant.

The guys slowly crawled into bed; Noah cautiously began to remove his clothes while they watched.

Mike reached out to him with his right hand. "C'mon, Noah. Don't be afraid."

Noah tried to smile, but his lips were frozen. He reached out with his hand, and Mike guided him toward the center of the bed. He rested between Mike and Randy; Angelo was to the left of Randy, and so Noah wouldn't feel left out, he leaned across Randy's torso, holding Randy's dick with his left hand and began to lick Noah's full erection. While Angelo licked, both Mike and Randy leaned forward and stuck their tongues into Noah's mouth. Noah stretched his arms wide, wrapped them around the shoulders of both strong men, and stuck out his tongue, so both men could taste it. Then, in a bold, but completely instinctive move, Noah lifted both his smooth legs, spread them wide and lowered them over Mike and Randy's bodies. A clear invitation for Angelo to begin fingering Noah's pink hole.

Mike smiled. "Are you a bottom?" He was rubbing his palms together.

Noah stared at him, unsure how to reply. "Why? And why are you smiling like that?"

Randy laughed, and Mike said, "There's one thing I didn't tell you about us ... not the most important thing about us, but something you should know. We love each other very much, and share everything about our lives, but while we have learned to be versatile in bed, we all prefer being on top."

"Yeah, man," Randy said, "Sometimes we even draw straws to see who's going to get plowed."

"Sometimes we just mark the calendar, and we each take turns on the bottom for a week," Angelo said. He was still holding Noah's cock; licking the shaft between words.

Noah's eye's bugged. He wasn't completely sure about versatile, dominant top or submissive bottom, but he had a good idea what it all meant. With his old Mike it had all been so clear. Mike would always be the one to fuck. But Noah wasn't an idiot; and he wasn't a liar either.

"Guys," he said, "I've only had one man in my life so far. He was married, and we only screwed around secretly in the backseat of his car, but I can promise you all, without hesitation, I'm strictly a bottom." Then he arched his back and spread his legs as wide as they would go to prove to the boys he was willing to please them all.

Angelo rose to his knees and shouted, "Yes, look how he arches his back!" while he made a fist and pulled his arm down as though he were pulling a string to get off at his bus stop.

Mike grinned, with a naughty gleam in his eyes. "Men, looks like we got us a sweet little package here."

"I wanna go in first," Randy said, rising from the pillow and practically pushing Angelo out of the way.

"Now, play nice boys," Mike said, "You don't want to scare him off on the first night."

Noah reached for Mike's cock and said, "Guys, I think there's plenty to go around."

There was foreplay that seemed to last an eternity. Mike shoved his cock into Randy's mouth while Noah took a full mouthful from Randy. Angelo continued to lick and suck Noah's dick, and eventually wound up eating his ass, getting it soaked and spongy and ready for three big dicks. When both Mike and Randy decided to press their dicks to Noah's mouth he gobbled both cock heads at the same time. Though both dicks were too large to suck off together, he managed to take care of both guys without playing favorites.

For the first time, he realized that all cock tastes unique; Randy's lingered with salt and vinegar, while Mike's big dick reminded him of peppered meat. When Angelo sat on his chest and pressed his dark uncut cock to Noah's face it was amazingly sweet with a hint of apple vinegar. Noah couldn't resist running his tongue under the foreskin. Though his previous Mike had preferred fucking, and shooting up his ass, every now and then, Noah had taken Mike's load in his mouth, too. He liked the taste of cum, and tried to suck as much pre-cum from the guys as he could. Angelo wasn't much of a pre-cummer, but Randy and Mike were, and when they saw how Noah was lapping up the juice they began to milk themselves so that Noah had big drops to swallow.

At one point, when the action was heading toward a peak, Mike rose, placed his palm on Noah's stomach and guided him into a fuck position. Noah didn't hesitate. In the middle of the bulky bed, with two guys at his side and one coming up behind, he went down on all fours doggie style and arched his back so that his smooth ass would be high in the air.

"You really want dick, man, don't you?" Randy teased.

"Yeah, c'mon guys," Noah whispered playfully, leaning over so that he could lick Randy's hairy legs. Long, sloppy licks, sticking his tongue all the way out, so he could taste the thick fur from ankle to the thigh. He liked Randy's sense of humor; his bad boy attitude reminded him of the old Mike.

Mike, who was now slapping cock on Noah's smooth ass, slowly pressed the head to the pink opening. Because he hated getting fucked, and dick up his own ass had always hurt so much, he expected Noah to flinch, or wince when the head entered. But to his shock Noah moaned in ecstasy, and his sweet little hole swallowed the big dick as though he had a vacuum up his ass. Actually, Noah didn't even wait for Mike to push the big dick all the way in; he instinctively backed into it and began to ride with Mike's large hands holding his waist; guiding him all the way in and all the way out. Mike clenched Noah's thin waist, his eyes bugged. Usually the guys he'd fucked didn't like it when the cock pulled all the way out and then was shoved back in again; they said it was painful and made them feel like they had to take a shit. But not for Noah, his ass begged for it – to be shoved and rammed as hard as possible, too.

While Mike banged hard, Noah began to take turns sucking off the other two, taking their big dicks all the way to the back of his throat and moaning while the other big dick filled his hole.

Randy, always the kinky one, leaned over and whispered into Noah's ear, "Do you like dirty talk, dude?"

With Angelo's dick in his mouth he nodded, and Randy began to whisper all the things he'd always dreamed guys would do to him. "That's a good boy, take that big fucking cock. We're all gonna get a piece of that pretty ass ... shoot our fucking seed right up that pretty fuck hole. You're a good little bitch, a good little whore who loves to take big cock up your ass. Don't you, boy?"

"Fuck yes," Noah moaned, "Fucking bang me hard, boys."

"I'm gonna shoot," Mike began moan, "here it comes."

"Go man," kinky Randy yelled, "Fuck the bitch ... fill that pussy with cream."

The fucking became more intense, with Mike's hard thighs banging against Noah's; his large hands squeezing Noah's waist. Noah's hole clamped down on the big cock, and Mike shot a full load and didn't stop fucking the ass until every last drop had been deposited. He climbed off, his dick still dripping with juice, and Angelo quickly shoved his cock as deeply as it would go. Noah noticed the difference at once. Angelo's cock, though not quite as long as Mike's, was thicker and made the lips of his hole vibrate.

"Fuck the bitch," Randy shouted to Angelo, his voice deep and hoarse.

Mike, who was still dripping with juice, went alongside Noah, and Noah did something he'd never done before. He opened his mouth and began to suck on Mike's semi-erect cock. It tasted of ass juice and cum, salty and ripe – a taste so unfamiliar and brilliant Noah began to swallow in large gulps.

Mike, holding on to Randy for support, didn't move. "Damn," he said to Randy, "He really does love dick. I've never seen anyone swallow this shit with such relish before."

Angelo's face began to contort; his eyes closed tightly. "I'm gonna blow."

Once again, the fucking became hard and rough; Noah continued to suck on Mike's dirty cock while Angelo deposited another full load of seed up his ass.

Noah assumed that Randy would climb on top next, but Randy had another idea. "Get flat on your back and spread your legs, dick slut. I wanna fuck you like I'm going to breed you while the other guys hold your legs up in the air."

Noah followed Randy's directions to the letter (he would have done anything for Randy at that point), and while Mike and Angelo held his legs wishbone style, Randy went between them and shoved his cock into the wet hole as deeply as he could. He then ran his hands over Noah's flat stomach and began to squeeze Noah's chest muscles until he made a fist. "You really work that chest out, baby," he whispered, "Like squeezing a handful of tit." Then, with his pelvis pressed against Noah's ass Randy began to plunge all the way in and then all the way out again. Mike and Angelo lifted and spread his legs higher, so his ass was now in the air, about a foot off the bed. Randy's cock felt different, too. About as thick as Angelo's, but the longest of all three; a slight curve that seemed to be hitting a very sensitive spot the others hadn't been able to reach.

"Oh, man, yeah, open me up," Noah whispered, his toes curling toward the ceiling, "Randy, man, just keep doing that, and I'll shoot without even touching my dick."

"I want you to cum with me," Randy said, "When I shoot my load up that pretty ass, I want you to shoot yours. Grab your cock and start jerking it off."

"No, I don't need to touch it … as long as you keep fucking hard and fast," Noah said, "I can cum better without touching my dick."

"Fuck," Randy said, while he plowed away, "You have the softest hole I've ever fucked. It's like the lips of your hole bubble out and vibrate while I'm fucking … like your ass is giving me a blow job."

Noah didn't reply; he knew how to control his ass muscles on purpose. But he began to moan, turning his head to the right so that he could suck on Mike's big toe while Randy fucked. The cocks were too far away, and he needed to taste and slurp the skin of a man. Randy was bringing him close to climax; the big, curved dick was hitting the anal cum spot, and there was no turning back. Even the lips of his hole began to rise with orgasm. The only other times Noah had felt this type of climax about to happen was when he'd practiced with a dildo.

"That's it, baby," Randy whispered into his ear, "I'm close, too, … gonna blow my load any minute."

Randy began to slam it hard; the smacks against Noah's ass sounded brutal. The bed shook, and Angelo nearly lost his balance. Randy's pounding continued, and Noah felt the beginning of climax. "Here it comes, bitch," he shouted. While the other buys held his legs in the air, Noah then reached out with both hands and grabbed their legs for support so that he could lift his whole body a foot off the bed.

Randy reached down and placed the palms of his hands on the bottom of Noah's ass for support, fucking with more intensity, and when he couldn't hold back any longer shouted, "Fuck, man, here it comes."

"Yeah, fuck me," Noah moaned, "Fuck me hard."

They both came at the same time; Randy up Noah's ass and Noah blowing a load so high the juice landed on his bottom lip. Mike and Angelo lowered Noah's legs so that his ass would rest on Randy's thighs. With the curved cock still up his hole, Noah wrapped his legs around Randy's waist and squeezed hard.

Randy took a deep breath. "Buddy, you are something else. Did you really shoot while I was fucking you? My eyes were closed, and I missed it."

"Of course I did," Noah whispered. And then, so all three could see, Noah licked all the cum from his bottom lip and swallowed it in one gulp.

Randy smiled. "I like that. I never got a guy to do anything like that before. This is really fucking cool."

"That was really hot," Mike said.

"The best piece ass I've had in a long time," said Angelo.

"I hate to pull my cock out," Randy joked, "It feels so warm and friendly in there, but my legs are starting to cramp."

Noah released his legs from Randy's body, and when Randy eventually did pull out, the guys took turns taking quick showers while Mike changed the sheets. Noah remained in the shower with each guy; he liked soaping them up and rinsing them off, especially making sure their floppy cocks were clean and fresh. And they liked kissing and feeling up their new bottom boy. He did things he'd never even considered doing with the old Mike; like holding Angelo's dick and pointing it toward his legs while Angelo took a piss, and licking the wet, black fur in Randy's arm pits. By then it was after midnight; they'd been fucking and sucking for hours and hadn't even realized the time.

Noah was the last one to leave the shower (he wanted to soap up his hands so that he could shove a couple of fingers all the way up his hole to make sure it was clean and fresh). Randy had the foresight to actually hand Noah a used hair color bottle so that he could douche and clean out all the cum: three full loads; some of it had dripped down his legs but there was still a lot up there. He knew how to hold it back, too, but knew it couldn't remain there forever.

By the time Noah was out of the shower, the other three were in bed under the covers. "I guess I'll go to my room," Noah said.

"What the fuck?" Mike asked.

"Yeah, man," Angelo said his eyebrows creased.

"What?" Noah asked.

"We all just assumed you'd come to bed with us," Randy said.

Noah's eyebrows rose. "You really want me to sleep with you. I mean, I wouldn't be in the way?"

"Just come over here and get into bed, baby," Mike said.

When Noah was under the covers, between Angelo and Randy (Mike snored, they warned him), he reached beneath the sheets and took two handfuls of cock and balls. "Can I ask you guys something?"

"Sure," Mike said, half asleep by then.

"Are you guys really all tops ... I mean ... none of you like to get fucked?"

"Yup," said Angelo, "We hate it, and can't imagine how anyone could like it."

"But it feels so good," Noah said, "Seriously, I can't imagine NOT getting fucked."

"Baby, you just bend over and arch that pretty back, and you're gonna have all the dirty dick you want for a very long time," Randy said, leaning over to nibble on Noah's ear. "Now go to sleep, bitch."

Noah smiled and closed his eyes. "I think I'm going to like living in the city."

Doesn't Play Well with Others
By Stewart Lewis

From the moment I stepped off the bus in front of the dorm, I knew everything was going to change. My life up to that point had been too structured, and something was telling me I needed to get lost in order to find my way. There was a distinct eagerness inside me, and I knew that these would be the years that would shape the rest of my life.

During the first few days, the students naturally gravitated into social groups – the stoners and the punks, the geeks and the freaks – but I felt suspended, like a hovering insect unsure of where to land, which is why when it came time to pledge for fraternities, I knew it was my chance to belong.

Andrew, the pledge leader for Sigma Chi, spoke with a veiled urgency, trying to appear nonchalant. I could sense that underneath the slight twitches in his face was a world of mystery, a brain plotting rapidly. His eyes were a clear green, cutting through behind erratic strands of jet-black hair, and they locked into mine periodically. I found myself lost in his gaze and not really listening to what he was saying, but I knew his was the frat I would pledge. I secretly hoped Andrew would be the doorway to the distraction I craved. Every time his eyes landed on me, I could feel myself sinking. I had only been in college for a week, and high school seemed like another lifetime, a blurry vision I could barely recall. Now was the time to really become myself.

I couldn't sleep the night before the new pledges were announced, and in the morning when I saw my name on the printout outside the house, my heart did a little dance in my chest. I was a chosen one.

Sigma Chi was a different kind of fraternity. There were no stellar jocks, no preppie trust-funders, no 80s rock meatheads. Sigma chi was the frat for the misfit toys. The ones with the box "doesn't play well with others" checked on their fifth grade report cards. I was too young to see the irony.

As Andrew welcomed the new pledges in the house lobby, I surveyed the scene: a dyed-hair, tattooed muscle-boy whispering into his cell phone, a mousy but attractive young man on a laptop, and a fair-skinned, distinguished-looking intellectual type pressing the eraser of a pencil gently against his cheek while holding a flat, sexy stare.

I swam back into the depth of Andrew's green eyes. As everyone dispersed, I lingered, hoping he would personally congratulate me. He only nodded and mentioned a party on the top of a mountain, starting at midnight. He smiled and turned, a rip in the back of his T-shirt revealing a small part of his smooth spine. Intellectual Boy got up and followed him, the two of them so lithe and languid that they might as well have been on a runway, modeling their disheveled preppie look. I watched them in a trance until someone bumped into me on his way out, knocking my backpack to the floor.

During afternoon classes, all I could think about was Andrew, his blend of calm and mystery, and how he smelled of something spicy. Later that afternoon I changed outfits four times in my room and my roommate said, "Jeez, you're like a girl. Got a date?" I ignored him and settled on a V-neck sweater that showed a little skin.

The party was crowded. Everyone drank cheep beer out of plastic cups and talked really fast, as if their ideas elapsed faster than their speech patterns. I couldn't find Andrew or Intellectual Boy anywhere. I hung out with someone who called himself Judge – we smoked some pot, and he told me about his sister who was a rock star in Germany. After some time, the crowd started thinning out, and I noticed a structure up in a tree, a small flickering light piercing out through slats of wood. I got closer and touched the trunk. A rope came down and hit me on the side of my head, and I heard someone laugh. Without seeing him, I knew it was Intellectual Boy.

"Come on up, pirate," he said, still giggling. I could hear Andrew's voice from inside, and when I got up I could see his silhouette. He had a slight, lean body, and as I rubbed up against him to pass I felt myself getting hard. I pushed at the bulge with my fingers to calm it down, but that had a reverse effect. My erection was ready to break through my pants, and I was starting to sweat.

The inside of the tree house looked like a Japanese tea room, with embroidered pillows on the floor and branches draped along the walls. In the center of the room sat a bong and two bottles of Pellegrino. Andrew was smiling behind the light of the single lantern. He looked phosphorescent and slightly sinister. He slowly took his shirt off, and I could see all of his muscles turning and straining beneath his skin. Intellectual Boy took off his glasses and put his lips up against my neck and let out two long breaths. Andrew slowly began touching himself while staring at me with such an innocent, pleading look it was all I could do not to scream. I took it all in, feeling heat in the tips of my fingers, swells in my heart. It wasn't the lingering effects of the pot I had smoked earlier. No, this was a new kind of drug – feeling the breath on my neck, watching beautiful Andrew, drowning in the moments that seemed to slow down and expand. He flicked his finger at me, and I bent forward and kissed him while letting my penis out of the zipper of my jeans. I felt a power unleash, a virility and strength that was finally free to let go. When I came, my sperm shot so far it hit the ceiling. Andrew laughed and stood up, parading his cock around. It was huge for such a small guy. I watched him cum into Intellectual Boy's mouth, who jacked himself off into his own palm. Afterward, we just sat there breathing. I barely knew them, but I had never felt so safe, suspended in the warmth of that tree house, with the sound of crickets and a few drunk people singing in the distance.

A few nights later at the pledge dinner, I was gutted to see that Intellectual Boy and Andrew both had girls by their sides. In fact, I was the only one there without a date. Andrew's girl was short and pretty, and kept staring at me. I turned away, nibbling on my pizza and trying to seem disinterested. After dessert, Intellectual Boy walked up and whispered something unintelligible in my ear. Before he scurried away I said, "What's your name?"

He turned and smiled, his dirty blond hair falling in front of his chiseled face.

"Iliad," he said, "but people call me Ice."

I could see his eyes flicker behind his glasses, as if he were turning a switch that shot out little bolts of electricity. I wondered, among other things, where the nickname came from.

As I was leaving, Ice palmed me an invitation to an upcoming after-hours party at a club outside the city. I walked around campus for three days with the invite in my pocket, touching it with my fingers all day, to the point that when the night finally came I could barely read the address.

The place was a converted warehouse with a super modern, almost futuristic interior. Everyone seemed to be in their thirties, and once again I couldn't see Andrew or Ice anywhere. I sipped a beer and stared at all the gorgeous people, mostly men. A handsome older gentleman in a suit approached me and said, "Hello there, you must be Andrew's friend."

"How did you know that?" I asked.

His hair was white, and his eyes were sky blue. He looked like a small boy caught in a fifty-year-old body.

"Follow me," he said.

He took my hand and immediately I was hard again. I couldn't help it, with his big dark hand squeezing mine just a little harder than expected. I wanted him to lead me on and on, to surrender to him completely.

We slinked through a red velvet curtain, and there they were: Andrew, Ice, and some other guys I didn't recognize. They were all sitting on a large gray ottoman sharing a joint. I took a hit and caught Andrew's eye, remembering that wonderful, vulnerable look that had been burned into my memory. Here though, Andrew was poised and demure, and Ice even more so. I wished to become them, to walk into their skin, to cover myself in their beauty.

The white-haired guy, Price, brought me a Popsicle. I started eating it immediately, and he watched me from the corner of his eye. I slowed my tongue way down, letting each lick last. For the first time in my life, I felt sexy.

Andrew stood up and asked me to dance. I followed him to another room that smelled of tangerine and sweat, and we danced with our bodies barely touching. We each had mounds in our pants, and every once in a while we'd inadvertently rub our jeans together. For hours we danced, lost in the DJ's beats. When the music finally faded, Andrew grabbed me and held me close, our bodies clinging together. I thought *please, don't stop; let me stay here forever.*

When I moved into the Sigma Chi house, everything changed. I was given the only room that was in the attic, and Ice and Andrew lost their subtle charm and became very demanding.

Ice would periodically come up late at night and order me to masturbate. "Touch yourself," he'd say, deadpan. At first I laughed but his expression didn't change, cold as his name implied. In response I, too, became serious, touching myself slowly and tenderly. It was on those afternoons that I was beginning to see what I had wanted all along, this feeling of surrender, and this opening of myself.

Each time I did it with more and more care and precision, hoping he would join me, but he never did. He just watched. One time however, while watching me, he reached down and felt himself through his pants, and I let out a soft groan, and he said, "Stop." He walked over to me and put his lips against my neck like he had done on the first night in the tree house. He kept on, silent except for his breathing, and without even touching my cock, I shot onto my stomach. He slowly cleaned it up for me with one of my dirty T-shirts and left the room in silence. I lay there for most of the night, naked and breathing, at times shaken with the aftershocks of pleasure.

By the end of the first year, I still hadn't seen much of Andrew but was constantly reminded of his look that night in the tree house. A look of such pure desire that I had never witnessed before, especially toward me.

The day before summer break, I saw him sleeping in the library on one of the big brown chairs. I watched him for a while, and then woke him up by touching my pen to his hairless arm. He opened his eyes, two emeralds glistening as if he had been waiting for me all along. He ran his hands through his hair and said, "Let's go."

He led me back to the tree house and opened a secret compartment, taking out a bottle of red wine. We cheered and drank in silence until he turned my head towards his and kissed me while running his fingers delicately down the line of my cheek.

He pulled back and said, "You are an old soul."

He kissed me again with sweet, full wine lips, and I once again began to drown. Dusk was descending, and I could hear creatures coming out of hiding. He began to hum, and I fell in and out of sleep, my head on his leg.

One must get lost in order to be found. This was the experience by which all of my future experiences would be based. I knew what it was I wanted. I knew who I was.

He kissed me again, and again, on my chest, my hips, the insides of my thighs, and the face of my feet. He devoured my every inch, and I sang to the sky. I sang to all the birds under the sun, and I sang to the coming of the night.

Stepbrothers
By Mickey Erlach

With spring semester over, Adam headed home for the summer before his senior year at State University. His mother had remarried a month prior, and she and her new husband were still on their honeymoon, so Adam knew he was coming home to an empty house.

After a three-hour drive, he was happy to be pulling up in front of the house, and he noticed the hatchback parked in the driveway and figured it must belong to one of his new stepfather's kids, who might be checking on the house.

Adam pulled his suitcases out of the trunk and walked up the walkway, let himself in, and walked right up the stairs. After a long drive, he was in no mood to talk to anyone.

He put the suitcases in his room, and the first thing he noticed was how hot it was in the house. If one of his new step siblings was there, why didn't he turn on the AC? Adam shook his head and took off his shirt.

Adam had been lifting weights since he was sixteen. His body was perfectly proportioned and nicely muscled at five-foot-eleven and 185 lbs. He inherited his mother's smooth dark skin and his father's large round ass, among other large assets.

He walked downstairs to turn on the air conditioning. While adjusting the thermostat, he heard the front door open and someone saying goodbye, followed by a car speeding away. He remembered his stepbrother from the wedding. Louis was a little taller than Adam at six-foot-one, but he was leaner. His nineteen-year-old stepbrother had thick black hair and dark features much like his father's, with black eyes and thick lips that begged to be kissed.

Adam remembered talking to him at the wedding and wondering if it would be incestuous to lay his new stepbrother.

"Hey, Adam," Louis said as he extended his hand. The two of them shook hands.

"Dude, what's with not turning on the AC? It's like a fucking oven in here," Adam asked.

Louis shook his head and headed upstairs. That was when Adam remembered that Louis was not much of a talker, and from what he gathered from his mother and Louis's siblings, he was not always playing with a full deck either.

Nutty or not, Adam still wondered if the boy liked to play.

He headed back to his bedroom and unpacked his bags. After putting away the last of his clothes and putting the suitcases in the closet, he headed back downstairs to the kitchen for some water. His mother always kept a large jug of water in the refrigerator, and he decided to forgo a glass and drink it straight from the jug. As he was guzzling the water, Louis walked into the kitchen.

"Adam, the man," he said.

Adam quit guzzling for a second and looked at Louis who had stripped to his boxers. The boy was long and lean, built like a swimmer with broad shoulders and a six pack. This pissed Adam off because he knew Louis never worked out, but he did hold out hope that Louis would end up fat when he hit thirty!

"So, Louis, are you living here now, or are you house sitting?" Adam asked him.

"Wouldn't you like to know, bro," Louis said, and he grabbed a soda and headed back to his room.

Adam rolled his eyes and finished the jug. He filled it with tap water rather than filtered, put it back in the fridge and hoped it was full of bacteria for Louis to enjoy.

Adam headed upstairs, walked into the bathroom, stripped and stepped into the shower. While he was soaping up, he thought of Louis, the weirdo, standing in the kitchen wearing nothing but his boxers, and his dick started to grow. Adam had not cum in a few days, so he took hold of his favorite toy and rubbed out a big load, barely taking a couple of minutes to do the deed, and hardly making a sound in the process as he learned to stay quiet while jerking off in the dorm.

He finished his shower and pulled the curtain back, grabbing a towel at the same time. Adam was startled to find Louis there flossing his teeth. *The house has three full baths, why is he in this one?*

Adam tried his best to conceal his cock, which was still half hard. It was difficult enough to hide when it was soft. However, Louis paid no attention to him, so Adam thought he would take one more stab at conversation.

"So, Louis, are you working or going to school?"

Louis stopped flossing and turned around to look at Adam, who had since wrapped the towel around his waist. Then he faced the mirror again.

"No," Louis said. He finished flossing and went into the guest room, shutting the door behind him.

"What a doofus," Adam said to himself. "I hope the little asshole isn't here all summer."

Adam brushed his teeth then crawled into bed.

At three in the morning, Adam was startled awake by some strange sounds. He thought there were cats fucking outside his window, but he soon realized the sounds were coming from the next room. He heard squeaking then high pitched moaning, more squeaking then Louis's voice saying over and over again, "Good boy, good boy, good boy."

Adam never heard anyone come in. Who the hell was Louis talking to? Then he heard him yell, "Ahhh ahhh ahhh," so loudly it shook the walls. Adam buried his head in his pillow to keep from laughing. Once the screaming stopped, he then heard Louis saying, "I'm such a good boy, oh yeah, good boy, good boy." Then, there was silence.

Adam was still laughing as he thought about his strange stepbrother masturbating and congratulating himself. Then he got hard again himself, but he was too tired to jerk off, so he rolled over and went back to sleep.

Adam woke up early the next morning and decided to make himself a pot of coffee and work out in the basement gym, provided it was still there. After locating his extra large mug, he filled it with the freshly brewed coffee and headed to the basement.

Since it was still pretty early, Adam decided to work out in just a black cotton jock strap, crew socks and cross trainers. The jock hugged his round butt and displayed his big basket perfectly, and he wished there were someone there to enjoy the view.

Once in the basement, he was happy to see that for the most part his equipment was still where he left it.

He loaded a couple of plates on the bar and secured them with collars. He decided to stretch a bit, and when he bent down to touch his toes he looked through his legs and saw Louis, stark naked and standing right behind him. Adam immediately stood up and turned around.

Louis was standing there with his dick hanging limp but low accompanied by two big, equally low hanging balls, and he was holding a cup of coffee.

73

"Adam the man," Louis said. "I took some of your aromatic java." He then turned around and headed back upstairs.

Adam stood there dumbfounded and was pissed because he would now have to brew more coffee although he did enjoy the view of Louis's bubble butt making its way up the stairs.

He slid under the bar and pressed the weights for twelve reps, and he sat up after the set and admired himself in the mirror he had mounted across from the bench. Adam ran his hands over his chest and down his six pack abs. He then flexed both biceps, displaying the high peaks that always earned him attention in the gym at school then he lay back down and did another twelve reps. With each set, he looked in the mirror and flexed his pecs, bouncing them before doing another double bicep pose. Adam loved being his own audience, watching himself get pumped and flexing.

Adam stood up and removed some of the plates and curled the barbell for ten reps very slowly, keeping his eyes on the vein that ran up his arms. Watching his biceps pump full of blood always turned him on, and his jock was beginning to get tighter.

He put the bar down, and flexed again, doing a crab pose, flaring out his lats and finishing off with another double bicep pose. He then did another set of curls.

During his third set, he heard Louis coming down the steps again. Adam finished the set and put the bar back. This time Louis was sitting in front of the mirror drinking another cup of coffee, blocking Adam's view of himself. *Fucking asshole*, he thought, *Drinks my coffee and interrupts my workout*. However, Adam didn't confront him because Louis was still naked.

"Can I help you, Louis?" he asked.

Silence.

Louis just stared at Adam, studying every inch of him. Adam noticed how Louis was looking at him and didn't know what to make of it.

"Louis, you're sitting in front of the mirror, and I can't watch myself when I work out."

Louis turned and looked at the mirror as if he hadn't noticed it was there. He stood up, walked across the room, and leaned on an old dresser that was placed in the basement a decade before.

"Louis, are you just going to stand there?" Adam asked him.

Again, silence.

Adam did another set of curls, watching himself in the mirror when he noticed Louis was now standing behind him. Louis reached around and felt Adam's biceps with each curl of the bar, running his hands over the pumped muscles. Adam was only startled for a split second then continued his set, enjoying the feel of his stepbrother's hands on his muscles, and he started to get hard again.

Adam curled until he was exhausted, then he put the bar back on the rack. As he looked at himself in the mirror, Louis continued to explore his body with his hands.

Louis felt his stepbrother's lats, tracing his fingers up Adam's muscular back, then he squeezed Adam's softball sized shoulders, and as one hand made its way up Adam's neck the other reached around to feel Adam's pumped chest.

As Louis continued exploring his body, Adam's breathing became heavier. He let his stepbrother enjoy every sweaty, pumped inch of him, and finally, Louis's hand was running down his six-pack then inside the black cotton jock strap and going for the prize.

As Louis released his stepbrother's enormous boner, he stepped around and brushed his lips against Adam's. Adam opened his mouth and reached around Louis's head drawing him in and kissing him deeply, tasting the coffee the asshole had taken without permission. With his free hand, Adam reached down and grabbed the weirdo's hard dick and was impressed with its length and girth. Adam slid his hand up to the swollen head and slicked it with the precum Louis's big dick generously provided.

Louis had managed to get Adam's jock down around his ankles, and they continued to make out while stroking each other's dicks. Louis's free hand continued to explore Adam's pumped body and found a nipple giving it a hard pull, and Adam moaned, but he did not let go of Louis's mouth. Those lips were too good to let loose even for a second.

He let go of Louis's head and flexed his right bicep while his stepbrother felt it with his left hand, as they continued to kiss. Louis obviously liked the feel of flexed muscles because his dick would swell and pulse emitting more precum whenever Adam flexed. This in turn made Adam's thick cock swell up, and he didn't know how much longer he could last.

Their breathing increased, and the stepbrothers were getting closer, but they never unlocked their lips.

Finally, Louis pulled away from Adam's lips and screamed, "Ahhh ahhh ahhh," so loudly it startled Adam. Then he shot his load covering Adam's belly and chest with pints of cum. The site of his stepbrother's load on his pumped chest made Adam shoot all over Louis, who groaned while Adam was shooting, "You are such a good boy, oh yeah, good boy, good boy."

Then, there was silence.

They pulled away from each other, and Adam grabbed a towel to wipe himself off, but Louis stopped him. He bent down and licked his stepbrother's body clean. After he finished his breakfast of cum, he winked at Adam, turned and walked back upstairs without saying a word.

Adam stood there with his half hard cock hanging out and his black cotton jock at his ankles and watched Louis's round butt bounce as he walked up the stairs once again.

What a fucking nut job, Adam thought. Then he smiled and hoped all his workouts would end like this one.

The Masseurs
By Lew Bull

I picked up a copy of the newspaper and turned to the classified ads. There I saw a heading, Massage. I skimmed through the lists of adverts and noticed how many included items such as "Man to Man," or various sizes such as "10 inches" or "8 inches." I realized that these adverts were not simply for massaging, but for little, or in some cases large, extras. I had never experienced a massage, with an "extra bit" thrown in, but at this present moment, I was feeling extremely horny and in dire need of some sex.

Having gone through the ads, I went back to one that had caught my attention; which read:

FUN IN THE SUN
Many hot guys waiting for you!
Brad – young, hung, hunky 9"
Mark – hottest butt in town
Clint – thickest 10" of passion
Gary – body-builder 8"
Eric – sexy stud to tease
Chad – muscular 9" both ways

The reason this advert caught my attention was that if I was going to get a massage, plus a bit extra, at least I could have a choice among a number of young guys, who all sounded like Adonises; after all, one should always keep one's options open! Underneath the advert was a telephone number, so I picked up the telephone and dialed the number. A soft-sounding male voice answered at the other end of the line and said, "Fun in the Sun, good morning. How may I help you?"

I replied hesitantly, as I had never done this before.

"Hello, I was just phoning to enquire about the massages. What are your hours and how much is it?"

Obviously the voice on the other end was used to questions of this nature, so there was no hesitation on his part.

"We're open twenty-four hours, and it depends whether you want a half-hour or full-hour session."

Before I had a chance to reply, he continued, "Why don't you pop around and come and meet the guys and see if you like anything."

With an invitation like that, and feeling as horny as I did, I thought, to hell with the cost, let's go.

I, however, decided I would go in the evening, maybe, so that no one would see me.

Early that evening, I had a shower, a bite to eat and left for the place, having been given directions by the man on the phone.

I drove up to the gate of a fairly large house and pressed the intercom button. I heard the same voice I had heard earlier on the phone and introduced myself as the guy who had phoned earlier and was coming for a massage. The gate opened, and I drove my car into the grounds and parked in the demarcated parking area. I noticed that there were a few other cars already parked there, so I knew there had to be other customers. I walked up to the front door, which was smartly opened before I could ring the doorbell by a young guy of about twenty-two years of age wearing only a pair of running shorts. I think my mouth dropped open as this was not quite what I had expected, however, I did like what I saw.

"Please come in, and welcome to Fun in the Sun. I take it that this is your first time here?"

"Yes," I stammered, still not being able to take my eyes off of the guy. I thought, well, if the rest are as good looking as this one, then this should be a very interesting evening.

"Come through to the lounge," he said, closing the door behind me and then leading down a long corridor. As I walked down the corridor, I noticed quite a few doors leading off it. At last we entered a lounge that was tastefully furnished in a mix of modern with touches of art deco and had a few young men sitting around, half naked, casually chatting to each other.

"Would you like a drink?" asked my host.

"Thank you," I replied, "just a beer."

He disappeared for a moment and returned with my beer, which he handed to me.

"The first drink is on the house," he said smiling at me, and we both sat down.

"Now," he continued, "my name is Fred, and if there's anything that you want, please don't hesitate to call me. Are you looking for anyone in particular?"

"I don't know," I said rather sheepishly. "I don't know any of the guys."

"Well, I'll tell you what, why don't I take you to one of the rooms, and I'll send the guys in one at a time and if there's anyone that you particularly want, you simply tell him, and we stop the 'parade' there, and he'll be your masseur for the evening."

"What about the cost?" I asked.

"That you negotiate with your masseur, whether it's for an hour or for less. Would you like to try?"

"OK," I replied, and off we went down the corridor toward some of the bedrooms.

I noticed that the farther down the corridor we went, the darker it seemed to get.

Eventually, we entered a room which had a double bed situated in the center of the room and a TV on a stand against one of the walls; other than that, the room was bare. There were no lights on in the room, and the only light that filtered in came from the glow down the corridor. Although the room looked gloomy because of a lack of light, it still felt comfortably warm.

Fred led me over to the bed and said, "Make yourself comfortable, take your clothes off, and I'll send in the first of the guys."

He then exited the room, closing the door behind him. It was now pitch dark inside the room, so I ventured to where the curtains had been. I pulled them apart slightly in the center, and a little moonlight came in through the crack. I took off my clothes, folded them and placed them on the floor next to the TV set, and sat on the edge of the bed to wait.

Eventually the door opened, and the first of the guys came in. I could see in the corridor glow that he was young and very well built. He came into the room wearing a pair of loose fitting track-suit pants and a white vest looking as though he had just finished doing some training at the local gym. He introduced himself as Chad and then proceeded to tell me about himself and what he liked doing. I wasn't quite sure what I was supposed to say or do, so I simply said, "Thanks Chad. I like what I see, but I'll look at the others and then make a choice."

My God, I sounded as though I was at the market trying to choose some beef rump and being not quite sure which piece I wanted, but after all, one should never rush into things, one should always think things over. So off he went and in came Gary.

He stood in the doorway, and I could see the silhouette of an incredibly muscular man. He stood there wearing the shortest pair of shorts I had ever seen, with muscles bulging everywhere. He introduced himself, but before he could continue, I said, "I can see you're into your bodybuilding." That must have been the cue for him because he suddenly started to flex his muscles in front of me. Now I have no problems with that, except, it does make my choices a little more difficult.

"Do you like what you see?" he asked flexing his biceps virtually under my nose.

I caught a scent of manliness and sweat, which turned me on, and I replied, "Oh yes, I'd like to see more, but I really should be fair to the others as well. As Gary turned to leave I couldn't resist squeezing his butt. By now my cock was standing at attention, and I thought, thank goodness it's dark in this room, and no one can see my hard-on.

The door reopened, and in strutted Mark. He had a very pleasing, young face from what I could see in the dim light, and I remembered that the newspaper said that he had the hottest butt in town. By this time I was no longer feeling as though this was my first visit to a massage parlor and had become bolder in my questioning.

I said to Mark, "I believe that you've got the hottest butt in town, is that true?"

"Well that's what they say," he replied.

"But seeing is believing," I added. "How about showing me?"

"That's not part of the deal," he said.

"Maybe not, but as the customer, I need to see what I'm paying for." I couldn't believe that I had actually said that.

Without much hesitation, Mark turned his back to me and pulled down his shorts to reveal a very sexy bubble-butt. "Well, are you satisfied?" he enquired.

"Very," I replied truthfully, and I thought to myself how great it would be sliding into that butt and making love to it. "Thanks, Mark, could you send in the next please?"

There was a knock at the door, and I got up from the bed and opened the door. There stood the most beautiful young guy of about twenty-five dressed only in a Speedo costume. I think my jaw dropped open when I saw him. He looked me up and down and said, "You look as if you've seen some nice things already." I realized he was looking at my cock throbbing in the air.

"Come in," I said, "and who are you?"

"I'm Brad. I'm twenty-six years old, horny and I've got a nine-inch cock."

"Is that when you're hard or soft?" I joked, because I could see from the shape and bulge in his Speedo that he wasn't small, and he didn't have an erection.

"Oh no, that's when it's hard, and sometimes I can get it to go a bit bigger, depending on whom I'm with." The mind boggled.

"Are you cut or uncut?" I asked.

"Rub your hand along here and you tell me," he replied, pointing to his cock in his Speedo.

I couldn't believe this was happening to me. I gently put my hand on the front of his Speedo and ran it along the length of his cock. I could feel it beginning to stir inside his costume, and I realized he could see how erect mine was getting.

"Well, what's the verdict?" he smiled.

"Definitely cut, and I reckon I could get it to grow longer than nine inches. How many more guys are there for me to see?" I enquired.

"I think there's only Clint."

"What's he like?" I asked. "Is he bigger than you?"

"When you say bigger, do you mean in cock size or in build?"

"Well, both, if necessary," I quipped.

"His cock is ten inches long and much thicker than mine, but I think I've got a better build than he. However, that's just my opinion, but we're the best of friends."

Now I had a problem; which young guy to pick. "Brad, I think I'd like to have a massage with you, if you don't mind!"

"I'd be honored," he replied. "You won't be disappointed. How long do you want?"

"Could we have at least an hour, please?"

He told me how much it would cost, and I agreed on the price. Then he said he was going to get some towels, creams, and supplies, and then he'd be back, but to make myself comfortable on the bed and wait for him.

After Brad had left, I lay on my stomach on the bed and waited for his return. While I lay there I thought, so much for fun in the sun, this is more like fun in the dark, but I had already made up my mind that I would return to this place on another occasion and try out one of the other guys. While I was dozing there on the bed, I heard the door close, the towels being dropped onto the floor with the other supplies and felt Brad get onto the bed.

"Right, are you ready?" he whispered.

"Oh yes," I whispered back.

He knelt astride my legs and I felt the cold trickle of massage oil being poured onto my back. Slowly he began to rub the oil all over my back. This felt good. His whole body seemed to lie across my back as he stretched forward to rub my shoulders. I could feel that he was still wearing his Speedo costume, but I could also feel that his cock was no longer limp.

"Why don't you take off your costume?" I said. "At least it won't get ruined with oil." He slipped from the bed and pulled off his costume. When he returned to the bed, he positioned himself between my legs and started rubbing oil up and down them. As his hands moved up my legs, I could feel them slide in the crack of my ass and then rub over the cheeks of my ass. This continued for a while, and then I felt his whole body stretch across my back, and he rubbed his whole body over mine. I could feel his cock slide up and down over my ass while his oily hands explored under my chest for my nipples.

After a while, he said, "I think it's time for you to turn over and let's do the front."

He rolled off me and waited for me to roll over onto my back. When I had done that, he began to rub oil over my chest and down my stomach.

His firm hands wandered over my stomach and continued in a downward movement towards the pelvic area. I could feel my cock throbbing in the dark. Slowly his hands moved closer to my crotch, and I waited in anticipation for that moment when the massage would probably end and the sex would begin. I felt a finger gently rub against the stem of my cock, which gave a little jump. Then I felt another finger, and so on until his hands were wrapped around the stem of my throbbing cock. I gasped with pleasure. While he held onto my cock, I felt his tongue start running over my nipples. He gently tugged at them with his teeth and licked them, and then he continued his tongue journey down my chest, onto my stomach until he reached my cock. A tongue flicked over the tip of it and then ran down the stem until he reached my balls, which he carefully caressed with his tongue. He then worked his way up again and took the head of my cock into his mouth. His tongue licked round the head, driving me crazy, then he slowly sank his mouth down my long shaft engulfing my whole cock in one go. He held his mouth there for a while, letting his tongue run up and around the shaft, and then he proceeded to slide his mouth up my cock. When he reached the top of my cock, he let it fall from his mouth, and leaning close to my face, searched for my mouth in the dark. We found each other's and began kissing passionately. After a moment, he released my tongue from his mouth and said, "What do you like doing?"

"Whatever you'd like to do," I replied. "You're making me so happy that I'll do anything that you want. If you want to fuck me, you may, or if you want me to slip into you, I'll gladly do it."

All he said was, "OK, you just enjoy."

Brad continued to kiss me while I felt his enormous erection. I decided that I needed to repay him for the pleasure that he had been giving me, so I rolled him over onto his back and began to lick and kiss his nipples. I then started working my way down his tightly muscled body, licking him all over until I felt his pubic hairs. I continued down his hard-on, which definitely was at least nine inches, if not more, until I reached his balls which I gently plopped into my mouth one at a time, swirling my tongue around them and listening to Brad groan with pleasure. This movement had brought me to the bottom of the bed, so I slid off the bottom and dragged Brad a little way down the bed, so that I was able to stand bent over at the bottom of the bed and lick between his legs and up his balls and cock. As I stood there with his cock now in my mouth, I felt another cock, very hard and very large press against my butt. I let go of Brad's cock and stood up straight to see if I could see who was there. Brad's voice came from the bed, "I told you just to enjoy."

"But someone else is here with us," I said.

"That's right," said Brad, without sounding panicky, "It's just Clint, you know the guy I told you about."

"What's he doing here?" I asked.

"I thought I'd give you a real treat since this was your first visit here. I hope you don't mind?"

"I suppose not," I said lamely; what else could I say?

"Shall we carry on," said Brad, pulling my head back down onto his cock. I started sucking him again, and as I did so, I felt Clint's barge pole poking at my ass waiting to enter. I had no idea what Clint looked like, but what I felt against me, I liked.

"Have you got some cream?" I asked, but before I could get an answer, I felt Clint's huge fingers sliding cream into my butt. He left his finger there and felt his way around inside my ass. Suddenly, I froze, because I could feel that he was rubbing my prostate, and I knew that if he continued like that, I would shoot my load.

"What's the matter?" said Brad.

"If Clint carries on doing what he's doing to me, I'm going to cum."

"Well, then we'd better slow down. Would you like Clint to take you?" asked Brad.

From what I could feel, I would say that Clint definitely had a bigger cock than Brad, and I admired size, but I had seen Brad, and I liked what I had seen. I was in a dilemma as to whom I wanted to fuck me, so I did the noblest thing, "I'd like both of you to fuck me," I said.

"Are you sure that you can take two big dicks," said Clint. This was the first time he had spoken, and he had a deep sounding voice, which gave me the impression that he could be rough.

"I won't know until I try," I replied, trying to sound casual about it.

"OK then," said Clint, "bend over and suck Brad off."

I duly did as I was told and proceeded to take Brad's beautiful cock into my mouth once again. As I did so, I could feel the thick, bulbous head of Clint's monster cock forcing its way through the muscles of my ass. I could feel the pain, and I tensed. Clint waited for me to relax and then tried again. This time he entered me, and I shouted out in pain, letting go of Brad's cock.

"Do you want me to pull out?" asked Clint.

"No!" I exclaimed. Although it was painful, one has to have a little pain in order to have pleasure, I thought. "Let me take control. You just stand there and let me slide onto you."

Slowly I pushed back onto Clint's dick, feeling it slide all the way into me. I could feel myself getting dizzy and thinking that I was about to pass out, but I fought this dizziness until he was completely impaled in me. I waited for a moment so as to get used to his huge size, and then I bent over Brad's cock and started sucking him off again.

Clint held onto my hips with his massive hands and breathed heavy breaths down my neck as he plunged in and out of me, slowly at first and then quickening later. I could feel my ass being pounded, but as I got used to it, so I began to push back onto Clint, meeting him with every thrust that he made. All this movement was making me work faster and harder on Brad's cock. He was writhing on the bed, groaning and pushing his cock deeper into my mouth. I knew that he was getting excited with this movement, and it was drawing him closer to his edge and that he wouldn't be able to hold on much longer. Suddenly, his body tensed, and he let out a gasp. A flood of hot cum shot into my mouth as Clint kept pounding me from behind, while Brad was unloading his stock into my mouth. I could feel his cum trickling out of the sides of my mouth and down my chin, and still he kept shooting. I didn't believe anyone could have so much in him. At last he relaxed on the bed, panting, while Clint continued pumping in and out. I had got used to his size by now and was enjoying this. I pulled off of his cock and threw myself onto my back on the bed beside Brad. I lifted my legs until my feet were behind my head. Clint re-entered me and carried on from where we had left off, but while he fucked me, Brad got busy on my cock, sucking gently at first. Clint was so deep inside me that I could feel his ball slapping against my ass every time he pumped me. I felt my asshole and realized that no part of his shaft was out of me and that all ten inches was imbedded into me. This was true pleasure.

I heard his breathing getting heavier and realized that he was about to cum, so I prepared myself for an avalanche.

He gasped and grunted, "Oh fuck!"

He started pounding as though the world was coming to an end. I could feel him blasting into me, and as he did so, Brad held onto me, encouraging us the whole time. I realized that this was a team effort. Although it was dark, Brad had enjoyed me being fucked by Clint as much as I had. When Clint had exhausted what was left in him, he slowly pulled the ten inches out of me, gave me a squeeze and fell onto the bed with both of us. I leaned across and felt both their cocks to give them a squeeze and was surprised to find that both were still rock hard.

"One down, one to go!" exclaimed Clint feeling for my nipples and pinching them.

"What do you mean?" I asked.

"Don't tell me you've forgotten, or are you giving up?"

"Forgotten what?" I replied.

"You said you wanted both of us," said Brad. "Clint's had his turn, now it's mine. Kneel over Clint's chest and let him suck you off while I fuck you."

"OK, but then Clint's left out," I said, feeling sorry for the guy who had given me such pleasure.

"Oh no he's not," said Brad, laughing, "While he's sucking you off and I'm fucking you astride Clint's stomach, Clint's cock is big enough to reach me and fuck me." I was dumbstruck. No wonder Brad had said they were best friends; they had obviously tried this before. Just the thought of the three of us knotted together made me horny. I had to be able to see this.

"It's so dark in here, and I don't want to miss this, do you think we could open the curtains or put the TV on so there is some light in the room."

Both agreed that they didn't have a problem with that, so the TV was switched on, not that it mattered what channel it was on, and the curtains were opened so the moonlight could flood in. It was then that I saw Clint for the first time. This guy was huge. He was like a giant both in build and cock size, however Brad had a more defined body.

Brad creamed himself in readiness for Clint's barge pole and knelt astride Clint's stomach. He held Clint's dick in his right hand and slowly lowered himself onto it. He was obviously used to its size because he didn't have to get used to it like I had done. Once he was impaled on it all the way to Clint's balls, he said, "OK, now you come in front of me astride Clint's chest, and I'll slip into you."

I positioned myself across Clint's stomach and chest and felt Brad's cock behind me searching for my entry corridor. I lowered myself onto his cock and sank straight to the bottom of his shaft. I felt no pain because Clint had loosened my asshole, and I was still wet from where Clint had creamed me. I began to rise and lower myself on Brad's cock while I could feel him doing the same on Clint's. At one stage, we were going in unison, both Brad and I riding up and down at the same time with Clint's mouth wrapped tightly round my cock. I felt Clint lift his knees slightly, which forced his cock deeper into Brad, which in turn pushed Brad's cock deeper into me and forced my cock deeper into Clint's mouth. This was truly heaven. I would never have thought this was possible.

Because of the light in the room now, I was able to see every expression – in fact I could even see sweat drops on Brad, if I turned my head to kiss him. This continued for quite a while with everyone enjoying every moment of it. I noticed that Clint's grip on my cock had got tighter, and I wondered if he was close to coming.

"Are you close, Clint?" I asked.

There was a grunt, which I took to mean yes. When Brad heard that he started riding Clint's cock even faster and tightening his ass muscles around Clint's thick shaft. At the same time, Brad's movements pounded into my ass, and I rode him like a bucking bronco until I knew I was going to shoot.

"Fuck me! Fuck me!" I shouted as Brad increased his pace.

I could feel my balls were ready to explode. I couldn't hold on any longer. I gasped and shot one load after another down Clint's guzzling throat. Brad kept pounding my ass, and I heard him groan in ecstasy as he shot his load, pumping me full of his hot cum. Clint kept sucking my cock dry and pounding in Brad's ass. I thought there had been an earthquake because suddenly Clint's pelvis thrust up, forcing both Brad and me high into the air, but without any of us losing contact with the other. He gave a low growl and speeded up his pounding in Brad, which caused Brad to pound me again, but never did Clint take his mouth away from my cock.

At last, he let go of my cock and panted heavily. I slowly lifted myself from Brad's wet cock and rolled onto the bed next to Clint. Brad then released himself from Clint's giant cock and lay next to me on the bed. We were all breathing heavily from this exercise. I felt a hand come from either side of me and get placed gently on my subsiding cock.

After a while I managed to say, "Thanks guys. That was the best I've ever experienced. I don't think anything could top that."

I heard a snicker come from both sides of me.

"What's your name?"

"Joe," I replied.

"Well, Joe, you ain't had nothing yet," said Clint.

"That I can't believe," I laughed.

"Trust us, we mean it. When we get together, anything can happen," laughed Brad giving my limp cock a gentle squeeze.

We got off the bed and tried to clean ourselves as best we could and got dressed. Brad slipped his Speedo back on, and I stood and admired his beautiful shape, both in the Speedo and out. Clint looked on the floor for his clothes and picked up a pair of shorts. He poured himself into them and stood there waiting to be admired. His shorts were so short and tight that it was a wonder that his huge dick could fit in there, in fact when I looked, the head of his dick was sticking out from the waistband of them. I bent over and kissed the top of his cock that was sticking out. "I hope I see you again," I said addressing his cock.

They both laughed and said, "We hope that we see you again. As far as payment is concerned, this one was on the house – provided we see you again and you come to us."

I went out into the cool, moonlit night feeling as though I was on a cloud. When I got home, I felt satisfied, but deep down I had a gnawing question of what Clint had meant when he said, "You ain't had nothing yet?"

Maybe next week I'll go back and find out.

Hot Basement Sex
By Dan DeVeaux

From the time I woke up late in the morning, I knew it was going to be a good day. First of all, the sun was shining bright this May day. Second, it was a Tuesday, and I didn't have any classes at the community college where I was a nineteen-year-old freshman. I lived with my mother who worked full time, so I would have the house to myself. I woke up horny as usual with a good-size hard-on. But I thought I'd start the day by washing my car and delay having a good jack-off session until later. Not wanting to soil my good jeans, I went down to the basement to fish a dirty pair of cut-offs out of the laundry basket. Since I was alone in the house, I went down there in just my jockey shorts and loafers.

Being an old house, the basement had thirty-inch high windows which made it bright enough in the daylight without turning on the light switch. Besides, I only expected to be down there a few minutes. Our old house had what's called a "grade door" at the side. It opened to the same level as the driveway to a small vestibule; which was four steps below our kitchen door and seven steps above the basement. I didn't realize that on the day the meter reader came, my mother locked the kitchen door but left the grade door unlocked, so the meter reader could access the meter in the basement. And I didn't know that the meter reader came on the first Tuesday of the month. And this was the first Tuesday.

So, I was shocked when, as I reached into the laundry basket to retrieve the pair of cut-offs, I heard the grade door open, a voice call out "meter reader" and footsteps on the basement stairs. Wearing only my jockeys, and with my dick still half erect, I backed into the shadows, so I wouldn't be visible for the few minutes I expected him to be there. As expected, he walked to the wall where the meter was, entered the reading on his hand-held device, then turned and walked toward the stairway. All of a sudden, he stopped as if contemplating something, then put his reading device down on the workbench. Now facing in my direction, I saw that he was a real "hottie," early twenties, probably, with a great build, a handsome face with curly dark hair and a bulging basket. Yeah, that really intriguingly big bulging basket made my own dick jump in my jockeys.

I immediately began fantasizing about what a big dick he must have and how great it would be to take hold of it. Still being a virgin, I had never even seen another guy's hard-on, much less touched one. So I couldn't believe my eyes when he unzipped his fly, pulled his big dick out and began to pee into the basement floor drain. Even half erect, it was a monster. When he finished peeing, he didn't stick his dick back in his pants. Instead, he just held it out there for a while then began to run his hand up and down his dick shaft. I watched his dick grow to full length while he jacked it slowly. It was awesome. Of course, by this time my hand was in my own jockeys doing a number on my own swelling dick. When he pulled his pants down to his knees, showing that he wore no underwear, and began to jack off in earnest, I thought I would faint. I had never seen a guy jack off before except for the times I did it in front of my mom's full-length mirror. Now seeing the meter man jerk his meat in my full view, my knees felt weak, and my heart began to beat faster and faster. Wow, what a show he was giving me.

The meter guy picked up the tempo, throwing his head back in ecstasy as he pounded his meat mercilessly. In the shadows, I beat my meat just as furiously. I was so carried away that I stepped back too far, knocking a box of empty cans and bottles off a chair. It made such a loud crash, scaring me so, that I jumped out in the open, fully exposing myself to the meter hunk. At the same time, he jumped and stopped, momentarily, but never took his hand off his throbbing dick.

"Well, it looks like I have unexpected company," he said in a friendly voice. "I thought I was alone."

"I live here," I said stupidly.

"Oh really. I thought maybe you were visiting from Mars. Anyway, you've got a nice size cock there in your hand. Why don't you let me see it close up?"

I was frozen, unable to move. So he moved close to me, took hold of my dick and rubbed it against his. It sent new sensations through my body. It was surreal. My sexual excitement intensified rapidly.

"How do you like rubbing cocks, Dude? I think it's better than shaking hands, don't you? I have to admit you gave me quite a scare jumping out of the shadows like you did. But with a big cock like yours, I can't complain as long as I can eat it for lunch. Hand me a towel from that clothes basket. My name's Tony, by the way. What's yours, you young hunk?"

"Sean," I said in a weak voice, my breath still short.

I did as told retrieving a towel, which Tony dropped to the floor in front of me. Then dropping to his knees, he took my dick in his hand and nibbled on my dickhead with his hot tongue, which drove me crazy. Still pumping his own dick, he ran his tongue along the shaft of mine, coaxing it even harder. Then he pushed his mouth down all the way to the base of my dick and deep-throated me. I never imagined anything could feel so good. Up and down on my dick his mouth went, interrupting only occasionally, to suck my balls until I thought they would explode. I hadn't even known that you sucked balls, but I sure liked the sensation now that mine were getting full treatment.

"Nice balls, Sean. Great to suck. I see they're filling out big time. Looks like you're going to shoot a big load. Well, I'm going to swallow it, baby, so let loose whenever you want. Tony is ready for it."

I hadn't even thought about what I'd do when I was ready to shoot, but now with Tony's invitation, I let go a cum load that I only wished I could have seen. I could feel volley after volley of cum releasing from my swollen cock until it was running out of the side of Tony's mouth, and he was gorging on my man-pudding like it was a gourmet delicacy. I emptied my balls thoroughly, panting like a dog in heat. Wow. What an orgasm. What an unbelievable first experience. What a hot sex partner. This was far better than any of my fantasies.

Tony's sex pole was still sticking straight out full of anticipation. It was huge, had to be eight or nine inches. I marveled at both its length and its girth. His hand-jobbing while he sucked me had kept it hard as a rock and craving action.

"Now it's your turn, Sean. On your knees, baby. My cock needs some real affection. Show it a good time. Suck the hell out of it with that hot mouth of yours."

I had never sucked a cock before although I had fantasized about it many times, usually while jacking off. And often while looking at a gay porn magazine where all the guys seemed to have nine-inch dicks and were pictured in various positions of sucking and fucking. Real hot stuff.

"This is my first time," I admitted honestly. "Let me know if I do it OK."

"Just watch your teeth because they're sharp and can hurt. Use your lips. Do like I did and just nibble on my cockhead at first. Then lick my shaft up and down and, finally, take my whole cock in your mouth and suction as hard as you can. My cock will respond, you can

91

bet. I'll let you know when I'm ready to shoot and you can decide then whether you want to swallow my load or have me cum on your chest. So go for it and enjoy it as much as I will."

I did as instructed and was surprised how big his dick felt in my mouth. And how good. I didn't mind the musty smell of his crotch. In fact it was a turn-on. I sucked his monster dick long and hard, enjoying a new experience for me. I was a little shocked when the precum oozed out of his dick but took it all in stride. I sucked his big balls as well, taking them in my mouth one at a time and squeezing them with my mouth just enough to make Tony squeal with appreciation. Those big orbs started swelling up big time, so I knew he was building up a real head of sexual steam.

It wasn't long before he yelled out, "I'm ready to shoot, baby, where do you want it, mouth or chest."

This was my first blow job, and I really wasn't ready to taste another guy's cum pudding, so I opted out. Besides, I really wanted to watch him shoot what I knew would be a huge load. One that had been building up for forty minutes.

"Chest please," I said just in time as Tony's cum fireworks started the minute he pulled out of my mouth.

"Yeah, watch this load, Sean, watch me shoot the moon with a big cum explosion. Yeah, there it is. Aw fuck, fuck, fuck. Just like a fucking volcano. My balls are loaded, man, and I intend to empty them down to the last drop. Yeah, that feels great. I needed to unload those fuckers before they burst like punctured balloons."

Tony sure put on quite a show. I couldn't have imagined a cum load that huge. Seemed as if he just came and came and then came some more. His entire body shook as he lobbed his cum missiles toward me, hitting my chest, chin and even my forehead.

"Stick your tongue out, Sean, and I'll give you a little taste of genuine Tony cum pudding. See how you like it. Someday, you'll be begging for it I bet."

Reluctantly, I did as I was told and Tony laid a big blob of his hot cum on my licker. It was tart and nasty I thought and quickly decided it wasn't for me, but I had given it a shot, anyway. Anything for this hot sex animal I was servicing.

"Fuck, fuck, fuck," Tony bellowed as the last drops of his cock-juice left his still-stiff dick. "You worked me up an awesome load, Sean, and now I'm exhausted. Really shot."

"Me, too," I said, still recovering from the excitement of giving my first blow job. "Let's go upstairs and sack out for a while."

Fortunately, this was Tony's last stop for the day, so he happily agreed, and we went up to my bedroom where we both got naked, kissed a few times and then slid between the cool sheets on the bed and fell instantly asleep. About an hour later, I woke up to the feeling of someone sucking my dick, and saw Tony's head bobbing up and down on it. It felt great, and I watched as Tony got me fully hard again with his hot mouth working overtime but, obviously, enjoying it. I ran my hand through his curly hair to show my appreciation. What an exciting way to wake up, with a blow job. I decided I could really get into man-to-man sex.

"This was just for openers, Sean baby. Just to get you hot enough to proceed with our lovemaking. I've got my eyes on your cute little ass. I want to fuck you real bad."

"I've never been fucked, Tony. I don't know if I can do it." I said noticing the size of his already hard dick. "Your dick is so huge it might not fit in my ass."

"Not to worry, Sean. I'll go easy on you. I'll work my big missile up your chute one way or the other. But I need it bad, man. Real bad. Besides, I think you'll like it once you try it. Most guys do I've found. Now, have you got some lube?"

Actually, I did have some lube. Used it a couple of times to stick my finger up my ass and work it around for some cheap thrills but never anything nearly the size of Tony's huge fuck tool. So I fetched it, but Tony put it aside for the moment.

"Lie on your back, put your legs in the air and pull them back as far as you can so I can see that cute rosy hole of yours. Yeah, that's it. Your glory hole is sweet. Real sweet. Needs to be eaten as well as fucked. Now I'll put a pillow under your ass to get it up high enough for an easy fuck. But first a few prelims. Know what rimming is? I'm going to run my hot tongue around the rim of your hole to get you really turned on. Then tongue your hole to loosen you up. Here goes."

With that explanation, he started in on me. God, his tongue felt good as he probed around my sensitive hole – sensations I had never felt before. When Tony's tongue did battle with my sphincter, I thought I would go ballistic. What a sexual rush I got. Next he worked a well-lubed finger into my sphincter, and it parted to let the intruder in. Again I was feeling great new sensations as Tony's finger massaged my prostate although, at the time, I didn't know that was the cause. After he repeated this action with two fingers, I braced myself for the final assault from his impatient dick, still hard as rock. When it came, it was gangbusters. Even with all the foreplay and lubing, it wasn't an easy penetration.

"God, Sean, your ass is really tight. I thought working those fingers around in you would loosen you up, but your still tight as hell. Breathe in as I thrust against you. I know you can take me. And my stubborn cock won't take 'no' for an answer."

"Ow. It hurts when you push in me so hard. Lube us up some more. Maybe that will help. It feels like you're trying to shove a baseball bat up my ass."

"Yeah, your sphincter is stretching out like never before. Sorry for the pain, but it should abate before long and the ecstasy kicks in. It will be worth the slight discomfort. I know since I've been fucked a few times myself."

Deeper and deeper, Tony worked his massive dick into my glory hole until he had pushed his entire eight and a half inches past my reluctant sphincter into my hot chasm of delight. The pain was still there, but as promised, the ecstasy began as well. I had never imagined anything as sexually exciting as this. Gradually, Tony stepped up the momentum of his thrusts until he attained a fast fucking rhythm that started me jerking my own dick like a madman trying to keep up.

"Yeah, Tony, fuck me harder, give me all you've got, man." I couldn't believe what I was saying, but it suddenly felt so good the way he was pounding my ass. And Tony really threw himself into every thrust as my moaning and pleading inspired him. Wham. Wham. Wham. We were like two fucking animals rutting in the wild. No holds barred. It was awesome for both of us.

Finally, Tony reached his moment of orgasm. He pulled out of me and shot off like the Fourth of July. His cum shots sailed high in the air, hitting all parts of my body. I suddenly had a coating of his ball-jam all the way up to my chest. It seemed to take forever for him to empty his giant nuts, and he moaned with excitement and gratification as it went on. I watched in amazement at the fireworks, hardly believing my eyes, until the gusher finally stopped.

Exhausted again, we engaged in some deep, passionate kissing while still rubbing our cocks together because we didn't want the moment to end. After a while, we bowed to the inevitable as our dicks slowly shrunk. We staggered to the shower and turned on the water full force. It ran off our bodies in a sensual but soothing manner that was welcome and restorative. We kissed some more with the water still running off us. Tony grabbed my ass and pulled my body tightly against his. Our cocks responded but only for a moment. They had had their day. And so had we. More than we could have hoped for.

"I don't want to let go of you," Tony whispered in my ear. "I want to hold you forever. You gave me some of the best sex I ever had. And I think you learned a lot about it, too. And enjoyed it."

I felt the same way but was still too shy to express it. But I think my body pressing tightly against his and my hot kisses spoke for me. Besides, my head was still spinning from the hot sexual action. Finally, my virginity was lost forever and good riddance. With Tony, I had experienced passionate man-to-man sex, and it was better than I could have imagined. I didn't know where it would lead and for the moment I didn't care. I was still savoring the moments of extreme sexual pleasure I had been privileged to share with a beautiful, sensitive guy.

As I had earlier anticipated, it had been a very good day.

Many Happy Returns
By Jordan Castillo Price

Kenneth shot a plastic tab through the seam of a hideous sweater. He wasn't sure why he bothered. It wasn't as if the sweater hadn't been returned at least three times. Not that it was defective, per se. It was just so ugly that no one would ever want it.

But Kenneth was only there to earn enough money to buy a new computer. Part-time, seasonal work seemed harmless enough, or at least it had, the day he'd accepted the job of staffing the most obscure return desk in the least-known sub-basement of SaverPlus.

He shot a plastic tag through a baseball cap, and wondered what type of person would return a hat. Someone with a head that was really big, or really small? He decided that he thought too much. Always had.

The clock clunked. It was an industrial piece of electronics, circa 1953, and it was far too retro to simply tick. Eight fifty-nine. He turned around and looked at the piles of clothes that had accumulated during his shift. Time to fold up the ugly returns and punch his timecard.

Forty-two years old and punching a time clock. Kenneth tried not to spiral down into a haze of self-pity by distracting himself with another thought, since his brain was so insistent on thinking.

Flat screen monitor. Bluetooth keyboard. Relax. Breathe.

The sharp ring of a call bell sent images of new computer systems scattering to the edges of Kenneth's mind. He looked up at the return desk, startled, and found a man in a leather jacket with spiked blond hair leaning over the counter on both elbows, chewing gum. He smiled at Kenneth. More of a devilish smile than an expression of actual happiness.

"We're closed," Kenneth said. "They've shut the lights off."

The customer peeked back over his shoulder, as if something had snuck up on him while he was trying to get Kenneth's attention.

"Sure," he said. "But look, maybe you can do me a favor."

Kenneth resisted the urge to roll his eyes. He couldn't imagine what would prompt him to do a favor for a total stranger, particularly at this purgatory of a job and especially at 9:01 pm.

"This shirt," the customer said, swinging a plastic bag onto the counter. "I need a large."

Kenneth sighed through his nose and reached into the bag. He had a big enough pile of returns. If he had the shirt in a large, he could scan them, swap them, and send the gum-chewer on his way.

He pulled the shirt onto the counter. It was, in Kenneth's opinion, the only decent shirt that SaverPlus carried. He owned three, himself.

"Whoa," said the customer, pointing. "You're wearing the same one." He levered himself up onto his palms, leaning over the countertop, into Kenneth's personal space. "That's pretty wild. Don't you think?"

"We haven't got this in a large," Kenneth said. "Not in black, anyway."

"But I need black," he said. "The shirt's from my mom. And she'll get all weird if I don't wear it the next time I see her."

"I'm sorry, sir ..."

The customer snorted, "Call me Crash." He squinted at Kenneth's name tag. "Kenny."

Kenneth composed himself. Bluetooth. DVD-RW. Five-hundred gig hard drive.

"These shirts are sold out in black large. They have been since November. If you'd like the shirt in mocha, I can do the exchange, but ..."

"Gimme yours."

Kenneth blinked. "What?"

Crash leaned farther still over the counter. He was tall and slim, and he had a very long reach. He stared hard into Kenneth's eyes and then reached up, fingering the collar of Kenneth's shirt. He had amazing eyes, pale, pale green. "Your shirt," he said. "It looks like a large. I would make it worth your while."

"You can't have my shirt."

Crash cocked his head to one side, and ran a tongue stud back and forth over the top edge of his lower teeth. "Everyone's got a price, Kenny. What's yours?"

Kenneth swallowed hard and got ready to tell Crash to go to hell – not a very festive SaverPlus farewell, but Kenneth was just a seasonal temp, after all – when Crash got a knee up onto the counter and started clambering over it toward Kenneth.

"Are you crazy?"

Crash grinned wide and flashed his tongue stud.

Kenneth almost called security. Almost. Except Crash wasn't particularly threatening. He crawled across the return desk like a stripper, his pale green eyes fastened on Kenneth's face the whole time. And when he oozed over the far edge of the counter, he kept on going down, sinking to his knees right between Kenneth's feet.

"What's that shirt worth to you?" he said, unbuckling Kenneth's belt.

Kenneth grabbed the edge of the counter and tried to will his knees to stop shaking. Before he could even register what was happening, his slacks pooled around his ankles.

"I can't believe you're just going to ..."

Crash ran his palms up Kenneth's thighs. He had silver rings on every finger, and the metal felt smooth, gliding over Kenneth's skin, hot from its contact with Crash's fingers. "What, no one ever ambushed you before? You're a good looking guy."

Objectively, maybe. But Kenneth had always managed to put a "don't bother me" vibe out there that resulted in him being left alone more often than not.

Crash tugged Kenneth's boxers down to his knees.

"And you're totally hung," he said, face so close that Kenneth felt the warmth of Crash's breath ghosting along his balls.

Kenneth meant to get another hand on the countertop to help hold himself up before his legs gave out from under him, but instead he found himself cupping the side of Crash's face, running his fingers over the crunchy spikes of hair and tracing the line of silver studs and hoops in Crash's ear.

Crash had a hand on each of Kenneth's thighs. He leaned in and pressed his face into the crease of Kenneth's groin, and Kenneth felt his cock throb, getting hard, fast. It brushed Crash's cheek, standing away from Kenneth's body in no time flat.

He gasped at the touch of Crash's hot, wet tongue. He swore he could feel that tiny metal stud playing along the veins on the underside of his shaft. Kenneth's fingers fanned over the side of Crash's face, tracing the sinew of his jaw as his hot, wet tongue stroked its way up, and down.

"You wanna feel the inside of my throat?" Crash asked teasingly, looking up from his crouch with his face nuzzled alongside Kenneth's hard-on.

Kenneth had a hard time forming a reply. Even a single-syllable word.

"You gonna give me your shirt?"

Kenneth nodded.

Crash raised one eyebrow. "Then take it off."

Kenneth looked out over the counter. The return desk faced a hallway, mostly, a dingy hallway that hadn't been painted in years, or redecorated in decades. He could see some of the sales floor if he craned his neck. And the guards had never bothered him in the past as they made their closing rounds, other than to yell, "See you later," as they passed the hallway entrance.

Crash's tongue darted between Kenneth's balls, and Kenneth had to clench his jaw to keep from yelping. "Your shirt," Crash said, forming the words against Kenneth's scrotum.

Kenneth peered out over the counter again, toward the darkened sales floor.

"What do you care if anyone sees?" said Crash. "It'll be totally hot if they do." He tilted his head back and fit his lips around one of Kenneth's balls, cradling it with his mouth and teasing at it with the tip of his tongue.

Kenneth squirmed. His cock was so stiff now it almost hurt, and his balls were tight. If he was so turned on already, how amazing would it feel if he were buried deep in that wicked mouth?

Kenneth pulled his shirt off with one quick tug, and let it fall to the floor beside his foot.

Crash smiled up at him, then reached into his mouth and pulled out the wad of chewing gum. He twisted around and stuck the gum beneath the counter. "Good choice," he said, and turning back to meet Kenneth's gaze again, he wet his lips with a long, slow swipe of his tongue.

Crash's hands slid up the backs of Kenneth's thighs, grabbing his ass, squeezing it, pushing Kenneth's hips forward so his cock sank deep, deep into Crash's hot, slick mouth.

Crash just held him there for a moment. Good thing, Kenneth thought, both hands clutching the counter so hard that his knuckles went white. He was in the midst of a giant head rush that threatened to leave him sprawled on a pile of ugly, poorly sized, or just plain unwanted holiday gifts.

Crash's tongue moved, an unhurried slither that dragged the smooth ball of his tongue stud tantalizingly over the bottom of Kenneth's stiff dick.

"Oh, God."

Crash grunted a reply. Kenneth thought he sounded pleased with himself.

Crash began to suck, and Kenneth's world tipped on its axis. His legs started to quiver, at first just a slight trembling, and then a full-on shake. Crash held his ass more tightly, sinking his fingers deep into the flesh, driving Kenneth's dick deeper still into his throat. Kenneth felt the softness at the back with his sensitive cockhead, felt Crash hum, and swallow, and use every trick in the book to make him explode.

Kenneth's hips started flexing, rocking his dick in and out of Crash's mouth, the root sinking deep and then revealing itself again, over and over, shining with spit.

Kenneth took a deep breath, and even though he wanted to just grab the back of Crash's head, feel a handful of that stiff, spiky hair as he crammed himself in as far as he could, to fuck Crash's face until that dam burst and he was coming straight down that talented throat – even though he wanted that more than anything else, Kenneth stopped. He held himself very still.

Crash pulled off Kenneth's cock with a slurp so loud it practically rang through the sub-basement. He poked his head up above the edge of the counter to see if somebody was watching. "What?" he whispered.

Kenneth's eyes darted back toward the entrance to the sales floor to make sure there wasn't a guard listening in. "Show me your dick."

The sly grin spread over Crash's face again. He grabbed Kenneth hard by the waist and pulled him down onto the floor behind the counter. The carpet was threadbare and dirty, but there were enough piles of clothing there to cushion them.

Crash's jeans were so old and tight that they hugged his long legs and slim hips perfectly, with no need for a belt. He faced Kenneth, kneeling, as he yanked the fly open.

Crash grabbed Kenneth's hand and stuffed it down the front of his pants. It was too tight in there to feel anything specific, yet just the thought of it, having his hand on some total stranger's hot, hard cock, made Kenneth's breath catch.

Crash eased his tight jeans down over his hips and his dick fell free, perfectly stiff. He wove his fingers through Kenneth's, and they stroked it together as Crash stared into Kenneth's eyes.

It was too intense for Kenneth. He needed to look away. He stared down at his own hard-on and took it in his other hand, stroking it alongside Crash's.

Crash pulled his hand free, leaving Kenneth with a stiff dick in each fist, one wet, one dry, stroking them both. A bottle of cheap hand lotion was tucked beneath the return counter. Crash grabbed it and shot a generous squirt of lotion on both of them.

The sensation changed from good to incredible as the lotion oozed through Kenneth's fingers. Crash draped both of his arms around Kenneth's shoulders and pressed their foreheads together. "That's right," he said in a hoarse whisper. "Jack me off."

Somewhere on the sales floor, a guard's keys jingled as he made his first rounds of the night. The lights were still on over Kenneth's desk, which wasn't so uncommon. Sometimes he had a little trouble shutting down his register.

"Have a good one," the guard called out on his way past the hallway.

Kenneth's eyes peeked over the top of the counter. He'd stopped stroking momentarily, though of course the situation would be compromising enough if he were to be caught, whether or not his slippery hands were moving up and down.

He blanked out what he'd normally say for a horribly long moment, and then shouted, "You, too," thinking that his own voice sounded alien.

He looked back at Crash's face, eyes almost too close to properly see. Crash's grin was a mile wide. He tilted his head to the side and fit his lips to Kenneth's. "Get me off," he said against Kenneth's mouth.

Crash's closeness was overwhelming. Kenneth wanted to back up, but there was nowhere to go. And the feel of Crash's mouth on Kenneth's lips made his dick even harder. Kenneth's hands moved faster, and Crash gasped. It felt good to wrest control from him, even in that small way. Kenneth concentrated on his strokes, making them even and regular, focusing on the way Crash breathed against his face. He wanted to make that breathing go ragged. He wanted to make Crash moan.

Kenneth gripped Crash's cock just a little harder, and Crash seemed to melt into him. Their mouths crushed together, and Crash's pierced tongue parted Kenneth's lips. Crash sighed a spearmint breath into Kenneth's mouth as the muscles in his thighs tensed.

Crash pulled his mouth free and buried his face in the crook of Kenneth's neck. His breath was hot on Kenneth's collarbone as he squeezed their bodies together, murmuring, "Yeah, oh yeah, mmmm, yeah," into Kenneth's shoulder.

Crash gasped and his hips jerked. Kenneth felt the wetness of cum, hot and sticky on his belly. Kenneth slowed his strokes on his own dick, concentrating on making them perfect, and basking in the feel of this man draped against him, breathing hard and making satisfied noises against his shoulder.

One of Crash's hands fell from around Kenneth's shoulders, slipping between their bodies to cradle Kenneth's balls. They pulled tight to his body, and the steady climb to the brink turned into a sudden rush. Kenneth felt the first crest of pleasure surge down to his groin, and Crash's mouth covered his again.

Kenneth bucked against Crash, their hands, wet with lotion and sticky with Crash's semen, tangling together to milk his pulsing dick. Kenneth came hard, his fluids mingling with Crash's between their bellies. He let himself moan into Crash's mouth, and Crash welcomed it, clasping Kenneth to him tight with his free hand, grinding their bodies together in a moaning, writhing mess of lotion and come.

Crash held Kenneth against him until Kenneth's hips stopped thrusting, and then he pulled away and sat back on his heels. His lips were swollen and his T-shirt was spotted with dark blots of lotion and telltale ropy strings of ejaculate.

He grinned and stood, offering Kenneth a hand up.

"I had a feeling you'd be fun," Crash said.

Kenneth had no idea how to reply. He was naked, except for the slacks around his ankles and the sticky mingling of cum growing tight as it dried on his skin.

Crash hitched his fly shut and turned to leave. "Wait a minute," Kenneth said. "Your shirt."

Crash looked down at the black ball of fabric on the floor. "Oh, that. I just wanted to make you take it off."

"But ... your bag."

"I pulled that one off the rack on my way in. My mom would never buy me a black shirt. She thinks I need more color in my wardrobe." Crash winked at Kenneth, and treated him to one more grin. He whistled to himself as he made his way down the dingy little hall and out onto the dimly lit sales floor of the lowest sub-basement of SaverPlus.

Kenneth waited until the whistling faded away then looked around at the sad piles of unwanted clothing on the floor as he zipped up his fly and buckled his belt. He'd need to work at least another hour to get the return desk to the point where he could close up. And he'd have to "accidentally" throw away anything that might be splattered with lotion, or worse. He tried to conjure up images of a gorgeous, flat-screen monitor and a printer/scanner all-in-one to take his mind off the time, but found that hardware wasn't doing a very good job of capturing his imagination at that moment.

Pale green eyes, spiked blond hair and a tongue stud were another story entirely. Kenneth picked up his black shirt from the floor, held it to his cheek, and sighed.

Morningwood – A Novella
By R. Forestier

The Prologue

In the fertile mind of a twelve-year-old boy, adventure is only a split second deviation from reality. A slapped-together "fort" in the backyard becomes a castle, a cowboy bunkhouse, a spaceship cockpit or simply a place to hide-out, a place to get away from the prying eyes of parents and neighbors. I enjoyed such a sanctuary, which I shared with a few of my closest boyhood friends. Its rustic nature made it no less precious to us than the elegant country clubs our parents loved to frequent. So, when my dad announced his intention to build a log cabin in the forest on a lake called Morningwood, it seemed to me to be a perfectly reasonable undertaking. He and four of his closest buddies, all long-time friends of our family, would form a partnership that would assure them the complete privacy of their get-away place.

It would be six years before I learned the truth about Morningwood.

One

Birthdays are always supposed to be special, sugar-coated events in our lives that mean we have advanced to a higher plateau of maturity. As I awoke this morning, the first thought to enter my mind was that this day, the beginning of my nineteenth year was going to be one that changed my life forever. Never mind the cake, cards and presents, this was going to be the day that I would be made privy to the secrets of Morningwood.

The cabin at Lake Morningwood had always been somewhat of a mystery to me. Why didn't Dad ever take me and Mom up there? After all, he spent a month there every year. There were also those many extended weekends.

His explanation was that he and his four partners, my "uncles," Jack, Bruce, Russ and Marc, had an inviolate rule: "No wives, kids or girlfriends allowed at the camp." It was promised that once I had achieved sufficient maturity, I would be welcomed at Morningwood.

As plausible as that had been, it never did much to calm my juvenile longings to be "grown up" and to be included in something slightly forbidden – something only adult males could be a part of.

Picturing my life as a banquet, once I was mature enough to form such an analogy, where each course was a new experience to be savored, Morningwood would be my dessert, and I had a very powerful sweet tooth.

Dad always came back from these trips with tales of the fish he and the guys caught and how they roughed it by cooking their catches over open campfires and how afterwards, they would sit around drinking beer and playing poker or bridge and just totally unwinding from the rigors of earning a living in the city. Mom never seemed to mind these periods without Dad. She probably enjoyed her own brand of solitude.

* * * * *

I am Donald Oscar Crowley. Dad probably thought it would be cute to give me a name with the initials D.O.C. especially if I followed in his footsteps and chose medicine as a profession. Visions of embroidered guest towels, glassware, handkerchiefs and cocktail napkins no doubt ran through my mom's head. The "O" was handed down to me in honor of my paternal grandfather. Dad and I shared that honor though I doubt that Grandpa and Grandma attached any significance to Dad's monogram "J.O.C."

Like my dad, I have a nice head of jet black hair, which I choose to wear in a style reminiscent of 60s college frat boys. Not long, not short, but just a nice manageable length. Deep blue eyes accentuated by my rather fair skin complete the picture.

My physique is nothing spectacular, weighing in at about 150 lbs at five-ten. Thanks to my love of swimming, my chest, waist and ass are smooth and tight. So far I haven't much body hair to speak of. The "treasure trails" many of my friends take for granted, I desperately covet. Dick-wise, I'm deeply proud of my nice uncut six inches, which was probably spared the indignity of circumcision because my dad is similarly intact.

James Crowley, MD, is a well-respected Urologist at Forsythe Medical Center located in Forsythe, Wisconsin. We live a very comfortable life in our mission-style home situated on a half-acre lot in a subdivision called "La Foret." I don't consider myself spoiled – more privileged since I've had the privacy of my own very large bedroom since I was old enough to walk. On my seventeenth birthday, I was allowed to get my driver's license, and Dad took me shopping for my first car, a maroon, 2001 Chrysler Sebring convertible. At that point, I felt sure my life was complete. The next milestone was my graduation from high school, which coincided with my eighteenth birthday in spring 2002. I had pretty much spent that first spring and summer goofing off with my friends who, like me were trying to "find" themselves. It was during this down time that my best buddy for many of those school years, John Rocco and I "found" ourselves in a way that would change my life forever.

My mom, Elizabeth, is a homemaker, and she is very good at it. She has her clubs and church activities that keep her busy; Dad has his medical practice plus the outside activities he enjoys with the group of partners who, together, own the cabin at the lake.

Dad spends a lot of his spare time in his basement workshop/lab tinkering with various mechanical and electronic instruments. He has never been one to share information on what he is working on or what he has successfully invented. He has always discouraged Mom and me from even visiting his private little world. We leave him alone. After all, he works hard at the medical center and deserves a little peace and quiet.

Mom and Dad had met just after graduation from high school. They were just nineteen when they married. Dad already knew he would enter the field of medicine. They must have forgotten the condoms one night since just about nine months later, I was born. The difficulty of supporting a wife and a child at such an early age while starting on his medical schooling apparently hadn't occurred to either of them. They managed somehow and were now enjoying the benefits of the years of hard work.

At thirty-eight, my father is a fine specimen of manhood. The few specks of gray starting to appear around his temples only serve to enhance his handsomely mature face. He usually sports a natural tan on his very athletic body.

Entering my teen years, whenever I got an opportunity to see him shirtless or better yet, naked, I had to suppress some very strange feelings. I found myself wanting to be near him at these times; even wondering what it would be like to touch his firm stomach or chest and to have his strong arms hold me close. He was not much of a hugger, and the most I usually got was a pat on the shoulder or head.

Dad had not yet had the "talk" with me about sex, so all my information was obtained from my schoolmates, fountains of misinformation as usual, so I didn't have a clue as to what was going on in my mind and body. I got my information from whatever I read in a few medical journals and magazines I found around the house.

My discovery of masturbation at age eleven was a total surprise as I am sure it is to most guys. Nothing ever compares with the first time.

On that happy day, I was sitting on the toilet and proceeded to get a hard-on. This was not unusual, but for some reason this day's woody felt different. As I gripped my hardening cock, instinctively my hand started sliding my foreskin back and forth, covering and uncovering the head of my now very sensitive penis. The sensation was so incredibly good that I could not stop, and I damn sure didn't want to. I was in heaven and really couldn't comprehend what was about to happen as the wonderful sensation became even more intense. Suddenly, my cock exploded with a gush of thick white liquid, leaving me in a state of absolute awe and exhaustion. What had I done? What had been lurking in my groin just waiting for me to bring it to life? Was my precious little jewel damaged? I sat stunned at the wonder of the event. Never had I felt anything to compare with it. Slowly, I raised a semen coated finger to my nose. The smell was not what I expected. It was sort of like the odor of fresh washed bed sheets. Quickly running to the sink, I carefully washed away any traces. The combined feelings of relief, bewilderment and extreme pleasure occupied my mind for several minutes – then an epiphany! This must be what the big boys called cuming.

Reasoning that I was not the only kid to have experienced this magical moment, my mind popped back to reality, my heartbeat returned to normal, and I resolved to do some research the following day, and the day after that, and up to this moment, I am still conducting "research."

Through further experimentation, it didn't take me long to find out that this was a renewable resource to be enjoyed anytime, day or night and as often as I felt the need.

Naturally, I couldn't wait to share my new knowledge with my best friend Phil and assorted guys in the neighborhood. They all seemed to be as amazed by my discovery as I was and no doubt passed along this knowledge to their friends. Scout camp was probably a lot different that summer. Oh, to have been a fly on those tent flaps.

After a few years of dating various girls and getting nothing from them but an occasional kiss and maybe a quick feel of tit, I found that I was looking more and more at other males as objects of my sexual fantasies.

At eighteen, I had my first truly passionate affair with another guy, John Rocco, and it changed my life dramatically (more about that later). It was a bit hard for me to accept, but now the realization that I was "queer" set in. As far as I knew, my parents had not a clue that I was gay and that was fine with me. Sooner or later they would figure it out.

* * * * *

Now, here I am at ripe old age of nineteen, and my libido is running wild. I can get a hard-on from eating a banana. For sure, this summer was going to be anything but dull now that I was to be introduced to life at the cabin on the lake.

"Happy Birthday, Don … now go pack your bag, we're leaving for the cabin in the morning." Dad was beaming as he spoke those magic words.

I had arrived.

There were four other members of the group plus my dad. Since they had been part of our family life for many years; I had grown to regard them as benevolent "uncles." All of them were about the same age as Dad and were more or less successful in their professions.

My favorite was Bruce O'Reilly, a red-head of Irish descent with a great sense of humor. I guess what made him so appealing to me was his ability to entertain me and my friends with an endless stream of jokes and stories that he told in a fake Irish accent. Solidly built, about five-ten with well-muscled arms and legs, he had his own architectural practice and was still single. Bruce appeared to really enjoy his life as a bachelor. This intrigued me and caused me to wonder about his sex life. Could he be …?

Then there was Russ Gordon. A pretty ordinary guy, brown hair, cut short in a military style. I suspect this was a holdover from his Army days. Married, but no children, his wife, Barbara, was somewhat of a recluse and never appeared at any of the picnics or other social functions the group held. This was a sexless marriage for sure. Russ didn't display a muscular build, but more lean and tight like a seasoned swimmer. He had some vague connection with a stock brokerage firm.

His biggest feature in my young eyes was his sexy, red Jaguar XK convertible, which was probably his solution to a mid-life crisis.

The bear of the group was Jack Braun, who was six-feet tall and about 220 lbs, partially bald with just a ring of blond hair around ear level. Jack lifted free weights three times a week and was very proud of his ability to impress his fellow muscle boys as well as his alleged stable of "hot chicks." He was big, but well proportioned. I was always intrigued by the amazing amount of hair on his arms and legs and could just imagine how the rest of him looked. More than once, Jack had been the object of my masturbatory fantasies. By far, he was the easiest for me to talk with since he was the most down-to-earth type of guy. Not surprisingly, he was the managing partner of a local gym, which catered to the big guys. At his insistence, I visited the place a couple of times. You could practically peel the testosterone off the walls. It was a bit over the top for my taste, all that posturing and preening, and I seldom went back.

Finally, there was Marc, short for Marcel. A Frenchman by birth, he had been in this country since his teens and was now a U.S. citizen. He taught French at my high school where I just graduated a year earlier. He was quite thin and wiry and only stood about five-six. His light brown curly hair and short stature gave him a very boyish look. His marriage ended tragically when his wife and five-year-old daughter were killed in an auto accident. He remains a widower.

As different as each one of these men was, they had one thing in common; a strong masculine magnetism that was irresistible to me.

Being a forever horny little bastard, my dream plan for the summer at the cabin was simple. Along with the fishing, canoeing and swimming, I would try to have sex with each one of these men in such a way that each of them would be left with the impression that they were the only one seduced. At no time would I be excessively aggressive. I wanted them to want me, but most of all I wanted to learn how to properly satisfy a man. They say experience is the best teacher. I was ready to be taught. My biggest problem would be setting the bait at just the right time and in just the right place. Learning their individual habits and favorite activities around the cabin would be crucial to the plan.

The trip in my father's GMC Suburban took about five hours. Marc and Russ got the front passenger seats, and I ended up squashed between Jack and Bruce in the back seat. The rear was packed with luggage and coolers. This was not a totally unpleasant situation for me.

The tightness and the heat from my two seat mates' shorts-clad thighs, coupled with the motion of the car caused my dick to stay hard for most of the trip. If either of them noticed, it was not apparent.

After turning off the highway onto a narrow dirt road, we stopped while Dad unlocked and then re-locked a security gate. We traveled a couple more miles, lurching and bouncing over the ruts until suddenly there it was. Shangri La! Xanadu! My pleasure palace for the next four weeks.

The cabin was of log construction and sat on a low bluff overlooking the lake. The air was sweet with the scent of pine, reminding me of the wreaths Mom always hung on our front door at Christmas.

The surface of the lake was marred only by the slightest of ripples. I jumped out of the car and ran for the shore eager to start my explorations. My youthful exuberance was soon interrupted by my dad yelling for me to get my ass back to the car and start unloading our gear. Well, every pleasure has its pain … in the ass.

It didn't take us very long to get the car unloaded, and the guys tackled the job of putting everything in its place. The coolers held dozens of packaged casseroles, meatloaves, soups and who knows what else that my mom had prepared and frozen weeks before our departure. They had things under control, so Dad suggested I take a look around the place to get my bearings.

The ground floor consisted of an enormous living room with stone fireplace, an eat-in kitchen fitted out with some very fancy appliances and a dining room, which doubled as a TV lounge. I noticed that there were little cameras located near the ceiling in every room. Some sort of security system I supposed. Very nice, but I was more interested in checking out the sleeping arrangements.

Upstairs, there were three bedrooms. Two of them held pairs of double beds. The third had only one bed but it was king size. This turned out to be my dad's digs. No doubt who was the "alpha male" around here.

At the far end of the hallway was a bathroom unlike any I had ever seen outside of a YMCA. Along one wall was a counter with three sinks. Opposite that were two little enclosed toilet stalls complete with doors for privacy, plus, in one corner was a urinal. At the end of the room was a wide-open, tiled shower room with four spaces, each fitted with an elaborate multi-head fixture. Damn, I could only wonder what this place was like when everybody decided to do their thing at the same time. Soap-dropping would be high on my to-do list. My cute little ass had never let me down in spite of the fact that it was still virgin territory.

My next stop would be the shore of the lake, but that would have to wait until morning. Darkness was coming on fast, and I smelled food.

After a great meal of Mom's meatloaf and baked potatoes, we all headed for the TV room and caught *Gentlemen Prefer Blondes* on Turner Classic Movies. For me, it was a dated bore. They loved it for the shots of Marilyn in all her platinum blonde glory.

The guys finally called it a night and went off to their respective rooms: Bruce and Marc in one and Jack and Russ in the other. Dad suggested we do the same, and we headed up to the king size bed. "I hope you don't mind that we are sharing a bed, Son. It's big enough for both of us, and I'm a pretty sound sleeper. If you have any problem with it, we'll work something out. It may be only temporary anyway as you'll find out later." Problem? Hell, this was better than I ever imagined. The only problem would be how to keep my hands off my sexy bed partner.

Rationalizing my sexual interest in my father was easy: I'm a young hot-blooded gay guy, and he is a mature, good looking stud-muffin. This was made all the more difficult by the fact that he traditionally slept in the raw.

"You should try it. We all like the feeling of freedom it gives us. Don't be surprised if you see a few naked bodies around the house any time day or night. It's also one of the reasons we are very selective when it comes to visitors."

The sound of running water coming from the direction of the bathroom caught my attention. "Hey dad, a shower would really feel good right about now."

"Sure, Son, go ahead, I'll wait 'til morning."

I stripped off my sweaty clothes and made my way down the hall. Sounds of snoring were already coming from the other two rooms so that would mean the showers weren't all taken. Steam was drifting from the entrance to the shower room, clouding my view of its occupant. Once inside, my delighted eyes took in the sight of Bruce in all his naked glory. His rear was to me, so I made a little noise with my throat, alerting him to my presence.

"Hey, Donny! Come on in and make yourself at home."

He was in the process of soaping his upper body and seemed to be having some difficulty reaching his back.

"Today, while unloading the gear I must've pulled a muscle in my shoulder, and it's giving me a hard time." The sight of his soap and sweat covered body sent an electric shock to my prick, which went to a full hard-on in seconds. I quickly formulated a plan.

"Uncle Bruce, I'm not much of a masseur, but at least can help out with the soaping part, so you don't aggravate the muscles any further."

"No thanks, little buddy, I think I can handle it. One thing though, I dropped my soap. It's somewhere on the floor. See if you can find it."

Picking up the bottle of body wash, I reached around his muscular torso, past his upper arm and lightly brushed his right nipple as I handed him the soap. My rock hard prick was now inches away from his slick, wet ass.

"You're sure you don't need some help with those tough to reach places?" Something told me he was weakening.

"Maybe you could just do my back and shoulders. I am kinda sore, and since you're here, you might as well make yourself useful."

Taking the bottle of soap from his hand, I squirted a nice glob on my palm. As my hands worked the lather across his broad shoulders and middle back and up into his hairy armpits, he sensed the direction my lathering was taking, raising his arms to give me better access. "Oh yeah, Donny, now work my shoulder blades some more. Those hands of yours got talent. You sure you haven't done this before?"

Accepting that invitation to continue, I gave his upper back a smooth, gentle massage. There was only one direction to go from there, and it was down. As my soapy hands made their way to the top of his furry ass cheeks, he seemed to tense, but then relaxed as I massaged the lather onto those gorgeous globes, working my fingers between them very slowly and gently until the tip of my left index finger barely touched his hot little rosebud. The heat of his ass against my fingertips was causing my head to spin, and I was out of control. He reacted with a sharp intake of breath and a tight clenching of his rock-solid butt cheeks. My heart was pounding with excitement; my cock was throbbing and primed for action.

Not wanting to go too fast and maybe ruin the moment, I backed off and allowed my soap-slicked hands to proceeded down his powerfully muscled thighs until, falling to my knees, I found my face directly in line with his seductively round and deliciously pink ass. The warm water cascading down his back and over those sweet cheeks washed away the suds except for the area deep within the crack. Gripping both mounds, I spread them apart giving me a perfect view of the tight little hole and its ring of ginger-red curls, while the water washed away any traces of soap.

"Ahhh, D-d-donny what are you doing down there, little buddy?"

Damn! Even my virgin tongue was hard at this point; wanting to reach out and lick some man-butt even though I hadn't even heard of rimming at that point in my life.

"Just makin' sure you're good and clean. Why do a half-assed job?" I snickered.

He got the joke and said, "Well, little buddy you are doing a hell of a job." With that, he turned around, presenting me with a delicious slab of cock-meat at full hard stand. His foreskin was pulled back revealing a smooth, deep pink head on a seven inch staff. For a moment, neither of us made a move. Looking up into his half-closed eyes, it was clear to me that he was ready and willing. My tongue snaked out and lightly caressed his cock-head, followed by my eager lips sinking down to the base; meeting the soft wetness of his golden-red fleece.

He groaned softly, "Ooooh man … sooo good … suck it … take it deep," and I thrust forward to get more of his throbbing cock down my throat.

"Yah, that's it, take Uncle Bruce's prick all the way in … oh man, your mouth is so hot. You're gonna eat my cum, Donny-boy." He grabbed the sides of my head forcing my lips and tongue to hungrily swallow him again and again while I stroked his tightening ball sack, a sign that he was approaching the point of no return. He hoarsely whispered, "Donny, I can't hold it … cummin' ... take my load … ahhhhhh!"

The gush of hot cream filled my mouth to overflowing. I swallowed again and again and still had enough left to savor once my lips reluctantly left its source.

Judging from the thickness and intense flavor of his cum, he had been saving this load for weeks. Moaning faintly, he fell back against the shower wall and slowly slid down to a sitting position on the cool, wet tiles. Fascinated, I watched as his softening cock receded into its nest of pubic hair; the reddened head, still dripping drops of nectar, disappearing within its silky envelope. Waiting for a reaction as he got back on his feet, my reward was a big goofy smile and a kiss on the top of my head, followed by a deep, contented sigh. No more was said. We finished our showers and headed off to our beds.

Dad appeared to be sleeping soundly. As I drifted off to sleep with the taste of Bruce still on my tongue, it didn't matter that my own need hadn't been taken care of. I was floating on air, but could hardly believe it had been so easy to land Bruce.

I awoke to the aroma of coffee and the sound of laughter coming from below. Dad was nowhere to be seen. A check of my bedside clock told me it was almost 9:00 am.

Suddenly, the events of last night hit me. Had I gone too far too soon? Would Bruce tell the others about me sucking his cock in the shower? Could that be the cause of the laughter around the breakfast table? Naah. It was doubtful he would brag about his best friend's son giving him a blow job no matter how good it had been. Thanks to my old high school buddy John, I had acquired considerable talent in that department.

Pulling on a pair of shorts, I went downstairs determined to be as casual around Bruce as if nothing unusual had occurred.

My fears were unfounded. Everyone was engaged in an animated rehashing of last summer's fishing mishaps. To my amazement, they were all naked!

"Hey, good morning son, come on and sit down. I'll get you some eggs and bacon in a minute. Meanwhile have a cup of coffee and feel free to take off those shorts. I told you we were very casual around here."

Why not? I figured what the hell, might as well join their little nudie breakfast club. The conversation resumed, and no one seemed to take any notice as I dropped my shorts and took a place at the table.

The talk turned to the day's activities. Dad was planning to do some work on his laptop for most of the morning. Bruce and Marc were going on a morning hike, and Jack decided to try his luck fishing from one of the canoes. Russ picked up a novel he was in the midst of reading and was going to relax on the front deck.

I offered to clean up the dishes and generally tidy up the place before taking my tour of the property.

As each one got up from the table, I was able to get a quick view of their bodies. Bruce was no surprise. Marc had a nice sized cut prick about three or four inches soft, which stood out because of his very slender build and a pair of low hanging balls that I knew would feel great resting on my chin. His ass was a bit skinny but well shaped. More impressive was the beautiful symmetrical hair pattern on his chest which continued right on down to his groin.

Jack had muscles on top of muscles. His body was heavily furred all the way down to his pubic area. His massive pecs and prominent nipples made my mouth water; then my eyes focused on his cock and balls.

Unlike many weight lifters, this guy was hung. My view was quickly blocked by Russ as he headed out to the deck. I only got a quick look at Russ's goodies as he went by, and they seemed about average. Plenty of time to check him out later. By then, Jack had gone out the door and out of sight but not out of mind.

My attention turned to Dad. It seems hard to believe, but he and I had rarely seen each other naked. When I stripped in front of him, it was usually in the course of having my annual physical and that was all business. Occasionally, I would catch him going in or out of the shower at home. Now, I had ample time to take in his masculine beauty, but my old feelings were starting to take over, and my cock throbbed to life. Quickly retreating upstairs, I headed for a cold shower.

Two

I figured it was now time for me to do some exploration of my new, if temporary, home.

Pulling on a pair of shorts and T-shirt, I went down to the kitchen and grabbed a bottle of water from the fridge. Dad cautioned me about wandering too far away from the shore of the lake due to the thickness of the woods. A guy could easily get lost since there were few marked trails and no other cabins within several miles of ours. Taking his advice, I headed down to the shoreline and followed it to the left. The cabin seemed to be situated on a large inlet or bay, which gave it privacy from the rest of the lake shore. Ahead of me was a large rock outcropping which would be my first destination.

It took me about fifteen minutes to reach the rock and to climb up to its summit. Once there, the sight was spectacular. The day was clear, so there was nothing to mar my view of the entire lake including the land on either side of the bay. No signs of human habitation other than our cabin could be seen.

A faint rustling of leaves and the whisper of breeze through pine boughs were the loudest sounds to reach my ears. Suddenly, a chipmunk popped his head out from under a nearby log and as quickly disappeared back into his home.

I resolved to bring him some treats when I next visited this tranquil spot.

Often, when hearing people speak of having a "religious experience" I scoff at the notion. How to define such a thing? This Sunday morning, sitting atop that promontory, surrounded by fragrant woods, I may have become a believer.

Rested and spiritually refreshed, my journey continued along the sandy shore. The sun was rising quickly over the tree tops behind me, and the heat of the day was reaching an uncomfortable level. Finding a convenient log to sit on, I stripped off my clothes and gingerly stepped into the crystal clear water. Yipes! It was dick-shrinking cold! Never in my life had water that cold touched my skin. It would be enough to turn my nuts into snowballs. No thanks. The fresh air on my naked body felt good, so I continued my walk burdened only by my beat-up tennis shoes and water bottle. My shorts and shirt could be picked up on my way back.

Previously unnoticed, there were two sets of footprints heading in the same direction. Maybe Bruce and Marc were somewhere ahead of me. It would be nice to meet up with them and learn more about the local terrain. Being naked in front of these guys no longer bothered me since it appeared to be the norm around these parts.

About a quarter of a mile down the shore, the prints made a turn to the left onto a narrow pathway. Following the path a short distance led me to a clearing, in the center was a rustic gazebo-like structure.

There they were, seated at a low table engaged in a game of chess. I couldn't contain my laughter. Bruce looked up from his game: "Hey Donny boy, what's the matter – never saw a couple of naked chess players before?" Marc motioned for me to come on into the little pavilion. "I see you have decided to get into the spirit of the jungle," pointing to my obvious nakedness and taking the opportunity to check out my youthful package. "Looks like you're not a *garcon* anymore, Donny."

Bruce interrupted by offering me a seat at the little table. Mercifully, he acted as if nothing unusual had happened between us. My respect for him jumped up a few notches, but I couldn't help

117

stealing a glance at the cock I had dared to suck last night. He must have caught me as there was the undeniable beginning of an erection, causing him to shift in his seat, moving in closer to the table. He quickly continued the conversation, sensing my curiosity about this spot and hinted that there were several other surprises in store for me as I explored their little piece of paradise. I watched them play for awhile but soon got anxious to continue my walk, especially now that the promise of new discoveries had been made. Anyhow, they were more interested in their game than bullshitting with me.

Returning to the shoreline, my tour was cut short by the intensity of the noonday sun, which was making things uncomfortably hot and would fry my pale city-boy skin. Heading back to the cabin, reclaiming my clothes en route, I decided to call it a day.

Jack's fishing trip proved to be a terrific success. He had come back with five large bass, which Russ was in the process of cleaning. Dinner tonight would be out by the campfire, and I could hardly wait for some of the guys home cooking. Bruce and Marc hadn't come back yet, so I decided to take a nap.

Dad must have had the same idea, and I found him sprawled across the bed at an angle wearing only a pair of my gym shorts. They were the ones with the embroidered D.O.C. monogram Mom had ordered from the Lands End catalogue. See, I told you she was a sucker for kitsch.

My arrival caused him to awaken. I gave him a rundown of my hike, the rock climb, my encounter with the chipmunk and meeting up with Bruce and Marc at the gazebo. "They probably told you that our little retreat holds many surprises, the least of which is the little summer house you visited. You may have noticed that there are security cameras located around the grounds and in each room. These enable me to keep an eye on the property when we aren't here."

My curiosity was again aroused. What could these surprises be? My sweaty body was becoming even offensive to me, so I headed for the showers.

When I returned to the room, Dad was busy doing something on his laptop.

"Don, I just realized you were due for your annual physical last week. While we are here at the cabin, it would be a good time to bring you up-to-date. The rest of the guys usually use this time to get their male-specific plumbing checked out. My lab isn't equipped to do blood work, but that can wait until we get back home."

Lab? What lab? He had never mentioned having a lab at the cabin. Could this be surprise number two?

We decided to take care of me the following morning.

Jack and Russ really knocked themselves out preparing a great fish dinner, plenty of good cold beer plus a couple of bottles of white wine, which I later learned was a good Napa Valley chardonnay.

The site, down at the waters edge was ideal for a cookout. A slightly drunken contentment settled over the camp while we relaxed and watched the fire slowly burn itself out. Life was really getting good at Morningwood. Impulsively, I leaned over and put my arms around Dad's shoulder and thanked him for making me a part of this really cool group of friends. He returned my hug and gave me an uncharacteristic peck on my forehead.

Three

The next morning, I woke up about 7:00 am. While I took a quick shower, Dad had wheeled in a portable massage table.

"Stay naked and jump up on the table and lie on your back. Now I want you to push yourself forward so your ass is at the edge of the table and bend your knees up toward your chest. The first thing I'm going to do is a digital rectal exam, focusing on your prostate."

He must have noticed the look of panic on my face, so in his best bedside manner, he continued, "Don't worry, I'll be gentle and use plenty of lube. You shouldn't have any discomfort."

Up to this point in my life there had never been anything larger than a thermometer stuck up there, so I was a little nervous. He was good at his craft and after pulling on a latex glove, his well lubed index finger slipped in easily as he gently massaged the interior of my virgin ass.

Then it happened. His finger tip applied some pressure to a particular spot causing me to let out a gasp, which he misinterpreted as pain. My cock went stiff in a flash.

He looked at me with a slight smile on his face and said, "Don't worry. That, my boy is your prostate gland." He then continued lightly caressing my deliciously sensitive gland.

Glancing down at my rock-hard prick he said, "I see the exam is having an effect. Don't be concerned, it happens to a lot of guys. Just relax, we'll be through here in just a few minutes." As he continued his gentle massage, all I could think about at this moment was if a finger

119

felt this good, how would a hard cock feel. He continued his probing, moving his finger against my prostate, applying a slight pressure as he slid his digit in and out. I was going nuts, that familiar pleasurable ache was forming in my groin. Never in my life had I felt anything like it. I knew any minute I was going to blow my load … and then it happened.

"Ohhhhh, Dad, I'm losing it … I'm c-cuming."

An explosion of semen hit my chest and neck, the remainder streaked my belly, filling the indent of my navel. I had shot the load of my life without even touching my cock. Looking at me with a smile on his face, he slowly withdrew his gloved finger.

"Well, you have just learned what every male should know about his anatomy. We guys come equipped with some erogenous zones that most men never discover. By the way, your prostate is in excellent shape. Now clean yourself up and relax, we'll finish your exam later today."

This was one anatomy lesson I intended to use, filed under "things to do."

I must have slept for several hours because when I woke up it was almost 2:00 pm. The house was quiet except for the sound of classical music playing softly from the vicinity of the TV room. Picking up my shorts from the floor, I headed for the bathroom to take a long overdue piss.

Downstairs, I found Dad again working at his computer. This seemed to be a good opportunity to ask him about the lab.

"Have a seat, Donny, this is as good a time as any to fill you in on the research project I'm working on. As you learned from your prostate exam this morning, stimulating that part of a man's anatomy can produce some undeniably positive results. For several years, I have been studying men's sexual problems such as low sperm count, impotence, and diminished libido. Some improvement in these conditions has been noted after manually stimulating the prostate gland and taking better care of our testicles. As a result of my research, a device, which replicates a massaging finger is being produced for me right now in China.

"In nineteenth-century Europe, this type of stimulation was used quite commonly by prostitutes to help their less than capable customers achieve a stiff erection and more powerful climax. Several books of the period made mention of the practice. *Memoirs of a Voluptuary* is one of the best. With the help of my friends and associates I have created a device, which is simple and in most cases, pleasurable to use."

At this point, I choked back my urge to burst out laughing. After all, I was still a teenager and the image of a sticking a mechanical finger up one's ass was almost more than I could bear. Not that it didn't have some interesting and entertaining possibilities. Seeing that he was quite serious, I stifled myself.

He then took a slender leather case from a desk drawer. Inside was a stainless steel probe with a number of joints much like human finger joints, but there were more of them, making it quite flexible. There were also several soft pink rubbery sleeves of differing thickness that were designed to cover the entire length, about seven inches and a diameter of one inch. A flange at the base would probably prevent accidental loss up the ass. My giggle fit was uncontrollable as I imagined it being used.

The kit also included a belt-like attachment that could be used to hold it in place when having sexual intercourse. It was powered by batteries located in the tiny control pad. I had seen dildos before in catalogs, but nothing quite like this.

"So, have Bruce, Marc, Jack and Russ all been guinea pigs?" I almost blurted out my first-hand knowledge that Bruce didn't need any mechanical assistance to have a memorable orgasm, but caught myself. "Sure, they all have been very helpful with their suggestions even though none of them really need any help at this stage of their lives."

Returning the device to its case and placing it back in the drawer, he finished up our talk by reminding me, "Our family stands to make a lot of money from this instrument once it hits the market, and you will be the ultimate beneficiary of its success, and oh yes, the product name is PROSAGE I. Without a doubt there will be IIs and maybe IIIs as we continually do research."

Today's events had given me a lot to think about. Was what Dad and I did this morning considered sex or just a physical exam? I damn sure enjoyed it no matter what it was. How much did the other guys enjoy using the PROSAGE I? Had they tried having anything else up their butt … like another man's cock? None of them appeared to be gay, but who can tell these days. Maybe Bruce had been planning to jerk off anyway, and I just happened to be a willing cock sucker. No matter, they were all candidates for admission to "Donny's Academy of Lust."

The rest of the day was uneventful, dinner from Mom's stash, a couple of poker games and then bed.

We had arrived on Saturday, and it was now Tuesday. So far, my first week was going almost too well. My Saturday night shower with Bruce had come as a real surprise. Not to mention my dad's finger-fuck session yesterday. Maybe I should cool things off for a few days and concentrate on further exploration.

The morning breakfast talk was mainly about each guy's plans for the day. Oddly, everyone was wearing some clothes. Had that first day's nudism been sort of an initiation rite for my benefit? Nothing sounded interesting to me, so it would be a good day to be out and about.

Jack suggested a light back pack with some bottled water and a snack might be a good idea.

This morning, I would get an early start and try to avoid the heat of the day. Of course, there was always the lake to cool off in if things got desperately steamy.

Minutes later, I was at the shoreline and decided to go to the right and cover some new territory. The sandy edge widened until there was almost a beach before me. This made my progress a lot easier since now my Keds were not so likely to get wet.

About a quarter mile from my starting point, I spied a log post stuck in the ground close by the tree line. Further examination revealed the carved letters "B.H" and an arrow pointing to a narrow trail leading into the thicket. This had to be checked out. The pathway showed signs of recent use. Several sets of footprints pointing in both directions were plainly visible. The pathway made a sudden turn to the left, and after a short distance, there was surprise number three – a good-sized building of similar construction as the cabin, but of more recent vintage. No sign of life and not a sound could be heard. I walked the length of the broad front porch, peeking through each window, but curtains blocked my view of the interior. The large front door was locked, but attached to the wall next to the jamb was a small metal lock box. It was the same type of key safe we had at home. On a hunch, I entered our house code, punching in 2687 on the key pad. Presto! The box opened and there was the key.

This place obviously belonged to Dad and the guys, so what harm could there be in my looking inside. Besides, a little rest wouldn't hurt.

Opening the door, the first thing I saw was an enormous bear skin complete with head, hanging on the opposite wall. The rest of the main room was typical lodge style: big stone fireplace, comfortable Indian print sofas and chairs and, of course, an antler chandelier. It was like a set from Bonanza. A doorway to the left of the fireplace led three steps down to a sort of recreation room with a big TV, billiard table and a reading nook lined with well stocked book shelves. Beyond this room was a small gym containing a few Nautilus type machines, and best of all, a good sized Jacuzzi spa, flanked by a steam room and sauna. This place was a fuckin' resort!

A big kitchen-dining room filled one end of the building. Upstairs was one large open "bunk" room containing six queen sized beds. Each was fully made up with fancy sheets and comforters, topped with those ridiculously large and generally useless designer pillows. The only concessions to privacy were hospital-type curtains made from fabric that matched the bed covers and could be drawn between each bed. Somebody had been reading *House & Garden* a bit too much. At the far end of the room was a doorway that led into a bath identical in every way to the one back at the cabin.

Returning to the main floor, I inspected the kitchen. The cabinets were fully stocked with household necessities. The industrial-sized fridge-freezer held enough food to feed an army.

What was going on here? Someone was expecting company. Why hadn't anyone mentioned this place to me? Of course, they hadn't mentioned the gazebo either.

On my way out, I spotted an aluminum-clad travel case on a shelf by the door. It was similar to the type used to carry photo equipment. My curiosity was fully aroused now. Close examination revealed an embossed nameplate – PROSAGE I. It was, of course, securely locked. Now, things were really getting interesting.

Returning to the cabin, I entered through the kitchen door. Russ was busy at the stove making up a batch of popcorn.

"Damn Russ, that smells good."

"Hey Donny … how was your walk today? See anything unusual?

I decided to play it dumb. "Ya, I visited the north shore and discovered a path that led to another cabin … wasn't expecting anything like that. Does it belong to you guys?"

He stopped his corn-popping, wiped his hands on his apron and thought for a moment before answering. "I think I'll let your dad explain about that. Good movie on tonight, *Ocean's Eleven*, don't miss it," and returned to his snack- making.

Cocktail hour was a very informal affair around the cabin. Usually about 6:00 pm everyone gathered in the living room and swigged down a few beers or glasses of pretty decent wine and talked about their day's activities. I chose this time to question Dad about the other cabin. "Well, I'm glad your time here isn't being spent just hanging out with us 'old' guys."

Dad then got serious and said, "I see you've taken it upon yourself to explore and learn about the place. Sorry I haven't had more time to show you around. Wait a few days, and I'll spend some time with you. You've got a lot to learn in a short time."

Marc settled down next to me on the sofa. "Listen to your papa, if you follow his advice and keep an open mind you will be very successful. Right now you may not appreciate the value of what you are about to learn, but be patient."

Dad spoke up, "Tomorrow, we will have a little 'family' conference and discuss the future of Morningwood. Now, let's hit the sack before we can't make it up the stairs."

Four

The pounding of rain on the roof brought me out of my wine-soaked sleep. A headache was my penance for last night's partying with the guys. Piss time. I managed to make it to the urinal in the nick of time. As I leaned against the wall enjoying the relief that comes only from emptying a full bladder, a naked Jack staggered in and headed for one of the stalls.

"Hey Donny, can't stop to bullshit, gotta take care of business." Seconds later, a horse-like splash came from his direction. The image of his muscle-man cock dispensing its liquid load, instantly gave me a boner that would need to be dealt with.

We both finished up at the same time, and as I turned around Jack was just coming out of the stall, his soft cock flopping up and down. I swear it was waving to me. Why waste a good opportunity to check him out. His clean-cut cock might not have the length of Bruce's, but he made up for it in thickness. This would not be the tool that would pry open my tight little virgin ass. This one would be saved for later.

124

"Gotta go back to bed, little buddy," and he swayed down the hall to his room, tight butt cheeks flexing with every step. Damn, now I was really hot! Making my way back, I stopped momentarily at Jack's open door. He was flopped out on his belly, already sound asleep. Russ was dead to the world.

One last glance at the muscular mounds of his tempting ass, then back to my room.

The sight that greeted me didn't help my condition. Dad had kicked off the covers and was spread out on his back with his soft cock resting on his low hanging balls. Quietly slipping onto the bed, I moved to within inches of his sleeping form to get a close-up view. His foreskin was partly retracted. Impulsively, my hand reached out and gently pulled back on the warm silky skin, revealing the moist, pale pink head. A faint musky odor reached my nostrils. That, coupled with the warmth his softened cock transferred to my fingers caused me to react with a renewed erection. Leaning forward for a closer view, beads of sweat dropped from my chest onto his well-muscled abdomen causing him to shift slightly in his deep sleep.

Lying back on my pillow, I watched as his flat belly rose and fell with his breathing. My cock, desperately needing attention, responded to my pounding fist with breathtaking spurts of hot cum. A roll of distant thunder seemed to signal my relief. The rain fell; sleep returned.

Five

Blazing sunlight woke me up. Checking the clock, it was almost 10:00 am.

After taking my morning piss, I threw on some shorts and went downstairs. The rest of the guys were sitting around the TV room having coffee and watching CNN.

Russ saw me approaching, "Donny-boy, get yourself some breakfast and come join us. We're going to have a little 'show and tell' as soon as you get settled."

Returning to the room with my coffee and bagel, I noticed Dad was setting up his computer to show something on the TV screen. "My boy, you are about to learn what we're planning for Morningwood and our PROSAGE I program. We've put together a PowerPoint presentation that will answer a lot of your questions."

What it boiled down to was that Morningwood was destined to be a combination research center and clinic where men could come and get help with their sexual dysfunctions. The patients would usually be an age-mixed group of no more than six. By coming to an isolated, but very pleasant location they were more likely to lose much of their performance anxiety and respond to treatment of their sexual problems. Of course, PROSAGE I would play a big roll in this therapy.

Shutting down the computer, Dad turned to me. "Here's the deal. The carefully hand-picked pilot group is due to arrive in two weeks. What I expect from you is some help in making the patient-guests feel comfortable. The presence of a young guy like yourself could go a long way toward putting them at ease. It would seem a lot less clinical with you as host at the bunkhouse. Your help would free me and the guys to work on the more technical aspects of the program. Oh yes, there is a small bedroom just off the kitchen where you could stay or you could continue to sleep up here with us. Your choice. We prefer you stayed at the bunkhouse, so you could keep an eye on things. What do you think?"

Marc spoke up, "Don't worry, we will give you a total course on the operation of the cabin, your duties will be outlined, and you will become very familiar with the PROSAGE device, so in our absence you can answer any questions or help with any problems that might 'arise' … pun intended."

Not wanting to appear too excited at the prospect of being given so much responsibility, so soon, I calmly responded, "Sure, I will be happy to earn my keep up at the bunkhouse. Start showing me the ropes anytime."

They were all relieved by my quick acceptance and set about deciding who would do what to get me going.

Russ would help me with the kitchen arrangements. Marc offered to guide me through the general housekeeping schedule. Bruce planned to handle the routine maintenance since he had designed the place, and finally, Jack volunteered to familiarize me with the exercise and spa equipment as well as the PROSAGE I. This struck me as odd. I fully expected Dad to do that. But what the hell – maybe Jackie-boy would prove to be a good teacher, after all, he was a licensed masseur. My dick got hard just thinking about it. This vacation was getting more interesting by the day.

Everyone agreed with Dad's suggestion that we all just relax for the rest of the day. The weather was perfect for a hike up to my rocky ridge. Packing up a beach towel, some water, peanut butter sandwiches and suntan lotion, I headed out. Reaching my spot, I found a nice smooth area to set up camp, stripped off my shorts and lay on my stomach enjoying the view of the lake. The warm sun on my naked body, gentle breeze and sweet smell of pine forest soon lulled me to sleep.

The crunch of leaves brought me fully awake. Looking up, there was Russ standing a few feet away, quietly taking in my naked boy-ass. He was also nude, so there was no way he could hide his stiff cock. I pretended not to notice.

"Hi Russ, you found my little hiding place."

He looked flustered, but blurted out, "Oh, this is one of my favorite spots, too, great for getting a sun tan, mind if I join you?"

"No, no man I like company." He spread his towel next to mine. Looking up at his naked body gave me an idea. I would casually bring up the subject of his wife.

"So the missus doesn't mind you spending time up here with the guys?

Glancing out in the direction of the lake, he replied, "To tell you the truth, Donny, I don't know if she cares or not. I mark the calendar with my away dates, and she just accepts it." A slight tremor in his voice betrayed his unease with the subject.

"A lot of wives would be pissed if their man wasn't around for them to sleep with every night. I guess it's probably tough for you, too, not having a warm body to make love to you when it's bedtime."

I watched his face for a reaction and at the same time noticed that his erection subsided when the subject of his wife came up.

Looking a little sad, he sighed and again looked away towards the lake and shoreline before responding.

"Well, Donny, all marriages aren't perfect. Barbara and I haven't been intimate for several years. She complains constantly of physical problems that make sex unpleasant for her. Not even your dad has been able to diagnose the problem. So I just gave up on her. Sorry to burden you with my tough story, but you're old enough to understand what I'm saying."

Feeling really bad for the guy, I needed to try to put him at ease. "Damn, Russ, I'm so sorry. I didn't mean to bring up such a personal subject. It must be tough on you not having a regular outlet for your sex needs. Won't she even give you an occasional blow job or at least jerk you off? Maybe you should try watching some porn flicks together."

He smiled and said, "No way ... she thinks porn is disgusting and akin to devil worship. Hey, how do you think I keep my pecker happy? My private stash of videos helps me a lot. She never questions why I spend so much time in my basement study. You probably do the same thing I do, you know ... take matters into your own hands."

Looking up into his eyes, I softly said, "Ya, but that gets old after awhile, there's nothing like having someone else's hand takin' care of business."

Letting that sink in, we both were quiet for a few minutes before I broke the silence. "Russ, I forgot to put on my suntan lotion, would you mind helping me out."

"Ahh, sure, Donny, maybe you can do the same for me." He reached for the bottle of Bain de Soleil I offered.

There was a touch of nervousness in his voice. This gentle man deserved something special, and I was horny enough to give it to him.

"Put on a good layer, I haven't been to the beach this year, and my pasty white bod needs all the help it can get."

Licking his lips, he replied, "Yah, I can see that," as he squirted a large cool blob on my shoulder and slowly smoothed it over my upper back and neck. It felt so good to have a man's hands working on my body; my cock stiffened under me. As Russ's hands made their way down my back, I raised my ass, freeing my cock to spring up toward my belly button. He hesitated before continuing, but after a moment, gently moved on to my ass cheeks.

I cautioned, "Maybe you should use a lot more on my butt since it never sees the sun."

"Sh-sh-sure. Can't take a chance with your light skin."

I felt another large splash of lotion, followed by his now trembling hands. My tight little ass was getting a lot of welcome attention, and I decided to see how far I could take this. Spreading my legs apart allowed him a nice view of my nut sac; slowly his hands went down the length of my crack; his finger tips stopping momentarily at my lightly furred balls.

Clenching and unclenching my butt cheeks was all it took. Next thing I knew, his fingers were moving from my balls to deep within my ass crack, gently stroking my hole, looking for an entrance. He found it; slowly massaging my pucker, then gradually inserting a well oiled finger until it reached my hot spot. I gave it a welcoming squirm and ground my prick into my towel. I knew then, I had him.

"Do ... do ... you like that, Donny?"

His voice was quavering, his breathing was becoming strained with excitement.

"Yessss, I never felt anything so good," I lied, thinking back to Dad's finger fucking.

"Do you want me ... to ... continue?"

His voice was really shaking now.

"I ... I ... think I know how to maybe make us both feel good."

My response was to raise my ass to meet his probing fingers. He took the bait; pulling his finger out of my ass, he rummaged through his rucksack and found a condom, rolled it over his slender, hard, shaft; straddled my back and gently eased his prick into my very willing ass.

I winced as the first few inches entered my tender passage, but then the head of his cock reached the glorious spot my dad had so recently introduced me to with his prostate exam. I was in heaven and flexed my ass muscles in appreciation and encouragement.

"Oh, Donny, you're ass is so tight and warm and I'm so fucking hot, it's been months ... ahhhh ... ah ... oh ... sooo ... hot and ... tight."

He worked his cock deeper; pressing his hot sweaty chest to my back; his fucking reached a fever pitch, and I loved every inch of cock he pounded into me, thrust after thrust, panting into my ear muffled little cries of pleasure until he suddenly stopped mid-lunge; bellowing like a bull, "Ohhh my Gaaawd!" He shot his hot load into my steaming hole, all the while, gently biting the nape of my neck in the throes of his climax.

Collapsing his whole weight on my sweat-soaked body, we lay still for several minutes, enjoying the euphoria that follows great sex. He gently kissed my neck before rising and slowly releasing his cock from my still pulsing ass, which hungered for more. A sticky wetness around my lower belly made me realize that I had also blown my wad.

We were both still panting from the excitement and passion when I told him he was my first man fuck.

Russ nuzzled the back of my ear and whispered softly, "Thank you. Then we were both virgins up until a few moments ago. I never would have thought it could be so good with another guy."

"Me either, Russ, thanks for making it nice for both of us."

As I sat up and looked around toward the lake, I caught sight of my little friend from my first visit poking his head out from under the log. "Damn ... busted by a chipmunk."

Russ looked at me with a puzzled expression and then smiled as he said, "He probably thinks we're nuts."

Gathering our stuff, we headed back down to the lake shore, looking forward to a cooling dip that would jolt us back to reality.

After our swim in the chilly water, we rested on the sand, getting our breath back.

Russ had a worried look on his face as he spoke, "Donny, please don't ever tell anyone about what we just did up on the rock. I was so desperate; I weakened when I felt the softness of your naked ass in my hands; you seemed so willing. Please understand ... it won't happen again. I'm not gay, Donny, and I don't think you are either. We were just two guys who needed some release. Your dad would kill me if he knew I had seduced his son; Jack, Mark and Bruce would probably throw my ass out of the group."

Taking his hand in mine, I gave it a gentle squeeze and said, "You didn't seduce me, I wanted it as bad as you did. Don't worry, what happened up there is our secret, but if you ever feel the need again, just ask me to take a walk. I'll understand."

He looked relieved and gave me a sweet and grateful smile as we rose from the sand and headed back to the cabin. I'd scored again. Would Jack and Marc be so easy?

Meanwhile, there was a lot of work to be done, and I was busting to get going on Project PROSAGE.

Six

It was Friday already. The time had flown by, and a hell of a week it had been, but we had hardly started. Today, Marc was going to walk me through the housekeeping routine up at the bunkhouse.

My main responsibilities would be to keep the place spotlessly clean. Linens and towels would have to be washed at least twice a week or more depending on how sloppy our guests were.

Fortunately, there was a small guest laundry facility in addition to the commercial units I would use. They could wash their own stuff if necessary.

All of the appliances were top of the line, even a built-in vacuum system. Marc explained how everything worked in the kitchen

130

even though I would not have to do much actual cooking. Russ would be on hand to do most of the prep, and my job would be setting up and serving. Almost every meal would be made up primarily of gourmet-quality frozen prepared products.

Each evening there would be a cocktail hour starting at 6:00 pm, which I would host. My bartending skills were nil, so Marc gave me a book and video put out by Old Mr. Boston. It would give me the basics. He had made up a schedule of duties for me to follow and gave me a lot of encouragement that I would do just fine.

"Just be your sweet, charming self, Donny. The guys will love you. Just remember, they are each paying $3,500 for their week up here. We want 'em to feel that they're getting their money's worth." And he gave me a little slap on my behind.

What was that all about?

My mind started spinning. What would they expect from their experience? Dad had said he would fill me in on the details of the PROSAGE program, and Jack was going to give me a hands-on training session with the device. This was either going to be a fun or frustrating week.

As the guys had suggested, I set myself up in the staff bedroom at the bunkhouse. Even though there was a week to go before the program started, I might as well get used to the place.

Back at the cabin that night, Dad sat down with me and explained the program.

The first day, each man would get a physical, an evaluation of their condition and counseling. Dietary recommendations would be made as well. This would be followed by a massage therapy period conducted by Jack. The rest of the day could be spent any way they chose. On the second day, they would be introduced to the PROSAGE device. That would be Dad's job. The rest of the week would follow pretty much the same schedule minus the physical. If the program proved to be successful, the plan was to continue with Dad as Medical Director, and a professional staff would be assembled for a full-time operation during the spring, summer and fall months. During the winter, an in-town, outpatient service would be offered.

Seven

Saturday – this was a lazy day that we all could use to do whatever we felt needed to be done. I decided to spend some time up at the bunkhouse, getting familiar with the various toys that would be available to my guests.

The pool table occupied my time for about an hour then into the spa followed by some steam. By late afternoon, I was limp as a rag and probably dehydrated from the dry sauna.

Dragging my tired ass back through the kitchen to my new room, I flopped out on my queen sized bed and immediately dozed off.

The sound of a door closing woke me up. Looking at the clock, it seemed that about two hours had passed. Jack's voice from the kitchen got me fully awake.

"Donny, you in here? It's Jack. We're wonderin' what happened to you."

"In my room, Jack. I kinda overdid the steam, spa and sauna and just about passed out. What's up?"

He appeared in the doorway wearing some denim cutoffs and a bright yellow "Jack's Jym" athletic shirt and looking very tasty even to my blurry eyes. He sat on the edge of the bed, and gripping my shoulder, gave me a gentle shake.

"C'mon guy, get your ass up and back to the cabin, it's almost dinner time and we're wait'n for you. Why don't ya take a cool shower and you'll feel better. I'll see ya' back there."

After he left, all I could think about was our encounter in the bathroom the other night and seeing him stretched out asleep with his gloriously naked ass on display.

This hot stud was going to give me PROSAGE lessons. Damn, life is good!

The subject around the dinner table that night was about a business trip to Milwaukee. Dad, Marc, Bruce and Russ would need to be there early Monday to meet with some prospective supporters in the medical community. The plan was for them to leave Sunday morning and return on Tuesday. Jack would stay behind to keep me company and to do some work around the cabin.

How cool was that? Jack all to myself for the whole weekend. No telling where that could go.

True to their word, the guys left right after breakfast the next day.

The mood in the cabin changed dramatically. Jack and I both felt the wonderful freedom that seems to come from being left alone after a full house of company has finally departed or the boss is away.

Jack is sometimes like an overgrown teenager. We communicate on a level impossible with my dad. He is the most down-to-earth member of the group.

Coming from rural Kansas and a family of farmers, Jack lacks the sophistication and education the others possess, but that's his charm.

We relaxed most of the day, watching TV, snacking instead of doing a full lunch.

The weather was perfect for a canoe excursion, so we dragged out the old fiberglass scow, packed up some life vests and pushed off onto the lake.

Jack knew the lake well and directed us along the shore and around the bend of the bay. The beauty of the place, the serenity, and incredible silence gave me such a feeling of contentment that couldn't be expressed with words. I turned my head to look back at Jack, and he just gave me a smile and a nod showing me that he understood what I was feeling.

We spent the next hour or so just slowly drifting along the shore. Stopping briefly to munch some snack crackers and down some Cokes. Naturally, I eventually had to take a piss and wondered how to do that in a canoe. No way I could stand up and do it over the edge without tipping the thing. Finally, Jack must have read my mind.

"In case you have to take a piss, there is a p-can under your seat. Just fill it up and dump it over the side. Just don't forget to rinse it out when you're through." I should have known these guys would think of everything.

Returning to the cabin, we both needed a good cool shower and a nap. Jack let me go first, saying "I'll take my shower later on. Right now I'm going up and crash."

Disappointing, yes, but we had the whole weekend ahead of us. Take it easy, Donny, I admonished myself. Jack might not be the push-over Bruce was. After a quick shower, I stretched out on Dad's king size bed. Sleep came easy.

Waking up to the sound of the Bee Gees "First of May" took me by surprise, but remembering that Jack was my only housemate, it made sense. He was lost in the 60s much of the time.

Throwing on a pair of gym shorts, the same ones Dad wore last week, I headed downstairs.

Jack greeted me enthusiastically, "It's about time, 'twas getting lonesome down here, but kinda nice at the same time, I mean without all the guys hangin' around."

Deciding to make myself useful, I offered to fix supper.

"I know what you mean. How about if I fire up the grill and burn some meat tonight?"

He walked over to me and wrapped me up in a bear hug, "You got it, Donny boy. It's all yours. Go to it."

I thought, do that again and we won't get to eat.

Being early May, the nights were still pretty cool. After dinner, Jack offered to light up the fireplace. That really topped off a perfect day, but the best was yet to come. While I was getting us some coffee, Jack had spread a big fur rug out in front of the hearth. Grabbing a couple of floor pillows, he said "If you don't mind, I'm going to make myself comfy and stretch out down here. You're welcome to join me. It's a lot warmer close to the fire. Before you do though, hand me that bottle of Jack Daniels, so I can sweeten up this coffee. Yours, too, if ya like."

I like.

This whole scene was enough to bring back the memory of my first real one-on-one sexual experience, which involved my buddy, John.

Eight

It all started out innocently enough. Our family had moved from an adjacent town to Forsythe, Wisconsin, which meant a new school district. This was right after I completed junior high school, placing me in the eleventh grade. Being somewhat shy and having no friends at my new school made my life difficult. My hero turned out to be a big Italian boy by the name of John Rocco. This guy was everything I was not. Very mature for his age, he had a husky, muscular build, was active on the school football team, very popular, and a good student to boot.

For some reason, we developed an "odd couple" type of friendship. Maybe he felt sorry for me. His home was within walking distance of mine, so we often rode the bus from school together. During one of these trips, the subject of our courses came up. We had both elected to take French rather than Spanish. This proved to be the thread that brought us together for study sessions in his basement party room.

At the time, I was fascinated with electronics, particularly vintage equipment such as the old- timey wooden consoles that were as big as refrigerators.

John mentioned that there was an old RCA Victrola monster that had been in his family since the early 40s, sitting in his basement. Would I like to come over and take a look at it after supper that night? I jumped at the chance.

The beast worked perfectly, even had a built-in 78 rpm record changer and a cabinet below for a small collection of records.

This developed into a regular thing. I would arrive about 7:00 pm. We would go to the basement, turn on the RCA and listen to some music or play around with the short wave frequencies. A little French study would get done, and then we would just hang out, usually talking school gossip. For the next three years, John and I had a very supportive kind of friendship. Supportive for me because of the sense of belonging he gave me just by being willing to freely associate with a non-jock. In return, I provided him with an outlet for his more intellectual interests, reading, music, the occasional trips to museums and just quiet hanging-out moments. Whether or not he ever sensed that I was maybe a "fairy" remained a mystery during this time period. He just seemed to accept the fact that I was different and respected me for that.

Several weeks after high school graduation, we were hanging out as usual down in his basement, discussing our futures now that we were over eighteen and free to make some choices. The talk turned to sex. Who was doing what with whom, which girls put out, etc. The talk got more and more into details – tits, ass, cunts and finally, which of the guys on his ball team had the biggest dick. Now that caught my interest. Not being on the team, my knowledge in that area had been limited to what I had been able to see in the locker room after gym class.

I commented, "Well, in all the years I've known you we've never seen each other bare-assed, so for all I know you might have the biggest one." He smiled and said "I'm pretty big, but Billy Cardozo beats me by at least three inches."

"You got that right … last week a bunch of us was hanging out in the park after dark. I don't know how the subject of dick size came up, but anyway someone says to Cardozo 'Hey Billy, take out the champ and show him off.' With that, he unzips and whips out this snake. The damn thing must have been a foot long, and it was still soft.

I said something like 'Holy shit, what a monster cock.' Someone in the crowd said, 'What's up, Donny, you never seen a cock before?' Maybe I showed too much interest in Billy's cock, I don't know."

John said, "Don't worry about it. Those jerks are always pulling shit like that."

He looked at me kind of funny and after a minute or two said, "So do you jerk- off much? ... I do. Especially when I am down here alone ... no one to bother me. I've got a stash of *Hustlers* and *Playboys* hidden away and can really get off on some of those tit and ass shots. Want to see 'em?"

Of course, I sort of wanted to see them, but even more, I wanted to see my old study-buddy jerk off.

He went to an old dresser under the stairs and pulled out a small stack of mags.

As he crouched down, selecting his favorites, my eyes focused on his nicely rounded butt. The elastic waistband of his gym shorts had stretched down, revealing a thin trail of black fuzz leading to the first few exposed inches of his ass crack. I was hypnotized by the sight, feeling like I was getting away with something a little kinky by spying on his ass, and at the same time, a little jealous. How come he had hair down there and I didn't. After all, we were both about the same age. In spite of all the jokes about plumbers under sinks showing their butt cracks, I was totally turned on by the sight.

My spell was broken when he stood and plopped a *Hustler* in my lap.

"Oh man, check out page 31, it's one of my favorites, just watch out for the cum stains."

He wasn't kidding. There they were. One had even landed on the spread-eagled model's face. My buddy was a real pervert, and I couldn't be more thrilled.

After years of mostly solo masturbation, maybe my sex life was going to get more interesting.

John sat down on the carpeted floor and patted the space next to him, indicating he wanted me down there as well.

"Come on, make yourself comfortable, and why don't you take off your jeans, so I'm not the only one practically undressed around here ... besides, if you get a boner it might break, crammed in so tight."

I protested that it would leave me in my jockey shorts and "what if someone came down from upstairs. Wouldn't it look a little weird?"

136

"Bullshit, we can hear anyone coming because the door is as squeaky as the stairs, besides, I'm the only one who ever uses this place."

He seemed pretty sure of himself, after all, he was just wearing those stretchy gym shorts and a T-shirt.

While I was pulling off my Keds and jeans, John stretched out on the floor, his head on a pillow and a magazine in his hands, just inches away from his face.

My gaze wandered down his body; stopping at his mid-section. Oh man! He was getting hard, and his dick was starting to stretch almost to the waistband of his shorts. Even without touching it, his cock was twitching under the influence of whatever he was looking at.

"Here, take a mag and lie down ... there's another pillow for you to use," he insisted.

Not wanting to wrinkle my sport shirt, I took it off, leaving me with just my tight-whiteys and sweat socks for cover. This was feeling very weird. Here I was practically naked in someone else's house, with his parents upstairs watching *Leave It To Beaver* reruns. That got me to thinking; wondering if the Beaver and Wally ever did the deed together. That would make such a cool episode:

"Mom! Wally shot his spooge all over the clean sheets."

"Boys, how many times have I told you to use the nice box of tissues I left by your beds when you masturbate. I'm going to have your dad give you a stern talking to as soon as he comes home ... Now get cleaned up for supper."

Just the thought of it gave me the giggles.

John was clearly annoyed by my laughter while he was getting off on a porn mag.

Suddenly, he dropped his magazine; jumped up and flipped off the light, leaving the room lit only by the bright golden radio dial. He lay back down on the floor saying, "Sorry Donny, I just gotta jerk off. These cunt pics are just too much, and I'm ready to pop."

With that, he pulled down his shorts, revealing his fat 7 inches of uncut Italian salami. Its grayish-brown color fascinated me. It was so unlike my pale pink shaft.

Looking down at himself, he said, "Not bad stuff, huh? Come on, we can both do it at the same time ... don't be such a pussy!"

Laying my head back on the pillow, I could feel the heat from his body just inches away from mine. His faintly masculine body odor

137

was starting to get to me. My cock was now straining at the seams of my jockeys as he reached over and pulled them down below my balls.

"That's better, now relax and let's have a good fist fuck. See, you're as ready as I am and not a bad piece you got … and unclipped just like mine," as he reached over and gave my stiff prick a quick squeeze.

Compared with me, John was a giant. My eyes couldn't leave the sight of his beefy hand sliding his foreskin back and forth, covering and uncovering his deep purple cock head. On the up-stroke, the supple skin gathered into a dark, wrinkled bunch then retracted, again revealing the silkiness of his glans. I was mesmerized.

Grasping my own stiff dick, we soon got into a rhythm and within minutes, our heavy breathing signaled our simultaneous orgasms. Shot after shot of our thick hot cream splashed onto our stomachs and coated our hands.

After we got our breaths back, John got up and brought me some Kleenex to clean up with.

"Damn, I really needed that."

I replied in a shaky voice, "Yeah, that was great. My load was the biggest yet. How about you?"

"About average. If I don't do it at least once a day, it starts leaking on its own."

Guessing he meant he had wet dreams, I agreed.

Hearing footsteps upstairs, I figured it was time for me to leave. As I got dressed, he said, "Don't forget, you can 'come' over anytime." He emphasized "come" and grinned, adding, "You know what I mean, no invitation needed."

My visits became a regular routine, and it usually ended with us both having a jerk-off session, sometimes helping each other out. I was totally happy with this arrangement then things took a surprising turn.

John called me on a Friday afternoon and was really excited.

"Hey, my mama and papa are going out of town for a wedding this weekend, and I'll have the house to myself tonight and tomorrow night. Why don't you tell your folks you're going to crash at my place. Mine said it was OK for me to have company as long as it wasn't one of my girlfriends. Mom even made a big pot of spaghetti and meatballs, so come over for supper tonight."

This sounded like a dream come true. I couldn't wait to tell my mom and dad about my weekend plans. They thought it was a great idea, especially since John was considered a good influence on me. Little did they know. With a little luck, my old study-buddy just might turn into my new stud-buddy.

That evening, he met me at the door wearing a "Kiss the Italian Cook" apron. For a moment, I thought about taking him up on the offer, but chickened out. We might be jerking off together, but kissing was a no-no for sure.

At this stage in my life, I didn't think of myself as a gay boy. Messing around was just something guys did sometimes. Someday, a girl would come along and we'd go steady, break up, and another would come along. Sure! Just like in the movies.

He grabbed my gym bag with its cargo of extra clothes and toilet things and led me to his bedroom. I had never spent any time in this part of the house, so was interested in seeing how my friend lived.

The room was very neat. An assortment of sports and rock band posters were tacked up on the walls. The only real surprise was a framed program from one of Enrico Caruso's performances at Carnegie Hall. This intrigued me, and I made a note to ask him about it later.

Seeing only one double bed caused me to wonder if we were going to share it, or was I going to be exiled to another room.

Mama Rocco was a hell of a cook, and we put away a lot of food, washed down with a couple of glasses of "guinea red" wine his uncle had made. John drank his like water. My only exposure to alcohol had been a glass of champagne at Jacob Goldstein's bar mitzvah a year before, so I took it easy and enjoyed a nice buzz.

We watched TV until about 10:00 pm, when the food and wine finally took its toll, and we decided to hit the sack.

"Which side do you like?" Oh great, we're going to share the bed.

"Doesn't matter to me, whatever you're used to." He opted for the side nearest the door. I got the wall side. When I returned from brushing my teeth, John was already in bed and flipping through one of his Playboys. I stripped down to my jockeys and crawled over him to my side of the bed, pulling back the covers in the process; discovering that he was stark naked. He saw the startled look on my face and laughed. "Hey, I always sleep bare-assed. Who needs clothes in bed? They only get in the way in case I need some relief in the middle of the night."

His body was totally sexy. For a guy so young, he had an almost fully furred chest, accented by nipples that stood up proud from their little brown rings. Jet black belly hair led down to a bushy cluster at his groin. His soft, dark brown cock lay atop his balls which hung loose in their wrinkled sac. The foreskin completely covered the head, with a little left over. No wonder he was such a chick magnet.

Snapping out of my trance, I slid under the sheet and pulled it up over us.

"G'night, Johnny."

"G'night, Donny, sweet dreams."

He rolled over to his side of the bed and put out the light.

Waking with a start, it took me a few minutes to realize where I was. It was just starting to get daylight outside. Too early to get up, so I rolled over, saw that John was still sound asleep, and decided to catch some more

The sound of snoring very close to my ear woke me up the second time. John had shifted in his sleep and was pressed up against my back, the full weight of his muscular chest pushing me up against the wall. His arm was resting on my thigh and a leg was wedged between both of mine. The heat from his body was incredible. Should I wake him up or just lie there and hope he would move on his own. Aroused, my cock needed release from its jockey-short prison. I whispered, "John, John, wake up, you're crushing the breath from me."

He moved slightly, muttering in his sleep. More drastic measures were needed. I twisted around enough to grab his arm and give it a shake. This worked. He opened his eyes and looked at me as if he was surprised to see someone else in bed with him.

"Oh crap, Donny, sorry to hog the bed."

"No problem, but I was starting to have breathing problems." I smiled at him, and he knew everything was cool.

Rolling onto his back, he pulled the sheet off our bodies. Looking down at my jockey shorts, he gave an evil laugh and reached over and grabbed the elastic and pulled them down to my knees. If this was going to turn into a wrestling match, I was ready. Pulling them off the rest of the way, I flipped over on top of his chest and grabbed his arms, holding them above his head. As he squirmed under me, my now hard cock slipped in between his legs, poking into his ball sac, the firmness of his hot cock pressed into my belly. He was able to free one arm and grabbing the back of my head, forced my face down into his hairy armpit, causing me to inhale a lungful of his musky odor. That weakened me long enough for him to throw me over on my side and

140

the next thing I knew, there was very hard Italian cock pushing up against my ass.

"I got you now pussy-boy, do you surrender?"

"Yes, yes," was all I could say. He relaxed his hold and rolled onto his back.

Turning over, I gazed at the beauty of his prick at full stand. The foreskin was pulled back, revealing a dark, moist head; a drop of precum poised at the tip.

Grabbing the shaft, he shook it in my direction. "It's all your fault, you shouldn't have shown me your cute little ass, Donny boy. Now look what you've done. I think you're going to have to help me out with this problem, maybe a hand job would work or maybe even ..." and with a leer, "a ... blow job. Take your choice."

My experience was limited to giving and receiving hand jobs. Cock sucking was something only "queers" did; yet, I was suddenly excited by its possibilities.

"OK, you got me." My trembling hand reached out and grasped the firm cock shaft and slid the dark, velvety skin up and down, covering and uncovering the glistening head. Pre-cum was already leaking from the tip, making juicy little sounds as I worked the length of this beauty. John's soft moans were only making my job easier. My other hand slid up his thigh and gently stroked his balls as my pace increased. A tightening of his sac told me he was getting very close, and two more slides proved it.

"Oh ... oh ... cumin ... don't stop ... suck it for me, Donny, pleeease suck it."

The rush of cum from his shaft was amazing. Pulse after pulse shot his cream across his furry chest and ran down my fist. On impulse, I raised my hand to my lips and licked a drop of his semen into my mouth. My first taste of cum, and it was surprisingly sweet, and I liked it.

John looked at me in awe. "You ... you ... ate my cum!"

Without hesitation, I leaned down and took the length of his softening prick deep into my mouth, giving it a thorough tongue-bath, my nose buried in the wrinkled folds of his ball sack. His whole body convulsed in reaction to my swirling tongue. I was in a cum-and-cock induced trance as I relished the thrill of giving my very first head job. A cock-sucker was born.

Later, at home, I got to wondering about the taste of John's cum. What made it so tasty and easy to eat?

Digging into some of Dad's medical books, I discovered that semen is almost fifty percent fructose. No wonder cock sucking is so popular! If those weight-loss plans knew this, no guy would ever get head again while the wife was trying to shed those extra pounds.

John and I spent a very happy summer, becoming "best buddies" in more than one way. He never did return the favor of a blow job but was always grateful for my willingness to take care of his needs. Following that summer, we would part. He chose to go on to take some phys-ed courses at our junior college while I thought about studies that would prepare me for college. We probably would never see each other again, and I felt a real loss when I realized my "study-buddy" was gone from my life.

Nine

Whiskey laced coffee, coupled with the warmth of the fire, lulled both of us into a deep relaxed state of total contentment. The feeling I had as I looked at Jack was unfamiliar to me. It wasn't my usual horny little brain working, but something deeper. A peculiar, but not unpleasant ache deep in my gut made me wonder if this is what love felt like. This man next to me was so strong and rugged, but at the same time a gentle teddy bear. Resisting the urge to reach over and touch him, I curled up with my pillow and dozed off, thoughts of what was happening to me occupying my mind.

Awakening, I glanced at the big grandfather clock in the corner. A couple of hours had passed. Jack was sound asleep on the floor next to me. The fire had burned down to just a few embers, and a chill was taking over the room. We needed to call it a night. Tapping Jack on his arm caused him to wake with a start. After realizing where he was, he stretched and slowly got to his feet.

"Bedtime, Donny, I'll see ya in the morning," and he dragged himself up to his room.

After cleaning up our dinner mess, I headed upstairs, took a piss and walked back down the hall to Dad's room. As I passed Jack's room, I couldn't resist stopping and looking in on him. He lay naked on his back, covers thrown to the floor. In the dim light, his cock was visible, nestled within its pale gold bush. The familiar feeling in my groin overtook any fear of discovery, and I moved close by his bed.

Kneeling on the floor, only inches away from his sleeping form, I let my eyes feast on his masculine beauty. Not daring to take matters any further, I rose and lovingly covered his nakedness.

Morning came with a bang, literally. It was Jack, unloading firewood from a wheelbarrow, tossing the logs onto the back deck. It was cool in the cabin, so I threw on some sweats and went down to see if I could help him. By the time I got there, he was finished.

"Good timing, Donny-boy. Well, at least we won't freeze tonight." I thanked him for his efforts and grabbed a couple of coffees for us. "What's the plan for today?" I inquired.

He thought for a moment and remembering something highly important, he brightened, "Today, my friend we are going to give you some PROSAGE lessons. I promised your dad we'd put this quiet time to good use. Don't be too worried about it – I think you'll find it a pretty fun way to spend a few hours."

Trying to sound as nonchalant as possible, I yawned, "Sure thing Jack, I need to know how the thing works, and we don't really have that much time before the guests arrive."

Inside, I was as excited as if we were going to Wisconsin Dells, my favorite amusement park. It was decided that we would have a leisurely breakfast, then relax for a while before starting my education.

When the time came, Jack suggested I go upstairs, take a shower, and he would meet me in his room in a few minutes and not to bother with getting dressed. When I got to his room, I noticed he had arranged his bed with several fat pillows and a couple of large towels spread out over the sheets. He had changed into what looked to me like pale blue nurse's scrubs. Thoughtfully, he had turned on the electric heat in the room, so I was OK with being bare-assed naked. Jack patted the bed indicating he wanted me to sit on the edge. Opening a case just like the one I saw up at the bunkhouse, he removed its contents to a small table close by.

Picking up the device, he gave me a detailed explanation of how it worked, what to expect and most of all how to control it for the best results. That done, he placed the least thick latex sleeve onto the "finger" and covered it with an ordinary condom.

"You'll notice that there are various thicknesses of sleeve. This is so we are able to accommodate most any body type. Some guys are tighter than others. As young as you are, you probably need the thinnest." He was right since I had only been penetrated once, not counting Dad's exam, and that was by Russ's pencil prick.

143

"Don't be embarrassed if you get a hard-on. That's the whole idea of using this thing. I am going to lube it and slowly enter your anus. Once it has passed through your sphincter, I'll turn on the pulsing action at a slow speed. Are ya ready? Just let me know if you feel any discomfort."

As instructed, I lay back against the pillows and raised my legs so they were bent at the knee and my hole was readily accessible. He then snapped on a latex glove and squeezing a dollop of KY on his finger, carefully lubed and massaged my hole.

Oh man, I was enjoying this already.

Once he was satisfied that I was relaxed and ready, he started the insertion. Out of sheer nervousness, my cock hung limp against my balls until he reached the magic spot and gently stroked the tip back and forth. He guessed, from the dreamy look on my face that I was ready for more. As my cock stiffened, he turned on the pulse feature. I groaned out, "Oh, damn, that feels so good."

Jack laughed and said, "I told you it would be kinda fun," and continued his gentle probing, going deeper each time.

As he slowly increased the intensity of the mechanical action, my need to cum became overpowering until I had to warn him, "Jack, I'm going to shoot." I gripped my cock and stroked it a few times. "Here it comes … ohhhh … aaaahhh…"

Blast after blast shot from my cock, some hitting my neck just below my chin. He slowly withdrew from my ass and handed me a clean-up towel.

As I lay panting from the experience, Jack said, "You did very well for your first time. Now that you know what our amazing toy can do, I'll have you go through a demonstration on me. Before we do that, let's take a break and have lunch."

How could he be so casual? He just gave me the next best sex of my life, and now he just wants to do lunch. I love this guy.

During lunch, he explained that it was important for me to experience the therapy since I would be spending a lot of time with the clients. There would be occasions when any one of them might need a little guidance as they learned how to properly enjoy their private PROSAGE sessions. I would be their on-site facilitator.

We decided to continue my training up at the bunkhouse since there we could use the hot tub and sauna to relax a bit before and after I worked on Jack. He also wanted to do some routines with the exercise equipment, which was an important part of the program.

We brought along several sets of scrubs for me to use during my work week. I tried them on and was surprised at how comfortable they were.

"You look like a real pro, little buddy." Giving me a sly grin, he added, "Let's use your room for your hands on experience." I didn't care if we did it on the front porch, I was ready to work on his muscleman ass. "The routine will be the same. Just follow my instructions and you'll do just fine."

He stripped off his sweats and lay back against the pillows, bending his knees; exposing himself as I had done. The sight of his muscular body in so vulnerable a position gave me butterflies in my stomach, and I felt my legs weakening as I prepared the tool and applied the KY as he had done. His prick and ball sac were hanging loosely, almost covering his butt hole. I hesitatingly asked if it would be OK if I lifted his package slightly so I could get a better view of my target.

He replied, "You're the doctor, do whatever you feel necessary." I gently lifted his ball sack, exposing the hairless, pink opening. After thoroughly lubing his entrance, slipping the tip of my finger in just a little way, I carefully placed the head of the tool at his tight little pucker, teasing the sensitive opening. Slowly, and with surprising ease, it slid in. When I reached that most sensitive spot, he let out a low moan.

"Ok, now turn on the pulse at low speed and slowly move it in and out, going a little deeper each time. Oh damn, Donny, you're doing great. You're a natural."

Just as mine had, his cock came to life and was soon pointing straight up his belly.

"Oh man, this thing works its magic every time. Now let go of my balls and take my cock in your hand and give it a few slides for me."

His silky ball sac felt so good I didn't want to let go but when my hand gripped the hardness of his cock, his pleasure was all that counted. Minutes later, my stroking hand brought him to climax, and he shot his load, soaking my hand in hot cum. I wanted so badly to see if his tasted as good as Bruce's, but not wanting to do anything that might damage the intimacy we had just shared, I didn't yield to temptation.

"Good job, Donny, of course you won't be expected to do that much work for all the guys, but thanks for helping me out." His smiling face was all the reward I needed.

We headed for the showers and then the hot tub, both of us needed to come down from our highs.

That evening as we lay naked in front of the crackling fireplace sipping our well-laced coffee, Jack suddenly sat up and leaned over toward me. "Donny, I just got to do somethin' I've been cravin' to do for a long, long time."

Leaning over me, he placed a big hand behind my head as he lowered his lips to mine, our tongues met in a soft, sensuous embrace, turning me into a wild and passionate animal as I returned his kisses, sucking the very breath from him with lips and tongue. When he spoke those wonderful words, "I love you, Donny," tears welled in my eyes and I responded with total sincerity for the first time in my life, "I ... I ... love you, Jack."

After we had time to reflect on what just happened between us, Jack fell back on the floor, taking me with him, cradling me in his massive arms.

"Donny, I hope you at least feel some of the happiness there is in my heart right now. I never knew how to express my love for another guy. It just was never in my playbook until now, when I suddenly realized my true feelings towards you. Once I passed that point I knew I had to tell you or bust. It struck me hardest when we were out on the lake, and the sense that you were feeling the same way I was about the beauty and peacefulness of the moment made me weak in the knees."

My fingers traced patterns through the dense blonde thatch of his chest while I gathered my thoughts. His nipples stiffened beneath my lightly stroking fingertips, sending tremors through his body and mine. Hardly able to believe that this handsome and virile man was offering himself to me, I finally asked, "But Jack, how did you know? What did I do to make you so sure?" He was quiet for a moment and then dropped another bomb on me.

"I've sort of known for years. All the signs were there. You never showed any interest in dating girls, or playing team sports, had very few close friends at school and you seemed to be happiest when we guys were around. The best day of my life was when you turned nineteen, and your dad said he would let you come here with us."

I rolled over on top of his chest, holding his handsome face in my hands. "You sure got that right. But what do we do now?"

"To be honest with you, I think your dad has a clue about you. He's mentioned several times the last few years that he thought you needed to be spending more time doing 'guy' things. That's why I kept trying to get you to come regularly to the gym. Actually, I just wanted to be near you as much as possible without appearing to be a dirty old man just after your cute little bod."

He leaned down and gave my chest a couple of playful licks. I squirmed and stretched seductively, hoping he wouldn't stop there, but instead he just lay back, pulling me down with him so that my head rested on his chest.

"I guess I wasn't much help then. So, you still haven't answered my question. What do we do now? Somehow just making an announcement at the dinner table when the guys get back might be a little awkward for everyone. 'Hey guys ... Jack and I are in love, pass the salt please.'"

He laughed and then said, "No, I think we can do better than that. First of all, I have a confession to make. In a moment of weakness, Bruce told me about your encounter in the shower."

I was stricken, and it showed.

"Don't panic. He and I have had blunt discussions about our sex lives before."

"Yeah, but they didn't involve me – why would he do that?"

"Bruce tends to be bi-sexual. His gay side reveals itself once and awhile, plus, he can't keep a secret. Haven't you noticed his bedside table is a stack of *Architectural Digests*, topped with a decoupage of *House & Garden* covers? I watched him build that thing, he lacquered and glued for days, he was like Martha Stuart with muscles. He was also the brains behind the design and construction of these cabins, so you can see he is a man of many talents. Too bad he just can't fall off either side of the fence. We never messed around, not that the idea wasn't enough to give me a stiff dick at times. He's a sweet and very sexy guy, but not lover material for me. Way too much baggage. Bruce is sort of like a cute Lab Retriever puppy. Give him a little attention, a pat on the head or a belly-rub and he's your friend for life. In your case, you gave him a lot more than that."

He paused, and then smiling, he added, "Oh, by the way he gave you high marks on your ability to satisfy a man. It was the best blow job he'd had in years."

Testing the waters, I said, "What about Russ and Marc?"

"Ah, nothing much to tell. Russ has a frigid wife, and for all I know his only sex outlet is his porn collection. Marc is still grieving over his loss of family and pretty much keeps his feelings to himself."

147

Thank God. At least Russ hadn't blabbed about our encounter on the rock. That would remain our secret as far as I was concerned.

Getting up and stretching, he looked down at me. "Damn, you're one sexy guy, Donny-boy, and I'm about to toss you into bed and show you what a muscle man can do to show his appreciation. Don't expect to get a lot of sleep tonight."

Ten

The faint light of dawn caused me to awaken. Reluctantly leaving the warmth of Jack's body, I made my way out to the deck. The scent of lake and forest was more intense than I remembered, but the cool morning air hitting my nakedness was enough to send me running back inside to finish what I had started – to take a wicked morning piss.

Sliding back under the covers; pressing my body into his caused Jack to awaken.

Taking me into his arms, we both sighed our contentment. Our first night together had been one of pure emotional and physical lovemaking. Not the kind I was used to – a quick jerk off session or a blow job in the back of a car, but one of soft caresses with hands and tongues, tasting and touching every part of each other's willing bodies until we reached the point where only total release could satisfy us. Teaching me the wonders of sixty-nine that early morning enabled us to feast on each others gushing orgasms. And yes, he was even sweeter than Bruce.

Damn! We suddenly realized that it was Tuesday morning – our weekend alone was shot. The rest of the crew would be coming back today, and I hadn't even started organizing my duties at the bunkhouse. Jack had some work to do up at the cabin, so I was left to figure out where everything was stashed that I would need to maintain order around the place.

The guys arrived back at the cabin around three in the afternoon and promptly crashed. Dad only told me that the meeting had been a success, and he'd give us the details at dinner that night.

While the house was quiet, I went about setting up a makeshift bar in the TV lounge, so I could practice my cocktail-making skills before the guys came down to eat. Shaken or stirred, up or on the rocks, did a martini include sweet or dry vermouth? Maybe they'll just want beer or wine; it was good enough for me. I picked up my *Old Mr. Boston* and crammed for a half hour.

148

Dad was the first one to show up. While I mixed him my first attempt at a Manhattan, he poked around in some papers from his briefcase. I grabbed a Coke and sat on the sofa next to him, expecting some information about their trip.

"So tell me, Don, how did your weekend go? Jack had an ambitious agenda set up for you. I hope all went as planned, particularly your introduction to the PROSAGE instrument." I must have visibly flushed red at that point. The questioning look on Dad's face left no doubt in my mind that he wanted details.

"Oh yeah, we went over all the exercise equipment, hot tub, sauna and steam room. We even had time to go out in the canoe."

He sipped his cocktail and continued, "That's great, I thought you two would get along just fine. Jack's a pretty laid back guy. More like the older brother you never had." I agreed and hoped that would be the end of the interrogation. It was not to be.

"I would really like to know how your familiarization sessions went. If you aren't prepared to help our guests, we'll need to work with you some more."

I was about to answer him when the rest of the crew strolled in and spying my bar, everyone ordered drinks. Putting me to the test, Bruce requested a Cosmo. Back to the book, but at least I was momentarily off the hook with Dad.

Dinner that evening was uneventful. The talk centered around the meetings they had in town and the news that some grant money might be forthcoming if all went well with the first few groups of men.

To my surprise and embarrassment, Jack could hardly keep his hands off me all evening. Sitting next to me on the sofa after I served coffee, his knee continually pressed up against mine. As I rinsed the dishes in the sink, he sneaked up behind me and massaged my shoulders. We had to talk. The other guys were sure to notice all this attention I was getting.

When I whispered to Jack to cool it, he just shrugged it off saying, "You worry too much, just relax and enjoy it. The others know how much I like you. We're just two guys expressing our feelings for each other."

Not convinced, I offered, "Yes, but Dad asked a lot of questions today and seemed to be pressing me to give him a lot of details about how our 'lessons' went. I know he'll bring the subject up again."

149

That night, neither Dad or I could get to sleep. After what seemed like an eternity of tossing and turning, he got up and turned on the light by his side of the bed.

"Son, can we talk about your weekend now?" At his insistence, I described being the patient and how fantastic it felt when my orgasm blew me away, and then how later I used the device on Jack, even helping him by jerking his cock while the massage was in progress. My candor surprised even me.

"And did that experience make you feel closer to Jack?"

Not really knowing where this conversation was going I said, "Yes, we felt we had really bonded by helping each other out. It was a really cool experience."

He was silent for a moment and then in soft voice, "That's good, son. Partners should always feel warm and excited when giving each other pleasure. I don't mean necessarily a married couple, but just two people, even if they are both men should be able to enjoy sexual pleasure together."

My mouth fell open in shock at hearing my dad talk about such a sensitive and divisive subject. He sensed my reaction, and as if to affirm his approval, leaned over and put his arm around my shoulder saying: "I'm proud of you, son, you'll grow up without all the sexual baggage so many men carry around with them all their lives."

One thing for certain, life around Morningwood would never be the same after this talk.

The pace of things was really picking up now that we were within a few days of receiving our first patients. The plan was for the group of six to arrive by charter plane at Rhinelander, some twenty miles to the south, and Russ would drive down in the Suburban and pick them up. They should be arriving at the lake by noon on Sunday. I would help everyone get settled up at the bunkhouse and along with Russ, fix lunch. The rest of the day would be spent familiarizing everyone with the facility.

Much to my happy surprise, Jack volunteered to spend the first night with me at the bunkhouse. Dad thought this was a very good idea and in fact suggested that Jack just move up with me as support as long as we didn't mind sharing the queen size bed.

I looked at Jack. The expression on his face did little to conceal his enthusiasm for that idea. More and more, it struck me that Dad was making a very conscious effort to enable Jack and me to be together.

Could he know that in the space of a weekend, we had become what I interpreted to be lovers? The answer to that was becoming obvious.

After dinner at the cabin, Jack and I gathered up our stuff and headed over to the bunkhouse. We were going to have four nights alone together and neither of us wanted to waste any time.

The sunset cast a rosy glow over the tranquil lake; as we walked along the shore. The aroma of the nearby woods, a mix of pines, grasses and from the darkest shaded areas, the damp mosses, was almost intoxicating, the unseen birds nesting in the trees for the night sang even sweeter. The realization that maybe for the first time in my life I was experiencing love, suddenly made me stop in my tracks. Jack took a few steps farther and turning around returned to my side, took me in his arms and softly nuzzled my neck, his breath on my ear sent a message that instantly caused my body to melt into his. I didn't need any corny violins and cherubs to tell me that, yes, I truly felt love for this man.

Eleven

Our days were filled with activity. Jack spent a lot of his time fine tuning the work-out equipment and at the same time kept up his own regimen with a combination of Nautilus and free weights. He finally shamed me into allowing him to set up a program for me, and I had to admit it was just what I needed to supplement my love of swimming. What this place needed was an indoor pool. I kept busy getting things ready for our guests. It was going to be like running a hotel, and I hardly knew how to keep my bedroom clean at home.

We spent as little time at the cabin as possible, going there only to have lunch and dinner and of course, to keep in touch with the rest of the guys. It was only a twenty minute walk away, but it seemed like another world now that Jack and I had become so close.

By Saturday, everything was as ready as it ever would be. I found a sunny spot on the deck and stretched out on a chaise, hoping to get some rays on my milky white body. It wasn't long before my rest was interrupted by Jack bounding up the steps. I looked up to the sight of his beautiful blond, furry body coming at me at full speed. He grabbed me up in his arms and carried me kicking and yelling into the gym, gently placing me in the swirling waters of the spa.

"What the hell are you doing to me?" I cried. His response was to put his big hands on either side of my face and pull me into a deep hard kiss, his tongue going so deep into my throat I thought I would pass out from loss of air.

"I'll show you what I'm doing. As soon as I drop these shorts I'm coming in there with you and we're going to make some lovin'. We might not have much time or privacy after today."

Once we were both naked in the comforting waters, I reached down to caress his stiffening cock. It felt so wonderful in my hand, its silky skin, covering the rock hardness of its shaft. My hand moved down to his balls, caressing them as they swirled gently in the turbulence of the spa. We kissed deeply again as I was picked up and placed in front of his waiting lips. He took my eager prick in one swoop, running his tongue over and under the sensitive head as he made his way to its base, burying his nose in the wetness of my pubic hair. Knowing that we were both experiencing the pure pleasure of lover-to-lover sex, I relaxed and let myself enjoy the incredible sensations pulsing through my body, until the moment arrived, and my climax gave us both the reward we were eager for.

Later, as we lay in bed enjoying the warmth of each others' bodies, Jack mentioned his business back in the city. For the first time, he seemed concerned about how things were going without his direction. I assured him that he probably had excellent people working for him that would take very good care of the gym and its members.

"It's not that I don't trust my guys to do their jobs, but my assistant manager has only been with me for two months. He's very capable and my trainers get along with him very well. John has my cell phone number, so he can get in touch any time he needs to. I guess I'm too much of a mother-hen and worry about nothing."

I thought for a moment; and suggested, "Why don't you call the gym and just chat about how things are – any new business, are the trainers getting some good clients? John would probably like hearing from you."

"You're right, hand me my cell, it's on the nightstand on your side." He punched the speed dial and hit the speaker phone button.

After a few rings, a deep male voice spoke, "Good afternoon, Jack's Jym, John Rocco speaking."

A sledge hammer couldn't have hit me any harder. Was this the same John I knew? How many John Roccos could there be in Forsythe?

Their conversation was a blur to me as I pondered the amazing coincidence that my old study-buddy and my new lover could be working together. I had to get more information.

As soon as Jack hung up, he smiled and said, "I made a good choice with John, he's young, about your age, and smart as a whip when it comes to running a gym. He relates so well with my customers, they all admire him for his sexy good looks and knowledge of bodybuilding. You'd really like him. It's a good thing he's straight as an arrow."

I softly answered, "I think I already do"

Sunday morning. I woke up to the overly jolly sound of Dad's voice coming from the kitchen.

"Get your lazy asses out of bed; it's after eight, and we still have some work to do before the guys arrive."

I untangled myself from Jack's burly arms and gave him a shake and headed for the john to take care of morning business. Dad had mercifully brewed some coffee and was busy doing a final inspection of the place. Satisfied, he came back into the kitchen just as Jack made his appearance. "Hey Jack, I hope you are as proud of Donny's work as I am. He has really knocked himself out to impress you and the guests."

"Yeah, I agree he's a quick learner. I'm going back up to the cabin. As soon as you get dressed come on up for a final briefing."

We finished our coffee and bagels in silence. Nothing was mentioned about my remark last night about John Rocco. Maybe he hadn't even heard my reaction. That made me happy because I was just not ready to deal with any complications in my relationship with Jack. What the hell, the worst thing that could happen might be John making some remark about me being his jerk-off study-buddy in high school. It wasn't as if we had a love affair, even if I had lunched on his tasty Italian pork a few times. Anyhow, thanks to Jack, I now know the difference between raw animal lust and real love-making.

Twelve

Right on schedule, the phone rang. It was Russ letting us know he was approaching the gate and would be at the cabin in fifteen minutes.

We did a quick review of the guests' profiles. This was the first time I had been allowed any information as to the nature of the guest-patients. Dad had omitted their last names for privacy concerns. True to what Dad had said, they were a real mixed bag. Just how mixed surprised me.

Reginald G., thirty-five, married but no children. A stock analyst by trade. He had not had a reliable erection for over three years. No apparent physical cause of his dysfunction. Hoped to save his marriage by taking advantage of the therapy my father had developed.

Bernard L., Owner-operator truck driver, fifty, divorced. Wife left him for another woman. Lesbian love was better than he could give her. Two grown off-spring had long left the nest. He felt inadequate and depressed because he could not satisfy the woman he still loved.

Herman A., sixty-six, retired Sears appliance salesman, still happily married but not able to function well in bed without the help of his wife stimulating his anus digitally. She did not like this at all, and her constant complaining did not help.

Buddy S., twenty-two, single, pre-med student. Suffered groin injury playing soccer. A good prospect for this study since his problem was injury related, and he is young.

Louis R., forty-six, bachelor, zoologist. Last sexual encounter was twenty years ago. Claimed to be unable to get aroused unless observing animals copulating, but has no desire to participate.

Mike S., thirty-nine, ex porn star, now a producer-director of gay-straight-bi porn videos. Believes he is burned out by all his early activity.

This week was going to be more interesting than even my twisted imagination could fabricate. But, the best was yet to come.

As the Suburban pulled up in front of the cabin, we all went out to greet the newcomers. One by one, the guys exited and were warmly welcomed, the sixth and last guy exited backward from the left rear door. It was then that I realized to my absolute astonishment that he was a little person.

Approaching me with his hand extended upward in greeting, he said those words that nearly sent me over the top as my mind projected a picture of the clown car at a three ring circus.

"Hi, I'm Mike."

Quickly recovering my composure, I shook his hand, and we joined the group heading into the cabin. The guys seemed to be very much at ease with each other, so I guessed the trip from the airport had been a good ice-breaker. My interest in Mike, though, dominated my mind. In spite of his small stature, he was a strikingly good looking man. Dark reddish-brown hair, a sharp squared jaw line and the shoulders and chest of an athlete. He was a stud. This guy must really have some stories to tell, but would he be willing to share them with me or this group of strangers.

My new-found professionalism took over, and I got busy offering refreshments and otherwise making everyone comfortable in the lounge.

Dad took over and introduced each of us and the role we would play in their week-long session. While this was going on, Russ had driven the Suburban up to the bunkhouse by way of a back road in order to unload the guys' carefully name-tagged gear.

Dad's talk went on for about an hour at which point he asked me and Jack to escort the group up to the bunkhouse. The short walk along the shore would also give everyone an idea of just how beautiful the place was. By the time we arrived, Russ had each man's bags placed in front of his sleeping area, so there would be no confusion about who slept where.

While Jack proudly showed the guys all the amenities, Russ and I got busy setting up for the evening meal. It was simple comfort food – fried chicken, scalloped potatoes and a spinach salad. Since everyone was kind of tired after their trip, thankfully everything went off without a hitch. Tomorrow, the program would get going, and I would probably not have much contact with the guys until meal times and later if they needed any "help" with PROSAGE.

By 11:00 pm, everyone had gone to bed, and Jack and I could finally have some time together. We were too tired to be horny, but just needed each other's warm body to hold. It had been a long day, and the week had just started. As we settled into our favorite tangle of limbs, the days' events suddenly came to my mind in a rush, and I could no longer control my snickering. It was contagious.

Jack turned his face to mine and choking back laughter, said, "Ok Snow White, you've met your first dwarf, now go to sleep."

Thirteen

"Ok, so I didn't give you all the details regarding our guests. It wasn't secrecy, I just didn't want you to form any opinions about the guys before you met them."

It was Dad responding to my asking why he kept the unusual nature of Mike from me.

"I'm cool with everybody, Dad. He just took me by surprise. Mike seems to be a very likeable guy, and I think, along with all the rest, we'll have a good week."

It was Monday morning, and the day's activities would be getting started right after breakfast. I had awakened early and gone up to the cabin to talk with Dad. Feeling better after our conversation, I headed back up to the bunkhouse to greet my guests.

Today, each man would meet with Dad for an hour's orientation. The program would be described to them in detail, and they would be issued their personal PROSAGE kit. Jack had set up appointments for their welcoming massage sessions and tour of the gym facility. Bruce and Russ had gone into the village for some additional supplies. I had some free time before setting up for lunch and decided to take a walk back up to my favorite rock. Gathering up my towel and water bottle, I set out along the shore.

The day was perfect for a little sunbathing and relaxation. When I arrived at the rock, I was surprised to find Marc stretched out on my favorite spot. He had never shown much interest in the natural features of the lake, so this took me slightly aback. He was wearing a red Speedo, which barely covered his tight little ass.

Resting on his stomach, facing away from me, my presence was concealed from his view.

All kinds of lascivious thoughts raced through my mind as I took in the sight, transferring themselves to my groin, which responded in its usual manner, clouding my judgment. I announced my arrival by purposely dropping my water bottle. He awoke with a start and quickly turned to face me.

Smiling, he said in his slightly French accented way, "*Allo*, Donny. *Ca va?*"

I responded in my mid-western accented French: "*Va bien merci.*"

He corrected me, "*Je vais bien, merci.*"

This was the first time we had a chance to just have a light conversation since arriving at the cabin. I liked Marc, but since he had been my teacher and was a good friend to my dad, we had a slight barrier to overcome.

Sitting up and assuming a yoga-like position with legs crossed before him, he continued, "It's nice to take a break on such a beautiful day. Do you come up to this rock often?"

My eyes were traveling down his torso, taking in all the details of his impressive chest hair pattern, stopping at the point where the black mat disappeared beneath the thin cloth of his Speedo.

"Donny? Ah! You are finding my chest hair of interest. This is not strange since you have none at all. Don't be embarrassed. Many men and women have found it fascinating," and then adding with a smile, "Or perhaps it is my new Speedo that has caught your attention."

At this point, I became tongue-tied and could only stammer out a weak-voiced "Sorry Marc, I … I … was just lost in thought for a moment."

We were quiet for a few moments, and then I got up the courage to continue, "Actually Marc I do find your hair pattern interesting. It forms such a perfect T, covering your upper chest; narrowing as it trails down over your belly and on to." I stopped short of mentioning his now bulging pouch.

Waiting for a response gave me a few moments of agony. Suddenly, to my happy surprise, Marc reached out and took both my hands in his and drawing them to his chest said, "Go ahead, indulge yourself, feel the softness, I know you want to very badly, and I really find it flattering whenever someone cares to touch me there."

He freed my hands, and I tentatively ran my fingers through the thick black fur, across his faintly muscular pectorals, lightly touching the small pink nipples hidden there in the matte, giving each one a gentle pinch, then down the center of his chest to a point just beneath his navel. I was trembling with a combination of lust; fear and expectation as my fingers barely brushed the waistband of his Speedo, wanting to go beneath the covering but not daring to.

My own stiffness was painfully caught inside my briefs, and I squirmed around until it was pointing straight up my belly. Marc caught my discomfort and laughed, "Donny, relax, I know you are stimulated, as am I, it is quite natural and not important. We have just shared a nice moment of intimacy between two people who very much like one another, and it is not more than that. To me, the human body is like a piece of fine artwork and should be admired and enjoyed by all lovers of beauty. I have known you since you were a little boy, and you are like a son to me. If I could make you happy by letting you explore my magnificent chest," and here he smiled, "so be it. You are not the first man or woman to have done so and probably will not be the last."

Sweat was pouring off my brow, a combination of the day's heat and the crazy-wild thing Marc had just allowed me to do. It was

157

clear to me that nothing further was going to happen, so I rose, picking up my water bottle and towel in preparation to get on back to the bunkhouse. "See you back at the cabin, Marc ... and thanks."

In response, he gave me a little wave of his hand and blew me a kiss. What an unusual guy he was. *Vive la France!*

Later that afternoon, as I passed by the cabin, Dad called to me from the deck.

"Don, I need a few minutes with you. You look like you could use a rest anyway."

Little did he know. I was still somewhat shaken by my earlier visit with Marc. Pouring myself a glass of iced tea, I joined Dad at the picnic table.

Pushing aside the papers he was working on, he spoke in a serious tone. "Don, I need your help with a little problem I'm having with one of our subjects, Buddy. He is not responding favorably to my attempts to get at the root of his problem. This morning I introduced him to the PROSAGE therapy with as much patience as I can afford to allow, yet he seems almost frightened to accept the help he needs. It is possible that he is intimidated by my being a doctor and equates me with the callousness of a hospital experience. He may also attach some negative homoerotic overtones to the anal aspects of PROSAGE. Would you be willing to undertake a little experiment for me?"

The image of Buddy, young, good-looking, athletic and studly popped into my mind.

"Sure. What do you have in mind?"

"It seems that each time I try to get him to relax enough to introduce the PROSAGE, he tightens up, and no amount of coaxing seemed to help. He may respond better to a young non-medical guy like you helping him to accept the PROSAGE therapy. He is after all, a pre-med student and is going to have to get over his squeamishness about such things. What I propose is that you spend some time alone with him in the privacy of your room. Watch some sports – maybe soccer, that's his game. Check the ESPN schedule. Jack has already agreed to spend the next night or two back here at the cabin. I don't care what you have to do or how you do it but try to get the guy to relax. I will give you a porn video that should stimulate some interest."

Waiting for my response, he gave me a smile and added, "I don't think you'll find this task too unpleasant."

I must have been blushing scarlet as I left the deck and headed up to the bunkhouse. Of course, Dad was right. Under most circumstances, what gay guy wouldn't jump at the chance to try to get a straight guy excited enough to display a hard-on in front of him. Still, something about this request was causing me to be very uncomfortable. Why had Jack agreed to Dad's request that he leave me for a night or two. I wanted to think that he had protested and would never give me up that easily. The feeling that I was being used by Dad and Jack just wouldn't go away. I had to talk to Jack. I found him cleaning up after a massage session.

"Dad wants me to try to coax a hard-on from Buddy. What's your take on this?" He looked a little flustered at my confrontational tone, maybe I hoped, a little guilty.

"Yeah, he brought it up to me this afternoon. I told him I didn't think it was a good idea. It would amount to having an unsolicited sexual move put on him by another guy, and it might set him back for who knows how long, but we finally agreed that for the sake of the program we'd ask you to help out. It would be a very delicate assignment for you if you agreed. Did you?"

"What could I say? To tell you the truth, I feel like I would be cheating on you if Buddy and I ended up having sex."

His expression softened and wrapping his big arms around me, he said, "Don't worry about that, I think we care for each other too much to let a little medical or psychological experiment get in the way. I won't try to make up your mind for you, but you might think of it as repaying your dad for all that he's given you over the years. This means a lot to him, and you mean a lot to me. Besides, it will give me an excuse to make it up to you. So there!"

I felt a little better about going ahead with my new duty after talking with Jack. It was after all, for the good of Dad's program, and I stood to benefit if it was successful. It was agreed that I would give it a try and invite Buddy to my room to catch that night's soccer game between Latvia and Bolivia. How exciting could that be? Maybe he would get bored, and we could get on with some other subjects, porn flicks for example.

Later that evening, after supper, and everyone had gone about their leisure activities, I found Buddy alone upstairs in the bunkroom. He seemed to be deeply engrossed in a copy of *Sports Illustrated* until he saw me approaching. Looking up and giving me a big smile at least made me feel welcome to his world.

"Just catching up on the big world of soccer, since I can't play anymore for awhile, I can at least enjoy the sport vicariously."

My plan was working even easier than I could have hoped for. He missed soccer, my TV would receive a satellite feed from ESPN, and there was a game going on right now.

"You're in luck my friend. Just so happens that there is a game tonight that I was planning to watch. You're welcome to come on down to my room and relax and enjoy the game with me."

"That's damn nice of you to ask. I accept."

Entering my room for the first time, he seemed impressed. "You've got nice digs down here, not that things aren't comfortable upstairs, but a whole lot more private." As he glanced around the room, a puzzled look came over his face as he saw that there was only one bed. "Don't you share this room with Jack?"

I calmly explained that yes, we are sharing but only on a temporary basis, so he can be here to help me out while the group was in residence. I also made it clear that Jack would not be spending the next two nights with me. This seemed to satisfy his curiosity. I closed the door *so as not to annoy the other residents*.

Planning ahead, I had removed the only chair in the room, so that there would be no place to sit but on the bed while watching the game. The stage was set.

As I predicted, the game sucked, and Buddy seemed to lose interest after the first hour. God knows, I had lost interest in the first two minutes. The time was not a total waste and had given me ample opportunity to check this guy out. Not bad stuff. He was about six-feet tall, not more than 170 lbs., close-cropped light brown hair, terrific legs and a very quiet, calm personality. It was hard to believe that this hunk could be impotent even with his sports injury, but maybe we could do something about that. I started out by asking him how life was around campus, are their lots of chicks available and so on. He seemed a little annoyed that I was asking about his social life but did open up a little bit.

"Campus life is just about what you would imagine. There are plenty of women available, but for the past two years, since my injury, I haven't been dating any of them. You can figure out why."

"Wow, that must be frustrating. I know if I don't shoot my load every day I'm like a caged tiger. Do you ever have wet dreams?" This question got his attention, and he opened up like a broken dam.

"If I could have a wet dream, I would be the happiest man on earth. Nothing ever happens. I sometimes think there must be a gallon of semen and sperm just waiting to be released, but no matter how hard I try to get my prick to do something, nothing works."

Looking very concerned, I appeared to be giving this problem some serious thought. "What happens when you watch a porn flick?"

"I don't have any pornography in my dorm room, and even if I did, there isn't enough privacy to enjoy it."

Picking up the tape Dad had given me, I presented it to him saying: "Here's your chance. I haven't seen this one, but what the heck, it can't be that bad."

Before he could protest, I popped the tape into the VCR and hit play and shut the bedside lamp off, leaving the room in partial darkness. I was now in charge.

"Here, grab an extra pillow and prop yourself up against the headboard, let's see what this is all about. If you don't mind, I'm going to make myself comfy by getting rid of these work jeans."

Stripping down to my boxers felt good. My cock found its rightful place nestled on top of my balls as they hung loosely between my thighs. Buddy was already wearing just a T-shirt and a pair of nylon tennis shorts, so I didn't want to suggest, just yet, that he get anymore comfortable.

The video title came up on screen. *Sluts of the NFL.* A lot of hot locker-room action took place between three cheerleaders and an entire fictitious football team, sucking, fucking, pussy-eating, you name it. Out of the corner of my eye, I watched Buddy for any reaction. His eyes seemed glued to the action, and after the first few minutes, he moved his left hand to his crotch and was lightly massaging his soft cock through the thin fabric of his shorts, seeming to forget that I was there just two feet away from him. In the dim light, I could see beads of sweat forming on his forehead. He was getting something out of this porn but no sign of an erection. After about twenty minutes, the video suddenly segued to another.

This time, there was an image of a large shower stall and a male figure barely visible in the steam. Another male enters the stall and immediately starts applying soap to his body while engaging the other in conversation. Bending down to pick up a dropped bottle of body wash, we get a good view of his nice little ass.

Wait a minute! That's my fuckin' ass! Holy shit! It's a video of me and Bruce! What the hell is going on here? Somehow, Dad had secretly caught us on tape. I knew what was coming next but could only sit paralyzed as I watched myself sucking Bruce's cock. I slowly

161

looked toward Buddy to see what his reaction to this man-on-man was. He was intently staring at the screen, his hand definitely moving more aggressively on his crotch.

Suddenly, he turned to me and with a look of utter disbelief he gasped, "Sheeeeit, Donny, that's you, and the other guy is Bruce! You're a queer?"

"No, no, Buddy, I'm as surprised as you are – I didn't know about this video, please believe me."

"Hey, I'm cool with gay, don't get me wrong, but I just never would have guessed."

"Look, I just happen to like giving another guy some pleasure. Call it what you like. Hey, relax, we might as well watch the rest of the show. Who knows, I may have a new career choice as a porn star." He laughed self consciously, but continued to gaze at the action unfolding in the shower.

I glanced down to his groin and swear I saw a hint of a hard-on. He quickly tried to cover it, but I decided to go for it; moving a little closer and slowly reaching out to rest my hand on top of his. Figuring a little reassurance might lead the way, I softly said, "Remember, Buddy, I am here to help you in any way that I can. Sometimes a guy just needs a little assistance to get his libido cranked up. I think I can do that if you'll trust me."

He let out a soft moan and pulled his hand away, leaving me to explore freely what could only be described as the beginning of a full world class boner. As the action unfolded on the screen, he stretched out flat on the bed, his head slightly elevated on the pillow, hands to his sides. I slowly drew down the waistband of his shorts, exposing his uncut jewel to my gaze. His erection had softened a little, probably out of nervousness and from the shock of his recent discovery, but I was determined to get things going again. Pulling up his sweat-soaked shirt, I lowered my face to his hairless chest, my tongue snaked out to his right nipple, lightly flicking the pink little nub, causing it to stiffen to a sharp point. This brought on another soft gasp and a slight tremor as my tongue worked its way south toward his deeply indented navel. I thrust the tip into its depth, leaving a pool of saliva as I further traveled toward my goal. My nose reached the warmth of his golden brown bush; the distinctive aroma of a fragrant and sweaty man-crotch urging me on. Encountering no resistance, my tongue found its way to that wonderful spot between scrotum and thigh where the scent of a male is most intensely concentrated into a mix of musk and sweetness.

I was drunk with lust as my hand caressed his tightened ball sac, rolling his pretty little nuts between my fingers. Pressing my lips to the delicate unsheathed cockhead, I consumed the entire shaft in one long suck. His body arched from the bed, and I quickly slipped my hand under his tight little ass cheeks, positioning my index finger at the rim of his virgin pucker, gently stroking its tight folds. His soft moans told me I had struck gold.

He squirmed and thrusted, sending his now rock-hard cock deeper into my throat until suddenly, he stopped, let out a deep "Ohhhhhh fuck!" and filled my waiting mouth with his pungent, steaming load. I swallowed deeply, enjoying the incredible taste of his long dormant spunk as it flowed onto my tongue. This was gourmet quality, and I now considered myself somewhat of a connoisseur in that department.

Brilliant sunlight awakened me. Glancing first to my left, I was happy to see Buddy, sound asleep, stretched out in almost the same position he was last night, shirt pulled up around his armpits, shorts down to his knees and what appeared to be a nice little pool of dried cum decorating his pubes. The now soft cock a far cry from its stiffened size, which was almost a twin of my own. After he shot his miraculous load, sleep must have taken over right away. Even though I hadn't cum, I was as exhausted as he was. One thing was for sure – his impotence might be a thing of the past, at least for now. I wondered how he would handle it. Even more interesting was going to be how Dad would explain the video to me and Bruce.

At my touch to his arm, Buddy awoke with a start. Looking down at his nearly naked body, and then at me, he burst out laughing.

"You little shit. How the hell did you do it! I shot a load from a hard cock for the first time in over two years. I know I didn't dream it because here's the proof," pointing to the dried cum spot tangled in his pubic hair. "How the hell am I going to explain it to Dr. Crowley."

"Let's worry about that after breakfast. Right now, the rest of the guys are in the dining room, and I'm neglecting my duties." As an afterthought, I added, "If you don't want everyone to know where you slept last night, slip out the side kitchen door and go around to the front. Everyone will think you just got up early for a jog."

"Cool idea. Thanks Don … for everything."

Fourteen

The new day's activities were not scheduled to begin for another hour, so I took the opportunity to run up to the cabin and report my success to Dad.

"Hey, how did things go last night?"

He was sitting at his desk working on the laptop. Continuing to enter some data and trying hard not to seem too eager to hear my story, he finally finished up. Leaning forward in his chair, he asked, in almost a whisper: "Did it work? I mean the soccer on TV, did you … aaah … use the video?"

"Dad please don't try to sound so innocent. You knew what was on that tape, and you knew I would probably run it." For the first time in my life, I saw my dad blush.

"Are you pissed off at me? If so, I am sorry for embarrassing you in front of a stranger, but I had a hunch that it would take something pretty strong to break through Buddy's insecurity about sex. If the *NFL Sluts* didn't work, the action between you and Bruce might. Did it?"

"Oh sure it worked, but how could you take advantage of me, your son, and Bruce, one of your best friends? If it hadn't worked and Buddy was totally turned off by seeing me sucking a guy's dick, things could have turned nasty. You really gambled on that one, Dad."

He looked sincerely sorry for the way he had handled things and gave me his promise never to do any videotaping without my knowledge. Then, almost as an afterthought he took me in his arms, giving me a genuine show of affection we rarely shared. Looking me square in the eye he let loose, "Donny, I've felt that you were gay for years, and now I've got a confession to make. My life is more complicated than you would ever guess. I love your mother very much, but I haven't felt passion for her in many years. When the opportunity presented itself to form this very private men's group with Bruce, Jack, Russ and Marc, I looked at it as a form of escape from the boredom of home life and the stress of my practice. Over the years, the guys and I experimented sexually with each other. Gradually, it turned into a 'research' project related to my work in developing PROSAGE. More and more, I realized that the company of men and the sexual opportunities it offered was what I really craved. Your maturity after turning eighteen allowed me the chance to introduce you to this, my other life. Watching you closely through the years had convinced me that you were probably homosexually oriented. Since arriving at Morningwood, you've passed a few of my tests. The first was the prostate exam. Believe me, my patients don't get that thorough treatment. The second came purely by accident when you caught me exposed in bed and you gently played with my cock. Trust me, I had a hell of a hard time pretending to be asleep and not getting a hard-on."

The ice was broken. We both knew this was needed badly. Our relationship could go on to a new level, not merely father and son but best friends and confidants.

I gave him a full rundown of the night's action, not sparing any details. He was visibly excited as my tale unfolded. There was no point in trying to hide the fact that I was gay, he knew that for sure just from catching the action on the video.

"I am so grateful to you son and relieved to hear that my theory proved to be correct and that Buddy's orgasm is evidence that there is no physical problem preventing him from having the pleasure of a sex life. The only problem that might surface is if I suggest to Buddy that he could be gay. Clearly, he associates the PROSAGE being inserted into his rear end with being homosexual. His denial prevents him from accepting that therapy. The success of PROSAGE hinges on it being acceptable to men whether they are gay or straight. Oh, by the way, that video was a spur of the moment idea. When you headed into the shower after Bruce, I gambled that something might happen, so I activated the security camera. The next morning, I simply edited the *Sluts* video to include your action. Just a hunch that paid off."

I tried to put on my best "hurt" look. "You can't blame me for feeling just a little bit used, though I guess in light of all that's happened, it's no big deal. Your son is a cock sucker. If you're cool with that then it's fine with me."

Well, there's one bridge crossed. No use pretending I'm anything but what I am, at least in front of Dad. But what's up with Dad? This is a side of him I never would have suspected. Morningwood seemed to hold a shit-load of secrets. I felt like I was a player in a kinky M-rated video game.

Later that evening, as I was cleaning up the dinner mess, raucous laughter came pouring out from the TV lounge. Mike's high pitched voice, somewhat akin to a *South Park* kid's was dominating the conversation. Finishing up my chores, I wandered over to see what the hell was so funny. It was Mike of course, telling about some of his adventures in porn.

"... so there I was, stark naked and lubed up for my assault on Mount Polly Plumppe. This broad weighed in at over 300 lbs, to my 120. The scene was for me to come running into the room, take a flying leap like a circus acrobat and land smack on top of Polly, thrusting my ten inches into her pussy."

At the mention of Mike's unusual penis size, an appreciative and envious "woooo" came out of the whole group.

"We were trying a new lube that claimed to provide 'The Slickest Slide for a Super Ride.' Off I went, charging through the door, leaping for my target. In mid-flight, I realized I was slightly off center and tried to correct, but no luck. As I braced myself for a landing, my right arm slipped down her colossal gut and right into the depths of pussy land. The impact was so strong and the suction so great that as my belly slid off to the side, my arm stayed embedded in her cunt, finally exiting with a loud sucking sound as I hit the floor. She was screaming every 'fuck' word she could find, the crew was in hysterics, and I was suffering a sprained wrist."

There was no doubt that Mike would have a tough time topping that tale. But, he probably would try.

It had been a long day, and I headed for my room, not even caring that I would be without my sweet man, Jack, for a second night. We would have plenty of time to catch up tomorrow. As soon as my head hit the pillow, the faint scent Buddy had left, hit my nostrils. It was enough to inspire a jerk-off but before I could work up a good hard-on, sleep took over.

A light tapping on my door roused me from my deep sleep. Glancing at my bedside clock I could see that it was 11:15 pm. Who the hell was messing with me now? I groggily asked who it was.

"It's Herman. Can I see you for a few minutes?"

What could I say? It was my duty to be there if any of the guys needed anything.

"Come on in, Herman. What's up?"

He quietly entered the room and not seeing anywhere to sit, asked if he could join me on the bed. Again, what could I say, but sure? The little bit of glow from my nightlight was enough for me to make out his features. I hadn't really paid much attention to him since the program had started. For a sixty-six-year-old guy, he was in pretty good shape. Possessing a full head of silver-gray hair and only a slightly paunchy mid-section gave him the appearance of a man who took good care of himself. I asked him how things were going, and he assured me

166

that the place was great and he had high hopes of getting the help he needed. But there was a slight problem with the PROSAGE device.

"And what might that problem be?" I cautiously inquired.

"Tonight, I decided that I should go solo with the device and did all the right things with the sheath and condom and lube, just as Dr. Crowley had instructed. As you may know, I am very anally oriented, so it should have been a cinch for me to slip it up my ass and activate the motor. What I hadn't considered is the problem I have with my back. Due to an old work-related injury, I can't bend easily at the waist. Reaching back there to use the thing proved to be next to impossible. I'm so used to my wife, Martha doing the work for me. Listening to Mike's wild stories tonight got me kinda horny, and I really need to get some relief, or I won't be able to sleep. I really hate to ask another guy to do this for me, but the doctor encouraged us to seek your help if we needed it."

It didn't take me long to figure out that the sooner he got his rocks off, the sooner I could get back to sleep.

"Tell you what, Herman, I am here to help out any way I can. Why don't you drop your drawers and lay back on the bed, and I'll see what I can do."

He quickly stripped down while I got the PROSAGE ready for action. Spreading a towel under his ass, I gently prepared him with a generous dollop of KY, making sure there was enough lube to do the job comfortably. The moment the tip of my gloved finger met his hole, he started to get a sizeable erection. Taking that as a good sign, I gently introduced the PROSAGE until I figured it was just about at the right spot to start the pulse. Bingo! He let out a contented sigh and started a humping motion that resulted in the PROSAGE going in to the hilt. He gripped his short but thick cock and jerked it frantically. In just a few minutes, a gurgling sound from deep in his throat signaled that the end was near. I gave the PROSAGE a few gentle thrusts, and that took him over the top.

"Aaaaah, Martha, don't stop, you're the best, Martha … here it comes …"

And there it came. Lots of it. After a respectable few minutes had passed, I removed the device and handed him a towel to clean up with. He needed it. This guy had shot a load worthy of a teen-ager.

He thanked me profusely, apologized for the reference to his wife, and as he left the room, paused in the doorway and with a smile said, "I don't suppose you make house calls."

The next morning, I trotted up to the cabin to report my activity to Dad.

"Hey Dad, what is tall and gray and comes in quarts?" Before he could answer my dumb riddle, I gave him the answer: "Herman!"

Fifteen

Later that afternoon, Jack returned to our little love nest. Not wanting to keep any secrets from the man I cared so much for, I gave him a rundown of the past two days events, including Dad's very personal confession to me. He was very relieved that Dad had come out to me, but was only mildly amused with the story of the video.

"Damn, I hope he doesn't erase that one. I want to give it my critique! It's been a year or more since Bruce and I swapped cum loads. How does he compare to me?"

"I thought you said you never had sex with Bruce, but wouldn't mind trying him out."

"Well, I held back that little piece of information, and for that, I am truly sorry. Besides you weren't ready to hear that little tidbit."

"You're forgiven, and just for your information, you are better than Bruce, and I don't intend to let you forget it. Now, I want you naked and spread-eagled on your belly in two minutes or else you might get punished instead of rewarded for your honesty."

"Hmmm … do I have a choice?"

"Not tonight. I'm calling the shots, and your hot muscleman ass is mine."

Letting Jack have a little time to think about what I might have in mind for him allowed me to take a quick shower. When I re-entered the room, the sight of his beautiful, muscular backside met my eyes. How lucky I was to have found a man who was so warm, sexy and loveable. At that moment, I wanted nothing else but to give him every ounce of pleasure my hungry mouth was capable of delivering.

Straddling his legs, the length of his body stretched out before me. The contented look on his face drove me on. Lowering myself until my lips touched the back of his thighs, my tongue danced lightly over the finely fur-dusted surface. Leaning forward, I approached my destination, the point where balls meet ass cheeks. Gently reaching under his belly, I grasped his semi-hard cock and pulled it back so that both cock and balls were now at my disposal. Flicking my tongue on the delicate membrane connecting the foreskin to the glans caused him to thrust his hips downward with the intensity of the sensation. Moving upward, my wandering tongue found its way into the warmth of his crevice, not stopping until reaching its ultimate goal, the crinkled pink-brown folds of his butt hole. The strangeness of what I was about to do gave me only fleeting concern. A whole new world of taste and scent was opened up to me at that point. He was so fresh and clean, with just a hint that he had earlier showered. Even if he hadn't, at that moment it would not have mattered. I dived in with all the enthusiasm of a gourmet trying an exotic dish for the first time. He bucked and squirmed as my tongue penetrated his most secret place, and I knew we both were enjoying the new and exquisite intimacy of the moment.

"Oooh ... Donny ... take me, baby, my ass is yours," he pleaded.

Slipping on a condom, I lubed up in preparation for my first man-fuck. The excitement over what I was about to experience almost caused me to shoot prematurely. Hardly daring to touch myself, I pressed down, rubbing my slick rod back and forth in the hot valley between Jack's cheeks. He reached back and grasping my cock, pointed it to his entrance. Slowly, I pressed forward, sliding easily into the depths of his ass.

"Ohh sweet baby ..." was all I could say as I experienced my lover's incredible tightness and heat. The massaging of his prostate was causing a rapid series of low pitched moans to come from deep in his chest. We were both near the end as he rose up on his knees and I plunged even deeper, reaching around and grasping his stiff cock, I swiftly jacked him in time with my thrusts, bringing us both to a gut wrenching climax.

Totally spent, we collapsed in a sweat-soaked heap. His final words to me before we both fell into a deep, blissful sleep were, "If ever there was an angel sent from heaven for the sole purpose of making another man happy, he has to be you. Thanks for choosing me."

Sixteen

The phone call had come at 2:00 am, which was 5:00 pm in Tokyo. It was Mr. Yamamoto the head of R&D at Fujitoy Enterprises, Ltd.

The news was not good. The factory in Osaka was reporting some very strange problems with the PROSAGE I's motor relays.

During routine testing for endurance, it was discovered that after one hour of continuous use, the little control mechanisms, the ones that regulate speed and intensity of the pulsing action were failing at an alarming rate. The devices would suddenly go completely berserk, flexing and bending and vibrating with sufficient force as to cause injury to the user. Furthermore, the batteries were overheating and leaking. Production had to cease immediately and would remain so until the problems could be worked out. No shipment would be made until further notice.

We were roused from our deep sleep by the insistent beeping of the intercom line. It was Dad. He wanted us up to the cabin ASAP for a conference.

As Jack and I made our way toward the meeting, a cold wind came in off the lake bringing with it a light drizzle. Not even the weather would help ease our anxieties this early morning.

Everyone was gathered around the dining table. Coffee cups had been set out, and Marc was just pouring the first round. Dad was trying to be as upbeat as possible.

"Hey guys, at least the damn things didn't explode in someone's butt. Better we find out these defects before distribution."

Russ spoke up, "We better gather up all the units we have on hand and remove the batteries. At least the things can be used as a simple dildo."

Dad brightened a bit, "Of course they can. I will simply explain to our guests that there has been a minor problem with the power supplies, nothing to worry about. They will receive replacement units as soon as they arrive from overseas."

Everyone agreed that they didn't have much choice. On Saturday, the last day of the program, everyone gathered in the bunkhouse lounge for a discussion of the program. Dad didn't want to characterize it as a group therapy session but more as a sharing of thoughts on the program.

We were lucky that all of our guests were extremely good natured about the whole thing. Almost to a man, they had experienced the improvement in their performance that they had come here for.

Buddy was the most enthusiastic about his success, giving me the benefit of a sly little wink as he thanked everyone for all the help he had received.

Mike had re-discovered sex as a personal gift to himself. For so many years he had performed acts in order to gratify his audience, never really enjoying a good old fashioned orgasm in private. Now, thanks to Dad's counseling, the PROSAGE I and Jack's very professional massages, he was a new man. Herman was likewise rejuvenated thanks to the wonders of PROSAGE though he did think he might have to take an extra dose of his arthritis meds whenever Martha wasn't in the mood to help. Later, he surreptitiously slipped me a card with his private cell phone number, whispering an invitation to call him whenever I was in town. I thought damn, I must be good.

Reginald was a more difficult case to crack. Apparently there was a strong relationship between the rise and fall of the stock market and his ability to perform in the sack. When his particular portfolios were not doing well, as they hadn't for about three years, he was impotent. This would take more than PROSAGE to cure. On the other hand, he did enjoy his newly discovered erogenous zones.

Bernie decided that he would entice his wife back into his life by introducing her to the wonders of the PROSAGE I. He figured she and her girlfriend were probably using a dildo anyway, so why not give her the best. He kind of liked what it did for him, too. Louis was a lost cause. He got a thrill out of using the PROSAGE but only when looking at the Animal Channel. Definitely a case for a psychiatrist.

Everyone was assured that their replacement devices would be shipped as soon as possible once the glitch had been resolved.

Russ would be taking the group back to town to meet their flights quite early Sunday morning, so we all decided to hit the sack at a reasonable hour. For me, that was now. I needed to make up for lost time with my beloved Jack. After helping Russ get the guy's gear ready for loading into the Suburban, we grabbed a bottle of Merlot and two glasses from the bar and headed to my room for a little R&R.

"Now, about that video," and he grabbed the remote.

When it got to the part where I was on my knees spreading Bruce's cheeks, I glanced down to see Jack's reaction. He was already sleeping like a baby. Returning my attention to the screen, what I had not seen then, but saw now was the big, knowing smile on Bruce's face as he turned around and presented his glorious manhood to my very willing lips. I rewound the tape, hit the record button and slept well that night.

Seventeen

The somewhat disappointing news of the PROSAGE problem did little to ruin the convivial mood as each of our guests said their goodbyes and headed home. As for the rest of us, it was relief time. We had all busted our butts to pull this thing off, and it wasn't a total loss. After all, I had accomplished my goal of seducing my "uncles," discovered my anal "happy place," fell in love with Jack and discovered that my dad was just as gay as I was. Whatever the summer had in store, it would have a tough time beating this spring.

Dad called for a family meeting up at the cabin. We all knew it would concern the failure of PROSAGE and the future of the project.

"I've made a few calls, and the consensus is that PROSAGE will have to undergo major re-testing and modifications before we can even consider continuing the therapy program. Meanwhile, we all can go about our business. Of course, Morningwood will be available for all of you to use as you see fit." Glancing in my direction, he continued, "My son and I have really gotten to know each other these past weeks, and I think you all know what I mean."

To my surprise, everyone smiled and raised their beers in an air toast. Jack appeared at my side and taking me into his arms, gave me a big wet kiss on the lips.

"Donny and I have something to announce. We've also gotten to know each other, and if I ever had any doubts about how I felt towards this guy they were dispelled by the happy times we've shared together at this beautiful place. I'm going to do everything in my power to make him happy for as long as he'll have me."

The group broke into applause, and with that vote of approval, Jack and I made a quick exit, heading back up to the bunkhouse and what was now "our" queen size bed.

Stretching out, hands folded behind his head, my beautiful man just smiled and said in his sexiest deep-voiced manner:

"I'm not moving a muscle, lover. You're going to have to work for it this afternoon."

I was more than ready for that challenge and straddled his hefty chest, slowly unbuttoning his flannel shirt, licking a trail down his furry torso as I went.

Reaching the waistband of his jeans, I softly nuzzled the hairy path as it entered the treasure spot below. Slowly lowering the zipper, I was happy to see he hadn't bothered to wear any cumbersome jockeys, and I could plunge straight to my target, which was now rising to meet my hot and expectant lips. Damn, he smelled and tasted like the sweetest honey on earth, and that was enough for me to forget about the banquet and head right for the dessert.

Morning came way too early, but being awakened by a handsome stud wearing nothing but a smile was my idea of heaven, but even heaven can be improved on if the stud is holding a nice hot cup of coffee as well.

"Rise and shine sunshine ... we've got some talking to do."

His demeanor suggested something good but serious was coming. I quickly got into an upright position suitable for accepting the welcoming cup and whatever else was about to be presented to me. "Listen carefully to what I have to say and don't jump to any wild conclusions. Last night I lay awake thinking about the bad news about PROSAGE. While I was mulling over how much work and money we put into this place and how now it would just sit here not benefiting anyone an idea hit me like a barbell gone wild. Why couldn't you and I work out a deal with your dad and the others to develop a spa-type get-away place for guys into heavy duty workouts along with some very relaxing activities? It's all here. All we have to do is organize it. I have a ready made customer base in my gym. We could even recruit my manager, John, to spend some time up here whenever I had to be taking care of business in town."

Jack's enthusiasm was infectious, but the mention of John's name caused me to momentarily freeze up. So many what-ifs popped into my head that my reaction was probably more subdued than he expected, but I agreed that it was an idea with exciting possibilities and that we should talk it over with the guys at breakfast.

My first concern was how John would react to meeting me again under some pretty powerful circumstances. You don't easily forget a buddy who so recently had provided head to you anytime you wanted it. Would he expect those favors again? Would I be able to resist the temptation of his incredibly sexy body and tasty salami?

My love for Jack should be enough to prevent any of this from happening. I hoped.

They bought it! Dad was particularly interested in the financial angle since it would quickly replace the lost revenue from PROSAGE. I caught Bruce licking his lips at the suggestion of muscle boys strutting their stuff around the place. The others just seemed to be content with putting the place on a money-making basis. So Jack's Jym @ Morningwood was born.

Eighteen

The adrenaline rush I experienced when Jack had revealed his plan for Morningwood was reignited as we lay in each others arms that evening. The peacefulness went unbroken now that we had the bunkhouse all to ourselves. This was going to be one of the last few nights we would have together before heading back to the city and the uncertainty of our new adventure. We made the best of it. The gentle stroking of Jack's big, yet soft hands covered every inch of my willing body. The light flicking of his tongue on my stiffening nips was followed by a slow progression down my chest, stopping briefly to thoroughly lave my navel before descending toward its target, my now throbbing cockhead. His hot mouth engulfed me all the way to my tightening balls, and I was in heaven again. The swirling of his tongue as he plunged and withdrew drove me over the edge in far less time than I would have liked. He was rewarded with a gush of my boy-cum that caused me to scream out in sheer ecstasy as shot after shot flooded his throat.

Raising his head, our eyes met. "Damn … sweetheart, that was the best you ever gave me."

Throwing my arms around him, I pulled him to me and our lips joined in a deep, hot tongue-kiss. The flavor of my own cum only made it better. I was on fire and had to return the favor before sleep grabbed us both.

My lover knew what I wanted when I stretched out on my belly and raised my hot little ass in the air. He wasted no time in getting me ready for the fucking I wanted so badly. His hot wet tongue thoroughly prepared me for the delicious probing of his finger. The gentle stroking of my prostate drove me nuts, and I begged him to replace it with his long hard cock. He knew all the moves that made the most of a butt-fuck. Time after time, he would get right up to the brink of orgasm, stopping at just the right moment so as to prolong our pleasure. I finally could not resist giving him those final cock-squeezing clenches of my ass muscles that I knew would send him over the moon. It worked, and we fell into a steaming, sweat-soaked heap. Immediately, well earned sleep took over.

It was Monday morning. At breakfast, Dad suggested we spend the day tidying up the place in preparation for our departure on Tuesday. I was cursing the fact that there was only one vehicle. It would have been nice to let the others go ahead. Jack and I could have stayed behind to do the clean-up. Of course how much work would have gotten done is up for speculation.

The trip back was uneventful. So much had changed in the last few weeks. The revelations about Dad and the other guys, the sex-fun I had, and finally discovering the miracle of falling in love with my beautiful man, Jack. It was almost too much for my young inexperienced brain to handle. Almost. I had grown up fast and was eager to continue my education in the real facts of life.

The hardest part of going home would be my separation from Jack. Some very sensitive negotiating lay ahead if we were to spend enough time together. How would Mom react if I were to suggest moving in with Jack? Dad would be no problem since he was encouraging our relationship.

That evening at home, he called me into his basement study for a little man-to-man talk.

"Donny, I am making things easy for you. I've already discussed with your mom the plan to join up with Jack in operating the cabin as a sports spa. She's very excited for both of you and thinks it would be a wonderful way for you to get some business experience before starting college in the fall. Believe it or not she actually is in favor of you staying with Jack so that you can work on the project together full time."

I never felt so much love and admiration for my father than I did at that moment.

A quick call to Jack brought an immediate invitation to pack my necessities and get on over to his place ASAP. Mom was a little disappointed that I wasn't at least staying a few days to be with her, but understood my excitement. After all, I was still her "little boy."

My Sebring convertible looked even better after our prolonged separation. I loaded my gym bag, packed with a wad of shorts and T-shirts, my shaving gear and my favorite bottle of jerk-off lube. That would have a better use for now on. Top down, I headed out for my new love's townhouse. The anticipation of what was to come made me light-headed, and I nearly ran a red light before coming down to earth.

Jack met me at the door looking sexy as ever in his favorite black silk boxers and nothing else. The minute the door was closed we fell into an embrace, him smothering my face with kisses, which I passionately returned.

He had prepared a welcoming fire and a low table set with two glasses and a bottle of champagne chilling in a silver bucket. "That fireplace isn't crackling just for effect. I wanted it warm enough in here, so I could strip you out of those clothes, and we could discuss our future in comfort."

I couldn't argue with that, so in a flash I was naked and in his arms on the thick llama fur rug that lay welcoming before the hearth. My life had become a succession of beautiful moments ever since that first night alone with Jack at the cabin.

We finished the wine and barely had the strength to make it up the stairs to bed. I lay awake for a few moments, thoughts of what tomorrow would bring when I was re-united with John Rocco at the gym. It didn't really matter anymore what his reaction would be. I felt secure in my relationship with Jack and nothing John could say or do would change that. He was a thing of the past. I prayed Jack would see it that way.

We made the short drive to Jack's Jym, arriving just as John was unlocking the front door in preparation for the day's business. The look on his face was one of surprise mixed with puzzlement. Jack immediately introduced me, and John quickly recovered his composure and broke out into a big smile, slapping me on the back and exclaiming, "Donny, 'ol buddy … how the hell are ya? Damn, it's been a while. You're looking great."

Jack looked a little confused, but then quickly figured we knew each other from school.

"So you guys know each other. Good. That will make things go a lot easier for all of us. I hope you weren't rivals. We need team work around here."

He was smiling through all this, so I figured so far so good.

John continued the conversation: "Yeah, Donny and I were great pals throughout school, he was a big help in getting me through the tough times, what with my sports schedule conflicting with my study times. He was a super study-buddy and a great teacher. He really taught me a lot about how to relax. It made homework a lot easier to take."

After speaking those words, there was the faintest trace of a grin as he looked into my eyes. I didn't think I'd have a problem with John. The momentary rush of blood to my cock I dismissed as just a fleeting bout with lust. Considering that he was the first male I ever tasted in that way, he would be hard to forget. We all went into the office, and Jack started filling John in on our plan to offer one or two week work-out programs at Morningwood. John was enthused right off the bat, and he and Jack started figuring out a basic outline of activities. I could see that this was going to be a long day. The gym was starting to fill up with the early-risers. Who the hell wants to bust a gut at 7:00 am? Apparently, a lot of guys. Making my way around the gym seemed a good way to pass the time and familiarize myself with the operation. The heaviest weight I had carried was my book bag, so there was plenty to learn. The eye-candy wasn't bad, so I had to constantly remind myself that I was a married man now.

Bruce must have had a hand in designing the showers. No partitions here. Just one big tiled room with ten shower heads. A glass door led into a six-man steam room. Conveniently, the adjacent sauna offered a clear view of the shower room through a large glass panel. Better than TV I thought. Funny, when I had visited this place a few years ago none of this impressed me at all.

Moving on, I stopped for a smoothie at the snack bar, then back to the office. They were still at it, now working on a list of potential customers. I was eager to know how I would fit into the plan. I really didn't want to be just a housekeeper. A note to self – talk to Jack tonight about this. Was I feeling a tinge of jealousy over Jack's closeness to John?

My momentary depression was relieved when, sensing my approach, Jack looked up from the scattered papers on the table and with a big smile, blew me a kiss, gesturing that I should join him at his side. From that moment on, I knew that our love would continue to grow, my future would be bright and nothing would ever interfere with my happiness with Jack. After all, I was 19.

It's About Time
By Jay Barbera

My face must have lighted up like a harvest moon when I opened the front door on that Saturday morning and saw him standing on the front porch. We embraced platonically as do old friends, and I invited him in. Had it really been fifteen years since that first time? While making a pot of coffee, my mind shifted back to that time.

* * * * *

"Well, I've been thinking about doing things like that for years," I shyly admitted and sat back to wait for Scot, the kid next door, to continue with what he had been wanting to discuss with me. We were sitting in my recreation room where he had just confided in me about having homosexual fantasies. What the hell, lots of people have diversified sexual fantasies. So, why not assure him they're perfectly normal.

"Really?" he said while seemingly surprised and placed a half filled glass of soda on the end table. "But you seem so manly," the boy continued with a thoughtful look in his eyes and a smile on his lips. He snuggled into the opposite corner of the sofa to hear more.

I briefly scanned downward from the sandy-brown hair, over the eighteen-year-old's handsome face to the muscular shoulders, arms and chest that were bulging through a tight T-shirt that matched his blue eyes. The weight lifting he had been doing for the past four years had definitely paid off. "There's nothing unmanly about it," I rationalized as if being an expert on the subject. But I was quick to add, "Not that I've ever had sex with a guy. I just don't see anything wrong with it."

Obviously more than mildly interested in the conversation he had been wanting to broach with me for the past several months, Scot took another sip of soda, put the glass down again and said, "But, what if you try to approach a friend and he refuses? He might go around telling everyone." The kid glanced at the lump in my pants, saw that I noticed and shifted his eyes back to mine.

"Guess you just have to be careful about that," I said with a shrug. What a tight body he had! With some of my recurring fantasies returning, a plan started to develop in my perverted mind. This might just work out.

But I needed a little information. "Have you ever had a blow job, Scot?" I asked, that being something I had been wanting to give to a guy for years.

A gleam flashed across his eyes and quickly faded. Then he looked embarrassed while saying, "No." Scot picked up his glass of soda again. "I didn't have much time for dating in high school. And now that I'll be going to college in September, I'll probably have even less free time." He shot a glance at my lump again and smiled. Maybe he was thinking in the same groove as I was.

"A hand job from a girlfriend?" I pressed on.

He shook his head and said, "The few girls I did go out with were all geeks. One of them didn't even want to be kissed, and forget about feeling them up."

I was getting excited about the possibilities. "What kinds of sexual fantasies do you have?" My homosexual fantasies had been getting more and more diversified, but I was ten years his senior. And, apparently, the kid was a virgin.

Scot took another sip of soda and twirled the glass in one hand while seemingly mentally debating whether to say what he was thinking or not. After licking his upper lip, he lowered his gaze to the floor and said, "Um, well, I sometimes think about jerking ... a guy off." He paused and looked at me before adding something I hadn't been expecting. "Well ... a couple of times I thought about doing that to you, too." He closed his eyes while a bright blush covered his handsome, boyish face.

This might definitely work out. Ironically, one of my fantasies had been to give a young guy his first blow job. And he'd never had one. I had to take a chance. Considering what we were discussing, the worse he could do was refuse. "I wouldn't mind going that far with you, Scot." I watched a gleam of interest invade his eyes. "How about if we just jerk ourselves off in front of each other to see if we like it?" I hesitantly asked while watching his eyes for a reaction.

"You mean it," he asked with a slightly raspy voice before dropping his gaze to my lump again. Then he swallowed, possibly to moisten his parched throat. Seeing me nodding, Scot said, "Yeah. I'd like to try that. You mean like right here? Like now?"

Wondering if that question had been the manifestation of some last minute reluctance, I decided to ease off a bit. We were going to do something with each other that day, but I didn't want to rush him. "We can do it here if you really want to." Remembering the first hand job I got from a girl, I smiled and added, "It'll be a lot nicer than both of us kneeling in front of a toilet bowl."

Scot grunted a nervous laugh before dragging out the words, "Yeah, I guess so." He took a slow, deep breath, which caused the muscles in his chest to take on more definition, and boldly said, "I'm ready if you are." This time, there was determination in his voice.

Neither of us was hard when we unzipped our flies a few minutes later – both of us were nervous. Being almost ten years his senior, the onus was probably on me to move this virgin through the paces. So I took out my penis and just held it loosely. His smile told me everything was cool so far.

Scot took his cock out while gazing into my eyes. Grunting a shy laugh, he admitted, "There were times when I thought about what it would be like to watch you masturbating." Possibly unconsciously, he started to stroke his dick.

"Want to just watch each other for awhile?" I was already slowly stroking myself, and it was already half hard.

"Sure," he said while his unblinking eyes were gleaming brightly and his lips were curled into a smile. He started masturbating himself a little faster.

"Don't rush," I cautioned, not wanting him to cum too fast. And I didn't want to cum too fast either. I was hoping to get the chance to suck him off, and I had never done that before. There was the possibility that I would lose my nerve after popping my load, that time when a man's level of sexual arousal drops.

Agreeing with a nod, Scot slowed the pace of his pumping hand. He watched my shaft reach its full length while I watched his do the same. "This is awesome," he said while never taking his eyes from my cock.

Suspecting the time might be right, I asked, "Want me to do you for awhile?" I was dying to feel his cock. It was kind of funny. You can go through twenty-eight years of life without having touched anyone else's but your own. You can shake his hand, but you can't shake his cock.

Scot smiled thoughtfully for a few seconds while staring at the rigid dick in my hand. Then he said, "That'll be cool."

"Why don't you just lie back and let me do it?" When he did so, I looked at the Adonis who was stretched out on my sofa, waiting to be pleased. And I had to suppress a moan of anticipatory excitement while sitting alongside of his hip.

His youthful, six-inch cock felt warm in my hand. Although it seemed strange to be holding someone else's, I slowly masturbated Scot and heard him sigh. His pale-pink head brightened even more and his shaft twitched.

Within a half minute, we were a lot more relaxed and smiling at each other. Both of us realized this was okay, even though his muscular chest was rising and falling from breathing slightly faster and my heart was beating as rapidly as his probably was.

I continued doing that slowly, knowing that the longer it would take him to cum the first time the more he would ejaculate. Hopefully, that would convince him that a man can please another man, something I had only heard but hadn't been sure about.

But saliva was filling my mouth. I wanted to know what it was like to suck a cock and even feel it ejaculating into my mouth. I had often planned on tasting my own semen, but had always chickened out at the last moment. Doing it with another guy, however, seemed like an intensely erotic experience, and I was ready to go the whole nine yards.

Noticing I had slowed my pace, Scot lifted his head from the sofa's armrest, blinked his eyes open and smiled at the sight of my fully hard cock. He didn't need an invitation to reach for it. "I wanna do you, too," he said, and there wasn't a hint of shyness in his voice.

"Mmmm," I moaned encouragingly when he closed a hand around my glans and slid it down to the base of my cock. Within seconds, we were keeping up the same slow rhythm while smiling at each other. "I hope you're enjoying this as much as I am."

I ran the tip of a finger around the rim under his glans; he did the same to me. I gently caressed his scrotum; he did the same to mine. Judging by our lack of timidity, it was hard to believe we had never done that with each other before. So far, everything was cool.

"I am enjoying it," he chuckled. "We can do this all day."

I agreed with him, but I wanted more, and I had to go for it. Surely he wouldn't object, judging by his apparent level of increasing excitement. It was time to take it to the next step.

"Scot?" I began. "I told you I've been having fantasies for years. I wanna know what it's like to give someone a blow job. Would you like that?"

The kid swallowed hard and squeezed my shaft nervously. He would later admit being apprehensive because he was afraid I was going to ask him to do that to me, too. Then his blue eyes suddenly gleamed like stars on a moonless night. "I'd love that," he shakily whispered.

The sensation of sliding my slightly parted lips over the spongy head of a hard cock for the first time was so indescribably erotic that my moans of delight were as loud as his. I took about four inches of his shaft in while being careful to keep my teeth out of the way, gave it a half dozen lust filled sucks and drew back to the rim. Then I went down another inch, almost gagged and realized my limit while gliding up and down on that length for about a half minute.

At the same time, Scot's hand just rhythmically squeezed my cock. He seemed unable to jerk me off because of his high level of excitement. "Oh, wow. That's fantastic," he whispered.

He may have thought what I was doing to him was fantastic, but he had no idea how fantastic it was for me. Although I had been wanting to suck a cock for years, I hadn't realized how highly erotic the act really was.

"I'm gonna cum," the kid whispered hoarsely about a minute after I had begun. He reflexively pushed a warning hand against my shoulder, but I shrugged it off and moaned encouragingly.

Wow! When that first powerful jet of hot semen splashed against the roof of my mouth and landed on my tongue, I went into total lust mode. I was suddenly engulfed in an air of ecstasy. I didn't even realize he was no longer masturbating me.

Scot clutched my shoulders with his trembling hands while the second, third and fourth ejaculations came so close in sequence that they seemed like one. "Oh, yeah," he sighed. "That feels fantastic."

I sucked his pulsating cock wildly, made loud slurping sounds, swallowed his cream and moaned as if it were I who were cuming. It was then that I silently vowed we would be doing that a lot more.

Scot, at the same time, was releasing a prolonged moan as if being relieved from a lifetime of pain. He even pumped his hips to force his throbbing cock deeper into my throat.

His youthful balls ejaculated eight times, some of which escaped from the corners of my inexperienced, lustfully sucking lips. His entire body was trembling. It was absolutely heavenly.

Instantly addicted to the slightly acidic, slightly salty taste of semen, I planned on licking what had trickled downward to the base of his shaft when we were done, but that wasn't necessary. I continued eating him until he completely wilted in my mouth and wound up capturing the rest. But even then I didn't want to stop sucking his cock, possibly out of concern that we would never get the chance to do it again.

"That was unreal," Scot sighed when I sat back. Without any hesitation this time, he started masturbating me again. "I never thought a blow job would feel that good."

Getting an idea, I asked, "How about sucking my cock?" and quickly added, "You don't have to let it cum in your mouth. You can use your hand when I'm getting close."

Without hesitating, Scot said, "I guess I can do that," and licked his lips to moisten them. He gave my shaft a quick squeeze and nodded as if agreeing with himself.

Seconds later, I was lying on the sofa with my jeans and briefs off one leg. Scot knelt between my knees and held my eight-inch cock straight up with both hands. He slowly lowered his handsome, youthful face. There may have been reluctance in the kid's movements, but there was also excitement in his gleaming, blue eyes.

"Suck it slowly," I whispered. "I want it to last." Damn. I couldn't get over how my heart was still trying to pound its way through my chest.

His warm, moist lips parted, slid over the bulging head of my cock and moved downward about three inches with determination. "Nice," I said softly. They glided up and down a half dozen times with a pressure that was too light. "Suck a little harder," I encouraged him. He did so. "Play with my balls, too." He did so and seemed to relax.

Within a minute, Scot was obviously enjoying what he was doing, but I was ready to cum. Watching his flared, sucking lips dripping saliva down the sides of my cock and feeling the teeth that were lightly scraping along my sperm duct had been getting to me. "I'm gonna cum, Scot," I groaned while placing a halting hand on his shoulder. "Jerk me off."

Scot's eyes were gleaming like the sun on a cloudless day while he was pumping my saliva coated cock with both hands and watching the hot semen splashing against the hair on my stomach and chest. He didn't even seem to mind what was oozing over his fingers. "Wow, this is like cool, man," he said through broadly smiling lips. He had finally sucked my cock, something the kid had only dared to fantasize. And now, he was making me cum.

After we zipped our jeans and while Scot was washing his hands in the kitchen next to my recreation room, I got a few more ideas. This had all happened so quickly, and I was quite excited over having sucked a cock for the first time. But there were still other things to try, and I knew his youthful balls could handle the job.

For the next half hour, we talked about how nice that had been and about things we usually thought of while jerking off. With no one to bother us since I lived alone, I said, "Why don't we take our clothes off and try a few of my fantasies?"

Scot readily agreed while admitting that he had always wanted to see me naked, not that my body was as muscular as his. During the next few years, he would be the all state wrestling champion in his college.

Scot didn't have much hair on his chest or balls, while I had a lot on my chest and kept my pubes closely trimmed. And what tight buttocks the kid had. Hopefully, I would be trying it before long.

Returning to the sofa, we slowly masturbated each other again while talking. "I'd like to try a lot of new things with you, Scot," I said while cupping a hand under his balls and gently squeezing his half hard cock with the other one.

"I'm game," he quickly responded without knowing what those things were. "I have a few fantasies, too."

"Ever wear a condom?" When he said he hadn't, I explained my reason for the question. "I'd like you to put one on and do me in the ass. Would you like to do that?"

"Oh wow! You mean it?" His eyes were beaming with excitement. "I'd love to do that to you." By the time he had finished that sentence, his cock was fully hard in my slowly stroking fist.

"Yes, I mean it," I said while thinking back a few years. "I used to have a girlfriend who liked to coat her finger with Vaseline and slide it in and out of my ass while she was blowing me. Once she even used three fingers on me." I grunted a laugh. "The only problem was that her fingers weren't long enough. So I'd like to feel what a real cock feels like in me."

"That'll be great!" Scot said excitedly. "When can we do it?"

When I told him I didn't have any condoms, he was disappointed, but I promised to have some the next day.

"That'll be cool," was Scot's only response, but it was obvious that the wheels in his head were turning.

"I want you to use one," I began explaining, "So you won't have to waste time washing up after you pull out of me." With his

185

youthful balls, I could probably suck him to another erection in a few minutes and even get fucked twice in the same day.

That possibility exciting me, I slid a palm under his scrotum and gave it a gentle squeeze before stroking up the length of his cock with a thumb and forefinger to judge its width. It was about an inch and a quarter, which I expected to be able to handle comfortably. Scot was like a dream come true.

Then I asked how come the idea of fucking my ass seemed to turn him on so much. I had tried it once with a girlfriend, but she didn't like it. So we didn't do it again. I guess some people are just not anal erotic. Well I certainly was, and I was hoping that he didn't just want to try it once to satisfy his curiosity.

Scot told me about the X-rated movie he had seen in which a man was fucking someone's ass. At the last minute, he pulled out and came all over the other guy's back. "That was such a turn-on that I've been wanting to do it ever since." He also admitted his excitement while watching me cum all over my stomach earlier.

"Hmmm," I said thoughtfully. "It's time to fulfill one of my recurring fantasies." By now, my cock was fully hard, too.

With me lying on the sofa and my knees hanging over one armrest, Scot knelt behind my shoulders while I explained the agenda. He loved it. Then I lowered his cock and made love to it as if I'd been doing that for years. My tongue swirled around his glans, licked up and down the underside of his shaft and bathed his tight scrotum. More turned on than I'd ever been, though, I had to resist the urge to bite the kid's balls. With my suggestion, he gently twisted my nipples.

"I love your hairy chest," Scot said when my lips slid over four inches of his throbbing cock. He stopped twisting my nipples long enough to grab some of the curly growth before returning to the sensitive buds.

Had my mouth not been occupied, I would have told him how much I loved sucking him off. Was this really finally happening? How could anyone not enjoy the act of fellatio? If some women can enjoy this act, why shouldn't men be able to enjoy it, too? Even his tight buttocks felt good when I grabbed them to pull about another inch of his cock into my mouth.

It wasn't long before I noticed Scot fucking my mouth and breathing heavier. "Ready?" I managed to mumble. This may have been his fantasy, but I was looking forward to doing it, too. At least he had an imagination, and I wasn't going to have to think of all the things to try.

"Yes," Scot groaned while sliding his cock out of my mouth, even though I really didn't want to release it. He inched forward on his knees while I guided his hips downward with both hands and opened my mouth widely. "I'm gonna cum now."

I sucked his entire youthful scrotum with its sparse covering of pubic hair while trying to bathe its every surface with my tongue. There must have been an electrical charge of sexual excitement running through my body because my hips spasmed, possibly brought on by my anticipation of what was going to happen within seconds.

Scot released a prolonged moan while watching his semen spurting all over the hair on my chest. "Oh my god," he sighed almost breathlessly and continued masturbating even after he had stopped cuming.

I slid my mouth off his scrotum and said, "Go ahead and do the rest. This was your idea." I replaced his hand with mine and pumped the slowly wilting cock that was going to give me so much pleasure in the months to come.

When I returned to gently sucking his scrotum, Scot swirled his fingertips around in the puddle of warm semen on my chest. He coated my nipples with the pasty cream and gave them a few stimulating twists. "Oh, wow," he whispered as if talking to himself. "I never realized how fantastic it is to cum on someone's body."

"Mmmm," was all I could say in agreement. It was then that I wondered what it would feel like to let him cum on my face, but that would have to wait for a future agenda. The thought of doing that, however, got to me, and I had to start jerking off.

Scot took control then. The kid fell forward and slid my cock into his mouth. I, wanting to suck all day and night by now, started blowing him again. We sixty-nined in that position for about twenty minutes, and seconds after he came again, I signaled him that I was ready to go off, too. So he masturbated me until my load was spent.

* * * * *

The next day, I found out how erotic it is to slip a condom onto someone's rigid dick while devouring his young, muscular body with my eyes. I gave Scot's scrotum a few caresses before reaching for the tube of KY-Jelly and saying, "This will make it go in easier." Not having known about prepping the anal canal first, I heavily coated his rigid shaft and got onto all fours with a smile of anticipatory excitement.

Surprisingly, Scot's glans entered my virgin anus with little discomfort. I told him to ease it in and out to stretch my sphincter muscle, and he did so while purring continuously. Since I had already sucked him to two orgasms, the kid wasn't likely to cum too fast this time. Or, so we thought.

I loved every moment of that wonderful act – the way the ridges on his shaft rubbed my anal ring and made it tingle, the way his thighs slapped against the backs of mine, the way he tightly held my hips. I didn't want to stop. "Oh, Scot, that feels so good. Keep fucking me just like that."

By the time his stiff, six-inch shaft had been riding in and out of my anal canal smoothly for about five minutes, he groaned and said, "I can't hold off anymore. I have to cum."

Keep fucking me fast," I practically begged. I repeatedly thrust my hips back to meet his every inward plunge while wondering why I hadn't begun doing this at a much earlier age. How could some people not like anal sex?

"Ah!" Scot cried out while plunging his cock as deeply into me as he could, which caused his balls to slap against mine. His strong hands gripped my hips so tightly that his fingernails almost dug into my flesh. "I don't believe this," he panted.

I thought I was going to cum just from the excitement of feeling his cock contracting inside of me. For some reason, mine had wilted, but I started jerking off anyway. "This is great, Scot. It's great. I love it."

With his load spent and his dick wilting inside of my ass, I got an idea. "Try to sit without letting it pop out of me."

He managed to slide his lower legs between my knees, pull my hips back and sit. Now we were both in a sitting position with me on his lap and his dick trapped in my ass.

"That was totally awesome," Scot sighed while I was putting his hand on my cock. He got the hint and masturbated me while we began talking about a few more things we could do together.

Ten minutes later, I was fully hard, and it only took a few more minutes for that young stud to get a full erection again. This time, though, he lasted much longer.

We took an uneventful shower together about a half hour later, got dressed and returned to my recreation room. I enjoyed having Scot around. Aside from the sex, he was a welcome relief from the pressures I usually had to endure at work. Maybe part of the reason was that I felt a lot more comfortable with him than I had felt with female friends.

When, during our casual conversation, I mentioned enjoying fresh water fishing, Scot's eyes lit up. "Really!?" he exclaimed. I used to love to do that when I was a kid."

"Why don't we spend some time drowning a few worms?" I offered. He readily agreed, and we also planned on taking in a few baseball games, too. This was turning out to be a great relationship.

* * * * *

It wasn't until two weeks later that Scot was lying on his side with me behind him. With my having used two heavily lubricated fingers to stretch his sphincter muscle while blowing him on a daily basis, I didn't expect this to cause too much discomfort.

He slid a thigh back over mine; I pressed the head of my heavily lubricated, condom covered cock against his anal ring. Being as gentle as possible, I eased two inches into him while caressing his balls. Probing slightly deeper with each inward thrust, I soon felt him relaxing completely. A minute later, the full length was in him, and I was slowly masturbating a man who was continuously moaning in ecstasy.

Scot had been a perfect male lover back in those days. He had a terrific body, a terrific cock, a pair of rapid recovery balls. He loved to suck and be sucked; he loved to fuck and be fucked. It was too bad that he had to move away after graduating from college to take a job in another state.

* * * * *

But now, Scot was back in my life since he had transferred to a local branch office. He was married but said something was missing in their sex life. I knew what he meant and had no objection to us spending some time together. So, what was to stop us from picking up from where we had left off?

It's Okay
By Jay Barbera

I guess it started one Saturday morning in a small boat on the Long Island Sound. Our luck hadn't been running too well, so Robert, a coworker, and I just talked about nothing in particular.

When I asked why he never dated any of the women in the office, he thought for a few seconds before giving me the first hint. "I guess," he began slowly while gazing off at the plastic ball near the end of his line, "you don't really know what I'm about."

The comment went over my head like a flock of gulls. "No," I said, "I don't know what you're about."

Rob smiled, giving that macho look to his rugged face. Then he clasped his hands behind his head, causing his arm and chest muscles to expand, and leaned back until he was resting against the bow of the boat. "Want to find out?" he asked, seeming to be daring me.

Although I said nothing, he must have detected some interest in my eyes. "I'm going to a house party tonight ... over on the Island," he said nodding toward Fire Island. "Why don't you come with me?"

* * * * *

By the time I had walked halfway through the spacious living room of that Fire Island mansion, I knew what Robert was about. I seemed to be the only straight person among about two dozen gay men and women, even though, judging by some of their mannerisms, I couldn't tell which was which.

It was about two hours later that I met Candy. Suspecting she was a lesbian, I didn't bother making a play for her, not wanting some bull dyke tearing my head off. So, we talked and talked and talked.

All the while, though, I was checking her out. What a shame, I thought. She was a blonde, about five-six, and had a pretty face, voluptuous lips, small but nice boobs, a slender figure and nicely shaped legs that showed themselves provocatively from the bottom of a snuggly fitting mini skirt. What a waste of flesh. That woman had been meant for a man.

"It's kind of warm in here," she said with a soft, sensuous voice that sent pulses of electricity through my nuts as if I had never gotten laid in my life. "Care to get some fresh air?"

* * * * *

Candy and I walked toward the boat dock without talking. When we got there, she sat on the edge and leaned her back against a post. I was about three feet away, facing her with a knee extended in her direction, possibly to assure her I would keep my distance.

While I was busy watching the moonlight reflecting off the rippling waves and washing over her cover girl face, she spoke. "So ... what do you think of the scene in there?" Her floating hand lazily pointed to the house.

Wanting to be honest with her, I simply said, "It's not for me."

"And," she asked, "what's with you and Robert?"

I returned her smile with the feeling of lust growing within me at the sight of her pure white teeth and perfectly shaped mouth. "I hadn't known before tonight that he was gay. Er ... that is, I guess he's gay, considering his other friends." I didn't want my remark to be interpreted as a derogatory one. Noticing the lack of hurt in her face, I continued. "I think someone like you is more my style."

"I'm ... not a woman," she said with no apology meant while her blue eyes pierced my heart.

Candy explained that the lack of hair on her face and body was from electrolysis treatments and female hormones, the latter of which had also developed her breasts slightly. Surgical implants had brought them to the thirty-four B size they were now. She also told me that she was living with a lesbian. "Ironic, isn't it?" she asked. "She loves women and wishes she were a man; I prefer men and wish I were a woman."

I was dumfounded and could only think of asking, "Wh ... why are you telling me this?"

When Candy smiled at me in that sensuous way, I still wasn't sure I believed her. I thought she was putting me on until she explained further.

"Well, inside the house, I got the feeling you wanted me as much as I want you. And I wouldn't want you to be disappointed if you were to kiss me and put your hand inside my skirt and find a pair of balls." She giggled lightly and put her fingertips in front of her mouth in a totally feminine manner.

I had to laugh with her, but our nervousness made us continue chuckling out of control for a few more moments. Then I could only escape behind a barrage of intellectual questions.

"Are your breasts sensitive like a woman's?"

"Definitely." Candy smiled and brushed the tip of her tongue across the edge of a sensuous upper lip in a way that would have forced me to kiss her had she not been a man. "In fact," she added, "if it weren't so dark now you'd see that my nipples are in quite an excited state."

I took a deep breath and reminded myself that Candy was a man. "But, can you still function as a male?"

"Sure I can."

"I mean, do those female hormones you take ... prevent you from ...?"

"No, I can still get an erection, and I can ejaculate." She looked at me, appreciating my interest. "In fact, that's the one big contradiction in me."

When I looked at her questioningly, she continued. "I like to be made love to by men, but I also love to perform anal sex on a guy." Seeing I still hadn't run away, she pressed onward. "Are you a virgin?"

"Yes," I said shyly, "with the exception of a woman's finger or two."

"Did you like that?" she asked, turning sideways and extending a knee toward me.

For a few moments, I looked at the part of her thigh that was exposed below the hem of her miniskirt and felt my mouth filling with saliva. I couldn't believe I was thinking like that while talking to another man. She's not a man, I tried to convince myself. She is a woman. And, besides, what's the difference whether you make love to a woman and suck her cunt or to a woman and suck her cock? Did I really ask myself that? I finally answered her. "I liked it very much."

* * * * *

The next day, although I still had some reservations, or maybe I was just nervous, Candy and I had lunch in my apartment. She had agreed not to push, and I had consented to our getting to know each

193

other a little better. After all, we had enjoyed talking the night before. We could be just friends. Neither of us was really starving for sex.

Candy filled a pair of jeans nicely, and her soft knitted blouse revealed the absence of a bra and the excitement of her nipples as she slouched into the corner of my sofa. While she was studying me with a provocative gleam in her eyes, her lips were pouting slightly, which made me want to kiss them, something I never would have considered doing before we had met.

With an uncharacteristic high degree of control, however, I managed to resist the urge to do that, even though I knew we were probably going to do something. But what? I can just let her suck me off. No, that wouldn't be fare. I can play with her tits while she does it to me, and she can masturbate herself at the same time. Would she be satisfied with that? Lots of street gays give blow jobs in men's rooms and get nothing in return. But she's nothing like them. Well, maybe I can give her a hand job. She knows I never did anything with a guy before and probably won't be expecting more than that. We'll see. She also knows I had enjoyed fingers in my ass. Is she expecting to fuck me in the ass? Hmmm that might be interesting.

"Do you like to get high?" Candy asked nonchalantly during a brief lull in our conversation.

Knowing where she was going with that one, I smiled while remembering the first girl I had fucked after having gotten her slightly drunk on beer. Then I realized that might be the best way to break the ice. "I haven't smoked pot in quite a few years." My eyes focused on her nipples. They had grown even more within the last few seconds.

"I have some in my handbag. Want to try? It may be just what you need to relax."

"Am I that obvious?" I felt myself blushing.

"I want you," she said seductively, "even if you don't want to touch me. Maybe, after awhile, you'll loosen up."

A few seconds after I agreed, she moved closer to my corner of the sofa, touched a match to the tip of a thick joint, held it between her delicious looking lips and took a few hits while staring into my eyes with a "come and get me" look. Then Candy leaned across my chest and dropped the match into the ashtray on the table next to me.

When she did that, a soft breast brushed over my arm, and I was up to sixty percent sure we were going to do something that day. I wasn't even stoned yet, but I wanted to grab Candy's tits and slide my cock into her mouth where that joint was. It took a few deep breaths to calm my racing heart.

Candy handed the weed to me. I took a long drag, held the mild smoke in for about a half minute, exhaled some and took some more. I needed it because I wanted her and didn't want to change my mind now.

When the reefer was too small for me to hold, Candy held it between her long fingernails and said, "Open your mouth." I did so; she took a hit and moved closer.

Knowing what she wanted to do, I parted my lips and accepted the smoke she blew between them. While doing that a second time, her sensuous mouth was only a fraction of an inch from mine, and my cock was getting hard. It was the third toke that did it, though.

After taking a drag that lasted about three seconds, Candy slowly passed the smoke to me. I don't know if I closed the gap between our mouths or if she did, but before we knew it, our trembling lips were sealed together. A purple cloud was surrounding our faces while her hand was resting against the back of my neck and mine were exploring her small, but soft, breasts. Damned if I wasn't kissing a man and loving every moment of it.

What happened during the next several minutes, I can only vaguely recollect. But soon enough we were completely naked. I sucked her tits while she combed her fingers through my hair. Somehow, Candy rolled me off the sofa, knelt between my outstretched legs and curled her delicate fingers around my fully erect shaft.

"My god," she sighed while looking at its nine-inch length. "What a man." Her lips were glistening with saliva as she continued staring at it, and I wanted her to suck it. I wanted her now almost as much as she wanted me.

Two skeins of blonde hair draped over the sides of my thighs while she continued stroking my shaft and rolling her lips around its throbbing head. Then I watched about five inches disappear into her warm, moist mouth. My breaths were coming in jerks, and my head was spinning from either the pot or the wonderful blow job she was giving me. Candy was certainly an expert at it, and I couldn't think of anything wrong with what we were doing. And, judging by the way she was sighing, she couldn't either.

I clutched bunches of her hair and gently pulled her upward. She followed my lead. We embraced while kissing. Instinctively, my hand slowly slid over her soft stomach and closed around her seven-inch erection.

Although still not sure of my feelings, I pulled her upward even further. Did I want to do this? I wasn't sure whether to stop or go for it. What would be so wrong? Candy was definitely clean, and no one else would have to know if I did do it.

Before I knew it, a cock was in my mouth. It felt wonderful. It was rigid, yet covered with soft flesh that caressed my lips. I sucked lustfully while wanting more and more. I didn't know if my moaning was louder or hers, if her excitement was greater or mine. We rolled to the side until Candy was on her back with her soft thighs draped over my shoulders and with about three inches of her dick in my mouth. I lustfully kneaded her heaving tits.

At some time during the next few moments, Candy must have reached into her handbag while clutching a bunch of my hair to force more of her penis into my mouth. I saw her head rolling from side to side while her hips were slowly pumping and her deep throated pants were drowning out my sucking sounds.

While sighing, "Suck me, baby. I'm getting close," she held a small vile to my nose. Recognizing the acidic scent of amyl nitrite, I inhaled deeply and soon heard her doing the same.

Within ten seconds, I was on cloud nine thousand. The soft, trembling thighs of a beautiful woman were rubbing against the sides of my face, and I was caressing the perfectly shaped cheeks of her firm ass with both hands. Yet, my mind was totally focused on the hard cock that was filling my mouth. It seemed like my entire existence was being consumed by her cock, which was sliding – no, it was gliding between my lips, and shooting jets of warm, pasty cream into my mouth.

I sucked and swallowed and rolled my lips around Candy's pulsating cock as it spewed a seemingly endless stream of semen into my moaning mouth. I wanted to swallow her entire length, and I think I did on a few occasions while only slightly aware of her distant moans of pleasure. That was my cock. I wanted to continue making love to it, and she was obviously enjoying the act as much as I was.

Somehow, with our hearts still rapidly palpitating from the drug or from what we were doing or from both, we twisted around and started sixty-nining. The wonderful things Candy was doing to my shaft and scrotum and anus were nothing compared to the pleasure I was getting from caressing her balls and lustfully devouring her cock.

By the time I was done ejaculating into Candy's faintly moaning mouth, her partially wilted shaft was completely in my mouth, and my savagely sucking lips were pressed against her neatly trimmed pubic hair. Talk about instant converts.

When I was flaccid, we stopped that wild scene. Candy slid her luscious lips off my cock and kissed its glans a few times with a silent promise of more to come. I twisted around and got on top of her. We kissed while tasting the traces of our mutual passion.

While we were taking a break, I was sitting on the floor with my back against the sofa. Candy was on her stomach between my outstretched legs, resting the side of her face on one of my thighs. For long moments, while she idly kissed my wilted shaft and glans, I ran my fingers through her fine, blonde hair, forgetting for the moment that she was really a man. Her body looked so good; her mouth felt so wonderful. I caressed the cheeks of her ass and lightly scratched her back while noticing how her soft flesh was rekindling the glow within me.

Suddenly, she started doing even nicer things with her fingers while sliding her warm, moist lips over my cock. It felt as though ten dainty feathers were dancing over the flesh of my scrotum in contrast to the pleasurable sensation of having my shaft playfully bitten up and down its length. The fingers slid back farther and teased my anus. I spread my legs to give her the green light, closed my eyes and rested my head against the sofa's cushion.

"Like that?" Candy asked between licks around my glans.

"Mmm hmmmmm," I moaned long and low, no longer high from the grass, but no longer inhibited either.

While tightly squeezing the base of my shaft with one hand and caressing my balls with the other, Candy kissed my glans about a dozen times before sliding the tip of her tongue into its slit. Smiling devilishly, she said, "Get that tube of stuff in my handbag next to you."

I had never seen KY-Jelly before, but knew what it was for. Handing it to her, I raised my knees and spread them a little wider to let her know it was okay, remembering how she'd told me the night before that she enjoyed fucking men in the ass.

Candy continued lightly biting up and down the length of my rapidly stiffening shaft, which had grown to seven inches by this time. She was also caressing my already aroused balls. "Relax, sweetie," her sensuous voice said. "You'll like this, too."

I suddenly felt the tip of a lubricated finger teasingly trace the outline of my rectum. That was nice as was the initial penetration of about two inches of her finger. To heighten my arousal even more, she licked around my throbbing glans and spiraled downward until reaching its base. Candy drew one of my balls into her mouth and then both of them. With my entire scrotum being sucked and caressed by her artful tongue and my now fully hard, nine-inch cock being masturbated and my anal canal being pleased by her twisting, plunging finger, I was in heaven and didn't want to do anything but lie there and enjoy the whole scene.

The next wonderful sensation was one I had never before experienced. I felt her warm tongue parting the lips of my tight, puckered anus and wanted to cum. I almost started jerking off, so great was the feeling.

Candy knelt between my legs and lifted my thighs with her shoulders before spreading my buttocks with the fingertips of both hands. Although I'd had fingers in my ass, they were nothing compared to Candy's tongue. I couldn't wait for her to stick her cock in me.

"Ohhhh, that's wonderful," I groaned while rolling my hips to increase the pleasure. The head of my cock was pointing straight up at me, and I thought it was going to erupt at any second.

"Want something to go deeper?" she asked, smiling up at me.

I didn't have to think about it. With a hoarse, exhaling voice, I said, "I'm ready whenever you are."

After inserting the tip of the tube into my anus and emptying half of its contents, Candy eased two fingers inward their full length and twisted her wrist to coat my anal canal with the greasy substance. Satisfied I was relaxed, she straddled my head with her knees, sat on my chest and said, "Make this a little harder for me, will you, lover?"

Although her erection was about three-quarters full and probably rigid enough to penetrate me, I didn't want to pass up the opportunity to suck it again. While staring at her beautiful tits with their excited nipples, I caressed her balls with one hand and unhesitatingly pulled her cock into my mouth with the other. I knew then that I was addicted to fellatio, even if it would only be Candy's cock I would be sucking.

I slid my lips halfway over her warm shaft and almost instantly felt it stiffening in my mouth. Will she let me swallow her cum once more before she fucks me? I wondered. And to think, only twenty-four hours earlier, I never would have thought of doing something like that.

"That's enough, buster," Candy whispered while removing her fully erect penis from my mouth, despite my unwillingness to let it go. "Get on your hands and knees … I'm going to give you the fuck of your life."

"Here," she said, standing in front of me while I was on all fours, "put some of this on me." She handed me the tube of KY and combed her fingers through my hair encouragingly.

The sensation from what I did next was unbelievable, too. After squirting a heavy glob of the grease into my palm, I smeared some around her glans and over her shaft. I felt every ridge while loosely stroking my fist up and down her length, and that caused my own cock to twitch from the excitement. Wanting to continue, I put more on and more and more until some of the stuff was almost dripping from her anxious rod. What a way to jerk someone off!

Knowing I was ready for the final step in my initiation, Candy gently spread my buttocks with the tips of her fingers and aimed her glans toward my anus. She circled the puckered opening with it a few times while breathing heavily. Apparently, her own excitement was as high as mine.

Surprisingly, the initial penetration of about two inches wasn't as painful as I had thought it would be. Her fingers had most likely done a good job of prepping me. Within a half minute, Candy was sliding about four inches of her rigid shaft in and out of my anal canal and the slight discomfort had subsided. "How does it feel?" she asked with a voice that was breaking up.

"Fantastic," I sighed. And it really did feel good. Fingers had never felt that good. "Get it in deeper."

Inch by inch, Candy slowly penetrated me deeper with each inward thrust. She was obviously being careful not to hurt me. Finally, her balls were resting against mine, and the head of her cock was poking something inside of me. Digging her fingertips into the tops of my shoulders, she hissed loudly while churning her hips and reaming out my ass lustfully.

What happened during the next five minutes could only be described as being heavenly. Candy started by holding my hips tightly and taking long, slow strokes with her super hard cock. Every time her balls slapped against mine, I thought I was going to cum. Then she started masturbating me while never slowing her fucking pace. My anus had never felt so good. And, as if that weren't fantastic enough, she used both hands to massage my throbbing dick and balls at the same time. Increasing the pace with her hips, she also did so with her hands.

"Ooooohhh," I sighed, not wanting her to ever stop. "I love it. Fuck me, baby. Fuck me ... I'm yours. Fuck me!"

Candy was grunting and moaning loudly with each inward thrust. "Mmmm. Mmmm. Your ass is so tight. I wanna fuck you all night, you gorgeous hunk." Her voice was shaky as she continued. "I want you to be mine, baby. I want to please you in every way I can. Mmmm. I'm gonna cum in your ass. Cum with me, lover. Cum!"

Candy was furiously masturbating me with both hands and riding her dick in and out of my ass its full length. There was absolutely no pain – just pure pleasure. Our pants and moans were synchronized with the rhythm of her hands and cock.

It was then that I spotted the amyl nitrite on the floor next to me. Quickly opening it, I extended my hand over a shoulder. She leaned forward, took a long hit and I did the same.

That familiar rush consumed us again as we spiraled up and up and up. The only thing in the world that existed was two cocks – one being frantically masturbated and one caressing the inner walls of my ass. I was so intensely focused on our genitals that I heard nothing and was aware of nothing else except the fantastic pleasure she was giving me.

Candy's rod stiffened even more inside of me and convulsed a few times. Knowing she was about to cum drove me over the edge, too. The sensation of her hot, hard cock in my ass and the fire in my balls caused me to start ejaculating a seemingly endless stream of semen.

When I felt dizzy and lowered my head, Candy started fucking me at a maddening pace. Her hot cream was bathing my prostrate and exciting me even more. I came and came and she came and came, and I knew I was in love.

After we rested for about two minutes, Candy made me stand. She knelt in front of me and sucked me off again until I came in her mouth. I didn't cum as much as I had before, But nevertheless, it was great to see that beautiful woman on her knees in front of me with her lively tits bouncing and her voluptuous lips sliding up and down the length of my cock in that loving way she did it.

* * * * *

That evening in bed, Candy taught me another way to make love to a man. After prepping her ass with the remainder of the KY-Jelly – I vowed to keep a generous supply in the house from then on – I waited for her to get onto all fours. Instead, she remained on her back and seductively whispered, "Get on top of me, lover." In that position, our kisses were even more passionate than they had been earlier.

"I never believed I would enjoy this so much," I mumbled between her sensuous, parted lips.

Candy smiled and slid her tongue across the inner flesh of my upper lip before saying, "I'm going to teach you lots of nice things."

Slowly, she drew her knees toward her shoulders while reaching for my stiff cock. Pressing its glans against her puckered anus, Candy whispered, "Push it in. Two men can fuck in this position, too."

The next half hour was unbelievable. With neither of us in a hurry, I fucked Candy's tight tunnel of love while alternating between lust filled kisses and sucking her responsive tits. All the while, I slowly masturbated her hot, throbbing cock.

By the time we were ready to cum, I was deep in her ass; her tender legs were curled around the small of my back, and each tongue was searching for the other's soul. With our hearts racing and our arms tightly embracing one another, we wanted to continue that act forever.

After our simultaneous orgasm was complete, we remained in that position. My stomach was bonded to hers with the help of Candy's warm semen. And, I was in love.

Buffed Bad Boy
By Bearmuffin

A few months ago, this hot little Mexican muscleman walked into the Pub, a hustler dive on Santa Monica Boulevard in Hollywood, where I was killing some time having a drink.

Now this stud had one of those rugged brute faces like a boxer and this sexy air about him that lured you to him like a magnet. He wore baggy black jeans, a blue baseball cap on backwards, and a black and blue checkered flannel shirt, which was rolled up to his big biceps and completely unbuttoned, so I could see his superb pecs and abs.

With his hot, muscular body and smooth milk chocolate colored skin, he looked like a Mexican Marky Mark. When I spotted him, I said out loud, "What a stud!"

He turned around and came up to me. "Hey, don't I know you?" he asked with a big sexy smile, exposing his glittering white teeth. His thick raven-black hair with a six-inch braid at the back was slicked back with brilliantine.

A thick but neatly trimmed mustache sprouted above his sexy brown lips. He told me his name was Carlos. He laughed when I called him Mr. Carlitos. He said he liked that.

I asked him what he wanted to drink, and he said a Tequila. So I bought him a shot of Cuervo, which he gulped down. He looked around for a second then told me to follow him to the men's room at the back of the bar. I waited about half a minute and then followed him.

When I went inside, Carlitos was standing in front of the toilet, leaning against the wall. He had stuck his shirt in his back pocket to expose his beautiful pecs, which were capped by thick, black nipples. His jeans were pulled down mid-thigh and his cock jutted out over his big brown balls. He was fisting it wildly getting it good and hard for me.

I sat on the toilet and started to lick his neatly furrowed abs and slab-like pecs. Then I stuck my face into his funky armpits. Fuck! His hot, smelly pits were ripe and musky, just like a real studman's pits should be.

I sucked the little Mexican stud's ripe brown cock for about five minutes. My nose was buried in his hot, musky pubes and the hot, man smell rushed up my nostrils as I took his sweet cock all the way down my throat. A few guys were coming in to take a piss, but Carlitos didn't seem to mind, so I kept on sucking his fat Mexican cock. After he shot a thick, sweet load of hot Mexican cum down my throat, he zipped up his Levis and said, "Give me some money, I've been good to you." I gave him ten bucks, but he asked for another five. He asked me for my phone number and said he would call me the next day.

The next morning around seven, I got a collect call from Carlitos. I accepted it, and we rapped for about half an hour. He told me he was from Acapulco, that he was working as a busboy in a downtown restaurant and that he lived with his family. He said he wanted to see me again and asked if he could come to my house.

Even though I didn't think he would rip me off, I was cautious. I told him we could meet somewhere else. I knew of this bathhouse on skid row. It was eight bucks for a room and no questions asked. I told him to meet me downtown.

Well, there he was in his black Levis again, the baseball cap, and his shirt wide open, so you could see his thick, juicy muscles. He was always smiling. He said he had a present for me and gave me a dirty, smelly T-shirt and a pair of undershorts he had been wearing for a few days. He also gave me a picture of himself posing like a muscleman and flexing his muscles on the beach. He said he gave them to me, so I'd have something to remember him by.

I gave Carlitos twenty bucks. I asked him if he was hungry and when he said he could use a meal, I took him to this Mexican restaurant around the block. After we finished our lunch, he said he wanted a cigar, so I bought it for him. He lit up the stogie and puffed on it as he leaned back with his powerful arms resting against the back of the booth and smiled at me. "I like to smell like a man," he told me. God, he was so fucking butch!

Afterwards, Carlitos and I went to the bathhouse.

After we got inside our cubicle, the first thing the stud did was light up a joint. After we both got stoned, he stripped and started to flex and pose for me. He said he had just come from working out at a gym. His muscles were thick and pumped up.

Fuck, he had a magnificent body! Then started to suck on my tits. He'd bite one nipple and twist the other one so fucking hard, I thought he'd rip it off. He never wore underarm deodorant, so his hot manly smell was exhilarating. I'd bury my face in his sweaty, hairy armpits and just breathe in those fantastic manly odors as I fisted my cock and he'd work on my nipples. After that hot tit workout, I shot my wad. Then he told me to suck his dick. His cock was fucking beautiful. It was thick and uncut with huge veins crisscrossing all over it.

He moaned hotly as I sucked on his cock. I'd get him to lie down on his right side, lift up one of his legs, grab his butt and pushed his groin against my face to let that beautiful cock slide all the way down my throat. His balls were huge, like two baseballs inside a soft leather pouch, and he loved me to suck on them while I stroked his sweet Mexican cock.

After a while, he said he wanted to fuck me, so I hunched over the little bed in the cubicle, and he shoved his hard, spasming Mexican cock right up my asshole. After about five or six short, brutal strokes, he laughed and shot his wad up my aching hole.

I saw Carlitos about two or three times a week after that, and I'd pay him between fifteen and twenty-five bucks a throw. I'd lick his muscles, lick his smelly armpits and suck his dick and balls. He'd work on my tits, I'd shoot my load and then he'd butt fuck me. He just shoved his cock right up my hole.

When I told him how much it hurt, he'd just laugh and he got off on it because it was like raping me. The last time I saw him, he let me suck his butthole. He squatted over my bobbing face, and I rimmed him for about ten minutes.

His sweet Mexican butthole was covered with all these sweaty little butt hairs. Carlitos moaned and groaned, really getting off on my licking his asshole. Afterward, he jacked off and laughed as he shot a huge load of cum all over my face that almost blinded me. Then he told me to lie face down. He started punching my butt really hard. He was getting pretty rough after a while, so I told him to cool it. He closed his eyes, whacked off for about three minutes then shoved his cock up my ass and raped me again, pulled out his cock and shot his hot load all over my sore butt.

After that last encounter, I stopped hearing from Mr. Carlitos. Maybe he lost my number. And then again, maybe the whole thing just ran its course. So, will I ever fuck him again? It's possible. I'm sure he's still out there hustling on Santa Monica Boulevard.

Beware of Greeks
By Mark Dante

He was a wiry little Greek, was Adrian Metropolis – built for speed. The girlie-girls thought he was pretty cute. So did some of the fellas.

Matter of fact, Adrian was damned cute: big brown eyes, curly dark hair, a full mouth with a crooked smile and straight teeth. It goes without saying he had a handsome Greek nose, and he kept his nifty little bod all shaped up with daily workouts.

The machos, however, were not too sure about Adrian.

He didn't care. He was as happy as he was gay, and though he didn't run with the pack, two or three times a week he'd descend on one of several bars he knew, pick off some cutey and take him home. This seemed to satisfy his basic needs.

At the moment, Adrian was enveloped in the arms of Morpheus, the Greek God of dreams.

Actually, Adrian was zonked. He'd stayed out too late, had one too many and spent several hours romping with the hunk who now shared his sack. At the moment his partner was wide awake. He was staring at Adrian's schwanse. It was starting to rise with the sun. The young fella was fascinated with the action of Adrian's cock. He had a nice one. Not huge, but surely big enough, with a tasty knob on the end when it was aroused. The hunk licked his chops, and his hand stole across the bed toward the lovely hard-on, the only thing Adrian had exposed. It was sticking out from under sheets that were drawn up over its owner's head.

The hand made contact with the cock. Its owner groaned and flung off the covers. He glared at the hunk.

"How dare you touch my cock without my permission?!" he squeaked.

"Hey, come on, man. Last night it was community property," growled his bedmate. "Didn't I pleasure ya nice?"

"You woke me from a most delicious dream!" moaned Adrian.

"Why dream, when ya can have the real thing? Look Mister Metropolis, honey. I'm hungry. Couldn't I have a bit of your sausage for breakfast?"

"Oh, shit! If you must, go ahead!" snorted Adrian.

He was just a bit jaded with this particular one-nighter, but a cock in the mouth is worth several in the bush.

While the young hunk had his way with Adrian, the Greek lay back and considered his good fortune. He was one of the lucky ones. He lived alone. He'd been raised by a doting grandmother who left him her posh brownstone on the west side and beaucoup in the buckola department. Adrian didn't have to work, so to occupy his time and mind, he went to school at Columbia.

"Hey fella, don't bite!" Adrian yelped at his tormentor.

"Ummm humph," came the muffled reply.

Adrian specialized in ancient Greek culture. He spoke and read Greek fluently and studied mythology and archeology. His studies went along with his hobby. He was obsessed with the collection of early gay Greek erotic art. After all, didn't the Greeks start the whole thing?

One day, his favorite art dealer called with what he thought was a great find. Adrian hurried over and was delighted to discover the dealer had procured for him a collection of rubbings from an ancient Greek bas relief. The pictures showed, in graphic detail, Greek athletes in every conceivable position of passion.

With his eyes bulging, Adrian flipped through the collection. "From where were these taken?" he asked.

"Ancient Sparta, Mr. Metropolis," was the dealer's reply.

"You're kidding!" beamed Adrian. "Why, the archeology lab is going on a dig there next week!"

"Ohhhhhh!" moaned Adrian. The hungry hunk was working his magic on the young Greek's tool.

"Ahh ... there's nothing like it," thought Adrian.

The pain was exquisite, and he held on as long as he could. Suddenly he grabbed the hunk by the ears and thrust his hard horn past the young hunk's uvula, as he let go a stream of cum that would have drowned a less experienced cock-sucker. The hunk continued to suck until he'd drained Adrian dry. Then the hunk withdrew and looked Adrian in the eye.

"Tasted even better than last night. Guess leftovers are always more flavorful the next day," observed the hunk.

"Yeah, yeah, Now that you've had your fun, let's get a move on. Cover your ass and get out. I gotta start packing. My plane leaves in five hours."

* * * * *

The next day Adrian was walking the streets of Sparti. (Modern Sparta). He was in pursuit of his favorite, make that second most favorite pastime, rummaging through old Greek shops.

In a dusty old shop, in a dusty old case, he spied a dusty old amulet. The dusty-crusty old shopkeeper saw Adrian admiring the piece and smiled knowingly.

"Ah, kind sir, an excellent choice. The amulet is enchanted."

"And that doubles the price, right?" glowered Adrian.

"Oh, kind sir, you wound me with your suspicious words. I can let you have it for two hundred drachmas."

"That's highway robbery, but the amulet is damned interesting. I'll give you one hundred," offered Adrian.

"One-fifty and done, then," beamed the shop man.

Adrian thought for a moment. He remembered what he knew about Greek culture and his own inner self.

"OK," he said finally. "Throw in a horn job and done."

"Done," exclaimed the shop man with an appraising glance at Adrian's perpetually lumpy crotch.

The dusty-crusty old man took Adrian to the back of his dusty shop. He held a dusty curtain aside and allowed Adrian to enter a dusty curtained room. Once inside, the old man motioned for Adrian to drop his drawers.

"Delightful," cried the shop man as Adrian unveiled his tool. Then the old man knelt and took the unique bulbous head of Adrian's cock into his mouth. The old man had no teeth and though the fastidious Adrian was appalled by the man's lack of hygiene, he had to admit it was about the best blow job he'd ever experienced.

The old man gummed the hell out of it. He teased and twirled it with his talented tongue until Adrian's balls ached to let go. Finally, the old man doubled his stoke, and Adrian came and came and came!

"Good work, old man," Adrian sighed when the shopkeeper had finished.

The old man grinned a toothless, cumey grin. "You Americans are simply delicious. Much tastier than our Greek boys. Why is that?" the old man inquired.

"Vitamins," Adrian volunteered as he took a spray can of Lysol from his shoulder purse and disinfected his genitals. "An ounce of prevention," his old Granny had always told him.

Adrian paid the man, popped the amulet into his bag and took off.

* * * * *

The next few days found Adrian slaving with the rest of his Columbia class at the site of Menelaus's palace outside Sparti. One evening, as he sat on a pile of rubble and watched the setting sun's reflection ripple on the River Euortas, a thought struck him, and he rummaged around in his bag until he found it. He'd just finished a joint and felt all giggly as he held the old amulet up to the sun.

"Enchanted," he snorted. Then remembering the old man, he smiled. What a blow job the old man had given him. He almost considered going into town for another, when he remembered the old man's instructions for the use of the enchanted amulet.

"Humbug," laughed Adrian has he held the amulet between his palms and aimed it toward the setting sun.

"Ah, Magic Amulet," he giggled, "Take me back to ancient Sparta!"

Suddenly, there was a burning sensation from the amulet in his hands and a great roaring in his ears.

The pain caused him to blink, and when he opened his eyes, he found the roaring sound was a cheering crowd, and he was sitting in a bright sun-drenched box overlooking an athletic field. Off to the left and right stretched thousands of applauding people dressed in the costumes of ancient Spartans.

Next to him sat a distinguished looking, middle-aged gentleman who must be pretty important.

"Oh, hello there," the man said to the dazed Adrian.

"Welcome to the games. My name is Menelaus. I'm the King hereabouts. At your service, sir. This is my wife, Helen."

"Not *the* Helen?" Adrian stammered.

The beautiful young lady seated next to the King gave Adrian a wink. "Is there more than one?" she asked.

Adrian shrugged. The girl was very pretty, but he was more impressed with what was going on down on the field. He had never seen so many beautiful boys. They were all apparently in their late teens. Even better, they were all naked, and to top that off, some of them were very well endowed.

"Smorgasbord," said Adrian to himself.

The King, who had been keeping one eye on Adrian and one on the field, remarked, "You seem to like our young men."

Adrian, not sure of the local customs, blushed, "Oh, sorry, King, but they are damned pretty."

"Would you like to have one of them?" offered the generous Menelaus.

"Well, golly gee, sure," replied the delighted Adrian. "Who wouldn't?"

"You look them over, and when the games are over, I'll make the arrangements," replied the King with a smile.

Adrian was highly pleased with the King's proposition. He clapped his hands together and grinned from ear to ear. Then he rested his head on his hands and began to study the boys. There was one who really excelled in everything. He was lovely to look at, and his sporting prowess was without peer. He won the discus and javelin throws and most of the running events. The crowd was also enthusiastic in their praise of the boy.

At last the games were over, and the young man had also won the decathlon. As Menelaus placed the laurel wreath on the young man's head, Adrian made his request, "That's the one, King."

"Xenephon? A wise choice indeed," smiled the King.

"He's my son by a former marriage. You may have him for a year. At the end of that time, he must go away and be married. He's betrothed to the princess of Athens."

"A year will be just ducky, King," smirked Adrian with a wink at Xenephon. Xenephon winked back at Adrian.

The royal party moved back into the palace. The young object of Adrian's adoration was called away for a few moments, and Adrian was taken to Xenephon's quarters. On a large dais was the bed. It was raised on a pedestal and looked roomy and comfortable.

The servant who'd escorted him excused himself and left Adrian alone. Adrian wandered aimlessly about the room, admiring the statuary and various weapons and trophies that must be a part of every well-to-do young Spartan's possessions.

Suddenly, Adrian froze. He stood before a giant bas relief that decorated one wall. At first glance, the carvings looked as if they were merely a random pattern like some of the wallpapers back home. On closer observation, however, the artwork revealed something altogether different and of particular interest to Adrian.

"Well, I'll be jiggered," he exclaimed to himself.

His eyes widening in recognition, the design was made up of many athletic young men who were, for the moment, engaged in activities other than athletics.

In fact, Adrian gasped as he identified the original sculpture from which his coveted book of Greek erotica had been taken. Once again, Adrian marveled at the imagination shown by the young men in the pictures.

Just then, however, he was distracted by someone behind him clearing his throat. He turned to see Xenephon standing close to him. The young man was also looking fondly at the carved wall.

"That was done last year. I had a bunch of the boys over, and one of them is quite an accomplished sculptor. I think the likenesses are remarkable. That's me on top in this one," said Xenephon, pointing to a trio in an astonishing position. "And here I am again on the bottom."

"Aaaarumph ... yes ... yes ... I ... I see," stammered Adrian, looking first at Xenephon and then at the carved images. His handsome eyes were bulging slightly as his vivid imagination pictured himself with Xenephon on the bed across the room.

The young prince could see that his eyes weren't the only thing of Adrian that bulged. He took Adrian's hand and led him to the bed. He motioned for the young Greco-American to sit. Adrian was, to say the least, excited by the presence of the young beauty and the prospect that Xenephon might show him a thing or two. He was disappointed when the athlete merely kissed his hand.

"Dearest Adrian. You must understand. You will enjoy all that I can give you, but not tonight. We do things with great ceremony around here. I must attend a celebration of my triumph at the games. You will just have to wait."

Adrian slumped in disappointment as the Prince went on.

"Tomorrow we will have our ceremony of betrothal, you and I. Everything must be done according to proper protocol. You will sleep here tonight. I must sleep elsewhere. I must bid farewell to my former lover. It is only fitting," he said as he stood up. "Until tomorrow, then, goodnight."

Adrian was livid as Xenephon left the room. He'd gotten himself all worked up over the prospect of having the boy to himself. Now the handsome turd was going to do it with someone else.

He lay down on the soft bed and tried to sleep.

Across from the bed, in the soft light of the lamp, he could still make out the figures on the wall. This did nothing to lull him to sleep.

It had been an exhausting day, however, and he finally fell into a fitful slumber. He dreamed of doing wild things with Xenephon all the long night long. Finally, the exquisite fantasy of the boy's soft lips caressing the taught skin of his cock sent him into a climax, and he awoke from a very wet dream as he sent bolt after bolt of cum over his stomach and chest.

He remembered little of the next day. All he could see was the face and torso of the Prince of Sparta.

The eyes and lips called to him, but the ceremony went on and on, and the feast that evening only heightened his passion. Finally, a group of Xenephon's friends escorted them to the young man's chamber and locked them in with gales of laughter and their best wishes.

At last the young Prince stood before Adrian. Each wore a short skirt with a wide belt. They were bare-chested and their beauty shown in the soft light.

Xenephon took Adrian in his arms, and the young Greco-American nearly swooned as the soft, warm, fragrant lips descended upon his. Adrian was already so aroused that the kiss set him aflame. He felt Xenephon unfasten his belt and suddenly he saw they were both naked. Xenephon led him once more toward the bed. They lay down, and Adrian looked down to the area of their loins. He had only seen the athlete's penis in repose as it swung between his legs during the games. It had been long and slim. Now it was incredibly hard, long and graceful. "A tool for love," he thought to himself.

What followed was beyond belief, for though the boy was only eighteen, he had been well schooled and was a genius at the art of erotica. His touch was, at first, light and gentle as he caressed and stoked Adrian from head to toe. His kisses were ambrosia, and his body was so beautiful, Adrian's heart almost burst with love.

That night, Xenephon drove Adrian to near insanity with his subtle and irresistible caresses. He stretched Adrian on a rack of exquisite pain, and as the hours went spinning by, the young man fanned the fires of Adrian's ardor then let the embers die down and glow a dull, dark red before he worked them again to white heat.

At length, Adrian screamed to be released, and the young beauty prepared for the final thrust of his mighty javelin. He laid Adrian on his back. Then taking a jar of oil from the side table, he smoothed it over his glorious cock and working his wondrous fingers into Adrian's rectum, he anointed all with the magic potion.

He pushed Adrian's knees up against his chest and slowly worked his marvelous manhood into Adrian's ass.

Whether it was the oil or the tantalizing movements of the mammoth phallus, Adrian could feel every vein and pore of the giant tool. As it touched and then slid over his palpitating prostate, Adrian groaned and thrust his shapely ass down full on the lovely pole.

Xenephon closed his eyes and moaned a soul shattering moan as he began to work slowly in and out. He breathed Adrian's name over and over, and the boy's fragrant breath fanned Adrian's face. The heat of their ardor caused them to perspire, but in their passion, the sweat smelled of rose water. The athlete continued to kiss and caress Adrian's face and chest as he worked. Adrian ran his hands all over the beautiful, muscular body that held him. He touched Xenephon's nipples, and the boy increased his pace.

The great cock stayed bone-hard as he shoved it in and out over the screaming prostate.

Adrian could feel his juices pushing toward freedom, and he pulled the boy to him as he met him thrust for thrust. Finally, in a last thrashing, pushing, rending shove, the Prince cried out and spilled his young seed into Adrian, who shot a bolt of semen across his and the chest of the wonderful boy. They floated slowly down to earth as Xenephon licked the milk of love from Adrian's chest. It was a moment to cherish forever. Afterward, the two young men nestled in each other's arms and dozed until early morn when the Prince took him again. The two climbed toward the summit together, and their climax was the pinnacle of Adrian's experience.

As the hours and days went by, their fondness for one another grew to a tender and often blazing love. For weeks, they did not leave the Prince's apartments.

Food was brought in to them, but often went untouched as they tasted the feast of love. The boy was an excellent instructor and found an apt and eager pupil in the ravenous Adrian. Twice during the weeks of their "honeymoon," Xenephon brought some of his friends over and treated Adrian to an orgy of new delights even the carvings on the wall were unable to portray. Usually the young men who visited them came in pairs, but didn't hesitate to switch partners. Fun and Greek games! Sometimes they would form a daisy chain and enjoy a mass blow job. There was something incredibly exciting about doing it in a group with equal interests. Adrian liked them all and found that each tasted different and had different and often kinky methods to their madness.

Above all, as in the games, Xenephon was the best.

The year of their passion flew by. But all good things must end, and finally, in a lavish parting ceremony, Adrian bid farewell to Xenephon, who sailed away to his princess.

Adrian was desolate. No one could console him.

Menelaus patted him on the back and offered him a replacement for the adorable Xenephon, but at the moment, Adrian felt there was no being on earth who could take the place of his beloved.

Helen hung around him and kissed him a little more than gently on the cheek. She whispered something about "a roll in the hay," but Adrian was too preoccupied with his own grief to notice.

He wandered the halls with his head drooping and his very soul in torment. He came at last to their room.

He thought of all the wonders that had been performed there, and as he gazed at the bas relief on the wall, he sighed a deep sigh.

Suddenly he heard a scurrying of feet. He turned toward the window. There was no breeze, yet the heavy curtains were moving in a most mysterious way.

Beneath them, he could see sandaled feet sticking out.

"Who's there?" demanded Adrian.

"Shh. Not so loud. Ya want to get me killed?" came a muffled voice from the draperies. Then a handsome blond head peeked out. "I'm Paris."

"Not *the* Paris?" Adrian exclaimed in a whisper.

The Prince winked at Adrian. "Is there more than one?"

Adrian shrugged, but even in the curtained shadows, he could see that Paris, the chosen of the gods, was as beautiful as his legend.

The famous troublemaker whispered again, "Hey, man, you're kinda cute, ya know."

"Yeah, I know, but you're gorgeous!"

"Maybe we should get together as soon as I get out of this mess," Paris offered.

"What mess?"

"Troy and Sparta have been arch enemies for centuries. My ship got smashed on those damned rocks, and I'm the only survivor. I made my way up the river, and here I am. If they catch me, it's curtains for ol' Paris."

Adrian thought for a moment. Then an idea struck him.

"What we need is a hostage. I'm going with you, beautiful. Let's see ... who'd make a good hostage?"

Just then, Adrian spied Queen Helen coming around the corner. She headed in their direction.

"Adrian, honey," she called out. "I've been looking for you. How about a roll in the hay?"

Adrian pretended he didn't hear the remark. "How about the Queen?" suggested Adrian.

"Now there's a history making idea," agreed the Prince of Troy with a look toward the approaching Queen.

"Who's he?" demanded the Queen, glaring at the handsome prince.

"Helen, I'd like you to meet Paris. Paris, Helen."

"Hi there," said Paris.

"Paris? A Trojan?" yelped the Queen. "I'll get the guards. Menelaus will have his head!"

"Helen, cool it," admonished Adrian.

"Oh very well, he's safe for now. But how about you and me have a little romp in yon hay?" she asked pointing toward the nearby bed.

"But your majesty, not in front of our guest," gasped the shocked Adrian Metropolis.

"Matters not," returned the Queen. "Ya got a cute little bod and I want it."

"What about Menelaus?" inquired Adrian.

"You mean his fuckin' Royal Impotence? He couldn't get it up for me if his crown depended on it," the Queen scowled a queenly scowl. "I've tried everything. I mean *everything*! I've twirled and stoked and sucked it. I even sat on it and did a three-hundred sixty degrees."

"Maybe ..." Adrian tried to suggest.

Helen went on unimpeded; growing angrier with every word. "Oh, he's horny enough for that heel, Achilles. I peeked through the door at those two one night. I couldn't believe it," she said to the fascinated pair.

"Can you imagine, Menelaus was fucking Achilles in the armpit!"

Adrian winked at Paris. "Oh, the old armpit caper."

The Queen turned her baby blues on Adrian and batted her eyelashes. "Come on Adrian, just a quickie?" she pleaded.

Adrian put a hand to his forehead. "I've got a headache. How about Paris here?"

Helen of Sparta – soon to be Helen of Troy – .she was the original jet-setter – spat a mighty spit. "A Trojan? They're poison! Besides ... they're all fags!"

"They are?" beamed Adrian at Paris.

The Prince of Troy winked at Adrian then said impatiently, "Say folks, while we're standing here playing with ourselves, the net's closin' in on ol' Paris."

"Helen," said Adrian excitedly. "Time's a wastin' look ..." then resignedly he made the sacrifice. "Look, I'll give you a roll in the hay that'll knock yer socks off if you'll help me rescue Paris here."

Helen gave him a suspicious look. "Now wait a minute. I thought this Trojan pansy and I were the only queens in this room. Are you sure you won't pull a Menelaus on me."

"Who me? Of course not," smirked Adrian.

The Prince of Troy smiled. He could see Adrian's fingers were crossed behind his back.

"I'll do most anything for a good lay," admitted the Queen. She thought for a moment. "We can take my barge. We'll dress this Trojan turd in one of my frocks and smuggle him aboard as one of my hand maidens."

The Queen worked quickly. She gathered her staff, and within a short time, they had enough provisions loaded aboard the elegant barge for a month's cruise.

Adrian had to admit, Paris looked adorable in drag, though his broad shoulders did make him look a bit bull-dykish.

About six hours out in the Sea of Crete, Adrian's conscience began to bug him. Finally, he decided he should give the Queen her due. He knocked at her cabin door.

"Go away!" came a pained moan from within.

"But Queenie, what about our roll in the hay?"

"I'm sick. I said I'd do anything for a lay. But, I hate ships, water and voyaging. Just wait 'til I get you on dry land, you little squirt. Now go away and let me suffer in peace."

Adrian sighed a great sigh of relief and moved his nifty little bod back to the ship's stern. He looked out toward the disappearing coast of Sparta. It was great to be alive, but he was lonely. Where was the lovely Paris? Oh, that's right, Paris had KP duty.

Just then he felt strong muscular arms reach around him from behind and press him gently against a broad chest. Sweet scented breath fanned his face as the Prince of Troy whispered in his ear, "Alone at last."

Adrian sighed as the Prince reached inside his robe and caressed his athletic chest. His able fingers touched and teased Adrian's nipples until he moaned with delight. Finally, the Prince turned Adrian to him. The young New York Greek could see that Paris had exchanged his dress for a loin cloth that showed off his brawny body to perfection. Adrian stood back and gazed in wonder at the choice of Aphrodite. His eyes lingered for a moment on the protruding crotch covering. Next, they traveled slowly up the muscled abdomen, then on to the broad chest with its protruding pecs and large tantalizing nipples.

Finally he came to the face. In the fading sun, he saw the glory of the gods revealed to him. Deep brown eyes gazed into his while the Prince's full sensual lips smiled the cutest smile Adrian had ever seen.

Adrian was drawn toward the lips as Paris took him in his arms and pressed their two bodies close. They could both feel their young manhood pulsating against one another. The glorious lips came closer and closer until they touched his. Adrian felt as if he was drowning in a sea of indescribable tenderness. The Prince's tongue crept from between parted lips and searched Adrian's for the surest way to passion. The kiss went on and on. It lingered, was given and returned for what seemed an eternity. As those profound moments in time passed, the Prince withdrew slightly so that he might study Adrian's face. The faint perfume of cloves warmed his face as the Prince whispered his name over and over.

"Adrian ... Adrian ... Adrian, I love you, my Adrian."

Adrian had never known such bliss. This was his destiny, the moment for which he'd been born. His heart nearly burst with the adoration that filled it, and as the young Prince of Troy took him by the hand and led him into the seclusion of stacked provisions, he sighed a blissful sigh.

They lay close together on a pallet of straw. Paris held Adrian close and caressed, and touched and kissed him. Finally, he took Adrian's hand, and with a moan thrust it into the folds of his loin cloth.

Adrian almost fainted dead away. In his hand was the biggest cock he'd ever felt, and he'd felt many of them. The shaft had to be nearly nine inches long and Adrian's tongue grew hard as he caressed it. Then he felt Paris take his own throbbing hard-on. Adrian once again considered how man was perfectly designed for making love. In the classic sixty-nine position –or as the Greeks refer to it, the zeta-omega position – erect cocks curved perfectly over the arc of the tongue. The cocks slid smoothly on a lubrication of saliva, and the lips could be contracted or expanded to meet any contingency. All the other modes seemed equally convenient. A cock in the ass was held firmly, yet allowed plenty of room for any size horn and a cushy tush felt good on the ol' gonads. Or if one did it face-to-face, one could sit in the lap of his lover and wrap his legs around his partner, and they could kiss and adore one another to their heart's content. All these thoughts, combined with the talented workings of Paris mouth, carried Adrian closer and closer to the brink. At last he could hold on no longer. The Prince could sense the moment was near and thrust his phallus deeper and faster until they were thrashing and throbbing in rhythm. Finally they came together. What bliss! What rapture!

After drinking one another dry, they turned and held each other. The kissed and adored and fondled one another in turn. And so their idyll continued for weeks on the Aegean Sea.

At length, almost sadly, the coast of Troy hove into view. The trio's arrival was celebrated with great rejoicing. King Priam and his Queen Hecuba greeted their long lost and presumed dead son with open arms.

There was some consternation at the sight of Menelaus's wife, Queen Helen. Paris' sister, the great prophetess Cassandra, pulled her robe over her head and ran around bare-assed, crying, "We're doomed! We are surely doomed!" As usual, no one paid any attention to her.

Helen tried her damnedest to resign herself to being surrounded by the poisonous Trojans.

Nothing dampened the great celebration that evening.

It was an orgy of food and drink. Most of the court, including Paris, finally passed out. Helen who had an enormous capacity for booze, ended up feeling all tittely. Whereas Adrian, who followed his grandmother's advice of moderation in all (or nearly all) things, sipped his wine and giggled as he watched Troy's royalty go under, one at a time.

He was disappointed that Paris also succumbed to the God of Wine, but before he had much time to worry about that, he saw Helen approaching. She had a predatory look in her eye, and he knew his time had come. Panic seized him as she lay down on his two-man (or two-women, or man and woman) sized couch and pressed her luscious lips to his. He felt smothered.

The sensation was not unpleasant, however.

"Fuck me, fuck me, you little squirt!" She panted as she rolled on her back and pulled him on top of her. Adrian's mind was in turmoil. "Come on Adrian, a bargain's a bargain," admonished the Queen.

Adrian had never done it with a woman before, and though he had a vague idea, it was all from clinical pictures he'd seen. He actually wasn't sure which end was up.

He reached with trembling hand toward Helen's crotch, and she pulled her robe aside to give him better access. He found a patch of curly hair, and as he dallied further, he discovered a tantalizingly damp hole. Surprise, surprise. He stuck his middle finger into it and found it warm and wet. Toward the top he discovered a teeny little weeny. He have it a twirl and Helen let out a delighted snort and moaned, "Yes, Adrian. Yes ... yes ... caress my clit. Oh, you are soooooo gooooood!" She pulled open the cleavage of her gown and exposed the two great moons of her bosom. Her red nipples beckoned to Adrian.

"Momma, momma," he groaned as he pressed sucking kisses on her blossoming buds.

She squealed and reached for Adrian's now throbbing cock. Adrian, who had a great deal of imagination for things erotic, could hardly wait to press his pulsating prick into her cavernous pussy.

Finally, he poised over her for just a moment and then plunged into her wet well. Helen let out a screech of ecstasy and grabbed his little ass as he started to pump. He pushed his cock all the way in as she wrapped her shapely legs around his back. She whimpered and moaned with pleasure.

With each thrust, Adrian plummeted deeper, and as he pulled back, he ran the bulbous head of his throbbing cock over the hardened tip of Helen's clit. And how she loved it!

"Oh, Adrian! You are the best! The very best!" she cried.

He road her far into the morning, and as he traveled his new highway, it occurred to him that it felt almost as good as Paris' mouth. And there were no teeth to get in the way.

Finally, Helen grabbed him by is curly hair and screamed as a wrenching climax tore through her body.

The excitement of the new adventure and empathy with Helen's ardor brought Adrian to fulfillment at the same time. He had to admit it was good – better than he'd ever thought it would be to do it with a female. He resolved then and there to enjoy both possible worlds. Naturally he wasn't about to give up the lovely Paris, but this new stuff was all right!

* * * * *

Weeks and months passed with Adrian leading a double life. Each night the adorable Paris brought Adrian new joys and pleasures. Then when they had flown through all the avenues of passion, Paris would, like any normal being, fall into a deep sleep. Adrian wasn't quite so normal. In fact, now that the ancient Greeks had shown the way, he was insatiable. While Paris slept he would steal down the hall to the waiting arms of Horny Helen.

Everything went just beautifully until that fateful night Paris awoke to find himself alone. Suspecting foul play, he rose and scurried down the hall to Helen's room. He opened the door very softly and peered in. Sure enough, across the room he could just make out someone's pumping ass in the moonlight. The ass looked familiar, and as his eyes adjusted to the light, he could see it was indeed the beautiful buns of his loving companion, Adrian.

Paris hesitated not a moment, but flung open the door and rushed to the bed. The Trojan prince was furious and gave Adrian a swat on his bare, pumping ass.

Adrian turned and gave Paris a big grin, while the Queen glared at the Prince.

"Come on in. The fuckin's fine," invited Adrian.

The Prince hesitated, but he was naked and when Helen got a look at his majestic and erect tool, she made a grab for it.

"Yum, yum, yum, let me suck your lollypop, Prince," she crooned.

Helen sucked Paris's big member while Paris kissed and caressed Adrian. Adrian, in turn, fucked the hell out of Helen. The three of them began to enjoy each other's company in and out of bed. They joked and played the whole day long. One of their favorite bedtime pastimes was Adrian in front and Paris giving it to Helen in the back side. She loved the game, and she loved her two fellas.

* * * * *

221

A couple of things happened at the same time: Helen discovered she was pregnant, and the invading Spartan Army pulled the "Great Wooden Horse Caper."

Cassandra warned the populace against accepting the Greeks peace offering. For once, at least Paris listened.

He and his two roomies were on hand when the horse was brought ceremoniously into the city. They watched while the celebrants became blotto, and the trio sat horrified and silent as a squad of Spartan soldiers stole out of the horse and let in the army.

While the Spartans sacked and pillaged and raped the Trojans, the great horse was left unattended. Paris helped Helen and Adrian inside and with a crow bar got the great animal rolling toward the main gates.

The Prince of Troy jumped aboard as the horse rolled out of the gates, down the beach and into the surf.

It was well constructed and floated out with the ebbing tide. Out they went past the thousand ships, which ironically, had brought the Spartan army to rescue Helen, and on into the open Aegean Sea.

The next day, Paris rigged a sail, and they proceeded through the Dardanelles, across the narrow sea to a deserted stretch of Grecian coastline. There they built a cozy cottage for the expectant Helen.

By the way, her exposure to her two companions' tender, loving care had completely rid her of her shrewish, viperous tongue. After the two men helped her deliver their son, Helen of Troy and Sparta turned out to be the sweetest mother and wife imaginable.

No one was sure which one was the father, but they didn't care. The trio loved each other in their fashion, and they adored their baby boy, Troy.

However, it must be remembered that most men will shove their erect cocks into any place that feels good; be it hand, mouth, ass, wet n' wild snatch or ... uh ... armpit, so Adrian and Paris serviced Helen regularly to keep her happy and agreed the three-way stuff was OK. Still, the two males were predominantly gay, and preferred their love-making one-on-one. Their tender togetherness giving them the sort of pleasure ordinary love can never bring.

Perfection – A Novella
By Kyle Michel Sullivan

He had the longest, smoothest, most perfectly shaped legs I'd ever seen, with hair the color of corn silk, soft like down and glinting gold in the morning sun as it swirled up skin tanned to just the right shade. His shoulders were broad, but not so much that they dominated his body, and his hips were slim, but not so much that they seemed narrow. More of the golden threads whispered up clean arms and even more lay gentle over his chest (well, what little of his chest that I could see above the few buttons he'd left undone). Further glints were visible across a smooth but firm chin (probably three days growth of beard for him), indicating how masculine he was even though his face was still unlined. He was at least six-feet tall, and longish hair crowned impossibly blue eyes that were still open to the world. He wore a white cotton shirt (long sleeves rolled up) tucked into an old pair of corduroy "OP" shorts that were so retro they were new, again, with Topsiders on his feet (no socks) instead of Nikes or boots, giving his casual stride just the right grace and making his proportions feel exactly right. And when I saw him on that April day under a cloudless sky, exiting one of those overpriced Lexus convertibles, all I could think was, "I've got to have you."

On canvas, that is. Nothing weird or kinky here. I'm too – what was that word my mom once used on me? – "risky-less" to get into something like that. Besides, I already knew better than to expect such a thing was possible because of the golden female "twin" who was driving the Lexus. I'd seen them both around campus, and you could tell from the way they clung to each other and kissed that they were anything but brother and sister.

Dammit.

I mean it's one thing to want to possess perfection; it's totally something else to have to compete with it for it if that makes any sense. Especially when you're like me.

Not that I'm ugly or vividly deformed or anything. I'm just average – in every way be it height, weight, looks or attitude. I can't tell you how many times I've been told by my jock brothers that if I'd just put some effort into it, I could have a good body instead of an okay one (and lose twenty IQ points doing it, I'm sure). And how many times my sister told me I could get any girl I wanted if I'd just talk to them and smile a bit more – "as if," to quote an old "Valley Girl". And how many times my mom told me that even though my skin freckles instead of browns, like theirs, it's no big deal (to them, maybe). Fact is I think the only time I ever heard my dad make a joke was when he suggested I was conceived by the Holy Ghost because I was almost that white (which for years made me wonder if what he was really saying was, I wasn't really his). No, the one problem here was I'm male and I saw zero indication Mr. Perfect-Man-On-Campus would be interested in anything like what I wanted him to be interested in.

If I really was interested in that.

I know, it makes no sense. After all, I've done things with guys. Older ones who picked me up and liked to be called "daddy" as they sucked me off (a crude way of putting it, but it was a brutally crude kind of fulfillment). And others about my own age who liked the fact that I looked five years younger than I really am (which was creepy) and who only wanted to get their rocks off and split before you were able to find out their names. I'd get a moment's satisfaction out of it, but I never really enjoyed it, never really knew if it was right for me, if it really was "my way."

Not that women ever did anything more than make me uncomfortable. I mean, a couple have, but I've only come close to going all the way with one, and she was a dyke in my high school who just wanted to see what it was like with a guy. Jeez, we got so freaked at just the heavy petting stage we both bolted from the bedroom and slammed *The Sound of Music* into the DVD player to keep from having to deal with it (I still sigh over Christopher Plummer singing "Edelweiss" at the end).

Anyway, there's the real problem. Here I am, a third year art major, finally and officially legal for anything and everything I could possibly want to do (at least, what I'd be allowed to do in Texas, it being such a fascist state), and I don't know what it is that I want to do – in anything, be it career, future, life or love. Not cool, to say the least.

And, on that particular day (period of time, really), I was in the middle of really regretting coming to this university because suddenly nothing I did seemed to please me or the idiots who call themselves "professors of art." My smooth, sweeping, monochrome landscapes were "perfunctory." My still-lifes layered in colorful oils were "derivative." My graphic art style portraits (sort of a more detailed Nagel with expansive color; a bit retro but I liked the feel) were compared to "second rate crap you'd see in a junior high public school." And as for history and geology and a course on Faulkner (of all people), they were off to very bad starts. On top of all that, my ridiculously over-priced dorm room was feeling way too small even if it was just me living in it and had piss-poor natural light available, and my folks were howling about the money vis-à-vis my mid-term grades.

But I think the capper was when my asshole former roommate who still swears he's straight got wasted on Tina and tried to rape me. When I wouldn't let him (probably the only time I ever successfully knocked a guy on his butt), he called my mom while he was still stoned and told her how I liked it up the ass, which I don't; I don't think; at least, I haven't, yet. I convinced her he was full of it, and what helped put it over was how his folks yanked him into rehab the very next day, hence my solitary quarters. All in all, not a banner year.

Anyway, there I was sitting on a bench in the quad, soaking in the last cool breeze of spring (there were already hints in the air of the usual eight-month Texas summer) as I waited to go to my horror of a life drawing class when he hopped out of the Lexus and "his twin" drove away.

Now, I'd seen him around campus before, and I've sketched him on so many sheets of paper (in pencil, in pen) that I've lost count, dashing off the feeling, grabbing the curve of his body under his clothes, adding the details from memory and usually turning out something good (well decent, anyway). You see, there was more than just physical attraction here (I don't usually go for blondes). I have this obsession with proportion. It's so rare to see every aspect of anything match just right – be it a building or tree or human body – that when I do happen upon something or someone that does, I freeze-frame and try to burn it into my brain by rendering it in some form or fashion. So it's not as if he was sudden or new to me.

But there was something about this one time and this one place with everything crashing in on me that seeing how he looked that morning, binging me a hint of peace. A sense of – I dunno – consistency, I guess. So I whipped out my sketchbook and pen, by habit, and glanced at him a few times as he passed, trying to get the feel of the moment as I let my pen dance over the page. Then he caught my eyes for the first time and smiled and nodded in that college-guy way of saying, "I've seen you around campus," and I forgot to breathe. I just sat there, my mind a complete blank until I heard a perfectly modulated Texas drawl purr, "What's that?"

225

I jerked around to find he was eyeing the few lines I'd managed to do in my sketchbook. He laughed, a bit embarrassed.

"Didn't mean to spook you," he said. "Just wanted to see what you're drawin'."

"Nothing," I mumbled. "Just trying to capture something on the fly."

"What?"

Numbly, I slipped the previous page over to reveal the last sketch I'd done – a felt tip scribble of him in left profile, smiling, his arms crossed. I didn't like it, much; it was missing something – a final spark to give it life, maybe, but he still grinned with pleasure.

"That's me. Wow, you're good."

I shrugged and said, "This was just a quickie – a ... a quick sketch," which was a lie. He'd stood still for a good ten minutes waiting for his girlfriend to finish talking with a girl she knew. "I've done better."

He leaned closer to look. "You still signed it."

"I ... I sign all my work, even the stuff that's crap."

"Uh-huh," and he flashed me a smile touched with a twinkle that suggested he knew I knew it was better than I said, then he looked closer at the sketch. "So you're Joe. You did that paintin' that's hangin' in the refectory."

A student leaning into his open locker, casually reading a textbook, done in shades of blue except for his skin, feeling a bit hidden and distant. One of a dozen paintings on exhibit from last semester's composition class, the only art class I did okay in. I was surprised he noticed it – that anyone did.

"Yeah," I croaked out. "One of my classes."

"Art major, huh?" He squatted beside me, those amazing blue eyes piercing into mine, that fan-fuckintastic smile on his face, those perfect legs seeming even more perfect in their sudden fullness, the golden down curling up his thighs to his crotch.

Shit, Joe, don't look at his crotch! Not when he's this close! I concentrated on closing my sketchbook and took a sip of the melted ice in my drink. I was having trouble breathing. My mouth would have made the Mojave Desert seem like a rain forest, and I was suddenly terrified about the tuna sandwich I'd just eaten. But he didn't seem to notice, so I nodded, hoping I didn't look like a monkey in heat, and said, "Third year."

"I'm dual ... sports an' communications. Name's Aaron Friesen," and he held out his hand. I took it, and just the fact that I was touching him in any way, form or fashion sent screaming lighting down my back to my thighs and brought about what has to have been the fastest erection in modern history. Thank God, I'm into briefs instead of boxers.

"Joe Martin." See even my name's average. Well not exactly. It's Joseph Allen Martin, also known as "Jam-The-Cat" in high school, and for none of the dumb reasons you can think of; just mostly because I was heavy into art and used that to keep the dicks who weren't afraid of my jock brothers off my butt. I'd do sketches of them for their girlfriends of the moment and that seemed to get them plenty of play in the back of daddy's car, so I was cool enough for that and for other reasons, and now I'm drifting close to hallucinating because of this gorgeous guy squatting next to me. Not good. Focus on Aaron, you dumb shit.

"Listen, Joe, I'm gonna be straight with you. (Pun intended?) I knew you're an artist. I've seen you workin' in your sketchbook and Andrea – that's my girl – her roomie's seen more of your stuff on exhibit in the art department. She says she saw one that looked a lot like me."

Yeah late autumn by the dorms, sitting under a pecan tree, three-quarters right, soft green T-shirt, tan Dockers, sunglasses, done in easy watercolors and – oh, shit, he's gonna bawl me out for being a fag and staring at him so much!

"I ... I just liked the composition of it," I muttered, "a student under the tree ... studying."

"Cindy liked it, too," he said, still even and smooth. "Fact is, I was wonderin'. My folks' anniversary's in a couple weeks, and I never know what to get 'em. And my brother, Josh, he always gets 'em just the right thing; don't know how he does it. Andrea says since it's their twenty-fifth, I should get 'em something silver, but I was thinkin', y'know, a ... a portrait or somethin' painted would be perfect, this year. So could I ... could I buy that one from you?"

I just looked at him, blank. I would never in a million years have expected him to want anything I'd done. Period. And he wanted to buy this second rate toss-off piece of crap from me? Man. All I could think to say was, "It's just a watercolor."

"I know," he said, looking bashful (Jesus, God, I wanted to hold him). "But Cindy, that's Andrea's roomie, she said she knew it

227

was me the second she saw it, and I think my folks'd like that. I could get it framed and …"

"I'll do a better one if you want."

He looked at me, taken as much by surprise by what I said as I was. "Really? You mean, like off a picture?"

"No," I said, without thinking, "no, pose for me and I could ... I could do something in oils on canvass. It'd take a couple of sittings, but it'd ... it'd mean a lot more. Be a lot more impressive."

"Wow." He thought about it for a moment then looked at me, sideways. "But how much'd that be? I don't have much money."

We could work something out in trade, slammed into my brain but I caught it before it hit my vocals, and all that came out was, "Forty bucks."

"You kiddin' me?"

"No. That'll cover the canvass and materials."

"But that's leavin' nothin' for you." And he had this little I-know-what-you're-up-to smile on his lips.

"I ... I'd get to work with a real model. I've never had one, before," which was a lie. I just never had one I wanted to pounce on before. But he seemed to accept it.

"A couple nights, you said?"

"Yeah. Uh, a few hours Saturday or Sunday then a couple nights over the next week to get the details down. And if it doesn't wind up perfect, I ... I'll give you the watercolor."

"Sounds great."

"Okay. When's good for you?"

"I dunno ... Saturday I'm interning at Channel Two till five ..."

"You could come by, afterwards. I'll have everything ready."

I wrote my dorm and phone number on a strip of paper and gave it to him, hoping he wouldn't notice how my hands were shaking. He chuckled.

"Rushin' Hall? That's across from the Phi-Delts, right?"

"Yeah," I said, smiling. "They keep reminding me every Friday and Saturday night."

"I been there. 'Bout six, then? Saturday night?"

I nodded.

"See you then, Joe. And thanks."

He stood up, and I let my eyes furtively sweep over him, again, then I looked up at him and said, "No big deal."

He smiled and sauntered away, and I watched him go. And I began blessing those little ol' OP shorts, and blessing him for wearing them in the face of a time where style demands that men and boys wear hideous clothing like those baggy half-pants which were, at the very least, a desecration against human anatomy. They fit his form just right, emphasizing his hips instead of his crotch as he neared me, and laughing over his magnificent rear as he strolled away. Now I use the word "rear" deliberately, because there was nothing vulgar in his movements, nothing crass, just the gliding motion of a panther wandering through its domain with a patient benevolence. It hurt me to watch him, to watch the smooth rolling of the shorts as they slid up and down the back of his leg, the golden hairs tickling away from the fabric then gliding back under, like waves whispering upon a gentle shore.

Suddenly, I realized I was about to ejaculate in my briefs. I pressed my legs together and let myself enjoy the sharp little sensations it sent all over my body. Then Aaron glanced back, caught me looking at his rear and turned away, smiling that little I-know-what-you're-up-to smile to himself again. I exploded right then and there. Came close to dying from the beauty of it. At that moment, I realized I could spend the rest of my life doing nothing more than painting this one guy and I'd be happy, just like Andrew Wyeth and his "Helga" pictures. What a dream of a world that would be.

Well, looks like I answered at least one of my questions, and caught a pretty good glimpse of the answer to the other. Only question left was did it really matter?

I don't remember much about the rest of the day, just that I went into this time warp where everything seemed to zoom past in slow motion. I mean, c'mon Aaron Friesen was coming to my dorm room Saturday evening! Aaron-un-fucking-believably-good-looking-Friesen was going to model for me! What else could I possibly care about?

Well, maybe that my place was a brutal mess. And I don't just mean the usual college guy junk of six week old pizza crusts hidden under piles of dirty clothes and text books plopped atop a dozen CD cases whose CDs hung from stick pins rammed into a cork bulletin board. Oh, I had that, sure with empty beer bottles and Dr. Pepper cans and juice cartons mingled in, but I also had sketches I'd crushed and slung aside in frustration or ripped in half and never picked up off that ugly gray carpet. And I had empty plastic peanut butter jars (I like creamy Jiff) I'd washed out and used to hold water for my acrylics or to dilute my oils with a dash of turpentine for a flat feel. I had colors from paintings I'd worked on back in September crusted on the rails of my unmade twin bed and artist's table, and my easel had nothing but a mass of smudges to prove I used it (no tubes of paint or used brushes or discolored canvas or indented pad anywhere in sight). Y'know, the only undamaged work of art in my room was a sketch of a guy in a Polo ad I'd started on a blank wall using a charcoal stick but had never finished. It was a caricature of the worst that a dorm room could be minus nude pictures of girls or posters of sports heroes or rocker boys taped to the walls, and I hadn't realized how bad it was until I came back to it after my last class. Brother. Couldn't have Aaron see what a slob I am, could I? Problem was where to start?

That's when I felt this wave of apathy sweep over me. I'd been feeling it a lot, this year, and that sketch on the wall was like a monument to everything I've been going through. Started but not finished. Interest lost halfway through. Critical eye taking over faster than the brush or pen could find completion. Even that painting that Aaron liked, the one hanging in the refectory, I hadn't completed the guy's backpack or locker; I'd just declared it done, even though deep inside I knew it wasn't.

That's why there were smudges of paint on my bed – from all the times I'd collapsed on it, brush still in hand, fingers coated with color, heart lost in disgust because my latest work was turning out to be crap. Perspective off. Color choices wrong. Original intent swallowed in the details of transcription. I had a thousand fancy phrases excusing me from achieving anything I wanted to and slamming myself for not making it happen, anyway. Typical.

I know where it came from – this growing feeling that my choice of careers was just not going to happen. I mean, who did I think I was, Picasso? I could be sloppy like him but not as emotionally connective. I liked to paint, but I had no burning need to. I enjoyed sketching, but for fun, not to focus the world on my vision. I knew I was good enough and capable of being better, but I didn't have the ego to proclaim myself a genius or say that I was the future of art. I was dabbling, playing with my minimal skills as if I could be the next Rembrandt or Degas or even Sergeant, since I really liked portraiture the most, while knowing deep down I didn't have the spark one needs for greatness. The fact is the only things in my room that even hinted at being good art were my sheets. They used to be white, but now they had this sort of Jackson Pollack feel to them from all the times I'd collapsed on them before cleaning the paint off. Wouldn't it be funny if

I get the most beautiful guy I'd ever met in here by promising to paint his picture and not be able to complete it?

Oh, great. That was *not* what I needed to contemplate.

To keep from thinking about it, I set about cleaning the place up. Nothing like self-flagellation to kick yourself into action. I pulled all my jars together and picked up the papers and long-gone food and made trip after trip after trip to the dumpster. I wound up with six loads of laundry, including pillows and comforters. I wash them because I found it cuts down on my allergies, though this year I hadn't cared enough to bother, and they hadn't bothered enough to bother me. As for the paint on my bed, I added more to make it look deliberate. My freshman art teacher once said, "All mistakes are deliberate ... and if they aren't, make it look like they are." I swept. I dusted. I washed away the charcoal sketch, though it didn't completely vanish, sticking around to haunt me, huh? By the time I got to scrubbing my bathroom, I was dirtier than my dorm ever had been.

I stripped off to do the shower. This was going to be the hard part. There was so much mineral residue from limestone in the water and some rather creepy looking fungus-type things building in the corners. I had an old tooth brush, so I used it and some dish soap to dig into the mess. I think it was close to midnight before I had it mostly gone and was sweating like a pig from the exertion and hot water I used to wash it away when I heard, "Hey," come from behind me. I jumped around, and there was Aaron, standing in the bathroom door, grinning at me!

"Didn't mean to spook you," he said. "You left your door open ... an' I knocked ..."

"Oh, that ... that's okay," I stammered ... and dammit, Joe, you're naked! Shit! I grabbed for a towel but hadn't brought any into the bathroom! "Uh, excuse me. I'll be right out."

He glanced me over then ran a finger over the dirt on my chest and smirked, "Maybe you better take your time." Then he showed me the tip of his finger; it was almost black.

I blushed and stepped back into the shower, muttering, "It'll ... it'll rinse off. Will you toss me a towel? They're in the big basket by the bed ... the door."

He strolled away, and I watched his rear roll under those OP shorts then started soaping up, fast. Oh, this was perfect. Aaron-un-fucking-believably-good-looking-Friesen comes wandering in when I look like something from the garbage dump and probably reeked like that, too. Shit. But then I wondered what I was worried about? He's got a girlfriend and what little gaydar I had was down at zero so far as he was concerned. Her? Well. Maybe it's wishful thinking. I mean, seriously – did I really think we'd wind up in bed?

He returned with the whole basket and set it by the bathroom door and kept looking at me. I could see him through the now almost clear shower door. "Got soap?" he asked.

"Yeah," I stammered. "Thanks. What's up?"

"Just thought I'd come by, see what you're up to. Spring cleanin'?"

"Yeah. I ... there wasn't anyplace to set up my easel, so I ... I got started making space ... and one thing piled on top of the other and here I am."

He laughed, and the deep sexiness of it ripped through me, and I couldn't help but get a hard-on.

"I was gonna ask you if you wanted t' head out for a beer," he said, "but ..." and he opened the shower door and glanced me over and his smile widened as he continued, "... looks like I came at a bad time."

I just gaped at him, surprised. I didn't realize my dick was pointing at him, as if at attention, until he ran his finger over the top of it and said, "You clean, yet?"

I jerked back, so startled I couldn't think of a word to say.

"What?" he asked. "You never had a jerk-off buddy before?"

"Y-yeah," I stammered out, "but ... but ..."

"But what?" he asked as he climbed into the shower, fully clothed except for his shoes.

The square basin was barely big enough for us both, and in seconds, Aaron's shorts and shirt were wet and clinging to his perfect body. I could see the darkness of his nipples under the white cotton, erect and ready and promising joy. The golden hair darkened under the effect of the water, and it playfully swirled over his chest and down the center of his smooth abs to a neat little "innie" of a belly button. And I could tell he was wearing boxers from the bulge in his OP shorts (it swung to the left). The beauty of it, the perfection, kept me speechless.

Impulsively, I grabbed his shirt and pulled him close, felt the warm wet cotton whisper against my body as I kissed him. Oh man, his lips were so, so smooth and moist and fit my own so perfectly. And his nose brushing the side of mine and his eyebrows mingling with mine gave me a rush like nothing I'd ever experienced, before. His hands trailed around to my back, strong hands, a guy's hands, and tickled down my spine and danced over my butt and crushed me closer to him. My erection slipped between his legs, so he pressed his thighs together, and the combination of the soft wet hair on them and the hem of the shorts tickling me almost drove me insane. I pulled at the buttons of his shirt, but he took my hands and stretched them down to my side and rammed his whole body against mine, pressing me against the tiles as he kissed me, even harder.

Through the shorts, I could feel he was as hard as I was. He was rubbing up and down against my belly, rolling under the material, and I wanted to hold him, to touch him, but he wouldn't let go of my hands. He just kept grinding his body against mine, the cotton and corduroy gliding over my skin and my tits and my pubes until I was sure I was going crazy. The water kept steaming, and his tongue kept probing mine, and his body kept rubbing me and suddenly I could feel him pushing harder and harder and jerking in spasms as he ejaculated into his shorts. Then I exploded between his thighs. I'd never done that twice in one day, before. He crushed even harder against me and the screaming lightning roared down the inside of my legs and – the hot water ran out!

I took a cold blow back to reality and Aaron vanished into the back of my mind as I slammed out of the shower with a yelp and smacked my hip on the sink at the just the wrong spot. Pain shot through my left leg, and I dropped onto the toilet. I put my head in my hands and, for a second, tried to bring back the picture of being with Aaron, but it was gone. Shit! Couldn't I even have a moment to enjoy the explosion I was feeling?

Man, right there, right there is the story of my life – lusting after a straight guy who wouldn't give me a second thought except that he wants something. And despite my hopes to the contrary, deep down I really knew all I'd ever get out of him was a jack-off fantasy, and that would be in a shower that went cold faster than it got hot. Irritating and typical and so damn depressing.

I finally rose and dried off and flopped naked onto my now clean bed (something I never do; I usually sleep in a pair of briefs) in my now clean dorm room and drifted into sleep, thinking about Aaron, knowing in the back of my little brain I was beginning to fixate on him and not caring that I was. Which was also typical and also depressing.

Why is it that all I ever want is what I can't have?

Well, now I had two of my questions answered beyond any doubt. I definitely wanted to paint (so long as Aaron was my model), and I was definitely into having sex with a guy (so long as it was Aaron Friesen). Dammit. I don't know why I thought deciding how I felt about those two concerns in my life would make things easier for me. Shit, I was even more confused than before.

I mean, seriously – would I be this hyped up over doing a portrait if my model was to be some ninety-year-old man or some radiant mother's six-year-old brat? So was I really interested in art or just the fantasy of it? The dream of getting a good-looking guy into bed with it? Was I aiming to be nothing more than a fag who paints pretty nude boys with nice hard erections and smooth skin and perfect hair and way too excellent muscles? What Tom of Finland did was fine for him (hey, I did a few little "illustrated stories" of my own when I was in high school and needed some way to pop off the steam), but their work was so – I dunno – so limited and a bit too laced with prurience for my needs. That was my word of the month – prurient. Hell, just about anybody can draw a decent looking naked guy with a hard-on. Why would I want to be just like them? Yet, having Aaron sit next to me – giving me the chance to paint just his perfect face and capture just his perfect smile and find just the right shade for his golden hair – God himself couldn't have told me that I was not meant to do at least this.

Which begs the question, so why do you still have questions, idiot? You're obviously psyched about this guy and can't wait to show off what little ability you have as an artist. And you had enough confidence in yourself to offer to show it, and not just because you think it'll get him into bed with you. It's something you'd enjoy doing, so what's the big deal? And the answer is I don't know!

You see, I've never really felt like this before. In fact, it's usually been the opposite. In my life drawing class, last year, the nude model was this viciously frumpy girl who had rolls of flab cascading down her bones. No, that's unfair; she was just overweight (by about forty pounds, I think) but I hated drawing her. I didn't mind that she was a girl; I was just irritated that she looked so sloppy. I felt the same way toward the nude guy we had on one or two occasions, who had next to no body fat and carried sharply defined muscles and was generally in good proportion, but who hid his face behind this scraggly beard and didn't believe in using deodorant. Guess that makes me picky or snotty or something like that, but I have to have a subject I can be proud to have painted, and I've only come close to having one of those.

It was a guy named Leon in ninth grade. Leon was a dick, to put it kindly. He pretty much ignored me in the few regular classes we had together, but he had some cruel fun with me in gym due to the fact that I was not as developed as the other boys. But he was headed toward being a good-looking guy, in a small-eyed cowboy kind of way, so I'd still done a couple sketches of him when things were slow in English.

Anyway, one day I was kept late after school (detention, actually; I got caught doodling during a geography lecture, for the twentieth time). I'd just called my mom, who said she couldn't get me for half an hour, so I went to some benches by the tennis courts to wait. And that's where I saw Leon sitting on one of those decorative rock formations that landscapers seem to think are so cool. He was scrunched up, arms across his knees, chin resting on his arms, looking mournful. He didn't see me, which was fine so far as I was concerned, so I sat down and started doing homework.

But I found myself sneaking glances at him, and not because I was attracted to him. (I hadn't fully figured out what my urges were, at that time.) There was just something about his position and the solitude around him that caught my heart, so I pulled out my sketchbook and snapped off a fairly decent rendition of the moment, using a soft pencil and handkerchief for smudging in some texture. In fact, I found myself praying that he wouldn't move before I got the position down and some of the details, and he didn't. Not until a beat-up old station wagon pulled up, and he slipped off the rocks and sadly plopped into the back seat. A tired gray woman was behind the wheel. My first thought was that she's his grandmother, and she did not even look at him. They just drove off. I don't think he ever saw me or ever even thought to see me; he was just lost in his own little world of misery and pain as are all fifteen-year-old boys, myself included.

Funny thing is here he was, one of the guys making my life hell, and suddenly I ached for him. I don't know why. Maybe it's because the old gray woman never even acknowledged him as he got in the car. Maybe it was the way he was sitting on the rock formation. Maybe it was just my own pitiful mood. Whatever it was, a couple days later I photocopied the sketch and slipped it into one of his books during English.

Leon was out of school for a couple days after that, and I forgot about it. Then he stopped me, a week later, and showed me the sketch and asked, "You do this?"

"No," I said. I was kind of scared of him.

"You know who did?"

"Nope. Why?"

He growled and turned to walk away then stopped. He didn't look at me as he said, "My momma died, couple days ago. Cancer. I ... I found it, today, in one of my books, second I opened it for class and ... and ... and ... it's like she ... she ..." He couldn't finish; he was too close to tears.

All I could think to say was, "Wow. I'm sorry."

He stiffened, glared at me and snarled, "You tell anybody 'bout this, I'll beat the crap out of you ... and ... and I don't give a damn about your brothers! You got me?"

I nodded. He stormed off. Never spoke to me, again. Not even to make fun of me in gym. I still have that sketch. And it's not perfect, perspective's off, his head's too small for his body, the feet look awkward, but my critique of it is gentle – not like how I can get with my work, today, and I can see a little quality in it. I guess I was hoping I'd find that, again, with Aaron.

So Saturday finally came inch-by-inch the clock neared 6:00 pm. I had everything ready – a comfy chair I'd "borrowed" from the refectory for him to sit in, a pair of lamps flanking the chair to give me decent light, Cokes and beer in my dinky little fridge, chips and dip and some Zero Seven on the stereo. The easel was positioned just right, a two-by-four pre-framed canvas resting on it, all treated and ready for oils to be applied. I had a pad of sketch paper for some studies, my Derwent pencils were sharpened (I only use #4b), and I had a fresh stick of charcoal to outline his position on the canvas.

I'd taken a shower at 4:00 pm and dressed very carefully in too-cool-artist-casual-chic – clean T-shirt with a slightly frayed collar and one tiny hole in it (for just the right feel), slim-fit jeans that were about four inches too long so bunched at my ankles, deck shoes with drops of paint on them. The way I was obsessing about how everything came across, you'd think I was prepping for a date.

And then came a knock at the door – finally! I opened it, and there was Aaron, still almost painful to look at. He wore a plain white shirt, Dockers and his Topsiders and looked so clean and fresh, I felt as if I hadn't bathed in a week.

"Hey, Joe," he said, grinning that fan-fucking-tastic grin.

"Aaron," I managed to say, "is it that time?" God, I was so proud of myself for being able to say that without a waver in my voice.

"Nope, I'm runnin' late."

"C'mon in," I said, and then I noticed the twin was with him. Dammit.

"Oh, Joe, this is Andrea," he said as if he had just realized she was there.

"Hi," she said. "You are so cool to do this."

I blinked. I was "so cool?" Jeez, where was she raised, on Saturday morning TV? Fortunately, the manners my mother beat into me as a child (figuratively, not literally; we don't have *that* kind of family) took over, and I smiled as I said, "Thanks. C'mon in. You guys want something to drink? I have DP, Shiner Bock, some kind of juice drink."

"You drink Bock?" Aaron asked.

"Yeah," I said. "Love it."

"Never tried it."

I pulled one from the fridge and handed it to him. "Try one, now. Andrea?"

"I'll just have some water, thanks."

I pulled out a bottle, twisted off the top and handed it to her as Aaron sipped at the Bock.

"Nice," he said.

"I got some chips, if you want."

"No, thanks," said Andrea.

"We're gonna grab a bite after I'm done, here," Aaron smiled.

Well so much for the thoughts that had settled in the back of my head despite my best efforts. Not that I should have been surprised; I already had a pretty good idea he thought I was gay, and the fact that he brought this female with him to act as chaperone just proved it.

Hey, I may be dumb, but I ain't stupid. Oh well, at least I'll get to sketch him.

"Then we'd better get to work," I said, making myself smile and glance at Andrea. "I have a stool at my art table, if you want to sit."

"Thanks," she said.

Hmmph, limited vocabulary, though I guess when you're blond and beautiful, you don't need to be able to understand anything deeper than *Nancy Drew*, huh, bitch?

I turned to Aaron. "This chair's for you. And I'll be here."

"Cool," he said, and coming from him it sounded like high praise. "How you want me to sit?"

"However's comfortable."

He glided into the chair, lounged back like a lion settling down to survey his pride, and looked straight at me. "This okay?"

"Fine," I said, fighting to keep that waver from my voice. "I'm gonna do a couple of quick pencil studies, first, to get a feel for your face."

"You ain't already got that?" he said, and his smile carried that same *I-know-what-you're-up-to* hint that I'd seen before.

"This time I don't have to do it on the fly," I smiled, looking straight back at him.

He shrugged, sipped his beer and took a deep breath. "Then let's get to it, boss."

So I grabbed my Derwent #4b and the sketchpad and got to work. And I did sketch after sketch after sketch of his face from a number of different angles and aimed for a number of different feels, trying to figure out the best ways to capture his beauty on canvas.

And it was the worst hour of my life! Not one friggin' sketch turned out right! Not one! Three-quarters left with shading, and his nose became this monster fit for Cyrano de Bergerac. Full-face line drawing and his eyes were off center. Profile swipes of full pencil made his neck seem too thin and the back of his head flat. Quick whipping circles made him look puffy. I tried doing an eye, just by itself, in the basic art school fashion, and it grew deformed. I focused on his chin, and suddenly it exploded into contours that brought to mind Picasso at his most second-rate cubist period. By the time I started trying to get just his mouth right, I was beginning to lose it.

I didn't know what the problem was, but I could not find a way to translate Aaron from my eye to my mind to my hand! A ten-second sketch I did of him once while he and Andrea waited at a traffic light was a better rendition of him than anything I was doing, that evening. By the time I'd torn the tenth sketch out of my pad and slung it over my shoulder, I was ready to jump out a window, I was so frustrated.

I think Aaron and Andrea felt it because she began picking up the sketches and saying things like, "Oh, this is good" and "Baby, he got your ears just right," and bullshit like that. And Aaron's smile kept getting smaller and smaller and less certain. Guess they thought I was locked in some kind of creative death spiral and were afraid I was gonna do the equivalent of a fired-worker rampage or something. I finally slung the pencil across the room, yanked a Bock from the freezer and guzzled half of it down just to shift my focus away from my exploding sense of failure.

I mean, shit, I wanted so much to impress him, to "wow" him and make him like me and become my friend and let me hold him or just be with him and enjoy the beauty of his light, and I was fucking it up, so perfectly. Now he'd know I'm nothing but a stupid little faggot who's just like all the other faggots who've probably come onto him, and I'd be dismissed like I was shit on his shoe. Just something to wipe off.

Aaron slipped out of the chair and sort of crept over to me and said, "Hey, boss ... you okay?"

"Yeah, I ... I'm fine ...I ...I ..." I muttered, then said, "I don't get it. I *can't* get it. I ... I've never had this problem before. I ... I can't get the sense of your face. The contours and life and ... and ..."

I couldn't continue. My stomach was churning, and I was tasting something far stronger than beer in the back of my throat. Oh, perfect – now I'm about to be sick in front of him.

Andrea took on this soothing expression (I could have killed her for it) and said, "Hey, Joe, it's okay. I know how you creative types can get ... and it's no big deal."

I turned away from her. I couldn't believe she said "you creative types"! That made me sound like some fucking lab experiment, and I was about to lose my manners with that bitch.

Aaron picked up one of the sketches and shrugged. "Really, Joe, it don't look bad."

"What the fuck do you know?" I snapped back, before I could censor the thought. "It's shit! All of it's shit! I don't know what the fuck I was thinking, saying I could paint you. I'm a fucking idiot."

He got this way too patient expression on his face and said, "Tell you what, why don't I just buy that watercolor off you for the forty?"

I was already ashamed of my outburst, so I nodded. "Lemme get it."

I went to a closet and pulled out one of my portfolios. I have one for every semester, and I make damned sure I get every piece of my artwork back, no matter how crappy it is. Nobody gets to mess with my work but me. I was already digging through it before I realized I was in the wrong one. I was about to put it back when I noticed a sketch I'd done in second semester drawing. It was a squiggly line drawing of a Chianti bottle with a candle stuck in it and wax dribbling down the sides, like what you see in cheap Italian restaurants. A nice little rendition layered in more emotion than I'd remembered. No great news, but it stopped me dead.

"Aaron," I said, not thinking (if I had thought about it, I'd never have said a thing), "lemme try something."

"What's that?" he asked.

I rose, holding the sketch of the wine bottle.

"My ... my second semester here," I said, "I took this experimental drawing class, where you try all sorts of things to jolt you out of old habits. One exercise was we had to blindfold ourselves and sketch something by feel. We didn't know what it was until the professor put it on a stool next to us. I wound up with this candle in a wine bottle."

He gave me a wary look and said, "Uh-huh." I think he already had an idea what I was going to ask, so I let it bolt out of me.

"Can I touch your face? Get a feel for it?"

Andrea finally popped in on what I was asking – the dumb bitch. "Wait, you want to what?"

"I want to close my eyes and run my fingers over his face and do a sketch, that way. Maybe that'll help me out of this artist's block I've got."

"You can't draw like that!" she said.

"I already have," I snapped back. I slapped the sketch into her hands and began digging in my box of supplies. "But I can't do it with graphite ... I need a Conte pencil. Something I can feel on the paper."

"That sounds kind of weird, Joe," Aaron said, and even though I wasn't looking at him, I could tell he was giving me his *I-know-what-you're-up-to* smile, again.

I found a good piece of Conte and turned to him.

"Head and shoulders, only," I said. "I won't go any lower. Andrea's here, so you know I won't try anything else." And that was my tacit acknowledgement that I knew he knew I was out to sleep with him.

Man, I was feeling bold, all of a sudden (or maybe it was desperate) but I *had* to break free of this growing feeling that I was an abject failure, and maybe this would help. It couldn't hurt, and no one was going to expect anything from it, anyway, not even me. "She can even blindfold me, to make it all correct. Think of it as a magic trick ... or stunt."

I wish I could have thought up a better argument, but hey – he cast a glance at Andrea, who was not looking too pleased then he slipped me that little grin, again, and said, "Should I sit back in the chair?"

"No, the stool," I said, and I popped my art table stool right beside my easel. Then I grabbed a paint cloth from the table and offered it to Andrea. "Will you do the honors?"

"Why do I feel like this is something David Copperfield would pull?" she asked as she came over and took the rag. Not a great joke, but not a bad one. Dammit.

I propped my sketchpad on the easel, again, and readied the Conte pencil in my right hand. Aaron sat on the stool, just inches from me, his wary expression still riding his face.

"Just be careful," he said, only half joking.

I spread my fingers and positioned them atop his left eyebrow, then Andrea blindfolded me. And, she did it tight, too, the bitch. I took a couple of deep breaths, ripped the realization that I was actually fucking *touching* Aaron Friesen's face out of my mind and made myself focus.

Okay, left eyebrow.

I ran my fingers over it, light and gentle, trying to translate what I felt with my left hand into what I was drawing with my right. Let's see, nice arch to it. Hair's smooth, not bristling. Neatly follows the shape of his eye socket. Not bad.

Slowly on to his left eye. Good form. Smooth flesh above the eye, and not too much, either. Lid creases back with a fraction of the lid remaining. Soft eyelashes in good order, too.

"This tickles," said Aaron.

I shushed him then followed the top eyelid around to the bridge of his nose. So far, he was perfect and smooth and felt exactly as I thought he would feel. And the bridge of his nose was no different. A small round dip from the forehead down to the top of his perfect straight – wait a minute! His nose isn't straight. The bone bulges a bit at the top then curls down in a slope, and the dip is more of a sharp circle that's been sliced into it.

I stopped and felt the sheet of paper, found the smooth waxy line of the pencil and made an adjustment where I thought I had drawn the bridge, then my left hand drifted over to his right eyebrow. It felt the same as the left. Nice arch to it. Hair's smooth, not bristling. Neatly follows the shape of the socket and –wait! It angles down more sharply than the other.

241

I stopped and let my fingers play over his skin, trying to get a better feel for the shape of his skull. Then I noticed the hairs on his eyebrow curled into each other more, and there was a slight crease running at a slant through them at the point where they danced down around his eye, and the texture of them changed, slightly. I stopped.

"You have a scar," I said.

I felt his face turn to me, just a bit.

"Yeah," he said. "You can feel it?"

I nodded. I heard Andrea come over.

"Where?" she asked. I could picture her bending in close to look. *Get the fuck back.*

"Right eye, where his finger is. Josh and me had just seen *The Three Musketeers* and we were havin' a duel with butter knives, and he got me, good. But that's back when I was seven. I thought it'd all healed."

"There's just a hint of it," I said. But it was something I had missed just by looking at him.

And then I started to understand my problem – I hadn't really been looking at him. I'd just been gazing upon him, like you do with a statue or some piece of installation art shit. I wasn't seeing him because I thought I already *had* seen him and had already formed him in my mind (if that makes any sense). He was cast in stone, and I was trying to translate something cold and impersonal into something alive, and that's not right.

Suddenly, I was noticing the little details that made him human instead of merely perfect. I drifted my fingers back over to his left eyebrow and felt it, again, and this time, I noticed the same pattern in the hair – it wasn't straight and smooth, not really; it also curled just a little, just enough to give it a wavy depth. And this time, I noticed there was just a bit of sharpness in the bone of his brow, meaning his forehead was not just smooth and even, but had curves and meaning all its own. Once again, lightning was screaming from my fingertips, but this time, it danced across my mind.

My hand trailed over to his hairline and along it to his sideburns and caressed the beginning of a sharp cheekbone and drifted down to where his jaw began, just in front of his ear. His skin was not merely smooth but carried hints of blemishes, still, as it rolled across the formations that build his face. I traced the line of his chin and felt the warmth of his breath on my palm as my fingers did their light little dance over the merest of clefts in dead center, directly below his mouth. His breathing seemed softer to me, deeper, and that warmth enveloped me in dreams and made me hesitate. And then I heard him lick his lips.

I stopped. I couldn't get a sense of where Andrea was, and I didn't want to continue unless I knew. "You're not looking at the sketch, Andrea."

I heard her move, slightly, behind me. She was.

"Don't tell me what it looks like," I said.

I heard her swallow before she said, "Okay," in a soft voice that had risen a couple of octaves.

I choked off a scream of joy. The way she said that one little word expanded reality within me, and I knew the experiment was working, and the sketch was evolving, and she was impressed, which is a good thing, even if it was her.

I drew my fingers up from Aaron's chin to his mouth, felt the hint of stubble peeking from his skin – *does your beard grow fast or do you just not shave every day?* His lips felt fuller than I had pictured, rounder, smoother, warmer, and then he licked them, again, his tongue glancing off my fingers.

This time, the screaming lightning ripped right down my back and slamming into my thighs. And this time it took the combination of both my briefs and my jeans to keep my erection hidden. But this time there was a million times more to it. Yeah, it was a charge to be touching Aaron like this, to feel his reactions to my caress, but I felt like it was beyond simple lust. I was finally connecting to him, and that connection was whispering from my left fingertips to my right ones and giving me a view of him I could never have imagined. Now he seemed to be part of me, and he was even more beautiful than before.

My fingers continued their exploration across his face. I found the tip of his nose has a hint of a point to it and little dents over the nostrils to keep them from being too smooth. And his left cheekbone curved a bit more than the right one, but the skin on his face had filled it in so that you would never notice unless you actually measured it. And his ears were colder than his cheeks, so they should be a hint bluer. And his earlobes were soft and rounded and creased under to his jaw. And his right eye was a bit rounder than his left. I felt the softness of skin between the prickly hints of beard above his Adam's apple and noticed how sharp was that point in his throat. And how the muscles of his neck blended together like tiny threads twisted around a straw. And the pulse of his blood through his veins was in unison with mine. And the little dip of bone at the base of his throat (the sternum?) was a half circle so precise, it could have been measured by an engineer. And the little hairs at the top of his chest brushed against me as if in welcome, and I felt a fullness in my throat and such joy and wonder, and I had to step back from the growing overload of sensation.

I yanked the blindfold off in a bit of a fog, or trance, maybe; I don't know. Even with the low light, I had a hard time adjusting them to where I could see. Aaron was in deep soft focus, but I could tell he was looking at me, unmoving. His breath was still and deep and quick. And Andrea was behind me, still looking at the sketch. I finally got my eyes under enough control to view what I had done.

And there he was in soft black Conte pencil against white paper. Oh, the lines were uneven in spots, and I'd doubled back over his features in a couple of places. And the shape of his head was indistinct (in fact, I hadn't even really tried to do more than get his eyes, nose, mouth and chin). But this sketch had captured his look. It showed his beautiful little *I-know-what-you're-up-to* smile. And his eyes were deep with feeling. And his nose, which I had tried so hard to make straight and perfect, curved a little and became more real than anything I had sketched before. And the line of his chin was in proportion to everything else. Even his ears looked just a little bit cold (I know it's crazy to say that, but I really do think they did). I was stunned into silence.

"Aaron," Andrea whispered, "you have to see this."

He hesitated then rose and stretched and looked at the sketch, and I looked at him and noticed his nipples were pressing against the fabric of his shirt. Without thinking, I glanced down. His left ankle crossed his right one, making his left leg jut a bit out, but it couldn't hide the extra bulge showing inside his Dockers – so, he *is* a boxers kind of guy. I looked up at him, still not thinking, and realized he was looking straight back at me, a hint of confusion in his eyes. I turned away, shaken. I still could not speak.

Somehow, Andrea set up the next session for Tuesday, 6:00 pm. Only reason I know is she wrote it on a slip of paper. All I could do was nod in answer as she and Aaron left.

I cannot remember one single solitary thought I had at that point. I couldn't even tell you for sure that I had one. I was a zombie caught in some deep black magic so soft and pure and quiet I didn't even know it existed. All I could do was gaze at the sketch, watch it gaze back at me, watch it seem to breathe and smile Aaron's secret little smile and wait for me to respond. And suddenly I was bawling.

Now this wasn't anything at all like weeping or crying or getting misty-eyed. This was gut-wrenching sobs that came from so deep within me it seemed they sprung from my soul. And they didn't start out of sadness or grief or happiness or any coherent emotion I could name; they came because I knew (without question I knew) that for the first time in my life, I had approached perfection. For the first time, I could understand the story of Pygmalion, who carved a statue so beautiful he could not help but fall in love with it. For the first time, I could understand the fascination with The Mona Lisa and her secret dreams. For the first time, I had looked into a sunset and seen the face of God. But instead of running from Him, I had leapt into the sky to shake His hand and wound up flying higher and higher from the sheer joy of my boldness. And even when I had looked down to see just how far I could fall, I hadn't grown afraid; I'd just become more certain. I was Icarus caught in the exhilaration of flight and stronger than the danger of the sun. I was an artist, a real honest-to-God artist, for the first time in my own mind, not some twit faking his way through classes and fooling people who didn't know better. I had only my own arrogance standing by waiting to send me crashing back to earth. I had the fire to be – just to be – and oh-my-God how terrible and wonderful it was.

All of these emotions tore through me at light-speed, careening off my thoughts and exploding into each other to create feelings I never knew could exist. Add to that the honest tensile sensations of my fingers exploring Aaron's face and the whisper of his warm sweet breath into my palm and the sound of his tongue licking his heartbreaking lips. It became so overwhelming and right, tears seemed the only appropriate sacrifice to the moment.

Oh, dear God, I would have died for him, right then. I would have taken a bullet. Would have ripped the head off anyone fool enough to want to hurt him. I was Thor ready to hurl thunderbolts at any threat to Valhalla. I was a lioness ready to protect her cub. Could that be love? I honestly do not know. All I did know was that an exquisite knife had slipped between my ribs and was caressing my heart. I could never feel this beauty and pain with a woman; it just wasn't possible. And somehow (I don't know how) I knew. I just knew he had seen the same truth.

He had. And he would not be back till Tuesday.

How could I live until then?

The next day did not exist for me. Oh, I dimly noticed the passage of night into day into night. And I do sort of recall the distant sounds of church bells calling people to services. This was Texas, after all, where even if the state doesn't have an official religion, people still wonder why you don't; I'm Presbyterian, for the record. I probably even ate something, though I couldn't tell you what. All I really remember of the day after Aaron's sitting is looking at the sketch I did. Gazing upon it from a number of different angles. Touching it. Feeling the gentle roughness of the paper give way to the quick smoothness of the Conte pencil. Smelling the black wax. It was as if I lost contact with the world and vanished into another existence where time had no meaning and God was replaced by this one tentative work of art. Could that be a form of insanity?

My mother had once told me that I was the least stable of her children. I know she meant it in a flattering way. She knew I could never be happy just getting a job and settling down and raising a family and becoming part of a nice middle-class world like my brothers and sister have, but it still marked me. Made me feel damaged. I wonder if she sensed that sometimes I quietly crash into a subtle psychosis whenever my life becomes overwhelming? Like with school not going well and my complete dissatisfaction with my current existence and that fucker who tried to fuck me. On more than one occasion this past year, I'd felt I was flirting with a Van Gogh phase and had feared for my ears.

But that Sunday it just vanished from my life, and I do not now believe – never really did – that there is anything wrong with that. It was like – like I dove deep into a cocoon of waking sleep and when I floated out of it, that is when I began my true life. That is when I had the first real notion of who I was and where I was going, and I don't remember ever coming to any conscious conclusion about it except that I could now see what was and was not important to me.

I mean, why was I taking a class in Faulkner? I hated his writing. Maybe he was important to an English major, but to an artist? Who cares if he never met a comma he didn't like? He was the epitome of unimportant.

And then there were my art classes. Failed painters and doodlers trying to tell me how to paint or sketch, so I could fail like them. All their moments were good for was practice, at best, and could actually wind up being harmful if not carefully managed. I could go anywhere for that kind of non-support, and for a hell of a lot less money than it was costing my folks in tuition.

I know these shifts in my psyche were seismic, but they still were not cognitive concepts in my little pea brain. They were mists drifting around my thoughts and obscuring them and altering them in steps and stages, so any action I took on my new beliefs was not deliberate. I just, oh, drifted. Like I drifted into Monday. Like I drifted into ignoring every one of my classes.

What did I do, instead? I began transferring Aaron's sketch onto my dorm room wall to obscure the Polo inspired one that was still hinting at my past existence. And in my boldness, I did it with a Sharpie instead of charcoal. Once it was on, it wasn't gonna come off. And if I screwed up? Hey, I screwed up; so what?

But I didn't, and somehow I knew I wouldn't. I popped a Yanni CD into the player (I don't care what you think; I like him) and got into a carefully gliding rhythm of sketch to eye to pen to wall. The smell of the Sharpie chased the Conte pencil's aroma from my senses and may have added to my feeling of euphoria. I never did do the paint-sniffing thing so I don't know. Didn't matter. All I focused on was the white paint tainted with a charcoal horror that was giving way to the mural that signaled my brave new world.

By late afternoon, I had a great rendition of Aaron's face gazing out at me, fuller, richer, with his secret little smile daring me to add color. Once upon a time, I'd have hesitated. Instead, I squeezed a half-full tube of unbleached titanium acrylic into one of my Jif jars, added dabs of burnt umber, portrait pink and a hint of cadmium red, mixed them with water and set to filling in the lines with my best camel's hair brush. After a moment, I realized the color wasn't exactly right and added a squirt of Azo yellow medium. And that was it.

I had the first layer down and was mixing up some color for the details when I heard a knock at the door. I didn't even turn to look who it was as I said, "Go 'way!"

Then I heard that gentle drawl say, "Sorry, boss. Didn't mean to bother you."

I spun to find Aaron in the doorway, leaning against the jam, looking very unsure of himself. He was wearing a loose athletic T-shirt and basketball shorts, his hair pulled back under a baseball cap that was on backwards, Reeboks and floppy socks on his feet. The beauty of the moment slammed the mural from my mind, and I all but cried out, "Don't move!"

He jolted, startled. "What you mean?"

"I mean, stay right there," I said as I wiped my hands off on my shirt (not even thinking that it was the same one I'd so carefully put on two days earlier), grabbed my sketchpad and a pencil and plopped onto my stool to sketch him. "Just like that."

"Why?"

"Isn't it obvious?"

He gave me a wary glance and muttered, "Joe, you are freaky," but he stayed put. Though he did nod at the sketch on the wall. "Y'know, you ain't supposed to do that."

"So?" I said, without really thinking. I was too focused on the sketch – on transferring the lines of his body and the curve of his legs and folds of his clothing and jauntiness of his cap onto paper.

"So they'll charge your folks to paint it over."

I just snorted in derision. "I thought you were coming, tomorrow."

"Yeah, well, Andrea went home to Houston an' she's not back, yet, an' nobody's 'round to shoot some hoops with ..."

That's when I noticed he had a basketball under his arm – very observant, aren't we?

"... and it's kind of borin' to do it by myself, so I thought I'd drop by to see what's up." And he gave a little shrug and smile.

"Now you know," I smiled back.

He eyed the mural, let a frown cross his face. "That's a little creepy."

"Why?"

He shrugged. "Just is."

"C'mon, Aaron, it's only a sketch. Besides, I'm doing a painting of you. This is good practice."

His secret little smile slipped back onto his lips and he said, "I know. You've done a lot of pictures of me ... an' it's got me wonderin'. Y'know?"

"Yeah," I said, finishing off the outline of the sketch, fluid; good proportions; even a little sexy but not overtly so. I started filling it in. "Am I your stalker? Guess you have a reason to wonder."

He nodded. "Uh, you ... you are gay, right?"

I smiled. He's as bright as Andrea, but on him, it's sweet. I kept working as I said, "Totally. And I think you're beautiful. But I'm not gonna do anything about it. I mean, look at you. If I did, you could break me in half." And oh, wouldn't I love it.

"Beautiful?" he sneered. "That's what you call girls."

"Attractive, then. Good-looking." But then I snapped to it and thought, What the fuck? "I still think beautiful is the best word. See?"

I turned the pad around to show him what I'd done, and he blinked. I had him, again on paper. His broad shoulders. His clean arms. His sleek body. His perfect legs. His neatly curled lips. All rendered in soft graphite tones and lightly shaded, giving him an ethereal feel. Even without studying it, I was proud of this sketch.

"Damn, Joe," he said. "An' I wasn't even here five minutes."

"C'mon in," I said. "I want to do some more. You want a beer?"

"Bock?"

"That's all I buy."

"Cool."

He sauntered in and sat on my bed instead of the chair. And don't you think I didn't notice.

"You're a funny fella," he said, accepting the beer with a nod of thanks.

"How?"

"I dunno. You don't act like the fags … uh, other gay guys."

I sat in the chair, propped my pad on my knee and noticed his left hand was draped over his left knee, a bit of the shorts – they were this neon blue with sunshine yellow trim – trapped under his wrist, the material stretched against his thigh. I started sketching that as I said, "What do you mean?"

He shrugged, sipped the beer.

"Is it because I haven't hit on you?" I asked.

He sort of nodded. I kept sketching. It's weird, but I wasn't getting nervous over how he felt about me. I was more curious to find out.

"Do you want me to?" I asked.

"No!" he said, shocked. "I'm not that way."

But something in his tone was sending me clues of self-doubt, and for the first time in my life I felt a true-life Jam-the-cat stir from his sleep. Okay, sure – I've had the nickname for five years, but I never felt up to it, you know? I just accepted it because it sounded great, and no one in high school really cared if I acted the part or not. But this time, I caught an image of a hungry tom in a dark alley thinking maybe he smelled a mousie, and I let my vocals rumble in pleasure as I answered, "Then what's the big deal?"

249

"I dunno. It's just ... well, when your hand was on my face, the other night, it felt ... it was ... well, you see, in my family, well ... fact is, if my daddy does anything more'n shake your hand and pat you on the back, you know he's had a few too many. Even Andrea doesn't ... well ..."

He shifted and the material fell away, drifting loose across his leg, tickling the hairs that swirled up his thigh. I ached to tickle them, myself.

"I can see where it spooked you," I said, "me feeling up your face, like that."

"What a way to put it ... but, yeah … little." He sipped the beer then looked directly at me, and I stopped drawing. "But I ... I liked it, too. An' that's got me all confused. I never even thought about bein' with a guy. It's got no interest for me. But here I am feelin' ... I mean not mindin' ... I mean ... aw, shit, I don't know what I mean."

He flopped back and put the cold beer bottle to his forehead. And you know what? I didn't even think about the fact that Aaron-un-fucking-believably-good-looking-Friesen was lying on my bed. I didn't cast one look at his legs or his crotch or his body as I stood up. I didn't even think about wanting to trail my fingers up his thighs – not then, anyway – or kiss the hair on his chest – as I'm thinking now – as I sat on the bed, beside him. The only thought that entered my head was comfort him.

"C'mon, Aaron," I said, "just because you liked being touched doesn't mean you're gay. Shit, you think it's contagious? That I infected you with queerness or something?"

"No ... but it's so ...weird ..."

"Why? Even if a guy *does* make a pass at you, it doesn't mean you're obligated to say yes. It's not like guys like me are diseased monsters out to force you into something that's not right for you."

"I know. It's just ... I ... uh, I got ..."

His voice trailed off, and I finally understood the problem. I'd forgotten the extra little bulge in his pants, the other night.

"It got you going."

He blushed and nodded. I just shook my head.

"Dude, haven't you ever had a massage?"

He looked at me with complete confusion. "What? No."

"Well ... I have. And it was at the hands of Olga, she-wolf of my dad's gym. That woman had arms bigger'n my legs, and she hurt me right and left as she rubbed and pounded and twisted me into a pretzel, once. *Not* what you would ever call foreplay. But let me tell you something: I got a real woodie off her."

"You kiddin' me?"

"Swear to God," I said, giving him the Scout's Honor salute. "And I mean it … she was *not* at *all* attractive to me. But there I was, lying face down with a hard-on as this big blond buff dominatrix smacked my ass and told me to roll over."

"What'd you do?"

"I told her, No, and pulled the towel tighter around me. So she grabbed it, gave it a good yank and flipped me sunny side up. And there I lay, totally birthday suit boy, the joy of my life pointed straight to the sky. Talk about embarrassing. But all Olga did was laugh and say, 'Vell, by Gott, ye'll have not'ing to vorry 'bout in der bedroom'."

"No shit?" he laughed.

I nodded. "Seems she'd also worked over my brothers. And while they may have inherited the brawn in the family, I was ... oh, compensated in other ways. In comparison."

Aaron doubled over with laughter and choked out, "Fuckin' shit, Joe!"

I chuckled, remembering the response my brothers had when I told them the story. They'd dragged me into the bedroom and yanked down my pants to see for themselves – the Neanderthal creeps – as if we'd never seen each other "nekked." And they both were pissed as hell when they realized how right she was. I still use it as a weapon whenever they get too pissy.

Finally, I told Aaron, "Everybody likes to be touched. In some way or other. My mom says that's why men used to get haircuts every week – for the feeling of it. Same for contact sports. It's a way of connecting with another guy. And that's what happened when I ran my fingers over your face … I connected with you and found a way to transfer you to canvas. And you felt that."

"An' that's the only reason you did it?"

"Yes," I said, with full and complete truth behind that lie. "I ... I didn't realize how nice it was until after you left."

"You think it was nice?"

All I could do was nod, in answer. The vision of him lying there looking up at me, arms up, hands cupping his head, I felt a quickness of breath that made me a little light-headed. I wanted so much to put my hand over his heart and send signals of understanding into it. He looked back at me, almost smiling.

"Guess it was, kind of," he said, and before the softness of his voice could register in my nimrod brain, he added, "So you ... you want to do it, again?"

"I've already got your face," I said – still being dumb. Then I snapped to and quickly added, "But I don't have your body."

"That a fact?" And he gave me his little *I-know-what-you're-up-to* look.

I got up, stretched, and man, I *did* feel like fuckin' Jam-the-cat: cool as ice and full of self-confidence. I wasn't just stretching; I was flexing my muscles in preparation to run for my supper, and "guess who" was most definitely the mouse. I *liked* it. I sat on my stool and said in what had to be the coolest voice I ever used, "You're right. It'd be weird for you, wouldn't it?"

He sat up, eyed me for a minute, took a long sip of the beer, and pulled off his shirt! And his body was even more perfect than I dreamed it could be: pecs like something you'd find on a statue of David, smooth round nipples standing at attention, a belly so tight that even sitting there were no creases or folds to it, silken threads whispering up the center of his abs to fan out over his chest. Oh, sweet Jesus, this little kitty was *so* ready to pounce! He stood up and strolled toward me.

"Think you're in my seat," he smiled.

I shifted to the chair before the easel, carefully removed his sketch from the pad to reveal a fresh sheet and grabbed an umber Conte pencil, this time. He sat on the stool, hands positioned above his crotch, his eyes sharp and warm on me.

"You better stop when you touch the top of my shorts."

"You got it, boss," I smiled back.

"Now close your eyes," he said.

"What?!"

"Do it right."

I sighed and placed my left fingers on his left shoulder, pressed the pencil to the paper, sat up straight and lowered my lids. The darkness wasn't as complete as with a blindfold, but it would do. It took me a moment to focus on just touch, focus on the idea that I was sketching him, not making love to him (not yet, I hoped). It wasn't as hard to shift away from my imagination, this time. Why, I don't know; I guess I just knew it wouldn't be the last time I got to do this, and that made me less needy.

252

I took a deep breath. The gentle aroma of soap – Irish Spring? Coast? – mingled with the scent of the wax. I could both hear and feel his breath whispering in and out of him. I could sense him watching me, waiting for me to try something stupid. Well I wasn't going to give him that satisfaction. This was going to be exactly what we agreed to – torso only, nothing lower – and what suddenly surprised me was that was all I really wanted, right then.

His skin was smooth, of course; I never doubted it would be. And his muscles were solid without being hard, which is also what I expected. I traced my fingers from his left shoulder up his trapezius to his neck, then down and around his throat and across to his right shoulder. There was a sharpness to his bones that I found surprising but right. Then I pulled back to his chest, felt the soft down whisper against my fingers as I followed the line of his right pec around to its nipple. All perfectly molded. I let my fingers circle it atop the bumpy little ridges (just noticeable under the hair) and then brush over the erect tit in the center of it all. He drew in a deep breath when I did that, so I did it twice more, making him almost gasp in surprise.

Mee-yow, pussycat.

"Keep your eyes closed," he said.

I smiled, and did, and proceeded to the left nipple to repeat my motion and got the same response. His breathing quickened. So did mine. Then he shifted in a way that made me think he was growing erect, and I finally felt a stirring in my own crotch. I began to wonder if I really had to stop at the top of his shorts. Time to find out.

My fingers drifted up the center of his chest, fanning out a little with the hair they caressed, then I let them slip down, down, down the middle of his abs, feeling the flowing smoothness of the taut muscles and laughing little follicles that surrounded his navel. I was still drawing and felt it gave me the excuse to send my hand gliding around his belly to his right side and trace up to his rib cage, to feel the ripple of small bones under elegant skin. Then I pulled my hand back across, slipping below his chest to his left side, and let the tops of my fingers trail back down to his waist. I heard him swallow just as I reached the cruel nylon top of his shorts.

"Keep your eyes closed," he said.

I did, but only because the sensation of touch had overwhelmed any need I had to see. I followed the waistband of the shorts, felt the ridge of elastic peeking through, noticed they grew tight and dipped, and before I realized it, I was touching hair.

253

I stopped and my eyes flew open without me even thinking, and I saw he had pulled the waistband of the shorts down with his right thumb and was holding them tight against his right thigh, exposing his pubes.

"Told you to keep your eyes closed," he said.

Suddenly, I felt betrayed, for some reason, and I jerked my hand away. "What the fuck *is* this, Aaron? You think you can play games with me? 'You can't touch my dick, but I'll fuckin' tease you with it!?' Shit!"

He blinked and straightened, startled by my outburst. "Sorry, Joe. Thought you'd like it." He let go of the shorts and they snapped slightly into place low around his hips. He was about to pull them up when – hello – my brain snapped into awareness and my hands snapped to atop his to stop him. My thumbs were resting in the curve where his leg curled away from his groin, at his tan line, touching skin that was smooth and creamy. Some of his pubes were still exposed, looking soft and inviting in the gentle light.

"I would," I said, my voice aching, "but not like that."

I knelt before him, as does a knight before his king, my hands still resting on his. He watched me, warily – no, maybe a little scared of me – but did not try to shove me away. And me – I was so full of my own sense of being, I didn't even think about what I was doing. I leaned up and took his left tit in my teeth and felt the golden hairs tickle my lips and chin and nose as I pulled at it oh-so-gently and my tongue darted across its top. He gasped and tensed but did not pull away.

"Like this," I said, softly, as I let my lips drift through the sea of soft down over to his right tit, then took that one gently in my teeth and slipped my tongue across it and got the same response.

"Holy shit, Joe," he stammered.

"Call me Jam," I said and then to my complete amazement, I rose and kissed him. His lips were everything I'd dreamed they could be – warm, soft, molding themselves to mine. I didn't try Frenching; it seemed wrong for the moment. I think that's why he let his mouth linger on mine, for a moment (for a lifetime), before he pulled back, pulled away, completely. He bolted to his feet and grabbed his T-shirt.

"I ... better head," he said, his voice shaking.

"Aaron ..."

"I'm not that way, Joe!" he snapped as he pulled his shirt on. "Never even thought 'bout it, an' I don't ... I can't ..."

"Nobody says you are," I said, rising to my feet. "I'm just like ... like an Olga to you, showing you how much you like to be touched." Man, what a lame argument! "Besides ... one ... one time doesn't make you queer. Not even two or three or a dozen, if at the end of it all, you still prefer girls. It ... it just means you're ... adventurous." (Oh, and that was even lamer.)

But he stopped by the door, his shirt only half on. I noticed the light had faded, outside, to the point where everything had taken on a soft sapphire hue and the world seemed calm and wonderful. I had no lights on in my room.

"Not ... not tonight," he murmured. "I ... I gotta think."

"I understand," I said. "You don't want to, that's fine. I'll still do the painting. But buddy, don't think this to death. People make too much out of things that just ... just happen. They politicize them and ... and label them ... and that's wrong. That's just wrong. You and me ... that won't mean anything but ... but you and me." And don't ask me to explain what I meant by that; I can't.

He eyed me, no trace of his smile or special look, just raw conflict. His breath was fast and sharp. He licked his lips a couple of times. I had to say something, say it now. Now!

"Aaron, I mean it: you put up a boundary, and I'll respect it. But I ... I really want to do more renditions of you. Watercolors. Acrylics. Oils. Pastels. Everything. I ... I look at you and I ... I see perfection, and I want to capture that."

He rolled his eyes, and I can't say I blame him. So I shut up. Probably the smartest thing I ever did. He closed his eyes, crushed them closed for what seemed like hours, or minutes, I couldn't say. Then they opened.

"If my daddy could see me," he laughed then seemed to make up his mind. He curled back against the door, clicking it closed, his hands at his sides. His eyes seared into mine. I think my heart stopped, for a moment, when he said, "I'm not turnin' queer for you."

I carefully slipped over to him. "I know," I whispered then I kissed him, again. And this time, he didn't break away.

What can I say about that moment? About drawing Aaron close to have his lips touch mine and feel his breath dance over my cheek? About my hands slipping 'round his waist to the small of his back to hold him next to me? About molding myself against him and knowing his strength and grace and beauty as it caressed my body. Even through two layers of clothing I could feel his exquisite muscles quivering against me. I began to shake from the intensity of the emotion as the meaning of it all overpowered my own concept of myself.

I'd never gotten even close to being with someone as gorgeous as Aaron, before, but that didn't seem to matter. The intimidation I'd felt so many times as I watched him cross the campus with his slow genial saunter – an intimidation I'd always believed was endemic to my makeup – vanished in the reality of his skin warm against mine. The understanding that I was bland or plain or average (choose your adjective, here) dissolved into nothingness like Santa Claus and the Tooth Fairy did when I learned my dad and mom filled the roles, respectively. My life prior to this moment was nothing more than myth-filled half-truths and misconceptions laced with fears and stupidity, and now none of it carried any weight. The only important thought was that he and I were together, even if it might be for just a few moments and then never again. I could have died right then and been happy.

I moved away from the kiss and let my lips dip to his chin and down his throat to his chest as my hands slipped under his shirt and slowly, carefully slid it up, up, up over his body. He raised his arms and let me guide it higher and higher, let my fingers tickle the sandy hairs under his arms as the material slipped past, let the palms of my hands caress his skin as I pushed the shirt off him, completely. Then I let my lips drift back to his right tit, let my teeth gently take it, let my tongue flit over it.

Instinctively, Aaron moved back, but then held still, letting me play with his nipple and pull it harder until he was cringing from the sensation and little whimpers of joy were escaping him. I could tell he was wearing briefs, this time (which only added to the sexiness of the moment, so far as I was concerned), but molded against his body like I was, I could also tell that the screaming lightning had launched itself from my mouth to his thighs and slammed him into straining hard against the cotton fabric. I almost moaned for joy when it became too much for him, and he breathlessly curled his right arm around my head and slipped his hand over half my face to guide my mouth away from his chest.

My hands were back around his waist. I began inching down his shorts, planning to remove them, but he put his hands on mine to stop me and guided them to my own shirt. I hesitated, let him give me a look of askance then I smiled, understanding. He needed a bit of a breather.

He leaned back against the door and watched as I pulled off my T-shirt. No hair on my chest. No real definition of muscle. No abs to speak of. Just the vague outline of my pecs and two tiny pink tits over a smooth belly. My shoulders were wide enough, I suppose, and I had next to no fat on me, but up to this point in time, I had only attracted older men and dip-shits who said I looked like I was still in high school (the perverts). And I'd expected nothing more up to that point. But then Aaron gave me his secret smile and pulled me close, and we kissed, again, and the world spun out of control, for an instant.

His arms were strong around me, the hair on them tickling my skin as he held me tight. Enveloped me in his grip. Oh dear God, I never wanted him to move, never wanted him to let go. He slid his hands down my spine, down to just above my butt, and stopped. I started to do the same to him, trailing my fingers down the small of his back to the point where his ass began to curve around, just under the elastic of his shorts, and he pulled away, shaking his head. Not just yet, boss. Not just yet.

No problem. I took his hands in mine and pulled him back into the room and drew him close to me. The room was growing darker in the night air. Pale light wandered in from the moon (was it a full one? It seemed that bright) and offered just enough illumination to see. He moved close to me, his gaze wary and expectant, and I shoved him onto the bed.

He fell back, laughing in surprise then I collapsed on top of him and held his hands above him. Now let's be real. All he had to do to get free was give me one quick shove. But he didn't; he just lay there and let me kiss him, let me lay on top of him, let me rub my chest against his and my tits against his and my belly against his and my crotch against his. Even through my jeans I could feel how rock solid he was, how ready. That's when I began tracing my lips down the center of his body along the path of pleasure laid out by his golden hair, he stretched back a bit to make the journey just a hint longer.

My tongue danced through the soft trail of down, gliding over and around the muscles of his abs, dipping into his navel, twirling through the patch below that slowly widened to meet the center of the universe. I let my hands drift over to his hips to gently pull at the shorts, and he did not stop me, this time. I tugged at them. They slipped down past his tan line and past the elastic to his briefs and kept gliding lower and lower until I had them down to his thighs. Now I could see

257

how big and full and wonderful he was under the white cotton that still formed around his hips.

My heart was pounding out an earthquake. I slid his shorts slowly, slowly, all the way down those perfect legs, using my thumbs to guide them and letting my fingers whisper over tiny gentle hairs that gleamed even in the moonlight. His muscles curved into his knees so exactly and rolled out again to form well-developed calves covered with even more of the golden corn-silk before curling down to solid masculine ankles.

I removed the shorts, lifting one foot and then the other, then slipped off his sneakers and floppy socks. Man, even his toes were good and strong and shaped just right, with hints of golden hair dancing across them. I got to thinking this can't be possible. I can't really be doing this. This guy can't be as wonderful as I think. I'm just obsessing and making too much over someone who's only good-looking, nothing more. There's something wrong here.

So I stood up and looked at him and everything about him. I dunno – it just fit just right. His shoulders and neck and chest and waist and hips and thighs and arms and head lying across my well-crushed sheets – the vision accentuated by a pair of new clean white cotton briefs and his calves draped over the bed's side. It hurt to see him lying there, looking up at me, waiting for my next move. Suddenly, I didn't trust my eyes, didn't trust my perceptions, didn't believe I was where I was and was doing what I was doing. It was all too overwhelming.

I reached down and gently took his hands and silently guided him to his feet. He almost spoke, but I put a finger to his lips, then closed his eyes, then slowly, softly allowed my fingertips to drift down his cheeks to his neck to his shoulders to his arms to his hands. Then I closed my eyes and slid down to my knees and allowed my fingers to wander over to his thighs. As I touched the hair that swirled up his skin, I envisioned flowing fields of grain on a brisk golden day. As I let my fingers follow the smooth form of his muscles, I pictured rolling hills after a gentle summer rain. As the backs of my fingers rose up the insides of his legs, gliding along the curls of his calves and small humps of his knees and the gentle build of his thighs, I saw a secret lake blessed with cool clean water laughing around a bright and happy shoreline.

I pulled my hands back around his legs at the last moment and let them curve to the back to where the hair grew soft and sparse just before his muscles leapt up and around to form his rear. I could feel the bottom of his briefs, tight against him, digging into the skin ever so slightly. The cotton rolled around tiny straps of elastic that held it in place at the junction of his legs to his hips. It was warm yet cool. I could feel him shivering, hear it in his breath. I hesitated only an instant before letting my fingers gently glide up and over the smooth roundness of his rear.

What did I picture then? Only how he looked. Only how he felt. Only the whiteness of fabric drawn taut over ivory flesh. The similes of image in my mind became this one reality. I knew if I opened my eyes, I would see exactly what I saw in my mind's eye, without question.

I reached up and took hold of the elastic with my left hand, caught it just where his cheeks flowed apart to blend into his back, felt the ridge of the seam were it joined, and I began to pull it down. He did not try to stop me, this time. My right hand gripped the left side of his briefs and also pulled. He did nothing. Now I knew we were connected. Now I knew we were one. Now I was ready.

I opened my eyes and watched the cotton and elastic slowly move down his hips away from a line where golden tanned skin gave way to alabaster then over his groin while still holding tight to his pubes then watched the base of his crotch surrender their hold and the briefs whisked away to reveal the world. And he was exactly what I had hoped for.

He wasn't so much long as curved in a gentle slope, and he wasn't so much thick as round and full, and he wasn't so much hard as ready for the next stage. His skin was like translucent sand, and his head was almost white pink, big and smooth, not oversized. He was cut (so am I, so I prefer it), the circle of a scar adding to his dimensions, and the veins in his shaft added depth to it all. The hair at the base was rich and sandy as it splayed out to dance up his abdomen and swirl down around his legs, and the neat balls (why can't there be a finer word for them than that?) hanging below it all were clean and inviting. Perfection, once again.

But this time at this point I believed in it. He was real to me, now, and not just because I could smell the vague muskiness of him or see the form of him or hear the shiver in his breath or feel the tension in his muscles as my breath whispered over him. No, he was now a part of me, and to make love to him, I just knew it would be like making love to myself and would be ten times more real than anything I had ever

259

done with a man, before, and it was to be everything I had ever wanted in my life, and I was so ready to complete the moment it hurt.

Except I – I couldn't go through with it.

My face begged to nuzzle him but would not move. My hands ached to fondle him but refused to leave his legs. My brain screamed to put my lips to him, but they froze. No matter what I tried to do to begin giving him what I knew would be the best blow job in the history of the world, I could not make myself do it. Suddenly, there was something wrong about it all.

Now know what you're thinking: Joe, you dumb fuck, what the *hell* are you doing?! You've been lusting after this guy since the beginning of the school year! You've been dreaming about him and sketching him and fantasizing over him as you jacked off in the fucking shower since the first time you saw him! And here he is, ready, willing and perfectly able to do what*ever* you fucking want, and you can't move the last few inches to actually make it all happen?! C'mon! He's fuckin' gorgeous and he fuckin' *wants* it, man! Just fuckin' *do* it, twerp!

And let me tell you. Had we gotten to this point before last Saturday night, there would have been *zero* hesitation on my part. I'd have pounced on him like a duck on a June bug (as my gran'mama used to say). But now after he'd lead me into a new world, a new belief in myself, a deep sudden realization washed over me that maybe, just maybe, he carried more meaning than just as an object of desire.

I think it was at this point my brain finally connected with my soul. I finally realized (or accepted or acknowledged or whatever) that if I had sex with Aaron, I wouldn't be able to paint him, anymore. What I saw in him would be gone, maybe even dead, and whatever took its place would be worthless to me. It would be like murder, and that is something I could never do, not to him nor to me.

I leaned back and sat on my heels, stunned. My hands were still on his thighs, still holding the white briefs. He was beginning to soften, making him even lovelier. I wanted nothing but silence, at that point, but then words floated into my space.

"Everything okay, boss?" I blinked and noticed he was looking down at me, frowning, confused.

I looked back at him with such intensity, he almost flinched then I asked, "Why do you want this?"

"Huh?"

"Why do you really want me to do this?"

He gave an incredulous snort and said, "Why you think?"

"I don't know ... but I don't want to do anything with you if the only reason you're doing it is to ... to get it over with. Like you have to do it for me to paint you."

"What?" He glared at me. "Shit, Joe, you want t' try makin' some sense?"

"Well, I ... I don't know if I can, Aaron," I said. "It's just ... there's something not right about doing this. It's like I'd be spitting in the eye of God after he's shown me the world or ... or something and I can't ..."

"Aw, for Christ's sake!" He hiked up his briefs and grabbed his shirt and yanked it on, almost tearing it. "You're really somthin', Joe! A real prick tease! You talk me into getting' all worked up then pull some psycho-crap before you even try to ... to ... shit, I thought you wanted to ... you said you wanted to do it and ..."

I rose to my feet, suddenly afraid he'd just leave, and I'd never see him, again. But also unwilling to let my connection with him be dragged into something as common and simple as lust.

"I did!" I said. "But I ... I think the only reason you're letting me is because you like to be touched. And held. And you need it so much you'll put up with anything. Almost anything."

"What!?" Man, for a second I thought he was going to hit me, he got so red in the face. "You freaky fuckin' faggot, you think I'm that screwed up?!"

"No! No. It's just ... I think you're lonely. I think you want something ... and you don't know what it is ... and I don't, either ... but maybe I can give it to you."

"Man, you are a true freak," he snarled. "This was one *big* mistake an' it's best t' cut it 'fore it gets any crazier."

He yanked on his shorts then started pulling on his socks and shoes, and I didn't even think to try and stop him. I just sat on my stool, eyeing him like a cat as I said, "I'm sorry. And you're right, it does sound crazy. But the fact is, your meaning to me is deeper than a ... a one night stand or ... or two nights or a thousand."

He rolled his eyes. I could tell, even though he wasn't looking up and tied his shoelaces with the fury of a strangler.

"Aaron, I mean it. If I ... I blow you, then you become nothing to me. You'd just be one more guy I gave a head job to and ... and I'd become exactly what I do not want to be – a queer artist who paints pretty boys just before he fucks 'em."

261

"I told you, I'm not turnin' queer for you!"

"And I mean it when I say I don't want you to! You're too important to me for that! But I didn't realize till now just how important! Aaron ... please try to understand ... the other night ... when I was touching your face ... I connected to something deeper inside me than just lust or longing. And I ... I ... I saw more to you than just the skin wrapped around your body. I saw more than just the public face you offer the world. And I saw that until that moment, I'd been trying to paint only what I saw – a dream ... and not a person ..." Shit, that sounded so lame. "... and everything I've done up to now reflects that ... that stupid, surface simplistic mentality."

He looked at me, slowly – warily – even more confused, and I can't say I blame him; I was now confusing myself.

"It's because of you ... through you that I found ... I've been wasting my time on nothing, and I can't do that. Not anymore. And I can't let you become nothing to me."

He finished tying his shoes and rose, his wariness increasing. "You ain't makin' one damn bit of sense."

"Fine," I said, moving towards him, "let me show you what I mean."

He backed away. "No, I ... I better head on."

"Aaron, please, just sit in the chair. I won't touch you. I don't need to, anymore."

He stopped before opening the door and eyed me as if I was from another planet. At that particular moment, I couldn't have proven to anyone that I wasn't. I backed to my easel and positioned the stool before it.

"We don't have to talk," I said. "You can keep an eye on me the whole time. And if I try anything, you have permission to smack me into next Sunday."

"Man ... you got me so fuckin' confused."

"I know. I know. I'm trying to explain something that I can't explain. Not with words. So please ... let me show you. It won't take very long. And you ... you'll get your portrait out of it. Okay? Then you can run clear to Tulsa, if you want."

He finally nodded and sat on the chair. "Let's get it over with," he muttered. Not the best way of putting it, but I wasn't worried about that, just then.

I scrambled to find the one clean sheet of illustration board I had and dropped it to the ugly carpet. I frantically swiped both sides of it with a wet sponge to prep them then pulled out half a dozen empty Jif jars and half-filled them with water. Then I realized it was dark, so I turned on my easel lamp, and I spun my desk lamp around to shine on him. I had a floor lamp by my bed that I moved to his other side, to give him a bit of fill light. Then I began mixing acrylic paints in their caps, using a different jar of water for each color, all like someone possessed. By the time I was ready, the board was dry and open to my use.

I didn't pay much attention to Aaron, during this, but I know he watched me flit around like a sketcher on a high. And any time I got too close to him, I know he tensed up and readied his fist. I didn't care. I was in some kind of art zone, and I'm still amazed at how easily I slipped into it.

The actual painting took a few hours, nothing more. I wish I could describe what I did, but it's so, it was so simple and straightforward, it would just seem boring and incomplete. Whipping through the outline of his head and shoulders. Putting down the first layer of paint and then the second. Working in the filler and then the details and then the shading, it sounds academic when it was really instinctive and sudden and almost, well, ephemeral. And even though I remember the chime of the school's bells (nine o'clock; ten o'clock) and Aaron breaking to grab a Bock and bring me one, too (I drank half of it before forgetting about it, completely) and ordering in pizza (which I ate, though I can't remember what kind it was) and taking a pee (winding up with burnt umber and portrait pink on my dick), I was not in this world as I wove and spun and conjured my new life.

Just past midnight with paint streaked across my body and layers of colors on my fingers and my jeans a full and complete mess, I was done. I don't know how I knew it was ready. I just thought if I add one more dot or line, it'll be ruined. So I signed it and stepped back, still in that netherworld of being here and beyond. I didn't have to say anything; Aaron knew it was ready. He slowly stretched and carefully joined me, and I stumbled back to this world an instant before he cast his first glance at my work.

Oh, and what a piece of work it was. Sweet Jesus, I had him. The thick and golden hair. The smooth and glowing skin. The bright and shining eyes. All in whispery layers of color that seemed more rich oil than flat water based. Lips with a hint of rubies. Cheeks with a bit of blush. The line of his neck. The flow of his shoulders. The sense of calmness covering a shattering want. This was more than just the combination of shades and tones that offered a photo-like representation of a good-looking guy; this was art. This was my explanation, my proof.

His eyes held layers of wariness and need and longing, all at one time. His secret smile was painful in its cool emotion. His posture was proper and correct yet demanding and distant. I could compare the effect to that of The Mona Lisa (give me a few more years of working on my ego and I probably will) in its simplicity and meaning. I could never be as proud of anything I did as I was of that portrait at that particular time; I just knew it.

Aaron did, too. I could sense the tension and weariness whisper out of him as he took it in. Oh, sure, he was impressed; I already knew he would be. But I needed to show him why my work also impressed me.

I drifted to my portfolios and dug through them for the best portrait I'd done up to that point. It was of the guy in my life drawing class, the one with the beard. It was an upper torso layout, from just above his navel to include all of his head. His eyes were closed, his arms were at his sides, and I'd made him to look a bit like Christ. It was good, but when I set it next to Aaron's portrait on the easel, it was like comparing the work of a child to that of Renoir.

Aaron looked at it, and I could tell even his untrained eye could see the difference. I slipped up behind him, put my arms around his shoulders, drew myself close to him, held him like a brother, and whispered into his ear, "You see? This is what you brought me to."

He didn't move, just let me mold myself against him. I lay my chin on his left shoulder.

"I now know that to paint ... to create ... I have to connect with the soul of my subject. You're the one who let me do that. You're the one who showed me there's a bridge that takes you from being a fool to being a king ... and that I was worthy enough to cross that bridge. You're the one who showed me that my paint is priceless, and I shouldn't waste it on nothing. Yeah, before I ... I knew you, I was attracted to you. And I thought it was just for your looks, but now I know it was because I sensed what you could show me. Where you could lead me. To have ... to have sex with you now would be a desecration."

Aaron took hold of my arms and held them tight to his chest. I could tell he was weeping lightly and still with some basic control, but enough to fill me with gratitude.

"I ... I'm sorry, boss. I really thought that's all you were after."

"So did I, once."

"Y'know ... that's all anybody's ever really wanted out o' me. The way I look. The way I act. My folks. My brother. Andrea. Everybody. They never me just ... just for ..." His voice whispered away. Finally, he cocked his head to look at me. "But you ... you're ... you're a funny fella, Joe."

I couldn't think of a nicer thing from him to say, so I just smiled.

He hugged my arms closer to himself and looked back at the portrait. "Is it really mine?"

I nodded. "Let it dry overnight, then I'll spray some fixative on it. You can pick it up after twelve. Get it matted and framed and it's ready for the parents."

"I'll let Andrea do that; she loves that crap." Then he looked closer at the portrait and glanced back at me. "You signed it 'Jam The Cat'."

"That's my name, now."

He gave me a hugely quizzical look and pulled away from me. I didn't mind; it was time for him to leave, and I was feeling the desperate need of a bath. We moved toward the door.

"My name's Joseph Allen Martin. At my high school, if your initials formed a word, that was your nickname."

"But 'The Cat'?"

"Well ... I tell people it's because I'm an artist and I'm cool, but the reality is … my junior year, I got into a shoving match with this jerk in calculus. He wound up pushing me through a window. We were on the second floor, so I did a back flip and landed on my feet. Broke a bone in my right foot. Might've been worse if I hadn't hit some grass. I was on crutches for weeks. Anyway, one of the kids who saw it said something like, 'Jam landed like a cat!' The name stuck."

He grinned and said, "Okay, boss. I can see that."

I stopped him by the door and said, "Aaron, I'm not your boss. And you are nobody's servant."

"I know that."

"Do you?"

He smiled and sort of shrugged. "T'morrow, 'bout noon?"

I nodded. Then he drew me close and kissed me, long and hard, with a deeper affection than he ever had before, and then he left.

265

He came back, the next day, Andrea in tow. And, of course, she rattled on and on so much about how great the portrait was. It was irritating. I think she wanted me to offer to do one of her, but she held no promise for me; too cloistered in her superficiality. So I borrowed a photo student's camera to shoot a couple of transparencies of it then handed it over to Aaron.

I didn't see him for two weeks. Not that it mattered. I knew he'd come back, again. I finished the mural of his face on my dorm wall, then contacted my folks and told them I wasn't returning to school the next year. "Oh and, just in case you didn't know, Mom and Dad, I'm gay." They already knew. Dammit. In fact, they were disappointed I didn't tell 'em after what happened with my asshole roomie. So much for any overwrought drama in my coming out.

Aaron finally dropped by one evening to show me some photos of his parents' anniversary party. His folks were nice well-off Republicans (scum of the earth) and his brother was an overweight chunk in comparison (tho' with him, I would have gone all the way). The centerpiece of just about all the photos was the portrait I'd done. It wound up hanging over the family's fireplace, which was a position of honor, according to Aaron. He even carried a nice handwritten note from his mother thanking me for doing it (well, at least she was raised right ... pun *not* intended). Then as he sat and I sketched (or painted or drew), we talked and ordered in pizza and drank Shiner Bock.

He got into the habit of dropping by two or three times a week, so I got to build my own little "Helga" portfolio. Faces. Hands. Torsos. Clothed. Nude. Face up. Face down. Whatever I wanted him to do, however I wanted him to sit, he did. We never again referred to our near death experience, and when the semester was over, he went back to Dallas, and I moved to San Francisco to invest completely in my new life. We haven't seen each other, since.

So here I sit in my overpriced studio, taking a break from my latest work (an old Jazz saxophonist with arthritic fingers and eyes that reach to heaven) happy as a cat that's caught his mousie. I'm seeing this photographer named Ric who's a few years older than I and who likes taking shots of me working; says he's trying to catch creativity as it sparks to life. He's still trying. He's not as beautiful as Aaron, but his meaning to me is deep and different. He tolerates my moods, and he brings me peace, and his eyes shine with the joy of a kitten discovering the world. I've painted him a dozen times. I want to do a dozen more. That alone should tell you how much I love him.

I'm slated to have my first full viewing of my work at a gallery in three months. My paintings of Ric will make up one section – Life. My portraits of old Jazz musicians from the "Beat Period" will make up the second section – Liberty. And the third section (if you haven't already figured it out) will be the first Conte pencil sketch I did of Aaron all by itself, but without a word to identify it, except for the one that flows from deep within my soul. And to those who ask why it has no title, I'll respond in the only way I can.

"How can you label perfection?"

About the Authors

Bearmuffin – A native Californian, Bearmuffin lives in San Diego with two leather bears in a stimulating ménage a trios. He writes erotica for *Honcho* and *Torso*. His work is featured in several Alyson and Cleis Press anthologies.

Dan DeVeaux – DeVeaux grew up, went to college, and now lives in the Midwest after living in eight states and Europe. His background is in advertising writing and straight fiction and poetry, some of which has been published. DeVeaux is new to erotica, but two of his short stories were purchased by *Mandate Magazine*.

Jay Barbera – Barbera has had twelve highly erotic books published on a variety of sexual topics. In addition, his short stories have appeared in dozens of adult magazines. Jay Barbera, who has been writing since 1982, lives in Cliffside Park, New Jersey.

Jay Starre – From Vancouver, Canada, Jay Starre has written for numerous gay men's magazines including *Mandate*, *Torso*, and *Men*. His torrid stories have also been included in over forty-five gay anthologies such as *Daddy's Boyz*, *Kink*, *View to a Thrill*, *Love in a Lock-up*, *Unmasked – Erotic Tales of Gay Superheroes*, and *Don't Ask, Don't Tie Me Up – Military BDSM Fantasies*. His steamy gay novel from STARbooks, *The Erotic Tales of the Knights Templar*, was released in autumn 2007.

Jordan Castillo Price – Price is the author of the *PsyCop* novels, *Among the Living*, *Criss Cross*, and *Body and Soul*. Price's short stories have appeared in the anthologies *Bloodlust: Erotic Vampire Tales*, *Got a Minute?* and *Torqued Tales*.

K. Appleby – Appleby was born in Sydney but moved to a farm in regional Australia at an early age. To his parents' horror, he became a vegan while working and growing up on the farm. He now resides in a small country town between the coast and the bush.

Kyle Michel Sullivan – Sullivan is an award-winning screenwriter with one published book to his name (available on Amazon.com). He was born in San Diego, raised in Texas (with only the usual scarring) and now lives in West Hollywood. He writes, sketches and paints, loves French films and plans to move to Ireland to write the world's greatest novel.

Lew Bull – Bull has been published in such anthologies as *Ultimate Gay Erotica 2007* and *2008*, *Travelrotica for Gay Men* and

Travelrotica Vol. 2, *Fast Balls*, *Dorm Porn 2*, *Treasure Trail*, *My First Time Vol. 5*, *Secret Slaves* and *Ultimate Undies*. He is also being published in STARbooks' *Don't Ask, Don't Tie Me Up – Military BDSM Fantasies*. He lives in South Africa with his partner of thirty years and should you wish to make contact with him, send an email to lewbull@hotmail.com.

Mark Dante – Dante is old enough to remember what it's like to face the terrors of a homophobic world, and he has written nearly a dozen short stories plus one novel on the subject. He is married to a charming and patient French lady, and they have a grown son and daughter who know his story and understand.

R. Forestier – Forestier grew up in Cambridge, MA, left at age nineteen in 1956, and quickly the learned facts-of-life. First stop, Houston, Texas, then New York City. Fifty years later, South Florida. Lots of casual sex, plus a few LTRs set Forestier up for his present and, hopefully, final relationship. Currently, a brief vignette of life in New York appears in the Apollo Network Library.

R.A. Padgett – Padgett lives in Ballard on the outskirts of Seattle, the land of lost souls and lutefisk with his partner of twelve years and their Boxer bitch. He has been published in *PUSH Magazine* and *Handjobs Anthology* and is a frequent contributor to various Websites.

Ryan Field – Field is a freelance writer who lives and works in both New Hope, PA, and Los Angeles, CA. His work has appeared in many magazines, anthologies and collections over the years. He is currently working on a new novel.

Sedonia Guillone – Multi-published, award-nominated author, Sedonia Guillone lives on the water in Florida with a Renaissance man who paints, writes poetry and tells her she's the sweetest nymph he's ever met. When she's not writing erotic romance, she loves watching spaghetti westerns, Jet Li and samurai flicks, cuddling, and eating chocolate. She offers more delicious M/M erotica at her Website: www.sedoniaguillone.com

Stewart Lewis – Lewis is the author of two novels: *Rockstarlet*, and *Relative Stranger*, both from Alyson books. He is also an accomplished singer songwriter. For more information, please visit www.stewartlewis.com.

Wayne Mansfield – Mansfield lives in Western Australia and has had his work published in many magazines both in the UK and the

United States. He has enjoyed writing since high school, where he won awards for his compositions.

About the Editor

Mickey Erlach – This is Mickey Erlach's first experience editing an anthology for STARbooks Press. His experience as an English and history teacher in a prison high school in Virginia prepared him for this undertaking.